MOUNTAIN AMBUSH

Just as it seemed the fighting was over, a dark-browed man with thinning black hair stepped out of the trees and fired his pistol at Jeff from fifteen feet away.

There wasn't time to be surprised. Jeff staggered as the first bullet slammed into his left thigh. A second tore across his belly and he spun awkwardly, crazily, to the ground, rolling into a heap beside a boulder.

"Well, he's done for," a voice announced.

"Lord, I hate to shoot the young ones," the dark-browed man said as he reloaded his pistol.

Jeff tried to regain his feet, but it was as if he were outside his body, looking down at everything. He swallowed the pain and fought to hold onto the shred that remained of his life . . .

VISIT THE WILD WEST
with Zebra Books

SPIRIT WARRIOR   (1795, $2.50)
by G. Clifton Wisler
The only settler to survive the savage Indian attack was a little boy. Although raised as a red man, every man was his enemy when the two worlds clashed—but he vowed no man would be his equal.

IRON HEART   (1736, $2.25)
by Walt Denver
Orphaned by an Indian raid, Ben vowed he'd never rest until he'd brought death to the Arapahoes. And it wasn't long before they came to fear the rider of vengeance they called . . . *Iron Heart*.

THE DEVIL'S BAND   (1903, $2.25)
by Robert McCaig
For Pinkerton detective Justin Lark, the next assignment was the most dangerous of his career. To save his beautiful young client's sisters and brother, he had to face the meanest collection of hardcases he had ever seen.

KANSAS BLOOD   (1775, $2.50)
by Jay Mitchell
The Barstow Gang put a bullet in Toby Markham, but they didn't kill him. And when the Barstow's threatened a young girl named Lonnie, Toby was finished with running and ready to start killing.

SAVAGE TRAIL   (1594, $2.25)
by James Persak
Bear Paw seemed like a harmless old Indian—until he stole the nine-year-old son of a wealthy rancher. In the weeks of brutal fighting the guns of the White Eyes would clash with the ancient power of the red man.

THOMPSON'S MOUNTAIN

G. CLIFTON WISLER

ZEBRA BOOKS
KENSINGTON PUBLISHING CORP.

ZEBRA BOOKS

are published by

Kensington Publishing Corp.
475 Park Avenue South
New York, NY 10016

First printing: April 1987

Printed in the United States of America

For my good friend Lee Zimmerman.

I. The Mountain

I

The wooden sign over the depot read THOMPSON'S MOUNTAIN. It wasn't an unusually large sign, nor was it particularly small, either. The station house itself was more or less identical to forty or fifty others that by 1880 clung to the rails of the Union Pacific as the line snaked its way westward from Nebraska through the Wyoming Territory.

The town that clustered along a narrow street was not unlike the other towns that had sprung up along the railroad during its construction twelve years before. Shops and stores were owned by McNamaras and O'Sheas, Kilpatricks and O'Haras, hard-working Irish who'd set aside their picks and sledges and taken up shopkeeping.

The air was still filled with smoke from the snorting locomotive, and the windows of the depot were black with soot. The trains had begun using coal for fuel, and the result was an oily black cloud that haunted the station before and after each train's visit.

"Takes a lot of horsepower to cross the ridge ahead," the stationmaster explained. "And the smoke passes away directly."

There was more than a little Irish to the man's speech, and when asked about it, he claimed a heritage dating from the hour St. Patrick drove out the snakes.

Thompson's Mountain had no attractions of merit, and the others hurried along toward the friends and relatives who awaited their arrival. No one had come to meet the loner. He shook off a boy who reached for his bags, then walked off down the tracks toward the bridge over the river.

"Odd, that is," the stationmaster mumbled under his breath. "There's nothing down that way."

But there was a freight train due in that morning from Laramie, and the manifests had to be checked. The stationmaster made a mental note of the stranger, then returned to his duties.

The newcomer continued toward the river. He trembled slightly as the smoke cleared and the simple beauty of the mountainside revealed itself. A small sign stood beside the bridge. It read MEDICINE BOW RIVER.

"Didn't use to need signs for a man to know where he was," the stranger grumbled. "Didn't use to need maps to tell the way or a compass to know north from south."

There was no one there to hear him. The words weren't intended for other ears. They served only as a reminder of another time, another place, another life.

The man inhaled deeply, spitting out the taste of oil and smoke. It wasn't what he had expected, not by half. Closing his eyes, he could hear the river beneath the bridge sweeping its way down the valley toward a rendezvous with the North Platte. Farther on that same water would surge across the broad prairies of Nebraska on its way to the mighty Mississippi.

Fort Laramie stood near the North Platte. The Cheyennes had signed the first great treaty with the federal government there in '51, the year before he was born. A second, greater treaty was signed at the fort in '68. That was just after . . .

He shook his head and turned around. He felt awkward, out of place. It wasn't cold, but a chill had come to his bones. The mountains had frozen him in some strange trance. He could sense something touching him, speaking to him in a way old Iron Hand had once mentioned.

It couldn't be the mountains alone. He'd seen other mountains, the Rockies near Denver and the high ranges that stretched across northern Colorado into the Wyoming Territory. He'd been through the valley of the Bighorn, too, where his cousin Dancing Lance had been killed fighting in the Fetterman battle. No, it wasn't the mountains.

But as he continued walking, the strangeness grasped him tighter than ever. He stopped his feet and stared out past the river at the countryside. Beyond the river was a clearing. In its center stood a small wooden cabin. He thought he heard someone chopping wood there, and a rider dressed in a bearskin coat flashed by riding a tall black stallion.

The visitor rubbed his eyes, and the vision disappeared. The clearing was overgrown by scrub cedar, and only a black scar hinted a cabin had once existed. Ground squirrels and a small deer now walked the mountainside.

"Things change," he mumbled as he stared at the mountain.

And as he stood there, shivering from a chill that had nothing to do with the briskness of the wind, he recalled something his father had once spoken.

"There's somethin' about a man's soul that brings him home, boy. A man's not cut out to be no tumbleweed, driftin' along at the whimsy o' the wind. No, a man's got to sink his roots into the ground to stand up to what gets throwed at him out here."

Roots? Yes, perhaps that was it. All his life he'd been lost. How long had he been away now, twelve years? Had it been that long? It was difficult to notice the passage of time when you were worried about filling your belly or keeping your hide in one piece.

"A man must never surrender the place of his birth," old Iron Hand had said just before the Cheyennes had joined in the Powder River War. "There is always something a man must fight for."

And so Iron Hand had ridden to war.

The stranger remembered that day, though in truth he hadn't understood. When news arrived that summer that Dancing Lance was dead, there'd been mourning in the cabin. He'd read prayers with his mother for the dead cousin who'd taught him to stalk deer. If he'd known what was to follow, he might have saved those prayers for himself.

The stranger shook his head to clear it of the memories. He hadn't come to remember. He'd come to do something, and there was an urgency to it. He headed back toward the depot, frowning as he saw the dark cloud of smoke curl up the ridge in front of him.

"Things do change, Pa," he whispered, somehow feeling his father's spirit close beside him just then.

Back at the depot, the stationmaster walked over and smiled.

"Could've told you was nothing out that way, mister," the Irishman said. "Would you be needin' a place to stay perhaps?"

"Is there a hotel in town?" the newcomer asked.

"Third buildin' on the left. Pat O'Hara's place. Mrs. O'Hara might be makin' biscuits for supper tonight, as it's Saturday."

"Is it? Well, that'd be fine."

"Yes, she's quite a cook, is Mrs. O'Hara."

With a parting wave, the stationmaster returned to his dank office inside the depot. The stranger turned and headed in the direction of the hotel. Once inside, a tall young man in a black coat and worn out necktie raced to the front desk.

"Good day to you, sir," the young man said. "We're most happy to welcome you to Thompson's Mountain. First time here, sir?"

"Uh, yes," the stranger replied warily.

"Staying long?"

"Just until I can find a house."

"Well, sir, now the Murphy place is up for sale. Just to the end of town, it is. A fine house, with nary a window broken. Mr. Murphy himself was laid out just last month, and the widow, dear lady, left only yesterday for her sister's in Grand Island."

"I'll inquire about it," the stranger said, taking out a small pocketbook and jotting a few words down on the first blank page. "Now, as to a room . . ."

"I've got a nice suite upstairs. There's a fine view of the river, and—"

"That would be fine. And a bath?"

"I'll have hot water and a tub sent up after supper, if that's convenient. Mrs. O'Hara will have biscuits ready at six, with roast beef and boiled potatoes."

"That will do quite nicely," the stranger said, inhaling the aromas seeping into the lobby from the kitchen.

"Might I ask what business you could be having here in town?" the clerk asked.

"I suppose you might ask," the stranger said, his eyes growing cold and dark. "But I won't be telling."

With a crooked right hand the man signed the hotel register. John Wilson, Denver.

"Welcome to Thompson's Mountain, Mr. Wilson," the young man said again as he rang a small bell. "I'm Brian Shea. If I can be of service, simply ask."

"Thank you," Wilson said coldly, "but I think I can handle things myself."

As Wilson took his key and started toward the stairs, a small boy of ten years or so appeared.

"I'll take that, sir," the boy said, grabbing Wilson's bag.

"There's no need," Wilson objected. "I can carry it myself."

"Please, sir, it's my job," the boy pleaded. "Mr. O'Hara won't feed me if I don't do my job."

"Well, I wouldn't care to be responsible for starving a boy," Wilson said, a trace of a smile appearing for the first time on his sour face.

"You've a kind heart, mister," the boy said, dragging the heavy bag along as Wilson marched up the stairs.

"You work here for your keep, do you?" Wilson asked when they entered the room.

14

"Well, sir, my ma and pa died, you see, and there's little work for a boy in this town. My sister Katy does sewing for the ladies, but there's little of that in the summer."

"Do you know horses, boy?"

"Rode my first pony when I was but eight. And my name's Jeff Kelly, sir. I don't take to being called boy, even if I'm naught but an orphan."

Wilson's hands trembled a moment, and his face turned pale.

"You all right?" young Jeff asked.

"Yes, it's just that I've come a long way."

"Won't take so long when they build the cutoff to Denver."

"Tell me something, Jeff. How'd you come by your name?"

"Oh, it's by way of my father's idea. He called my eldest brother Washington. Me, I got Jefferson. There's an Adams and a Madison in our family as well."

"So you're a regular American."

"With a bit of Irish to him."

"Still, you appear young to be lugging bags up stairs."

"Well, only other job to be had was at the saloon, and Katy put her foot down on that."

"Well, Jefferson Kelly, I might have something for you myself. Can you keep secrets?"

"By the good saints, I can."

"Then, find me a good horse to buy. And a rig complete with sound team as well. By noon tomorrow, and there's a dollar in it for you."

"Done," the boy said, extending his small hand to Wilson.

Wilson gripped the grimy hand firmly and gazed into Jeff's bright green eyes and reddish-blond hair.

"Have this for good measure," Wilson said, releasing the boy's hand and flipping a bright silver dollar toward the still-outstretched palm.

"Oh, sir!" the boy exclaimed. "Why, if there's a horse to be found west o' Laramie, it's yours!"

"Tell me, Jeff, are Mrs. O'Hara's biscuits any good?"

"Oh, like paradise, they are, but stay clear o' the turnips, sir. They cause your stomach to turn all the night."

"I'll keep that in mind," Wilson said, laughing. "Now get along with your duties."

"Yes, sir," the boy replied, turning to leave. "An' thank you kindly, sir."

The door slammed shut, and Wilson walked to the window. He swept aside the curtains and stared at the mountain. Clouds had gathered with the passing of midday, and he found himself remembering how welcome the afternoon rains had been in summer. He ran his hand through his long sandy-brown hair. It was an old habit that seemed to relieve his worries. It had little effect this time.

"I've come home, Pa," he whispered to the mountain.

Even as he spoke the words, he was chilled by the changes that had come to the world he'd once known so well. There was a bitterness in his heart as he stared at the long shiny rails that stretched out east and west from the town, that clawed their way into the mountainside and blackened the sky.

16

He drew out a small gold watch from his pocket and opened it up. A musical tune filled the air with its happy melody, and he smiled at the portrait inside.

"I had to come, Marie," he whispered.

As he sat in the room and tried not to remember the hard times they'd shared in the mining camps, along Shepherd's Creek, and, later, in Denver, he felt colder than ever. The laughter was missing, the tenderness and the understanding.

"It's happening all over again, isn't it, Pa?" he asked. "Like when Pike and I were alone after the soldiers left."

But this time was different. Before there'd been no choice. This time he'd come there with his eyes wide open. It'd been because he wanted to, needed to. And there was something else that had changed. This time he held all the cards. And the outcome would be different, very different indeed.

After enjoying Mrs. O'Hara's fine dinner of roast beef and biscuits, Wilson waited in his room for the promised bath. When a knock came at the door, he stood up.

"Come in," he said.

A young woman in her late teens carried in a brass tub. An older, larger woman followed with two buckets of steaming water. The second woman stared at him briefly, and Wilson felt uncomfortable. He felt no easier when he recognized in her dark, wrinkled face and bent nose the unmistakable features of a Cheyenne.

"Come on, old woman," the girl ordered, pulling the Indian along with her. "You'd think you never saw a

17

white man before!"

"I see before," the old woman said, gazing at Wilson with eyes full of pain.

"I'll send the boy in later to get the buckets," the girl said. "I'm sorry about this old squaw. She could go to the reservation, but Pa says she won't leave this valley. It has to do with some Cheyenne graveyard or such."

"It's all right," Wilson said. "I understand."

At the sound of his voice, the old woman examined Wilson's face more closely. Nothing was spoken, though, and when the door finally closed, Wilson began undressing.

I wonder if she really recognized me, he thought. He'd expected all the Indians to be gone, what with the Custer massacre and the army riding down every Indian it could find. The old woman couldn't really know him, anyway. He'd last visited the Cheyenne camps as a thin-faced boy of fifteen.

Wilson washed himself carefully, rubbing the old scars on his leg and belly as if that might somehow erase them. The pain from the bullet wounds had long since passed, and any twinge he felt now was due to memory. He suddenly felt old, more ancient than the wrinkled Cheyenne who'd left half an hour ago. He wouldn't be twenty-eight till October, and yet there were wrinkles etched in his forehead, scars on his chest. Only a week before, he'd torn three gray hairs from his head.

"Was I like this before I saw DeMoss again?" he whispered.

After all, DeMoss had aged him once before, turned him in a single instant from boy to man. But that had been long ago, in another lifetime almost. Now he was a different man, John Wilson, of Denver, Colorado. Or was he?

That night he lay alone on a big feather mattress beneath a canopied bed, gazing through the open window at a million stars. He couldn't remember John Wilson. He could only recall someone else, a small boy running across a virgin mountainside. Somehow the railroad and the town had been erased. There were only the mountain and the cabin and the boy.

II

The Indians had named it the country of the medicine bow after that weapon of legend touched by the warrior spirits of the plains. Atop the great boulder-strewn mountains spread great forests of pine and spruce. In the summer, patches of wildflowers splashed color across hillsides dotted with antelope and elk.

It was a virgin land then, crossed more often by majestic eagles than by the parties of Arapaho and Cheyenne Indians who sought poles for their lodges and meat for their bellies. The ruts of the white man's road to California and Oregon lay to the north while the great peaks of Colorado drew goldseekers farther south.

One white man did come to the Medicine Bow Mountains, though, a man strong like the mountains. His great, massive forearms resembled the trunks of the lodgepole pines. He was christened Ezekial Thompson, born on a black winter's night the year General Andrew Jackson drove the British army back from New Orleans.

Some said he came of age hauling cotton bales to a river landing at Natchez. Others told of how his father had come west with Pike's first expedition. It wasn't known how or when he'd first come to the Medicine Bow country or what convinced him to stay. But Zeke Thompson soon became as much a part of that land between the forks of the Platte as the mountains themselves. His name was known from Scott's Bluff to Fort Hall, and there were those who'd learned to step carefully and speak softly in his company.

By that time he was already past fifty, an old man for those times, even if his life had been a peaceful one. Streaks of gray could be detected in his full beard, and there was a thinning of the coarse brown hair that hung over his ears down to his broad shoulders.

Old Zeke stood well over six feet tall, and his girth was legend. Two full-grown men, it was said, could stand elbow to elbow in his shadow. His bent nose and the jagged scar on his left cheek bore witness to a life that had seen its share of fighting and dying.

If it had been possible to peer beneath the great bearskin coat that seemed always to be about Zeke Thompson's shoulders, other scars might have been seen. There was a great tear across his chest made by an outraged grizzly, the thin red lines carved by three decades of arrowheads and lead balls. And on his back, kept secret from all the world, were the telltale streaks etched by a stern father's whip more than forty years earlier.

Big Zeke had done it all. He'd worked for Fitzpatrick's fur company, trapping beaver in the Rockies. He'd scouted for wagon trains headed for the distant Willamette Valley in Oregon. He'd tried his hand at farming, been a post trader, even worked as a carpenter. Finally he'd built a three-room cabin overlooking the Medicine Bow River and settled down with his wife, Ruth, to raise two sons and live out his days.

To the boy running across the meadow toward him, Zeke had no need to be more than he was, the biggest and bravest man that had ever been. After all, that boy had watched Cheyenne chiefs stand in awe of his father, and such men as those feared nothing.

For as long as anyone could remember, the peaks of the Medicine Bow country had been nameless. But from the moment old Zeke cut the first pines for the foundation of his cabin, that mountain took on his name. Even the Cheyennes called the place Thompson's Mountain, naming it so on a treaty cloth even the army recognized. The boy expected, as indeed the Indians said, that Zeke Thompson would walk the mountainside as long as there was a sun shining in the heavens. It was the way of boys not to notice how with each passing year, the hand of change crept ever closer.

"Pa, did you shoot the buffalo?" the boy might ask. "Can I have a rifle of my own next summer?"

Old Zeke would reach down and pull his scrawny son onto the horse with him and growl.

"Boy, ain't you never goin' to grow some?"

"I grown some last spring, Pa," the boy would answer.

Then Zeke would spur the old horse and race to the cabin, howling so that the mountains themselves seemed to shake. A smile appeared on the old man's face as he found no hint of fear in the boy's eyes.

Standing like a sentinel in the door of the cabin would be the boy's mother, stiff like a board, wearing a look that hinted of violence in her solemn, half-Cheyenne eyes.

"I warned you not to be so rough with that boy!" she'd say as Zeke swung his son off the horse and dropped him to the ground below.

"You's tough, ain't you, Jeff?" his father asked.

"Tough as buffalo hide, Pa," the boy answered, smiling at the approval he read in his father's eyes.

The boy's mother would then pull him to his feet and scold him for being so reckless. Then he would fetch water from the river for drinking or washing or some such thing, and his mother and father would share a quiet moment alone before supper.

He remembered her fondly. Her father, the Reverend Jonas Ryland, had come west from St. Louis to spread the gospel among the heathen Cheyenne. He'd won few converts, but the little school he'd built on the Laramie River had brought the written word to the Dakota Territory.

Ryland had taken a Cheyenne wife. When a daughter had been born, he'd named her Ruth. In the Bible Ruth was a woman of great devotion, and the girl proved worthy of the name. Following her mother's death, Ruth served as the link between her father's ministry and the Cheyennes. Many times old Iron Hand, her mother's brother, had shielded young Ruth and her father during periods of conflict between the cavalry and the neighboring tribes.

Jonas Ryland later remarried, and Ruth worked as nursemaid and tutor to three brothers. Then Zeke Thompson offered to build her father a new mission in return for the favor of Ruth's affections. The reverend was somewhat relieved to turn over his half-Cheyenne daughter to a white man who could provide for her, and getting the new mission buildings in the bargain was the kind of shrewd bargain no frugal New Englander could resist.

Zeke never regretted the deal. Ruth was as loyal and hard-working a woman as her biblical namesake, and though her Cheyenne relatives sometimes regarded her as quarrelsome and pigheaded, Zeke excused her behavior on the grounds that she was usually right in the end.

She was tall for a woman of those times, straight as an arrow, with dark hair and warm eyes. She was taut, wound so tight Zeke half expected her to unravel the first time she took off her Philadelphia-made corset. But she was warm and comfortable, and the combination of her stern religious father and her proud Cheyenne mother produced a woman no less firm and courageous than her husband.

Often when the boy returned from the river with the water buckets, his mother helped him empty them into the big barrel beside the stove. Then she would sweep a long strand of light brown hair away from his large, walnut-colored eyes and hold him firmly by the shoulders.

"Are the chickens fed, Jeff?" she'd ask.

"Yes, Ma," he'd answer. "The kindlin's in the box, and I checked on the horses already. Time for lessons?"

"Time for lessons," his mother'd echo, grinning as the boy raced to fetch the ancient grammar and its companion, a book of stories they both knew by heart.

Those lessons drew them together. Ruth Thompson had never been able to impart her love of learning to Zeke, or to her older son, Pike. But in young Jefferson she'd found a willing, often eager pupil.

"Why pour all that book learnin' down the boy's throat, woman!" Zeke continually grumbled. "Boys ought to be runnin' through campfires and swimmin' naked in the river."

"An educated man has a future in this country, Zeke Thompson!" Ruth answered each time.

"Only future a book-learned man's got 'round here is gettin' scalped by Indians or bein' ate by grizzly bears."

Zeke Thompson's laughter rolled like thunder through the cabin, but Ruth just shook her head.

"Don't mind him," she told young Jeff as the boy opened the grammar book. "Deep down he's proud you can read and write."

Jeff sometimes had his doubts. If the reading drew him closer to his mother, it pushed him away from his father. There were days when Jeff wondered if Zeke Thompson would ever gaze down at him with the pride that had once filled those great, sorrowful eyes.

Things changed little as the years passed. Jeff spent a summer with his cousins in Iron Hand's camp, hunting and fishing and learning the ways of the Cheyenne. Iron Hand taught the use of the bow. The old man handed his twelve-year-old grandnephew a weapon that might have tested a full-grown warrior. For days Jeff strained to bend that bow, to pull the bowstring back to his ear. At times it appeared fruitless. But Jeff was the son of Zeke Thompson, and by summer's end the boy had mastered the bow and killed an antelope while riding full gallop on a half-wild pony.

Most of the lessons had come from Dancing Lance, the tall dour-faced cousin only two years Jeff's senior. Dancing Lance taught the merits of keeping hidden from the enemy. One afternoon the Cheyenne clipped a large lock of light-brown hair and grinning, hung it from a nearby lodgepole. Jeff took great care to prevent a second scalping.

Dancing Lance was unequaled as a hunter. The youth had won his name from the speed with which he could hurl a spear. It amazed Jeff that the young Cheyenne could get to within striking distance of a creature as swift as the antelope before hurling his weapon.

"I pray to the hunter spirit," Dancing Lance explained. "Don't say that to your mother, for she'll say I will burn in the pit for it."

Jeff never told, nor did he mention that he himself had prayed to that same spirit once or twice. It was, after all, a boy's way to try anything that might win him acceptance. When he brought into camp his first kill, a spring antelope, there was much dancing and celebrating among his Cheyenne cousins.

The recollection of those times warmed the heart of the man Jeff Thompson had become. The Powder River War had come, though, and the Cheyenne camps had moved north into the land of Red Cloud's Sioux. Even as the news of Dancing Lance's death reached the mountain, news of another kind crept in from the east.

It had long been the dream of the government in Washington to build a railroad from one end of the growing nation to the other. "Atlantic to Pacific" was the popular call. The Civil War had halted the plans, but in the year following Lee's surrender, rails had begun the long march up the Platte from Omaha. Soon the railroad was across the Nebraska border into the Dakota Territory, bringing with it people and civilization.

It was to that time that Jeff Thompson's memory was drawn, to the final days of his fifteenth summer. Many would have considered him still a boy had he not been the son of Zeke Thompson. The long, sunny days brought a strange, strawlike tint to his hair and a dark, leathery tan to his shoulders. His eyes darkened with flashes of growing confidence. At a glance he appeared frail, little more than a stick at times. And yet there was something rock solid about young Jeff, a touch of iron to his arms and shoulders. He could ride all day and all night. He never seemed to tire.

Jeff, like his father, was most at home under the open sky. He passed more nights along the Medicine Bow and North Platte than on the straw bed of the cabin. Nearing fifteen, his passions for the bright sky and the clear rivers were those of his Cheyenne cousins.

He wasn't small for fourteen, though at times it appeared so. He was still a full head short of his father, and half that shy of his twenty-year-old brother, Pike. Jeff, more than ever, was impatient to get his full growth, if for no other reason than to lay to rest the jests Pike and his father exchanged over the strange sound of his voice and the clumsiness that came with a body that was mostly legs.

That particular morning Jeff sat at a table finishing lessons his mother had assigned the day before. A new book of history had arrived from Peter Ryland, his mother's half-brother. The young man had taken over the Laramie River mission the previous year, and Ruth

Thompson had assembled a shelf of books as a result. The new book told all about the war against the southern states that had just been won, and it was as foreign to Jeff as might have been a tale of China.

"Still readin' that book, boy?" his father asked from across the room. "You'd think two books'd be enough for any man's lifetime. Woman, you've spoiled this boy for the mountains."

"Nonsense," Ruth said, stirring a large kettle on the stove. "You say yourself he rides near as well as a Cheyenne."

"Well, he's a long way from bein' the man Pike is," Zeke Thompson declared, gazing first at Jeff, then at the corner where Pike was still sleeping.

"Give him time, Zeke," Ruth pleaded. "Pike's already a man, and Jeff's still got years of growing."

"I was full-growed when I was his age," Zeke mumbled. "Too much soft livin' for him."

As Zeke went on to recount for the thousandth time some winter spent alone in the Rockies, Jeff finished answering the questions his mother had written on a small slate.

"I'm finished, Ma," Jeff announced.

"Then, put the slate in its place and shelf the book," she instructed.

"Boy, we look to be in need of wood for the stove," Zeke observed as Jeff returned the book.

"I'll split some," Jeff told his father. The boy then headed out the door.

He paused long enough to take the long, double-bitted ax from the toolshed, then continued on to the woodpile. As he took the first length of pine and prepared to split it into slivers for the stove, he wondered why his father found it so difficult to call him by name. Jeff knew, though, that he'd never ask, for fear of what the answer might be. Perhaps, he thought, Jefferson Thompson would never be more than just a boy to split wood or fetch water.

He drove the heavy bit of the ax into the wood, sending splinters of pine flying in half a dozen directions. The mountainside resounded with the steady slamming of the ax against the logs. Chopping wood had been Jeff's chore since he was big enough to lift the heavy ax over his head. In the beginning it had pleased him to have a man's work to do, but lately it had become tiresome. Still, splitting logs on such a perfect morning made his body feel fierce and lively, strong and vibrant.

He set the ax aside long enough to wipe the sweat from his forehead. Then he peeled off his shirt and let the cool breeze refresh him. Soon he resumed the work, splitting logs until he lost track of time. Once he'd amassed three kindling boxes' worth of stovewood, he returned the ax to the toolshed, then filled his arms with wood and carried it inside the house.

"Took long enough," his father commented as Jeff deposited the wood in the box beside the stove.

"There's more outside," Jeff said, returning to the bright sunlight. He made two more trips to the woodpile. When the kindling box was filled to overflowing, he sat at the table and waited for dinner.

"Jeff, the wash basin's not empty," his mother told him as she lit the stove. "You're not so old that you've forgotten to wash, are you? You might find a fresh shirt in your chest."

"Yes, ma'am," he said, heading for the basin.

"Pike, a change might be in order for you as well," Ruth told her older son as he rose, yawning.

Jeff glanced back at this older brother. Pike frowned. His eyes filled with that brooding silence usually reserved for an enemy. They all knew this would be Pike Thompson's final summer on the mountain. He was twenty now, and that was an age at which a man took up his own lodge and his own life.

"Surely, Ma," Pike said, the darkness leaving his eyes.

Jeff felt his brother's big hand on his shoulder and hurried to get himself scrubbed. There was a devotion behind those brooding eyes that could be missed. Though Pike and Jeff were as different as two sons of the same man and woman could be, there was a strange interdependence.

"Zeke?" Ruth asked as Jeff slipped a fresh shirt over his shoulders. Zeke Thompson answered with a harsh stare that silenced the others. It wasn't until they were assembled around the table for breakfast that another word was spoken, and then it was Ruth's daily grace.

"Pike, I'll be needin' the mules," Zeke said as they ate. "After breakfast you go an' bring 'em down. Best get that new saddle pony, too."

"Where are you bound?" Pike asked. "To the Cheyenne camps up north?"

"No, an' you best stay clear o' them your own self, Pike. They's ridin' with the Sioux, and that bunch'd as soon scalp a white man as look him over."

"White man?" Pike asked, rubbing the dark-brown flesh of his forearm. If Jeff's sandy hair reminded their mother of her father's Connecticut family, Pike's raven-black hair and sullen brown eyes were the legacy of her

30

Cheyenne mother.

"You going to the fort, Pa?" Jeff asked.

"Leave early tomorrow," Zeke answered. "Be gone maybe six weeks."

"Need some company?" Pike asked.

"Figure on takin' your ma along. Been a long time since she's seen her brothers."

"Pa, we could all go," Jeff said excitedly. "We last got to the fort more'n two summers back."

"No, best to keep somebody here," Zeke declared. "Pike's old enough to be on his own. Even you, boy, ought to get accustomed to dependin' on your own self some."

"It has been a long time since we've all been to Fort Laramie together, Zeke," Ruth said, offering another corncake to her husband.

"I know how long it's been, woman," Zeke said angrily. "If I was aimin' to take 'em, I'd said so. No, they'll be stayin'."

Silence settled over the table for a few minutes. Pike, as always, accepted his father's word as law. Jeff gazed pleadingly at his mother, hoping she might intercede. There'd been talk of him going to the fort alone, spending the whole winter there with his Uncle Peter. But the war that was being fought between the army and the Indians over the Bighorn country had swallowed that idea.

"Guess I could be bringin' them boys back somethin' from Laramie," Zeke finally said. "We got lots o' pelts to tote, and there'll be room on the mules for some goods comin' back."

"I could purely do with one o' them new Winchester rifles, Pa," Pike said. "I seen one when that cavalry patrol came through last winter scoutin' the trails."

"Might be a good idea to look into, Pike," Zeke said, scratching his bearded chin. "How 'bout you, boy? Got any wants?"

"Maybe a new book of stories, huh, Ma?" Jeff asked. "I just about got all the old ones in my head word for word."

"Books?" Zeke said, shaking his head. "Books? Woman, you never should've learned that boy to read. Books? A boy with fifteen summers under his britches ought to be askin' for trade whiskey and painted women."

"He's had his eye on a little gal down in Mornin' Star's camps, Pa," Pike said, grinning widely. " 'Course she's a full head taller and a mite more skilled with a bow."

"Best watch them Cheyenne gals, boy," Zeke warned. "I got myself half o' one, and she's been nothin' but trouble."

Ruth scowled as Zeke bellowed.

"Well, you can just get your own supper for that, Zeke Thompson!" she said. "It's bad enough to make fun of your own son, but to talk of me like that!"

"Was only jestin', woman," Zeke said, following her to the door. "You know I never had one thought o' goin' back on my bargain."

"Well, that's better. I'll see to the books myself, Jeff," she said, smiling at the boy. "Painted women indeed! You've been to one rendezvous too many, Zeke Thompson! There'll be fires waiting in hell for you, and that's for certain."

Pike and Jeff exchanged fearful glances with their father as Ruth launched a tirade against the evils of drink and debauchery. When she finally finished half an hour later, the sun stood high in the sky, and chores were waiting. The animals had to be brought in, and the packing for the long journey to Fort Laramie began in earnest.

III

As Jeff Thompson rode his tall black stallion through the valley, he glanced back at the cabin. His mother and father had been gone three days, and the silence that draped the mountainside was more than he could bear. The sun wouldn't be up for another hour, but Jeff knew the Medicine Bow country like his own nose, and there was no danger to riding along in the dark.

There was a heavy dew that morning that transformed the tall grasses to an amber ocean swaying in the mountain breezes. That same wind blew damp and cool against Jeff's face, and he regretted not wearing the heavy woolen coat his mother had woven for him the winter before. Pike's old deerskin jacket was usually perfect for such a day, but an unusual chill bit the air, and he found himself shivering.

"Best not dawdle, little brother," Pike called to him from somewhere ahead. "Them antelope ain't goin' to wait on us."

Jeff didn't bother answering. He just nudged the big black forward, and the animal picked up its pace.

"Figure there's anybody up to the Cheyenne camps by now?" Jeff asked his brother.

"Not likely," Pike said, spitting a sour taste from his mouth. "I was up that way last week, and there was nary a sign. From what them soldiers was sayin', the Cheyennes had themselves a busy summer shootin' bluecoats up on the Powder River."

Jeff gave his horse a second nudge, and the distance between the two riders closed considerably.

"I miss the Cheyennes," Jeff mumbled. "Seems too quiet for summer. Iron Hand promised I could go with him after buffalo in the north country this year."

"Iron Hand didn't know there was goin' to be war, though. I figure maybe the soldiers had 'bout enough o' that now. There's been some talk o' peace. I figure Pa'll let us know when he gets back."

"Guess so."

"You ain't missin' that little Cheyenne gal, are you?" Pike asked, grinning broadly.

"That's kind of tiresome as a joke, Pike. No, I was thinking about Dancing Lance."

"Does no good thinkin' o' the dead, little brother. They put him on his scaffold last winter. Better to think o' the livin'. Pa always says a man ought to keep his eyes to his own affairs."

They crossed several miles before either of them spoke again. Jeff was content to listen to the birds singing, and he could tell Pike had an eye on something else. There was little point to talking to Pike anyway. If it merited speaking, Pike would say it himself. When Jeff went to jabbering away, as was his habit, there'd often be a splash in the nearby river caused by the sudden arrival of a surprised fourteen-year-old.

"I saw close to twenty antelope up past them rocks

35

there," Pike said as they wound their way between two slopes. "Even a Kansas farmer ought to be able to hit somethin' if he keeps his ears and eyes open."

Jeff didn't reply. He knew the comment was directed at the poor aim he'd demonstrated on their last hunting trip.

"We'll leave the horses here," Pike said, leading the way to a small stand of pines. "Prime your rifle and keep to my right. I don't plan to get myself shot by my own little brother."

"I wouldn't be shooting at you," Jeff mumbled.

"Might be safer if you was," Pike joked as he slapped Jeff between the shoulder blades.

They then wove their way through the trees, bending over so as to offer no clue to their presence. The buckskin soles of their moccasins touched the ground so lightly that no audible sound resulted. Soon they were among the boulders where Pike had earlier spied the antelopes. They crept forward cautiously until they reached the edge of a mountain meadow.

Pike tapped Jeff on the shoulder, then pointed to the left. Jeff followed his brother's fingers to where the antelopes were grazing on the soft grass that surrounded a small spring. The animals seemed ignorant of the danger awaiting them.

"You take the second shot," Pike whispered as he leveled his old trade rifle and fixed the largest of the bucks in his sights. "Take the one on the right. Just below the shoulder."

"I know where to shoot," Jeff grumbled as he brought his long rifle to bear.

"Well, see you hit the mark this time."

A moment later the stillness was shattered by two

blasts. Powder smoke filled the air, and the antelopes flew into motion.

"You got him. That's for sure!" Pike declared. "Plugged him sure as I'm standin' here, little brother."

Jeff stared ahead at where the single antelope lay. A pool of bright-red blood spread beside its chest.

"You didn't miss, did you?" Jeff asked.

"You know I didn't," Pike growled as he started forward. "He moved just as I fired. My ball hit him in the neck. We'll have to trail him a ways."

Jeff followed his brother down a slight slope and on across the meadow.

"Best dress your kill," Pike said. "I'll drag mine back here. If you finish 'fore I get back, go down and bring the horses."

"Sure," Jeff said.

"You done good, little brother," Pike spoke before leaving. "Pa'd be proud o' you this day. Keep that rifle handy. I seen wolves up here before."

"I will."

"That was a fair-sized antelope, Jeff. Might be dark 'fore I bring him in. Wouldn't do no harm to have a bit of supper ready if I was to be late."

"Antelope steaks and fry bread," Jeff promised. "I'm only a fair shot, but I can cook just fine."

"See you don't burn the bread," Pike warned. "I best get started."

"Watch the rockslides, Pike."

"Always do," Pike mumbled as he headed into the forest in search of the wounded antelope.

It took Pike every bit as long as he'd suspected to find and kill the animal. Jeff had little chance to be concerned about it, though. There were the horses to be brought up, a fire to build, and the butchering of the antelope.

None of it was new to Jeff. He'd skinned animals and field-dressed the meat ever since he could remember. Zeke Thompson would never allow the boys to wash pots or clean house, but hunting and butchering were judged proper work for a man, along with fetching water and chopping wood, feeding stock, and such.

"Got that fry bread ready?" Pike asked as he emerged from the darkness. "I could eat a pine cone just now."

"Here," Jeff said, breaking off a corner of the bread and tossing it to his brother.

"Gave me quite a run, that one did," Pike said, pointing to the dead antelope he'd dragged back. "Must've bled himself past carin'."

"Guess so," Jeff agreed.

"Got camp set up, I see. How far you drag your kill off?"

"Close to a hundred yards, I'd guess. You sit down and get your dinner. I'll tend to yours."

"A man dresses his own kill," Pike objected, putting a firm hand on Jeff's chest to stop him. "I'll get to it directly. You go ahead eatin'."

Jeff smiled. Not long before, Pike would have turned over the dirty work without thinking twice. In an unspoken way it was an acknowledgment that Jeff was no longer a boy to be taken along to learn the ways of the woods. A wolf howled off in the distance, and Jeff pulled his rifle closer.

"Likely he's two, maybe three miles back," Jeff judged.

"It'd seem so," Pike responded. "Saw some tracks

back a bit."

"Well, I guess that means it's a wolf for sure. Better'n findin' out the Arapahos are back."

"You just hope it's not Utes. There's too much Cheyenne to your face for their likin'."

"Not so much as is in yours, Pike Thompson!"

"Well, you'll notice I sleep with a knife close-by."

Jeff nodded. He told himself it might not be a bad notion to wrap his rifle in a blanket and keep it handy that night, just in case a wolf or a Ute or whatever decided to pay them a call.

Pike skinned the second antelope and dressed its meat before rejoining Jeff beside the fire. Jeff filled a tin plate with fry bread and antelope steaks, then busied himself with clean-up. It was cool enough in the high country to keep the meat from spoiling, so salting was postponed till morning. Even so it was late when Pike kicked dirt over the last embers of the campfire and the two brothers spread out their blankets.

"It'll be a few days 'fore we need to do any shootin', little brother," Pike pointed out. "Especially to feed you."

Pike tapped Jeff's bony shoulder.

"I don't know about that," Jeff objected. "I eat like Ma's prize hog. I just run most of it off."

Pike chuckled a little, then slid between his blankets. The night was clear and quiet. Even the wolves observed the silence.

"I love nights up here," Jeff whispered. "I think a man could almost hear God."

"Does make you more mindful o' things, don't it?" Pike said quietly.

"Guess Pa'll be down to the river camps by now.

Likely he'll find the whiskey drummer first. Ma'll scream like thunder about that."

"They're a day at least from the river camps. Ma don't travel so fast as she used to, and Pa's mindful o' that."

"Miss 'em much?"

"Not so much. I figure to build my own cabin down where the Medicine Bow joins the North Platte this fall."

"That's a good place. Winter's not so hard there, and plenty of game and fish can be had."

"Trappin's fair, too."

"That what you figure to do, Pike?"

"Most likely. Thought 'bout soldierin', but I couldn't hardly fight the Cheyennes. Not with my face. Don't know I could go down to the towns and find a life. Mostly they need men who read better'n me. They don't take to red faces, neither."

"Trappin's a good life," Jeff said, sighing. "I wouldn't mind it myself. If you have a good place like this mountain, it doesn't take so much to make a life for yourself. We don't need much money, just a little to trade for powder and shot."

"An' for a new horse now an' again."

"Well, you can always catch a horse."

"Or steal one," Pike said, laughing.

The night closed in on them then, and both fell silent. Morning found them fast asleep in the dewy meadow, and it was only when a ground squirrel scampered through their firepit that they stirred.

"First time in a long time I slept past sunrise," Pike declared as he rubbed his eyes. "Best get up an' back to the cabin, little brother."

"You want breakfast first?" Jeff asked.

"I always want breakfast. No more antelope, though."

"Just so happens I have a bit of butter and some eggs. How'd that be?"

"You keep surprisin' me, Jeff. I might have to invite you to my cabin next spring."

"I expect by then you'll have a Cheyenne gal to do the cookin'."

"Well, I might need somebody to go huntin' with."

As they hurried to pack up the meat and break camp, Jeff felt himself smiling all over. It was the closest they'd ever been, closer than Jeff could have imagined six months earlier.

Jeff led the way back to the cabin. It was only an hour's ride, so he felt no urge to hurry. The only thing waiting for them there was work. The chickens needed feeding, and the hogs often escaped their pen. The antelope meat wanted salting, too.

"It's hot today," Pike said when they reached the river.

"I know a way to cool off," Jeff said, glancing back at his brother. "River's right here waiting for us."

"You sure you could stand gettin' wet, little brother?" Pike asked, laughing. They both knew Jeff liked nothing better than swimming that river.

"I could stand it, and you could use it," Jeff said as he climbed off his horse. "You smell like a dead buffalo."

"That right? Well, you ain't no better!"

"Never claimed to be," Jeff said, stripping himself. "I do take a bath once in a while, though."

"Then, take another one," Pike said, shoving Jeff into the river.

Jeff clawed his way back to the bank and began splashing Pike furiously. It was a mistake. A moment later Pike stormed into the water and grabbed Jeff in his massive arms.

"How'd you care to drown a little, Jeff Thompson?" Pike asked, pushing his brother's head under the water.

Jeff never even mumbled a protest. Instead the fourteen-year-old's hands worked themselves free. With a quickness Pike couldn't believe, Jeff bloodied the nose of his tormenter.

"You're dead, boy!" Pike screamed, diving after Jeff's flying feet. "You got to pay for that," Pike added, pinning his brother to the ground.

A year before, Jeff might have pleaded for mercy. That would never happen again. Instead Jeff squirmed and fought back as best he could. Two sound right hands in his belly knocked the fight from him, though, and he lay there lifeless as Pike stared in disbelief.

"How come you to fight me, Jeff?" Pike asked, his eyes clouding with confusion. "Lord knows I got twenty pounds an' six years' growth on you."

"A man stands up for himself. Pa says it often enough."

"Yeah? Well, you wouldn't see me take on no grizzly bear, little brother, an' it's near the same thing, you goin' after me like that."

"Maybe."

"You're crazy," Pike decided. "Pure crazy, Jeff."

"No, just wet," Jeff said, pushing strands on damp yellow hair back from his eyes. "Still want to swim?"

"Sun ain't quit shinin'. I tell you, Jeff. You gone and growed up on me! There's not much boy to you no more. You popped me just fine."

"You didn't do such a bad job on me," Jeff said, rubbing his tender ribs.

The icy water of the river quickly washed away the pain and the weariness, and the two Thompsons found themselves reborn. After splashing each other and scraping off a week's dust, they finally left the river and got dressed.

"Jeff," Pike said, pulling his brother away from the horses a moment, "I got something to say to you."

"What?" Jeff asked, blinking the last of the river from his eyes.

"I knowed it a long time, but I never thought to speak it. Guess now might be the time. Jeff Thompson, you're a better man than me. You can read books, an' you know things."

Jeff's smile faded, and he listened carefully for fear he'd miss something.

"But, little brother, here in the mountains only the strong an' the quick survive. Ain't no quick an' the dead, like Uncle Peter says down in the river camps. It's quick *or* dead. That's the choice. You get that knife o' yours and see to it you know how to fight your way out o' anything."

"I can take care of myself some!"

"Ain'ts 'nough. You got to get the cold eyes to you, look so you'd as soon kill as look at 'em. That's what keeps a man alive up here."

"I don't know as I could do that, Pike. I'm not sure I could kill a man."

"Then, you best go to the fort an' stay with Uncle Peter. Time'll come when there's killin' to be done for a man who'd build his lodge in this country."

"Ever kill a man, Pike?"

43

"Three times," Pike told him, the color rushing out of his face as he spoke. "An' Jeff, I could kill a man without bein' very mad at him if there was a need."

The words left Jeff pale and empty. It was all he could manage to get himself mounted and follow Pike back to the cabin. The air had grown cold and lifeless. Even the birds grew quieter.

IV

It was later that same day that they saw the fire. At first it appeared to be a mirage, a single thin spiral of black outlined against the clear blue afternoon sky. But then the smell arrived, an intruding scent of cedar that disturbed the natural state of the mountain.

"Can't be Cheyenne," Jeff remarked as he and Pike saddled their horses. "Not from that direction. Anyway, no Cheyenne would burn green wood in his fire."

"Strange we didn't smell 'em earlier," Pike said. "We couldn't been far from 'em last night. We'd heard a troop o' soldiers, and trappers know better'n comin' up Zeke Thompson's mountain uninvited."

"There's only one fire," Jeff observed. "Too small to be for cookin'. No old timer would build himself a fire for coffee in the summer."

"Likely some folks got themselves lost from the emigrant road."

"This far south?" Jeff asked.

"Well, better take your rifle along just to be sure. An' fetch Pa's pistol for me."

Jeff froze a minute as he gazed into his brother's cold eyes. It was that killing look he'd spoken of earlier.

"We chased men off this mountain 'fore, little brother," Pike reminded Jeff. "They run faster when you show up armed."

"Guess so," Jeff said, reluctantly turning toward the cabin.

It wasn't long before he'd gathered the weapons and returned outside. Pike took the pistol, then motioned toward the horses. As they rode along the river, Jeff felt himself shiver. It wasn't cold, and he wore his woolen coat besides. No, the chills came as Jeff read a grim determination in his brother's eyes.

"Killin' a man's not to be taken lightly," Zeke Thompson had said once. "You shoot a deer, well, that's the nature o' things. But shootin' a man breaks the Lord's covenant, an' it's best considered some. Once you put a hole in a man, it's too late to do the thinkin'."

Jeff recalled something else, though—words spoken to him only a year before.

"There is always a thing a man must fight for."

Old Iron Hand had said it the night his band of Cheyennes had packed up and headed north to join the Sioux in their war for the Powder River country.

"Each man is a warrior," Dancing Lance had explained when Jeff first learned to draw a bowstring. "Even the gentle ones such as you must hunt for food and fight the enemy. Life must be bought, just as flour is paid for at the fort."

Dancing Lance paid the price, Jeff reminded himself. Perhaps on this day Jeff and Pike might pay as well.

"We'd best cross the river here, little brother," Pike declared. "That way the wind'll be in our face."

"It's like trackin' deer," Jeff said as the horses splashed

46

into the river. "All except the killin', that is."

"Oh, that's not so different, neither. But we ain't ridin' out here to kill nobody. This is more of a scout."

Jeff sighed. It was somewhat of a relief to hear Pike say that. Sometimes it was difficult to know what was in Pike's head by looking at his face.

"I figure they's up in the clearin', just past Turtle's Head Point."

"It's flat there," Jeff said. "Perfect for a campsite."

"Poor for trappin', though. Ain't seen a beaver there in years. Stream's all dried up."

"Still, it'd be a fair lookout," Jeff said nervously. "You can see down the valley most all the way to the Platte."

"But not up it," Pike pointed out, grinning at the thought. "Guess maybe they don't know there's anything up this way."

"Maybe they don't care."

"Then, they'd best look to their hides," Pike said, his face taking on a crimson tint. "Zeke Thompson don't care for trespassers."

"Maybe Pa knows."

"He'd never tolerate nobody campin' 'round here without sendin' us word, little brother. That's for sure!"

Jeff wasn't as certain, but he held his tongue. It was safer keeping Pike's anger directed at the intruders.

The brothers wound their way through the rocks and trees of the mountainside for more than five miles before drawing close to the smoke. Voices could be heard on the wind, and Pike held up his hand in a motion that halted them both.

"They're speakin' English," Jeff whispered.

"Well, keep your rifle handy just the same," Pike warned. "White man can kill you just as surely as a red

47

one."

Jeff pulled the long rifle out of its saddle scabbard and rested it on one knee.

"Should I load it?" Jeff asked.

"Wouldn't do much good ridin' up there pointin' a empty rifle."

Pike paused a minute as his younger brother performed the complicated loading operation. It wasn't easily done on horseback, especially considering the unwieldy nature of the rifle. Fortunately the black horse was accustomed to Jeff's firm knees. The animal stirred only twice.

"Ready?" Pike finally asked.

"Ready," Jeff said, swinging the rifle forward and drawing back the hammer.

"Watch 'em careful, little brother," Pike instructed. "You hear me shout, you blow the head off the first one you see and ride like thunder for that fire."

"Sure."

"An' don't worry 'bout bein' able to shoot, Jeff. It comes natural enough at the moment of need."

They waited in silence for a few minutes. Then Pike led the way toward the mysterious campfire, onward into the unknown. The air was frigid, but perspiration dripped down Jeff's neck. Then the trees parted, and the two young riders appeared at the entrance to a small encampment.

Jeff half expected to be met by a flash of rifle fire. Instead he found himself confronting a half-dozen white men dressed in city clothes. One tall young man in the center stood, took a long cigar from his mouth, and glanced from Jeff to Pike.

"Howdy," the man said.

Jeff looked to his brother, but Pike merely nodded.

"You boys from around here?" the stranger asked. "I've been trying to hire a guide for weeks."

"We got a cabin a ways back," Pike answered.

"Well, that's fine news. Why don't you two climb down and warm yourselves? I never dreamed it could be so cold in the summertime."

"Night's a good deal worse," Pike said, rolling off his horse without taking his eyes off the man with the cigar.

Jeff followed suit, sliding off his horse. Pike gave a silent nod, and Jeff uncocked the rifle, then replaced it in the scabbard.

"Tie up the horses, Jeff," Pike instructed. "Guess we'd best have a talk with these fellows."

When Jeff returned from the chore, he sat down on a rock beside his brother and listened to the man with the cigar.

"My names's Henry DeMoss," the stranger said. "I'm chief engineer for the Union Pacific."

"The what?" Pike asked.

"The railroad," Jeff whispered.

"How come you to be here?" Pike asked DeMoss.

"This is my survey crew," DeMoss explained. "We're looking for the best route through the mountains into Salt Lake and California."

"Why come through here?" Jeff asked. "Everybody knows the best route for travelin' to California. You hug the Platte to the Sweetwater, then cross the high mountains past Fort Bridger."

"If you were going by wagon, I'd agree," DeMoss said. "There's water and grass. But a railroad needs a straight line. Our route comes along the South Platte, then swings due west. It's a hundred miles out of the way to even touch the North Platte."

"And there's Indians up there, too," one of the others said. "The Sioux and Cheyenne are making war on the whole army."

"There's a Cheyenne camp not ten miles from here," Pike told them.

"From here?" DeMoss asked, glancing around in alarm.

"They're all up on the Powder River just now," Jeff said.

" 'Course, if they was to hear you was buildin' a railroad through the heart o' their country, they just might come on down here," Pike added. "Real fast!"

"We'll be needing some help from the army," DeMoss told his companions. "This railroad will be built! You can bank on that, my friends."

"Not through these mountains," Pike objected. He stood and stomped his feet. "This land belongs to Zeke Thompson!"

"Thompson?" one of the men asked. "This Thompson's Mountain?"

"He's right, Mr. DeMoss," another one agreed. "You wouldn't want to take on this Thompson fellow."

"The man's half rock and half grizzly," a third told DeMoss. "I saw him kill three men with a knife down in the river camps a few years back. He's half devil!"

"Nonsense," DeMoss declared.

"You ain't never met the man," Pike said. "He's our pa, an' he's been here since the beginnin', when there weren't no white men in this country. Some say he grew here with the first pine trees. The smart thing'd be for you to turn 'round an' find another way to get to

California."

"You could swing north a bit more," Jeff suggested.

"That means building two bridges instead of one," DeMoss said, shaking his head. "No, this is the shortest route."

"Shortest route to gettin' killed," Pike warned.

"Needn't be that way, son. You don't know what a railroad does for a land. It brings in people and goods, churches and schools," DeMoss pointed out.

"Real schools, like the one on the Laramie River?" Jeff asked.

"Schools and towns, fine hotels, and industry. Why, it brings the future. You never saw anything like the magic a railroad casts on a valley. Whole new cities, like Omaha, crop up overnight. And for a man who owns land along the right-of-way, there's a fortune to be made."

"Ain't interested in no fortune," Pike declared. "We got all we need right here. Only want to be left alone. That's all!"

Pike turned and motioned for Jeff to follow, but DeMoss blocked their path.

"Stay to supper," DeMoss pleaded. "We've got plenty, and I could do with some company from hereabouts, somebody who knows his way around."

"We've got our own business, and we'd best get along with it," Pike said, angrily pushing DeMoss aside and continuing toward the horses.

"You best keep an eye out for wolves, mister," Jeff said as he started after Pike. "They've been known to lurk around this place."

"Oh?" DeMoss asked, raising an eyebrow. "Wouldn't be spinning a tale now, would you?"

"Take it as you choose," Jeff said, untying his horse from a small aspen. "I never wished a man ill, but it might do the wolves in this valley some good to have a meal off you."

DeMoss continued to speak, but Jeff ignored the words. He mounted his horse and followed Pike down the mountainside toward their father's cabin.

That night the two young men sat together on the porch, looking out toward the distant spark of light that marked DeMoss's camp. Two wolves howled, and Pike smiled.

"Guess maybe the wolves'll have a good dinner tonight, eh?" Pike asked. "A nibble or two might encourage them railroaders more'n a backside of buckshot."

"Maybe," Jeff said, sighing.

"You read anything in them books o' yours 'bout railroads, Jeff?"

"Some," Jeff said.

"You figure that man means what he says?"

"Well, I heard some talk of a railroad to California. Truth is, the best pass through these mountains *is* right here. You'd have to cross the river, but I don't figure that'd be too much of a problem. Once you cleared the Medicine Bow Mountains, it'd be a pretty easy thing to get to Green River."

"Pa won't like it. He don't take to people o' any kind, much less men that build roads and bring trouble."

"You figure there'll be trouble?"

"Don't you? 'Less them men go back where they come from an' build their railroad somewhere else, we'll have more of a war here than they ever dreamed of havin' up by the Powder River. The Cheyennes won't take to havin' the buffalo range crossed by more white men, and Pa won't let nobody through here!"

"Would he fight the army, Pike?"

"He'd fight the devil, I expect. Anyway, I guess we better let him know what's goin' on."

"How?"

"I'm goin' to ride to Fort Laramie tomorrow. I guess maybe I could get there in a few days ridin' hard. Little brother, you stay here an' tend to things. An' you might spend some time with them railroaders, 'specially that DeMoss fellow."

"Why?" Jeff asked.

"Learn all you can 'bout their plans. Take care, too, 'cause you never dealt with such men as those before. Keep your eyes open an' keep track of everything they say."

"I could ride to Laramie, and you could stay here, Pike. You know better what to do."

"No, it's for you to do, Jefferson Thompson. The trail to the fort's not one a boy should ride alone. An' the truth is, DeMoss wouldn't be too likely to trust me after today. You, well, I expect he'd tell you his life story, little brother."

"You mean because I'm only fourteen," Jeff said, frowning.

"Just on the outside," Pike replied with a grin. "That's your advantage. You could write it all down, too. I'd like as not forget everything by nightfall."

"You'll be careful crossin' the buffalo trails? Might be some Cheyenne huntin' parties down for the summer."

"I can tend to my own hide pretty good, Jeff. It's you that's got your work cut out for you."

It was true enough, Jeff thought. There were the

animals to be looked after, hunting to be done, and on top of it all, this man DeMoss to be scouted.

When Pike headed off that next morning, Jeff swallowed deeply. An unusual hollowness took possession of him. He'd never been out there all alone before. Even in the Cheyenne camps there'd been Dancing Lance and old Iron Hand. Now there were just the cabin, Jeff . . . and the long, terribly lonely summer nights.

V

Jeff did his best to fend off the solitude by keeping busy. It wasn't hard finding things to occupy his time. Tending the livestock usually took Pike and him half the morning. Doing it alone required half a day. By midafternoon, though, he'd chopped a week's supply of stovewood and stretched strips of venison on the drying racks behind the cabin.

And now? he wondered as he stared off down the mountainside at the river surging through the valley. On another day he might have taken advantage of the August sun to shed his clothes and swim that river. He'd passed many such an afternoon in quest of trout for the supper table. But that day his heart felt no surge of boyish enthusiasm. Instead he saddled his horse and made his way slowly through the tall pines that spread out across the broad shoulders of the mountain.

Jeff had no particular destination in mind. He'd left his rifle in the cabin, so clearly he was not riding in search of game. No, it was a certain restlessness born of isolation that sent him riding, like his Cheyenne ancestors, alone across the valley. He wove his way between the trees so that little more than a shadow of his presence could be detected.

Jeff's mind drifted to another time, another place. He was out beyond the Laramie River with Dancing Lance, riding a spotted pony atop a foreign ridge. The two young cousins watched from the cover of the aspen-studded hillside as a dozen wagons rumbled down the emigrant road toward distant California. Children chased dogs along the flank of the train, their bare, sunburned shoulders and light-colored hair contrasting with the tanned, hardened chests of Jeff and his Cheyenne cousin.

"Once the buffalo blackened this valley," Dancing Lance had said sadly. "Look now at how the white man has left his mark on the land."

Jeff had watched Dancing Lance trace the line of ruts left by two decades of wagon trains. Later that month Jeff had stood atop a limestone cliff etched with hundreds of names.

I used to think no one could own the land, Jeff had thought. But see how these men write their names on the rocks! Some things were beyond understanding.

Even now as he moved along the timberline, unseen save for a circling hawk, Jeff little understood what it was about the white men that drove them ever westward, that kept them from becoming one with the earth and the sky. He knew what had brought Zeke Thompson's wanderings to an end, recognized the zeal that brought his uncle, Peter Ryland, to the banks of the Laramie River.

But what of Henry DeMoss?

Long ago Zeke Thompson had taught his son that to learn a man's motives, you must learn about the man himself. Jeff admired the way his father could read men. Old Iron Hand had the talent, too. Jeff, though, best knew words and phrases, language and history. The hearts of men remained the greatest of life's mysteries.

Jeff located DeMoss's small band of railroaders a half mile from the river. They were spread out in a half-circle along the broad, wide curve of Thompson's Mountain. DeMoss stood clearly in the center, gazing through a small pipelike object mounted on a tripod.

Jeff slid down from the saddle, taking care to shield himself and his horse from view. He then sat in the shadow of a pine, waiting, watching, observing every detail, taking in the various movements of the strangers as they slowly made their way across the mountain.

Jeff understood almost nothing DeMoss did, but even a fool could see the railroad crew was setting red poles in the ground, marking a trail. Jeff noticed something more after a time. The trail followed the curve of the mountain so that the steepest slopes were avoided.

So, that's it, Jeff thought. He's picking the route. The tripod, the strange instruments DeMoss held in his hand . . . they helped him keep to his course. And as one red marker after another was nailed into the rich, warm earth of Thompson's Mountain, Jeff again remembered the deep ruts of the emigrant road etched across the buffalo valleys. Those ruts were so similar to the photographs his uncle had once shown Jeff of the great railroads that stretched across the East.

"Not here," Jeff whispered, closing his eyes and wishing DeMoss and his men away from the land loved no less by Jeff than by his father and mother, a land to which a man could belong, where he might be at home once and for always.

That night after eating alone in the cabin amidst a silence that threatened to swallow the earth, Jeff snaked his way back to DeMoss's camp. Quietly the boy avoided DeMoss's sentry and crept back along the route, slyly removing one pole after another. He relocated each so that the once-level trail now meandered here and there seemingly without purpose, without design.

For two days more Jeff stalked the railroaders, watching as the thin black thread that marked their campfire every morning reappeared each evening farther west. And at night more markers were changed. The morning of his fourth day alone on the mountain, Jeff was awakened by the whinnying of the horses in the corral outside. Instantly he jumped to his feet, pulled on his trousers, and raced to the door.

For a minute or two he saw nothing out of the ordinary. Then he detected a pair of riders weaving their way across the river below. From the clumsy way they rode and the wide-brimmed hats on their heads, Jeff could tell neither was Cheyenne. Too tall to be Pike and too slim to be Zeke Thompson, the riders nevertheless seemed intent on reaching the near bank of the river. And there was no other reason for crossing the Medicine Bow at that point than arriving at the cabin.

Jeff never hesitated. He took down his rifle from its resting place beside the hearth, quickly loaded the gun, and swung the long barrel toward the unexpected and unwelcome horsemen.

"Hello there," the first rider called out. "All right for us to come ahead?"

"No, it's not!" Jeff called out. "Stay clear. This is Zeke Thompson's land, and you're trespassin'."

Jeff swung the rifle out so that the morning sunlight glinted off the barrel. The riders drew up short.

"I come from Mr. DeMoss," the first stranger said. "He thought we might camp along the river today, have a parley, so to speak. Seems somebody's been tamperin' with our stakes. Whole survey's wasted. Got to start over again. You see anybody 'round who'd interfere with another man's work?"

"Oh, I suppose it'd make a difference as to whether that man's work was on his own land or not," Jeff said, stepping outside so that the riders could glimpse the dark scowl on his face. "We told you. This is our place. Take your railroad elsewhere!"

The two horsemen exchanged grins, then turned back toward the river. Jeff busied himself with the stock, pausing only occasionally to study the camp taking shape across the river. By midday DeMoss had his whole outfit there.

Pa's going to like that! Jeff thought. But at the same time there was some comfort to knowing DeMoss was close-by.

An hour later as Jeff plucked weeds from his mother's vegetable garden, he discovered just how close DeMoss could be. A twig snapped, and Jeff jumped to his feet in time to discover the surveyor standing beside the melon patch.

"Didn't mean to interrupt your work, son," DeMoss said, a wide grin spreading across his face.

"I'm not your son, and you're not welcome here," Jeff barked. "You and your fool railroad! Why don't you leave?"

59

"Guess I'm not the leaving kind. If only I could talk to your father. A man like Zeke Thompson, a man who's seen this country opened to civilization, would know his opportunities."

"You don't know him. If you're still around here when he gets back . . ."

"Back?"

Jeff shifted his feet and nervously scratched his ear. It was pure foolishness to jabber away like that.

"I suppose he's off hunting," DeMoss grumbled. "And your brother, the Indian boy?"

Jeff scowled. He and Pike shared the same Cheyenne grandmother, and neither of them had ever apologized for it. Now here was DeMoss, speaking the word "Indian" as if it were the worst sort of insult.

"You'd best pray neither one of them happen across your camp anytime soon," Jeff declared.

"So, I guess that solves the riddle of who's been moving my survey markers," DeMoss said, laughing. "I suppose I have to admire the way he slipped in there on us, pulled out the stakes, and set them up all over again." DeMoss paused long enough to smooth his long black hair. A smile still filled his face, and Jeff avoided the engineer's bright eyes. DeMoss was the enemy. It was best to stay clear.

"I've got my work to do," Jeff told the man. "It'd be best for you to get on back to your camp. Even better for you to head back to wherever you came from."

"St. Louis," DeMoss explained. "A fine city, St. Louis. Before that I was in Chicago, and before that Philadelphia. Oh, there are grand sights there, you can be sure."

"I only know these mountains," Jeff said, glaring at

the intruder. "It's enough."

"Is it?" DeMoss asked. "Wouldn't be for me."

Those words haunted Jeff the rest of the day. That night they rolled through his dreams like one of DeMoss's locomotives, belching smoke, screaming out with steam-whistle shrillness, ushering in progress like a fancy woman up from one of Trader Petrie's bawdy tents. Yes, that was it exactly. Progress would slink its way over, whispering promises, painting pictures of splendor. But the moment you couldn't meet its price, it would vanish like a July snowflake, leaving scarcely a droplet of water behind to mark its passage.

If Zeke Thompson, or even Pike, had returned that next day, Jeff never would have ridden to DeMoss's camp. But things being as they were, the loneliness welled up inside Jeff until he couldn't stand it. Worse, the aroma of roast prairie chicken and fresh biscuits drifted over from across the river. To a boy who'd eaten naught but smoked venison or fried trout and a few potatoes for close to a week now, the temptation was overpowering.

"Glad you happened by," DeMoss announced when Jeff rode through the shallows around noon. "Just in time for supper. Care to join us?"

"That's kind of you," Jeff said, dismounting.

"I mentioned before. I'm Henry DeMoss, chief engineer for the Union Pacific. I'm surveying the route for the railroad. And you are . . ."

"Jefferson Thompson, though my family calls me Jeff."

"Well, Jeff, make yourself at home."

Jeff couldn't help laughing at the remark. He *was* home. He kept his tongue, though, for a dinner guest ought not to insult his host. And the food tasted every bit as good as it smelled. To top it off DeMoss passed around cups of cider chilled in the river. The liquid ignited Jeff's throat, and it spread warmth though his entire being.

As the balance of the afternoon unfolded, Jeff did his best to restrain his interest. But as Henry DeMoss explained how the instruments could effectively measure great distances, how using mathematics and the stars a man could map the surface of the earth, how soon whole sides of mountains must give way to the expected path of the Union Pacific, Jeff found himself envisioning the new world that would follow. There would be towns with libraries and schools, maybe even a university like the ones Uncle Peter spoke of so glowingly.

On the following day DeMoss demonstrated the instruments, let Jeff himself plot part of the route.

"You've a natural head for figures, Jeff," DeMoss said, praising the speed and accuracy of Jeff's solution. "The Union Pacific can find a place for so bright a boy, I'm sure."

"I already have a place," Jeff objected.

"Hardly," DeMoss whispered to his companions. "No, you'll have a bright future indeed, especially once the deeds of transfer are signed."

"Signed by who exactly?" Jeff asked.

"By your father," DeMoss explained. "Or you, should he be unable."

"We know he's getting old," one of DeMoss's assistants added. "Sooner or later this railroad will be built. The key is who will build it, and who will grow rich in the process. Why not all of us?"

"Yes," DeMoss agreed. "But someone should talk to your father, Jeff, persuade him how profitable it would be for you. Once he understands . . ."

"No, Zeke Thompson will never let you go through here, not over his land," Jeff declared. "You don't know him. He's a man to have it his way."

"As am I," DeMoss said sharply. "I'm the future. He's the past. If the past isn't awfully careful, the present will roll right on over it. You use caution, Jefferson Thompson. Talk to him. Make him see it my way."

Jeff only shook his head. There was no talking to Zeke Thompson about such measures.

DeMoss's camp moved along that next morning, leaving Jeff to await the return of Pike and their parents. The survey continued, and this time, instead of setting out markers, great notches were cut in pine trees.

"You'll kill the trees that way!" Jeff protested.

"They'll be cut anyway," DeMoss explained. "Likely be used to build whole new towns."

Jeff only shook his head at the senselessness of it and returned to the cabin to await his father. Yes, his father would know what to do, what to say. Zeke Thompson always did.

VI

With the departure of Demoss's survey crew, Jefferson Pike found the loneliness of the mountainside worse than ever. Whether chopping wood, fishing for trout, or swimming away the hot afternoons, he couldn't help wondering why Pike and his parents were taking such a long time to return from Fort Laramie. At night, when the solitude smothered him with its overpowering silence, he imagined all manner of accidents. Perhaps a rockslide had blocked the trail. Maybe a band of emigrants short on provisions had set upon his family. But each dawn he'd shake off the fear and smile at the rising sun, confident that no disaster on earth could long deter Zeke Thompson from completing a journey.

Three long days after DeMoss had departed the valley, Jeff spotted a slender horseman riding alone beside the river. There was no mistaking the dark, Cheyenne hair or the sullen eyes of his brother, Pike. With a loud whoop and a surge of energy, Jeff raced down the slope.

"You'd think I was gone all winter," Pike said as Jeff climbed onto the horse behind his brother.

"Seemed like it," Jeff replied. "Pa comin'?"

"With the supplies. Ma, too, and Uncle Peter as well. Where's that DeMoss? You've been keepin' him in sight?"

"He's gone now," Jeff explained. "Was camped on the river till just lately. Guess he had his surveyin' done. Likely he's gone back to where the railroad is."

"Wish he was gone for good," Pike said, spitting a mouthful of tobacco juice onto the ground. "But Pa's sure he'll be back. Means to put the line through here, I'd say."

"He does. He marked his path with red posts, but I moved them around so that he couldn't make head nor tails of the route. Then he notched the trees. Pure waste to blaze tall pines like that, let their summer sap feed the birds and the bugs. Those trees'll be dead by next year's thaw."

Pike nodded, then nudged his weary horse on toward the barn. As Jeff tended the tired animal, he finally caught sight of his father. Zeke Thompson sat a horse as no man alive. His hulking figure dwarfed his mount, and the powerful shoulders that had for so long wrestled with the elements for survival filled onlookers with awe.

Ruth rode along with her fair-haired younger brother, Peter Ryland. The youthful minister seemed out of place with his light complexion and delicate features. Even Jeff seemed rugged by comparison.

"Well, boy, you appear to've survived," Zeke bellowed, giving Jeff a rare slap on the back with a bearlike hand. "I hear we've had company."

"Yes, sir," Jeff said, taking a deep breath and preparing his report on DeMoss. "They were—"

"Time for all that later," Jeff's father told him. "Now let's unload the supplies. Your ma'll want to get dinner started, and I for one am in need of a few moments off this horse."

Jeff helped his father dismount, then began assisting Pike with the supplies. Most everything was boxed or bundled, and Jeff tried to hide his curiosity. Only a long wooden crate still bore the freight labels. Out West the name Winchester Arms meant rifles, and a whole crate of them told Jeff that Zeke Thompson expected trouble.

"Your father worries these railroad men might bring trouble," Peter Ryland told Jeff as the two of them loosened ropes and removed parcels from the pack animals.

"And you don't?" Jeff asked.

"A railroad might well prove a godsend. It wasn't long ago Kansas and Nebraska were wild, unpopulated prairies. A railroad linking East with West will draw our country back together. It will give birth to cities. It will—"

"What about the Cheyennes? What about us?"

"You'll share in the progress," the young minister declared. "Your land will become valuable. You can't imagine the changes that will come."

"I don't want to," Jeff said, sadly glancing at the familiar timberline, at the peaks he knew as well as he knew his own toes.

"You don't understand . . ."

"No, Uncle Peter, it's you that doesn't understand. This mountain's our home, our life. Pa won't sell part of it to the railroad. He can't. He made a promise long ago to the Cheyennes that he'd die first, and Zeke

Thompson keeps his word. This railroad won't bring progress here. It'll bring death. It's goin' to be the Bozeman Road all over again."

"Your father's not blind, Jefferson. He knows the army's in force at Fort Laramie now."

Jeff scratched his head and stared at his father. Old Zeke, no less the mountaineer than he'd been twenty years before, stood beside the crate of rifles, mumbling to Pike about the survey crew.

"You don't know," Jeff whispered. "You weren't born here."

Peter Ryland was a man of faith and conviction. He continued to speak of the new world the railroads would usher into the Medicine Bow country. But talk of cities and farms was lost on his audience.

You don't know, Jeff thought again and again as the words tempted him with their dreamlike visions of the future. But there stood Zeke Thompson, inspecting the new rifles and cursing this Henry DeMoss who dared cross the mountain with his infernal instruments and red poles.

An hour before sunset Jeff took his father to De-Moss's abandoned camp. Ole Zeke picked through the ashes of the campfire, then followed the trail of the departing surveyor until it faded into the distant horizon.

"Well, I do suppose he's gone," Zeke grumbled.

"You seem almost disappointed," Jeff said. "Me, I'm glad he's left."

"You don't know that kind, boy. I've seen 'em before. He'll be back, and trouble's sure to follow."

Jeff nodded, and turned his horse homeward.

"Somethin' keepin' you, boy?" Zeke thundered, a

broad smile spreading across his bearded face.

"No."

"Then, let's do some ridin'!"

Jeff kicked his horse into a gallop, and the two of them tore across the side of the mountain together, chasing the sun across the western horizon as the wind stung their faces. For Jeff it was a rare moment of acceptance, of belonging. And when they fell out of their saddles back at the cabin, Zeke shoveled Jeff along toward the door of the cabin as the wonderful aroma of fresh biscuits and venison steaks flooded the air.

"You did just fine up here with the rest of us all gone," Zeke spoke softly. "Those railroaders'll have a time takin' this mountain with three Thompson men to defend her."

"Think it'll come to that?" Jeff asked nervously. "Fighting?"

"Sometimes it happens that way. Your mother's uncle, old Iron Hand, could tell you as much."

He has, too, Jeff thought as he followed his father to the wash basin. Each generation, it seemed, the Cheyennes had yielded ground to the encroaching whites. But what ground did Zeke Thompson have to cede?

Jeff cast the question from his mind as his mother set out platters of food on the table. After grace, the conversation turned to the Laramie trip. His mother described wondrous bolts of new checkered cloth and cast iron kettles purchased from the post trader. Zeke raved about the new lever-action Winchesters. Pike was more impressed by the city of tents spreading out across the river from the fort and the fancy women and gamblers who inhabited the place.

"The devil's workshops," Peter Ryland grumbled. "They'll go the way of Sodom."

Pike and Zeke grinned as the young preacher stood and proclaimed a dozen scriptural passages attesting to the reward awaiting the wicked. Jeff felt his mother's glaring eyes and did his best to keep a stiff lip. It wasn't altogether possible, though.

Jeff found more to his liking the news that two new books were among his mother's recent purchases. An old copy of Fremont's journal, along with a newer volume of stories, would provide hours of enlightenment and entertainment. And as if that weren't enough, his Uncle Peter had brought along a trunk of texts from the school.

As summer gave way to the first gentle breezes of autumn, life on Thompson's Mountain settled into its usual pattern of hard work blended with periodic diversions. For a time Jeff passed the afternoons studying with Peter Ryland, but in September the young minister returned to his little mission on the Laramie River. But while all seemed perfectly normal, an overpowering sense of uneasiness lurked in the distance. Once each day, Zeke Thompson or one of his sons would ride along the crest of the ridge, searching the distant slopes for any trace of intruders.

Sometimes stray emigrants would arrive at the river. Zeke would appear, rifle in hand, to correct their course. One or two might grumble, but knowing Cheyennes also rode the land of the Medicine Bow convinced most to shift direction.

The second week of September a different band of travelers arrived. It was Jeff who spotted the spirals of dust that heralded their arrival, but it was Zeke

Thompson who identified the visitors.

"Soldiers," Zeke grumbled. "They got no business on my land!"

Jeff squinted his eyes and tried to examine the distant figures. It wasn't possible to tell anything about the antlike shapes.

"You sure, Pa?" he asked.

"Don't need to see their faces, boy," old Zeke explained. "No other fool rides these mountains in column."

Jeff gazed again at the strangers and nodded his agreement. But when he accompanied his father that next morning, Jeff learned there was more to the group than a cavalry patrol.

"It's DeMoss," Jeff said, pointing at the smiling civilian among the soldiers.

"The railroad fellow?" Zeke asked.

"And he's not mappin' a route this time, Pa."

"No, he's here to parley."

When Jeff and his father arrived at DeMoss's camp, they found a thin, gray-faced cavalry officer, Lt. Ben Allen, in command.

"So, you're Zeke Thompson," Allen said. The lieutenant pushed his hat back from his forehead, revealing a steadily receding hairline. "I expected to hear from you before long."

"I'd say so," Zeke spoke sourly. "You come ridin' across my mountain with a squadron of dragoons. You could hardly expect nothin' else."

"I don't know that I like your tone, Thompson," Lieutenant Allen growled. "You old trappers are all alike. You sit out here on some mountaintop and think you own the world."

70

"I don't *think* I own anything," Zeke said, glaring at the cavalryman. "I *know* I own this place, that mountain, and everything as far as the river."

"I suppose you have a deed to show that," DeMoss said, stepping forward. "Because the territorial office has no record of such a deed. And without clear title, I have as much right to this acreage as you do."

"And I suppose these soldier boys are here to help you," Zeke said hatefully.

"It's the responsibility of the army to protect private citizens in hostile country," Lieutenant Allen said as if reading from a book of military regulations.

"Hostile country?" Jeff asked.

"There are Cheyenne Indians hereabouts," Zeke said, laughing. "Guess that's who you had in mind, Lieutenant. Don't know of anybody else that I'd call hostile. You, boy?"

"No, Pa," Jeff said, laughing along with his father as the soldiers' faces reddened.

"They're simply here to see that the law's followed," DeMoss said, motioning Lieutenant Allen aside. "Titles . . . well, all that's something a judge could decide. I'm here to see a higher justice served. I mean, as your son's no doubt told you, to build a railroad through this country. Now, I know you've been out here a long time, Thompson, and this is your home. That's why I'm prepared to make you a very generous offer."

"So you believe I own the land, do you?" Zeke asked.

"You're here," DeMoss said. "Let's just say I'm willing to be fair. You'll be a rich man, Thompson. Your sons will have a future."

"They have a future now!" Zeke roared. "Never knew no tin-plated horse's rear to offer anybody something

71

for no reason. Now you listen to me, Mr. Railroad. This is my mountain." Zeke nodded to Jeff, who walked to the horses and drew a small, time-worn square of deerskin from his father's saddlebags. Jeff passed the skin to Zeke, who then spread it out for Lieutenant Allen and DeMoss to examine.

"What is this?" DeMoss asked.

"It's a treaty cloth," Lieutenant Allen explained as he gazed at the combination of words and pictures. "I've seen 'em before. It gives Thompson this land."

"I don't believe it's legal," DeMoss complained. "There's no government seal."

"He doesn't need it," the lieutenant declared. "There's one on the treaty itself. This is just a cloth showing Thompson here's been given this country by the Cheyenne nation."

"What?"

"It's an agreement between Thompson and the Cheyennes. Our treaty is with the Cheyennes. It's as good as gold, Mr. DeMoss. It means he's got clear title to the mountain. Sorry, but there's nothing I can do for you here."

"Nothing?" DeMoss cried angrily.

"Afraid not," Lieutenant Allen said, shrugging his shoulders.

"Then, it's down to this," DeMoss said, turning back to Zeke. "I'll make you as fine an offer as you've ever seen. We can even talk stock in the railroad."

"A man doesn't sell his heart," Zeke said, smiling at Jeff, then gazing at the surrounding countryside. "No, you take your railroad elsewhere. The day I signed this cloth, I pledged never to let the white man build a road across the sacred land of the Medicine Bow. I keep my

72

word. Find another mountain."

"I can't do that," DeMoss declared. "The grade's all wrong north and south."

"I don't see where you have any choice," Lieutenant Allen said. "If he won't sell, Mr. DeMoss, you'll have to seek another route."

DeMoss nodded, but Jeff read no defeat in the engineer's dark brooding eyes. Jeff followed his father toward the horses knowing Zeke Thompson had also read those eyes.

"This settles nothin'," Zeke grumbled, kicking a rock across the camp. "We'll hear from that one again."

VII

A sense of foreboding hovered over the Medicine Bow Valley as the first chill winds of October greeted Thompson's Mountain. DeMoss had come and gone. No sign of the engineer or his survey crew was detected afterward. As for Lieutenant Allen, he and the rest of the cavalry were too busy with Red Cloud's Sioux and their Cheyenne allies up north in the Powder River country to spare time or worry for Zeke Thompson.

October was a golden time in the Rockies. The leaves of the aspens and cottonwoods, together with their cousin oaks, blazed scarlet and amber on hillsides overlooking winding rivers.

The sting of the morning wind warned of winter's approach as Jeff helped his mother dig the last of the vegetables from her garden. With Pike, he hunted the deer and elk which always seemed most plentiful just before first snow.

October storms could prove the equal of the worst December blizzard, so shutters were latched each eve, and any shingle on the roof that appeared suspect was replaced by a fresh one. Meat was smoked and salted, as were trout from the river and ducks shot on their annual pilgrimage to the milder south.

But if October meant work, it also afforded Jeff a rare chance for amusement. For it was in October's second week, amidst the worst early snow in a dozen years, that he'd been born. No actual day had been recorded in the family Bible, but old Zeke recalled it'd been the second week for certain. As a result a birthday celebration was always held then.

For the most part, Zeke and Ruth Thompson didn't devote a lot of time to idle merrymaking. Christmas and Easter were celebrated, as was Ruth's father's custom, but as often as not the Fourth of July came and went without so much as a nod. Birthdays, though, were cause for a day free from chores and a night of berry pies and tall stories. Best of all, Jeff thought, gifts were given.

But as each October day died in a fiery mountain sunset, Jeff became strangely unsure of the celebration. He was fifteen now, and Pike had abandoned birthday celebrations at sixteen or seventeen. With the shadow of the railroad still lurking over the horizon, Jeff wondered if his father would even remember such a trivial occasion as a birthday.

Birthdays never amount to much anyway, Jeff thought as the third week of October arrived. A few gifts, a bit of song and dance . . . what was that? And yet in spite of everything, he still hoped his father might pound the dinner table and declare that a terrible injustice had been done. Jefferson Thompson had turned fifteen, and the rest of the world had failed to notice!

As the days passed, Jeff shook off his disappointment and busied himself with chores. He was tending the horses an hour after dawn one day when he felt something scratch his ear. Instinctively Jeff reached back, but the horsefly he expected to snatch from the air proved to be a hawk feather held by his brother, Pike.

"Don't you have anything better to do than that?" Jeff growled, surprising both Pike and himself with uncharacteristic anger.

"What's got you stirred up, little brother?" Pike asked, balancing the feather on his nose. "Thought you might like a little entertainin'."

Jeff couldn't help grinning as Pike danced between the horses, causing the feather to sway one way, then the other. But each time it started to fall, Pike would dip his head or bend his back, allowing the gentle morning breeze to right the feather.

"You're close to as good as Dancing Lance," Jeff said, recalling how his cousin could balance three feathers at one time on his nose or forehead.

"Well, I'm only a quarter Cheyenne," Pike said by way of explanation. "Just thought you're entitled to a laugh on your birthday."

"My birthday?" Jeff asked. "It was days ago."

"Not by Ma's calendar. I never set a lot of stock in days and weeks anyway. But you got to know we'd never let you get off without a birthday shebang. Ma's makin' a peach pie, and Pa's busy polishin' somethin' that sure does look like one of them new Winchesters."

"I thought maybe I was too old for birthdays," Jeff said, wiping his forehead and laughing again as Pike resumed his feather act. "You don't go celebratin' yours anymore."

"I'm half a head taller'n you, and goin' on twenty

years old. If I rode with Iron Hand, I'd have my own lodge and wife as well."

"The lodge sounds just fine, but I don't know 'bout those Cheyenne gals, Pike. They can be mighty bossy."

"Mighty pretty, too," Pike pointed out as the feather finally fluttered to the ground. "I wouldn't object to winterin' with Reed Dancer or that little one with the pointed nose."

"Prairie Flower," Jeff said, smiling. "I like her myself."

"Well, her uncle, old Raven Wing, might give her to you for a pair of horses and a Winchester. Fifteen's old enough for some. 'Course you're awful skinny."

Pike lifted Jeff's shirt and poked him in the ribs.

"More bone than dog soldier," Pike taunted.

"Maybe she'll hold off till I grow some more. I think she's got an eye for me. Carved me a flute last spring."

"Who'd thought it?" Pike asked, laughing loudly. "My little brother takin' a gal to his lodge!"

Pike's jesting was only the beginning of what proved to be an eventful day. Zeke Thompson soon appeared to join in the merriment. Jests were freely exchanged, with most of them finding Jeff as their target. Jeff was too relieved at discovering his family hadn't overlooked him to get very upset, though. Soon Zeke administered the traditional Thompson family pounding, fifteen solid whacks this year, and the celebration continued.

Ruth Thompson stayed quietly in the background that morning as Pike and Zeke took charge. Jeff raced with them barefoot across the meadows, swam the river, rode the crest of the ridge, and, to top it all off, outshot Pike in a test of marksmanship, first with a Cheyenne bow, then with the new Winchester rifles.

"Guess I better get some practicin' done," Pike

declared when it was all said and done.

"No, the boy's got the true aim, Pike," Zeke said, a trace of surprise filling his voice. "Some do, you know. I've seen others practice till their fingers close to wore away and still not hit the side of a barn. But those that have the eye of the hawk, well, they're rare, so they say."

The birthday feast consisted of roasted duck, boiled potatoes and carrots, biscuits, and the promised peach pie. Jeff ate so much he wasn't sure he'd ever again be able to stand.

After the pie was devoured, Ruth Thompson started off the gift-giving by presenting her youngest son with a beautiful beaded buckskin shirt. The arms were fringed, and it was so soft Jeff almost hated to wear it.

Pike followed by handing Jeff an iron skinning knife.

"That's good for trout, beaver, or even railroad engineers that get too nosy," Pike said, laughing. "It's the best the trader had, said he's gettin' three buffalo hides for 'em from the Sioux."

Jeff took the knife and nodded his gratitude. Then all eyes fell on Zeke Thompson.

"A man, and fifteen's as good an age to start bein' a man as any other, ought to have a fine shirt and a good skinnin' knife, Jefferson, but it's more important he's got a fast horse and a good gun. You've never been shy of swift ponies, boy, but you've needed a gun to outfit you proper."

Zeke laid an oilskin on the table, then opened it so the shiny new Winchester underneath might be seen. Carved in the stock were the initials *J. T.* Jefferson Thompson. Jeff grinned as he realized his father had marked the gun that way.

"Let's hope the only cause I have to use it is to bring

in a buck for fresh meat this winter," Jeff said somberly as he gazed southeasterly to where the rivers and prairies of Kansas and Nebraska were already being tamed by the railroads and those who followed.

"Amen to that," Ruth told them.

"I wish it so myself, but it don't appear likely," Zeke grumbled.

At least it's calm just now, Jeff thought as he tested the rifle. And as the days that followed flew by, seemingly frozen in a spell of tranquility, it seemed that trouble might keep its distance. Then, as October's gentle chills gave way to a harsher November, a rider appeared at the river.

Jeff was the first to spot the lone, slim-shouldered figure. The visitor rode the bare back of a spotted pony, and a bright red-and-yellow trade blanket shielded him from the wind. At first Jeff wasn't certain whether a stray Cheyenne woman or some lost Sioux boy had stumbled onto Thompson's Mountain. But when the rider pulled the blanket away from his face, Jeff froze. The bright brown eyes that blazed on a forehead graced by midnight-black hair belonged to a distant memory, to a face now laid to rest.

Dancing Lance? Jeff asked as he gazed in disbelief. But it wasn't Dancing Lance at all. The figure was too thin, too young. The boy in front of him had walked the earth no more than ten summers. But the eyes, the hair . . .

"It's been a long time," the young visitor spoke in a quiet, weary voice.

The blanket dipped from the rider's shoulder, revealing three red scars etched in the dark reddish-brown flesh.

Not Dancing Lance at all, Jeff thought, his eyes suddenly brightening. No, Dancing Lance was still dead, but Little Heart, the child who'd once ridden behind Jeff on a dozen journeys through the hills and streams of the Medicine Bow country, was not.

"My father sent me," Little Heart explained. "He makes his camp not far from here."

"Iron Hand's nearby?" Jeff asked, helping his cousin down from the pony. "Is the war over then?"

"Over?" Little Heart asked, his ten-year-old eyes failing to understand.

"Has the fighting stopped?"

"No," Little Heart said sadly. "The bluecoats are in the north. But there is a new danger."

"What?"

"It's not for me to talk of. My father asks that you come to his camp."

"Where?" Jeff asked.

"I will take you."

Jeff nodded his understanding, then escorted his young cousin back to the cabin.

News of Iron Hand's return was met with a loud series of whoops by Pike. While Jeff tended Little Heart's pony, Pike asked the boy a hundred questions. Old Zeke put a stop to that, hoisting the underfed Indian on one shoulder and carrying him to the cabin. Ruth then took over, filling Little Heart with biscuits and gravy, a half-dozen eggs, and a slab of bacon.

"A blanket's little help in fending off the cold," Jeff said after Little Heart had eaten his fill. "I've got some old shirts and a pair of trousers you can have. They might be a little big, but you keep eatin' Ma's cookin', you'll fit just fine in 'em."

"The Big Horn country grows short of game," Little Heart explained as Jeff drew the clothes out of his trunk. "The bluecoats are everywhere along the river, and the deer has found other meadows. There are few buffalo near our camps there."

"But that's not what brought you back, is it?"

"No," Little Heart said grimly.

Toward dusk the young Cheyenne led Zeke Thompson's family along the winding trail to Iron Hand's camp at the mouth of Wolf Creek. The Cheyennes had spread out their lodges many times at that spot, and Jeff fondly remembered the laughter and the dancing that echoed through the surrounding hills. There was no celebration this time. Iron Hand's camp held only a dozen lodges, and it seemed to Jeff to be a mere shadow of what once had been. The old chief himself seemed terribly tired. His forehead was filled with a hundred lines, and his hand felt heavy, old, when it rested on Jeff's shoulder.

"I have grave news," Iron Hand announced as they gathered around a small fire. "The iron road creeps across our land."

"The railroad?" Jeff asked. A glance from his father silenced any further questions.

"They brought a survey crew across my mountain," Zeke told his brother-in-law. "Made us an offer for our land. I turned 'em down, said it was my mountain, and I'd not have their rails chew up the buffalo grazin'."

"And still they come," Iron Hand mumbled. "Always it's the same. They come with their roads and their people, driving off the game, taking what is not theirs."

The old Cheyenne reached out his hand and made a snatching motion at the air.

81

"How can a man own the land?" the chief asked. "Who can own the air or the sky? It is given to us all by the spirits. We walk it only a short time. It is still here when our bones are eaten by the winds of time."

"It's like I told you when we made the treaty cloth," Zeke said. "These white men've got to have papers to tell them what is. Their hearts are cold."

"Yes," Iron Hand agreed. "They don't feel the hunger of the women. They can't hear the cries of the children, don't taste the bitter tears I shed for my dead sons. They are blind!"

"We'll fight 'em," Zeke promised. "They won't cross my mountain!"

"Then, they will cross another mountain," Iron Hand said sadly. "I know of these iron roads. Our brothers in the south tell stories of how the bluecoats kill anyone who stands in their way. American Horse is Dead. White Antelope, too. Sand Creek flows red with their blood."

"So, what have you come to tell me?" Zeke asked. "You know I won't break my promise to you."

"Others have," Iron Hand said. "Some say you have the true heart, Zeke Thompson, but others say you are a white man, and a white man can wear many faces."

"Some can," Zeke said without anger. "Not me. My heart mourns with the Cheyenne, and my arm rises against those who'd cross the Medicine Bow. We'll fight!"

"We also," Iron Hand said, clasping Zeke's trunklike forearm.

"Yes!" the other Cheyennes yelled. "We also!"

But as Jeff searched the youthful faces for old friends, for warriors who'd spun a hundred tales of the buffalo hunt or of fights with the Crows or Pawnees, he felt a terrible despair. Only the very young and the old met his gaze. Bare chests revealed protruding ribs. The faces of the children were ashen with hunger, and soon winter would appear. This was no Cheyenne war camp. It was a village of the walking dead.

Zeke Thompson had noticed it, too. When he returned to the cabin, he set about readying its defense. A low wall of logs were built, enclosing the animal pens, the stable, and the cabin itself. Winchesters were kept at the ready, and the slightest noise brought alarm. Still, there was no sign of DeMoss.

"He's an educated man, Zeke," Ruth reminded her husband a dozen times. "He won't try to shoot us. He'll make another offer, and another after that. He can't afford to break the law."

"Which law?" Zeke grumbled. "Our law? He won't give a hoot for any treaty cloth. He'll make his own law, then do what pleases him. It's no different than the judge back in Mississippi who took Pa's farm. Book laws are for those who have the money to get them written. Out here the only law that matters is who's got the true aim and the most rifles."

It was a sobering thought, and Jeff tried not to dwell on it. But there was no escaping its truth, not even when his mother sent him to his Uncle Peter with a pack mule laden with animal pelts.

"I'm more than pleased to see you, Jeff," Peter Ryland said when the weary fifteen-year-old appeared at the little mission on the Laramie River. "It's not a good time to be riding this country alone, though. The Cheyennes are on the prowl."

"I'm in no danger from the Cheyennes," Jeff assured

his uncle. "Their blood flows in my veins."

"Maybe, but you don't look much like an Indian, even in that garb. Why, your hair's close to as light as young Jeremy Fitch's."

Jeff frowned as he glanced at his uncle's schoolroom. Gone were the dark-haired Sioux and Cheyenne children. A few long-faced Crows occupied a bench near the back. The rest of the room was full of pale, round-faced whites, most of them children of soldiers or the growing civilian population of Fort Laramie. Others were there temporarily, waiting with their parents for the Cheyenne menace to subside so the trail to California might be safer.

"I have near seventy, most days," the minister told Jeff. "A couple of boys help me light the stove each morning, and some of the girls lend a hand with the cleaning. What I really need's someone to assist in the teaching, though. Someone the Indian boys will respect. Like maybe you."

"Pa needs me back at the cabin," Jeff explained.

"Not so much as I do. Your ma suggested it. It'd give you a chance to study, to read all those books you're always pestering me to borrow. You're not like Pike, Jeff. He'll always be wild, like old Zeke. You, though, could find a future waiting for you here. There'll be a railroad through here by spring. A man who can read and write, who knows this country, will be in demand."

Jeff shook his head sadly. How could he explain? Peter Ryland wasn't born in the mountains, didn't know how the brisk winter winds and the hot summer afternoons touched the soul, etched their mark deeply on a person's heart.

"Think it over, Jeff," the minister suggested. "The

offer's always open."

"I'm honored you'd think of me," Jeff replied. "But my place is with my father. I'm not as different from Pike as some people think."

"Don't forget who you are, Jeff."

"I never do," Jeff whispered.

A week later, as he sloshed through the first winter snowdrifts, Jeff had a similar talk with Iron Hand. The old chief suddenly paused and reached out to Jeff.

"Are you all right?" Jeff asked.

"I was only remembering the first time I rode this mountain," Iron Hand said, panting for breath. "I was with my father, and he spoke of the earth and sky as if they were old friends to greet as the morning sun. Once I came here with Dancing Lance, and before that with Buffalo Robe and Three Owls. Now they are gone, and soon I will join them."

"Not for a long time," Jeff objected. "You still have Little Heart to see grown."

"All the young men die. It is hard growing old without the friends you knew as young men. It is hard to close the eyes of your sons."

"Dancing Lance was my friend," Jeff whispered, sadly staring northward. "I miss him, too."

Iron Hand's eyes searched Jeff's face, probing for some hidden truth. Then the old man ran a wrinkled hand along Jeff's smooth, hairless cheek.

"No beard," Jeff said, feeling the ancient icy fingers trace their way to his chin, then lightly dance across the thin, almost invisible hairs on Jeff's upper lip. "Pike plucked his," Jeff added, "but I've hardly got any worth worrying over. Besides, Pa has a beard, and his heart's true."

Iron Hand nodded, then rested his hands on Jeff's shoulders. Jeff felt the rock-hard grip, the power in those wrists that had long ago given a young Cheyenne the name he would always carry. Suddenly Iron Hand cried out to the sky. Snow resting on the branches of nearby pines sprayed the air with white powder, and the sound echoed around the whitened hills as if a hundred ghostly voices had suddenly been awakened from their rest.

Iron Hand then pulled off his elkhide robe and stripped himself to the waist. Jeff had no idea what the old man was doing, but Iron Hand's dark, earnest eyes bid the boy to do the same. The icy wind bit through Jeff's bare arms and shoulders like a dagger, and his head pounded from the sudden shock of the cold.

"Look, here," Iron Hand said, touching first his own proud chest, then Jeff's. "My father's daughter bore your mother. Within him the fire that burns inside you was first kindled. I feel it now, as the earth turns white with winter's touch."

"Yes," Jeff said as the numbing cold sent shivers through him.

"Sometimes I see only the yellow in your hair, and I forget the fire of your mother's eyes. Never forget you, too, are born of the Medicine Bow, that your heart is Cheyenne."

The old man's fingers wove their way across Jeff's belly, then slapped the hard, summer-toughened shoulders.

"I know who I am," Jeff whispered. "I will always remember."

"Then, know this as well. No people ever die who are remembered."

86

There was a distant, faraway look in Iron Hand's eyes, and Jeff fought to catch his breath. The old chief seemed undaunted by the cold. Perhaps he was off in a land of memory, hunting buffalo or playing his reed whistle along the river, hoping one of the girls would mirror his affections. Jeff hurriedly pulled on his shirt and coat, then draped Iron Hand's robe over the old man's shoulders.

"You thought I was gone, but I wasn't," Iron Hand said, smiling like an old fox. "Don't forget. No one ever died who was remembered."

"I won't," Jeff promised as he turned homeward. "And I'll always remember who I am."

As he made his way through the November snow flurries, the words echoed again and again through his head.

Yes, I remember, he told himself. I'm Zeke Thompson's son, and I always will be.

VIII

Winter descended on Thompson's Mountain with a fury. Deep snowdrifts choked the trails, and the energy of the Medicine Bow River was frozen as if by an incantation. Soft white smoke seeped continually from the chimney of Zeke Thompson's cabin, and except for seeing to the needs of the livestock and exercising the horses, Jeff rarely ventured past the log palisade that surrounded the cabin and its neighboring buildings.

November flowed into December, and December gave way to January and February, but little changed. There was no great blizzard of '67, just a long, perilous Wyoming winter fraught with the usual hardships brought by four months of frozen mornings and bleak afternoons. At night fog hung in great shrouds across the Rockies so that the land itself appeared to have been swallowed.

March witnessed the first thaw. The thick ice in the river began to glisten and crack as the midday sun bombarded it. Game reappeared, and the pines shook the snow from their branches. As to the country more than a mile distant from old Zeke's cabin, it might as as well have belonged to another world. No one could traverse the passes, for the best routes were still blocked with two feet of powder.

It seemed a good winter to Jeff, a pleasant interlude of peace after a disturbing autumn. Almost forgotten were Henry DeMoss and his survey crew. Iron Hand's little band of Cheyenne would appear from time to time, but no one else visited the mountain.

Spring always brought with it a sense of rebirth. In the wildflowers poking their heads through the snow Jeff saw that life continued as it always had, that the warmth of summer grew from the depths of winter freezes. And in his own broadening shoulders and deepening voice he recognized the man he was fast becoming.

"Growin' like prairie fire," Zeke commented as his younger son inched ever taller. "Any day now he'll catch Pike."

Jeff wasn't quite so sure. Five more inches remained before he reached Pike's six feet, and Jeff's body seemed in no particular rush to add them.

"Always the young men hurry themselves into old age," Iron Hand remarked more than once. "Oh, how I remember my own impatience. I never ran as fast or wrestled as well as my brothers, it seemed. But when the time to ride after buffalo came, I was the one asked to come along."

"I was to ride to the buffalo hunt last year," Jeff grumbled.

"Yes, and this old man who is your mother's uncle should have taken you," Iron Hand said. "Soon the white man will swallow the buffalo as he's swallowed the Cheyenne. And there will be no more of us."

Jeff laughed, but Iron Hand looked with such intensity that the earth seemed to freeze. He believes that, Jeff told himself. Afterward, he spent as many nights in the camp of the Cheyennes as he could.

Soon Iron Hand moved down the valley, though, and Jeff found himself busy mending the log wall or chopping wood. Fresh game was sought for the table, and ground for the spring garden had to be broken. The work seemed without end, but it brought with it a hardness Jeff was pleased to notice. And while hunting deer or rabbits with Pike, Jeff thought he glimpsed in his brother's eye a new respect.

Snow still clung to the woodlands when the elk returned to the mountain. Jeff never fully understood where the great lumbering beasts vanished each winter, but hunting them before they shed their heavy winter coats was vital. Ruth Thompson had made many a wonderful robe from the hide of an elk, and those not kept always brought a fine value from the post trader at Fort Laramie.

As Jeff loaded his rifle in preparation for the hunt, he couldn't help staring in wonder at the eastern horizon. The sun hung in the distance like a giant ball of yellow fire, tearing away at the heavy ground fog as dogs might attack a wounded stag.

A morning to remember, Jeff thought as he followed Pike outside. A day of importance. But at the time, his mind pictured the tall, broad-shouldered elk that would fall before his rifle and not the smaller, deadlier enemy that crept through the pines a quarter mile away.

"I expect to sink my teeth into a steak big as your

ma's skillet," Zeke Thompson declared as his sons mounted their horses.

"We won't disappoint you, Pa," Jeff promised.

"Rarely do," old Zeke said, waving farewell.

Jeff followed his brother toward the ridge, thinking that Zeke Thompson would rather have been riding after elk himself than staying at the cabin, feeding the animals, or splitting kindling. It's his way of making way for us, Jeff realized, letting the old give way to the young even as the tallest of pines often fell so that saplings might rise in its place.

"I saw one o' them elk yesterday," Pike said, slapping his thigh. "Little brother, I tell you he must've been a thousand-pounder easy. Why, you could make a whole lodge of his coat!"

Jeff started to reply, but the words were never spoken. Just ahead of them the thin carpet of snow was pounded into a muddy mush. At least a half-dozen different horses had passed the spot.

"Indians?" Jeff asked, more hoping than believing.

"No, shod," Pike pointed out as he drew his rifle from its scabbard. "You bring along a box of shells, Jeff?"

"No," Jeff said, nervously pulling his own rifle from its sheath.

"Best warn Pa. Might be better to lose the horses for a time. Make it easier for us to keep from sight."

Jeff nodded, then slid down from the saddle. A hundred thoughts battered his mind. Here was Pike, calling him by name for the first time in memory. Shod ponies had ridden across the mountain recently, but no one had announced their arrival. Before any of it could be digested, though, three shots rang out, and the trunk of an adjacent pine tree exploded with their impact.

"Get down!" Pike screamed as the horses raced off down the slope. "Get down!"

Jeff sprawled flat in the soggy grass as bullets again splintered the pine. He fumbled with his rifle, but his fingers suddenly grew numb. He couldn't seem to work the lever or point the barrel.

"Oh, God, the cabin!" Pike shouted, racing through the trees a dozen yards, then rolling behind a boulder as the air exploded. Bullets whined through the air, one hitting the ground no more than a foot from Jeff's left hand.

It was either the near miss or the smell of burning coal oil that lent wings to Jeff's feet. His own misfortunes soon dimmed in comparison with the peril facing his parents. As Jeff raced through the pines, his eyes caught sight of the cabin roof, now trailing flame and smoke. Bright yellow flashes erupted from the windows, attesting to the fact that Zeke and Ruth were not sitting idly by during the attack.

"So, what do we do?" Jeff asked as he crawled beside his brother.

"Try to figure out what's happenin' first," Pike said, staring in bewilderment at the shadowy figures that encircled the cabin. "Near's I can tell, there are three over behind the stable, two more on the hillside, and three or four up above us."

"We've got to get to Pa," Jeff gasped.

"Sure, only how?" Pike asked. "For now we'd best see if we can't spot the ones tryin' to shoot us. Then maybe we can lend Pa a hand."

"All right."

"Got any extra shells at all?"

"I loaded up the magazine," Jeff explained. "Thought fifteen would be enough for an elk. I didn't know . . ."

"Neither'd I," Pike said, touching Jeff's arm lightly as if to reassure him. "I only loaded ten. Pa's got a dozen rifles and the better part of a crate of ammunition in the cabin, but we can't get to it. Whoever's doin' this ain't stupid."

"No," Jeff agreed, following Pike through the pines in search of their invisible enemies.

For better than a minute the two brothers managed to hide their movements behind a swirling mist and several large boulders. Then the ambushers again located their prey, and rifles barked. Jeff barely dodged a shot that tore away a whole branch from an aspen just above his head. Powder smoke rose from behind a rocky outcropping, and Jeff nudged Pike. For once they had a target.

"You watch my right," Pike whispered as he crept forward. A rifle barrel protruded from the dense pines, and Jeff fired twice in its direction. The barrel drew back amid a storm of curses, and a third figure rushed through the pines to determine the cause of the commotion.

So, there are three of them, Jeff thought as he concentrated on the two in the pines. The one at the outcropping then rose to fire, and Pike shot the would-be murderer through the head.

"They got Hester!" one of the men in the pines shouted. "Watch out, Brooks!"

From the scurrying behind the outcropping Jeff knew there was a second gunman there. Pike knew it, too, for he halted his progress and motioned for Jeff to try and get behind the the remaining bushwhackers.

Jeff was amazed to find his composure returning. The numbness in his fingers passed, and he felt strangely at home, weaving through the trees, dashing in and out of the rocks, stalking men as he once had stalked deer with Dancing Lance.

"Remember, the only difference in scouting men or game is that men can outthink you," Dancing Lance had once warned. "You can turn from hunter to hunted in the time it takes the wind to turn a leaf."

That's what's happened, Jeff thought as he continued to weave his way across the mountainside. Those men were the hunters, but now they are quarry, rabbits to be bagged, deer to be shot.

Tracking the intruders was simple. Their heavy boots sent constant warnings as they snapped branches or stirred leaves. They smelled of tobacco and coffee, and half the time one was yelling at the other. Jeff worked his way around behind them, then cocked his rifle and took aim.

The rest was not as easy. His sights were filled by a tall, heavyset white man wearing a long gray slicker. Jeff had no sympathy for his victim, didn't recognize the man in the least. But killing . . . well, it wasn't done easily.

Jeff might never have fired but for the fact that the gunman back of the outcropping located Pike. The three gunmen opened up together, and Jeff's finger squeezed off a shot. It found its mark, blasting through the slicker and carrying its victim forward a full five feet before letting the man drop lifelessly to the ground.

"One of 'em's behind us!" the surviving ambusher in the pines cried out.

Jeff worked the lever down, then back. The two riflemen below left their nests and headed in panic toward their companions behind the barn. Jeff fired, rammed home another shell, then fired again. Pike did the same. Soon the hillside seemed alive with shooters. The two stumbling survivors of the hillside ambush got to within twenty yards of the barn before Zeke hit the one on the left, and the other fell to the storm of bullets fired by Jeff and Pike.

"You did that just fine!" Pike said as Jeff joined his brother at the outcropping.

"Now what?" Jeff asked.

"Nothing," Pike said, squeezing the trigger of the Winchester. A sickly click followed. "I've shot my load."

"Check the bodies," Jeff suggested.

But the dead men carried Spencer carbines, and their companions had wisely carried off any remaining ammunition.

"Keep 'em from leavin' the barn," Pike said, handing Jeff the empty rifle. "I'll see if I can get back of them."

"You never in your life crossed that slope without falling," Jeff objected, handing Pike the loaded rifle in return. "You edge your way along the trees. I'll see if I can't distract them."

Before Pike could argue, Jeff scurried off into the thick underbrush like a large rabbit, whooping and hollering like a hundred Cheyennes. The men behind the barn called out in alarm, and one blundered into the open long enough for Pike Thompson to shoot off an ear. The wounded outlaw's screams tore through the air like splinters of lightning, and Jeff saw one of the would-be killers head for the horses. Then, just as it seemed it all might be over, a dark-browed man with

95

thinning black hair and solemn green eyes stepped out of the trees and fired his pistol at Jeff from fifteen feet away.

There wasn't time to be surprised even. Jeff froze, then staggered as the first bullet slammed into his left thigh. A second tore across his belly. He tried to utter a warning, but his lips wouldn't move. He spun awkwardly, crazily, to the ground, dropping the useless rifle as he rolled into a heap beside a boulder.

"Well, he's done for," a familiar voice announced.

In spite of the pain that was flowing through his body, Jeff managed to gaze upward.

"Lord, I hate to shoot the young ones, too," the dark-browed man said as he reloaded his pistol.

"Had to be," Henry DeMoss said grimly. "They'd inherit, quarter Cheyenne or not. That uncle'd see to that. You know these religious fanatics."

Jeff's heart filled with rage, and he tried to regain his feet. But it was as if he were outside his body, looking down at everything. Only the fingers of his left hand seemed to work, and they were of little use.

"Jeff!" Pike called out, but Jeff couldn't answer. His eyes remained wide open, drinking in the terrible scene below, but he was powerless to affect its outcome. The cabin was half-consumed in smoke and flame, and old Zeke finally rushed out the door. For an instant it seemed the burly man might reach the safety of the palisade, but three shots in succession hit the old trapper. One leg went limp, and Zeke dragged himself on. The trio back of the barn took aim together. A quick volley knocked the man down, and a final shot from the trees finished him.

Ruth, screaming in rage, ran to the only man she'd

ever loved. She fired twice as she ran, but as to whether she hit any of the attackers, Jeff couldn't tell. He only saw her knocked sideways by the bullets that killed her.

Jeff felt new power reach the fingers of his feeble left hand. He worked his way along his leg until he gripped the shiny skinning knife in its boot scabbard. The Cheyenne blood burned, and he somehow managed to drag himself forward. Hatred was a strong weapon, and it gave him strength. But even so, he managed only a few yards before the pain overcame him, and his vision blurred.

"Pike?" he mumbled as the final shots died into memory. What had become of Pike? Was he dead as well? Oh, Pike, not all of us! Who will remember? Who will—

His thoughts were interrupted by a rapid crackling sound. Then an explosion rent the air, and he had to gasp for breath. The powder and shot in the cabin had ignited, splintering beams and planks and sending what was left of the cabin twenty feet into the air.

"So much for Zeke Thompson!" the dark-browed killer declared as he walked toward the old mountain man's lifeless body. "He was somethin' once, but now he's only food for the buzzards, just like the rest of us will be one day."

"No man can stand in the way of progress," DeMoss said, dropping his coat over Ruth's delicate face and narrow shoulders. "Should've sold, Thompson."

The killers tarried only long enough to set the barn afire and shoot the pigs. Then they mounted their horses and headed back into the dark woods whence they'd come.

"Pa?" Jeff called feebly. "Ma?" But as he watched the

flames devour what was left of the only home he'd ever known, he realized another page of his life had turned. He swallowed the pain and fought to hold onto the shred that remained of his life.

2. Renegades

I

Jeff felt himself drift in and out of consciousness. One moment his eyes would open, and he could stare overhead at a clear spring sky. He'd sniff the wildflowers on the hillside beside him and hear ground squirrels scurrying through the branches of the pines and aspens. Then the stronger, heavier odor of charred timbers, of ruined dreams and broken lives, would descend upon him like a shroud, and he'd return to a nether world of shadows.

A thousand memories of times gone by flooded his mind, mingling with strange sensations. Pain from his wounds mixed with the touch of cold, moist hands lifting, carrying off. Sometimes he'd glimpse faces . . . dark, sullen brows and deep serious eyes. He'd mumble words that had no meaning, falling apart like pieces of bread left out in the rain.

He floated along in that strange sphere that separated the living from the dead, whispering a feverish prattle and reaching with desperate fingers for someone, anyone, to hold onto. There was no one . . . nothing.

Jeff had no notion of how much time passed before he finally cracked his eyes open for good. At first his vision was clouded, smothered in a fog of pain and memory. When the haze cleared, he gazed up at the shining walnut-colored eyes of Prairie Flower, the slender daughter of Iron Hand's old friend, Raven Wing.

The girl said nothing, just stroked Jeff's bare chest with her soft fingers and smiled.

"Wh . . . what . . . where," Jeff stammered.

"You're in the lodge of your uncle," she whispered. "Little Heart brought word, and the young men . . ."

"Then, it's true," Jeff muttered. "My mother and father, Pike . . ."

"Not Pike," she told him. "He is well. My father and your uncle ride even now with him after the white men."

"I hope they kill every single one of them," Jeff said bitterly. "I hope they—"

"Iron Hand knows what to do," Prairie Flower said, placing a finger over Jeff's mouth to hush him. "The debt will be paid."

No, Jeff thought, picturing his parents lying still on the cold, hard ground they'd loved so well. There weren't enough white men in all the world to pay for Zeke and Ruth Thompson.

"We all share your sadness," Prairie Flower said, setting a small wooden bowl beside Jeff's forehead. "Our people know death well. You must think of life. Invite the spirits to heal your wounds, to return strength to your bow arm and swiftness to your feet. Here, this will speed you to your feet."

Prairie Flower dipped a spoon into the sticky liquid in the bowl. Then she touched the spoon to Jeff's lips, letting the cool liquid soothe his parched lips and snake its way down his throat. Soon his chest felt alive again. His breathing eased, and his head began to clear a bit.

"My mother picked the herbs herself," the girl explained as she continued feeding Jeff. "Iron Hand spoke the sacred words to the medicine bundle, and Two Humps marked your forehead."

Jeff tried to smile. Two Humps was an old man now, and his visit testified to the importance of Iron Hand in the tribe.

As his body began reawakening, Jeff fought to rise. He only managed to turn his neck from side to side and work his fingers. Even so he discovered that a moist poultice of river moss and sweet herbs occupied his abdomen. His right leg seemed all right, for he could move his toes. The left leg was numb, senseless below the hip.

My leg? Jeff tried not to think about it. He'd seen emigrants on the wagon road who'd fought in the great war against the Southern whites. Many sleeves were empty, and others walked on sticks for lack of legs. He'd often wondered what life would be like when one couldn't run across the meadows or jump across campfires. Now perhaps he would have to find out.

"So, you haven't died after all," Pike called out then from the narrow opening in the front of the lodge. "Thought you were dead for a time, little brother."

"They . . . did . . . too," Jeff managed to answer.

"It's not as easy to kill a Thompson as some'd think," Pike declared. "There are those whose bones attest to that!"

"It didn't help Ma and Pa, though," Jeff whispered. "They're gone."

"Well, for what it's worth, we caught up with three o'

them, little brother."

"DeMoss?"

"No, he got clear. We'll have to tend to him another day."

"The cabin's gone."

"Yes, and all the supplies. Even the new rifles. I rounded up five horses. We'll be safe for now with Iron Hand."

"Sure," Jeff agreed, sighing.

"It's not how I figured it'd be at all," Pike said, sitting beside Jeff's blankets. "Never dreamed they'd catch us by surprise like that. And you, little brother! You fought like a wildcat! Just look at you, plum shot to pieces."

Jeff raised his head slightly as Pike traced a thin line above the poultice.

"Bad?" Jeff asked.

"A near enough thing, yes, sir. Bullet cut across that belly o' yours like a hatchet, took a nice neat slice. If there'd been a bit more o' you, it'd killed you certain. As it is, you'll have a dandy scar."

"And . . . my . . . leg?"

"Not pretty at all. Took a ball through the hip, hit the bone, then popped up just above the knee. Raven Wing cut it out, but there's a hole as big as your fist. It's a pure miracle you didn't bleed to death."

"But the leg's still there."

"It is, but that won't be much help for now. You won't walk till first snow, I'd guess."

Jeff sighed and tried again to lift his head enough to see for himself. Pike bent over and helped Jeff rise until he could examine the wounds. The poultice spread across his entire belly, and the leg was wrapped in bandages. What flesh wasn't covered with cloth or moss was scraped and torn by briars and rocks. Jeff half wished he'd never looked.

"Now you know the worst," Pike said, easing Jeff's head back to the blankets. "Rest easy, little brother. All you have to do is let yourself mend."

Jeff nodded and closed his eyes. Within a minute an overwhelming weariness took possession of him, and he faded off to sleep.

In the days that followed, Jeff sometimes stayed alert for as long as an hour or so at a time. Then he would close his eyes and allow the numbing fatigue to carry him away. Gradually, though, he grew stronger. Prairie Flower removed the poultice, revealing a thin red scar half a hand long. The bindings on his hip and thigh were changed, and the wound drained. Even so, he could manage no more complicated movement than sitting up.

"It's well that you are stronger," Iron Hand told Jeff soon thereafter. "The iron road creeps closer, and the bluecoat soldiers come often to these hills."

Jeff understood the meaning of that news. Iron Hand would move his camp. It wasn't safe staying in one place too long while soldiers patrolled the creeks and rivers. Jeff recalled the nightmarish stories shared by Little Heart of the months spent dodging bluecoat cavalry through the Bighorns. So now that was the fate awaiting Jeff and Pike.

Iron Hand didn't break camp immediately. First old Two Humps appeared to inspect Jeff's wound. The medicine chief chanted and danced, then sprinkled powders over the discolored flesh. Iron Hand sang softly. Prairie Flower, Pike, Little Heart, and others formed a circle and joined in. The chanting and singing continued until Two Humps cried aloud. The medicine chief held his hands up toward the sky, then motioned for quiet.

"He's done what he can," Iron Hand told Jeff. "Now you must pray the spirits give you strength."

"Yes," Jeff said, closing his eyes and praying in the manner his mother had taught him. It wasn't the Cheyenne way, perhaps, but he'd always felt the same closeness for her God that old Iron Hand showed for his spirits. The sincerity of Jeff's prayer must have shown on his face, for Two Humps smiled, and Iron Hand gripped his nephew's shoulder warmly.

The following morning Pike and Little Heart built a travois of lodge poles and buffalo hides. Jeff was laid out on his blankets, and Pike strapped him in place using deerskin strips. When all was in readiness, the travois was tied behind one of Iron Horse's broad-backed mares, and the camp started its way westward into the heart of the Medicine Bow Mountains.

For three days the little band of Cheyennes wound its way through the hills and peaks between Wolf Creek and a high meadow hidden by the twin shoulders of a mountain. At its northern edge was a small pond fed by three springs.

"Here we'll be safe," Pike said as he helped unhitch the travois.

Jeff didn't care if it was altogether safe or not. Those three days had been an ordeal. The travois had jolted him every few feet, and his leg had resumed its bleeding. The pain at times had filled every inch of his being. Each night he'd lain beside the campfire, shivering from the chill of the April night and dreading the

106

next day's journey.

Jeff greeted warmly the news that camp would, at long last, be made. Lodge poles were arranged, and their deerskin and buffalo-hide coverings were stretched across the framework. In hours the meadow was transformed into an encampment.

Once the lodges were erected, Pike and the other young men headed off after game. Jeff waited anxiously each time for his brother's return. Sometimes Pike would reappear with a deer carcass. Other days the young men would ride in with news of railroad work crews, and Iron Hand would form a raiding party. Shouts would echo across the meadow, and a dozen horsemen would charge off down the mountainside.

In early May, Pike led a half-dozen Cheyennes out of camp. A short time later the distant mountainside resounded with the sounds of rapid gunfire, and a chill wound its way down Jeff's spine.

"What is it?" Jeff asked, dragging his stiff left leg along as he crept to where Iron Hand stood. "Soldiers?"

"No," Iron Hand, shaking his head solemnly. "They wouldn't fight the bluecoats, not so close to our camp."

Then, they must be trappers or some emigrant band lost in the high country, Jeff told himself. When Pike and the others finally appeared at dusk, the riddle was solved. A pair of sand- and sweat-streaked whites were dragged into camp. Their shirts had been torn from their shoulders, and neither wore boots. Both seemed petrified by fear. For good reason.

"We found 'em blazin' a trail down by the river," Pike told Jeff.

"Railroad men?" Jeff asked, trembling slightly at the effect those words had on Pike's eyes.

"Lookin' for a ford, most likely. Last time they'll be doin' that."

"You mean to kill them?"

"They killed our folks. And others. Old John Henry Flatt out near Miller's Creek. We'll have our revenge."

Jeff watched as the captives were bound to pine saplings. Soon the children began tormenting the captives, poking them with sharp sticks, lashing their backs with deerskin straps, tossing water on them, and pelting their chests with pebbles. Jeff expected to feel differently. He thought a sense of justice would fill his chest, that he would join the laughter of the others. But all he saw was the terror in the two men's eyes, the despair he felt himself.

For the first time since the ambush, Jeff was glad his leg prevented him from joining in. He sat on his blankets, massaging his withered thigh and trying his best to work the tendons of his knee. He only wanted it all undone. He found no comfort in the suffering of others. Jeff stared again at tormented captives, then frowned. Soon Little Heart joined him.

"It will take time to mend," Jeff's young cousin told him.

"Yes," Jeff agreed. "But I'll be walking before the hatred passes."

"They remember the soldiers who killed our people in the north," Little Heart said, pointing to the others.

"And you?"

"I remember, too. My brothers are all dead. My mother, too. My heart is black with sadness. I would kill them all. These could be the ones who killed your father."

"Maybe, but I'm not sure. Even if they were, I couldn't find much comfort in their deaths. It changes nothing."

"It's war," Little Heart said simply.

"Yes," Jeff agreed. "But what will it lead to?"

That night Jeff kept to his lodge while the captives were put to death. Shouts of triumph filled the night air, but Jeff couldn't help wondering what would happen next.

"How's the leg, little brother?" Pike asked that night after the celebrating had died down.

"Still stiff. I suppose we'll have to move camp again."

"It won't be safe for the little ones," Pike explained. "Iron Hand plans to return to the north country."

"And where will we go now?" Jeff asked.

"Deeper into the mountains for a time," Pike answered. "Maybe later we can work our way back to the Laramie River, visit Uncle Peter. You could stay at the mission till your leg heals up."

"And you?"

"Look at me, Jefferson Pike. What do you see? There's no yellow in my hair, and I don't belong in a room full o' books."

Jeff frowned as he studied his brother's somber eyes. Pike's long, straight Cheyenne nose and raven-black hair marked him, walled him off from the quieter life of trading posts or frontier towns. But Jeff saw something darker, more disturbing.

"You can't fight the whole world, Pike, and that's what it'd be," Jeff said sadly. "I hate 'em, too, but all you'll do is get yourself killed."

"Doesn't much matter. I feel half dead already. But

before I'm buried, I'll have my revenge."

"Then I guess you'll need help," Jeff whispered. "Won't be too long 'fore I'm fit to ride. Then we'll deal with 'em together."

"You? You're white enough to pass for George Washington."

"Only on the outside," Jeff said, touching his chest the way Iron Hand had, not so long ago. "But here, inside, I'm no different than you are, Pike."

"We'll be on the run, you know."

"Isn't that what we are right now?"

"Yes," Pike admitted. "And we're likely to stay that way."

Iron Hand sent scouts that next morning to check the passes to the north. When the riders reported the path clear of cavalry, the Cheyennes busied themselves breaking down the camp and preparing for the long and difficult journey. At dawn Iron Hand would start northward.

Pike had no intention of delaying his own departure that long. He helped Jeff onto a gentle mare, then turned his own horse south.

"My heart goes with you, young ones," old Iron Hawk said as Jeff followed Pike down the mountain-side.

"And ours are with you, Uncle," Jeff said. "May we meet in a better time."

"Or a better world," Pike added.

Yes, Jeff thought as he rode onward. But there was no better world in their future, only more terror and death.

II

Jeff had never noticed before how lonely the wind sounded as it whistled through the Rockies. There was something hollow, terribly cold and empty, about the way the breezes whined through the treetops. As Jeff and Pike rode from one hillside to another, never staying in one camp more than two days, Jeff felt a kinship for that orphan wind.

Once the mountains and rivers of the Medicine Bow had been home. Now everything seemed foreign, lost. If not for Pike's determination, Jeff might have abandoned hope, just stretched out on the hillside and given up.

"This is still our country, little brother," Pike said each evening. "They may think they've chased us clear, but they haven't. Soon enough they'll start to pay for what they've done."

Jeff rarely replied, just stared sadly toward the distant horizon.

"How long you goin' to just sit there like that?" Pike finally demanded one summer afternoon. "You think that leg's goin' to mend itself? You got to work it, stretch it out, get up on it!"

"I can't, Pike. It's shot to pieces."

"No such thing. I saw it after Two Humps finished bindin' it. All the tendons're still there, but they tightened up. You got to make 'em work for you."

"I can't."

"You can! Get up! Up!"

Pike reached out and grabbed his younger brother by the arm. Jeff winced as he hopped on his lame left leg, but Pike wasn't put off by protest or pain.

"Stand on it! Go on, walk! Your name's Jefferson Thompson. Act like you know what that means! Swallow them tears and walk on it. When it hurts, remember that smilin' devil, DeMoss. Remember how he killed your ma and pa, left you for a dead man!"

Jeff finally yelled and stepped forward. His left knee refused to lock, and he stumbled back to the ground.

"I can't," he said again as his screams echoed back at him, taunted him with his own voice.

"You can," Pike said, pulling him back up. "Now do it!"

Jeff was more careful this time. The pain throbbing through his leg brought a numbness with it. He trembled from head to toe, but still he dragged the stiff left leg forward, then set his weight on it until the reluctant tendons relaxed, and the joint locked into place.

"Now again," Pike urged.

Jeff swallowed the pain and took another step. As he came down on the tender left leg, it buckled, and once again he fell. This time Pike left him lying in a heap on the hillside.

"I can't get up," Jeff complained.

"Then, you'll have to stay there, I expect," Pike told him.

After staring bitterly at his older brother, Jeff took a deep breath and fought to bend his left knee enough to rise. Pain flooded the whole leg, but the joint moved slightly. He balanced his weight on his hands, then hopped onto his right leg. Finally he set down his left foot and stood on both legs together.

"I knew you could do it," Pike said. "Now tomorrow I want to see you walkin' around some. Best get that leg to workin'."

Jeff felt like his leg was on fire from the waist down, but his pride refused to let him admit the fact. Instead he did as Pike ordered. By summer's first dawn he was limping around enough that Pike trusted him in camp alone.

Jeff had been so preoccupied with his leg that he hadn't paid a lot of attention to the direction of their travels of late. But as he sat alone he couldn't help noticing they had left the remote backcountry and climbed to within a few miles of the Laramie River. From his vantage point he could gaze down into the valley below, where a troop of cavalry rode by in a textbook column of twos.

When Pike returned an hour before dusk, Jeff reported the soldiers.

"That's nothin' to what I saw today," Pike announced. "I saw hundreds of men shovelin' dirt, layin' iron rails for DeMoss's railroad. And I think I figured out how to hit 'em back."

"Hundreds of men?" Jeff asked. "Pike, there are cavalry patrols all over the place! We can't stop that, not with me barely walkin' and neither of us havin' more than a handful of shells for our rifles."

"I solved that," Pike explained, revealing three full boxes of Winchester ammunition. "I paid their supply office a sort o' unofficial visit. Just dipped my hat down to cover my face a bit an' strolled right down there."

"We can't win this kind of a fight, Pike."

"Maybe not, but we can sure bloody 'em a bit, make 'em hurt, slow 'em down so they wonder who it is that's got it in for the fool railroad."

"It'll take more than two of us to do anything."

"I know," Pike admitted. "There'll be others to lend a hand."

"Iron Hand's way to the north."

"Wasn't the Cheyennes I had in mind, little brother. Them rail camps're full o' Yankee dollars, and money can buy friends."

"The kind you can rely on?"

"No, the kind you can use," Pike said, grinning in a sly, calculating manner Jeff had never seen before.

But as they scouted the construction crews those next few days, Jeff gave it little thought. Pike was never far away, and he devoted most of his energies to convincing Jeff to work his leg harder.

"No man's lame on horseback, little brother, but a horse can get shot. You're not half as much use as when you could run like a July flood."

The next night as Jeff roasted a pair of snared rabbits over a fire shielded by a three-sided ravine, Pike walked to his horse.

"Keep a bit o' that warm for me, won't you?" Pike asked. "I have to see some folks."

114

"Who?" Jeff asked.

"Well, little brother, I didn't spend all my time in that supply office. I spoke with some people. I'll be bringin' back some."

"Who'd you find, Pike? Deserters from the army? Thieves? Whiskey runners? Not a very dependable crew."

"You'll see."

Jeff couldn't help feeling nervous as his brother headed off into the darkness. And as the minutes passed into hours, his concern grew. He finally hopped over to where he'd stretched out his blankets and drew his rifle from its scabbard.

I'll be ready if there's trouble, he told himself. But he also knew he could offer Pike little help.

The rabbits were heated and reheated a half-dozen times before Pike eventually returned. With him rode four others, none of them the type Ruth Thompson would have invited to Sunday supper.

"This here's my little brother, Jefferson," Pike said as he dismounted.

"Howdy, boy," the first, a heavily bearded man of near thirty, spoke. "Alf Depford's my name."

Depford extended a dirty hand, and Jeff reluctantly shook it. Depford wore the tattered remnant of a blue uniform coat, and his boots were of more-recent cavalry issue.

"These three're the Massey brothers," Pike explained, pointing to the others. "Tom, Charlie, Pat, this is Jeff."

Jeff nodded at the three. The Masseys removed their hats, and Jeff saw there was a clear family resemblance. Each had the same dirty blond hair and slightly upturned nose. The oldest, Tom, was maybe twenty-five. Charlie was close enough to it that he might have passed for his brother's twin. Pat was eighteen or so. Their beards were sparse and scraggly, and except for their eyes, they might have been judged younger than their years. Those eyes, deep blue and sullen, were old. Jeff had never seen colder, deadlier eyes, not even in the camps of the Cheyenne.

"Glad you saved some dinner for us," Pike said, taking the first rabbit off the fire and passing it to the newcomers. "My brother can sure cook, boys. Near as good as he shoots."

"These next weeks the shootin'll be of more help," Depford said, tearing apart the rabbit and hungrily biting into his share.

"Your brother's come up with quite a plan," Tom Massey explained. "We're goin' to make this railroad do some bleedin', yes, sir. They'll know we've come their way, and that's a fact."

"The Masseys've been partial to this railroad since it took their land back in Kansas," Pike explained.

"Seems we've been a boil on their backside, so to speak," young Pat Massey said. "Got posters on all three of us, three hundred dollars gold and no questions. That's more'n they paid for our farm."

Jeff found the news disturbing. These four, none of them washed, all smelling of horse sweat and damp leather, weren't much to inspire confidence. Worse, the Masseys were wanted. If Pike and he were in their company, the danger was that much greater than before.

"Tell him what you done, Alf," Tom said, nudging Depford.

"Sure, Tom, go ahead on," Pat added.

"I had some disagreements with a crew boss," Depford said in an accent that hinted he had not long ago lived in England. "The fool said I wasn't fit company for an Irish dog, so I swung my sledge onto his head. Improved the conversation quite a lot."

The Masseys laughed, but Jeff shuddered. Thieves and murderers, these four. They ate like pagans, ripping and tearing at their food. A tracker downwind would have no difficulty in following their trail.

Later, after cleaning up the bones and dousing the fire, Jeff walked off alone and stared at the pinpricks of light that marked the campfires of the railroad camps two miles away.

"You don't seem too pleased with our recruits, little brother," Pike said, joining Jeff. "It's not everybody who'd take on the Union Pacific, you know."

"I suppose."

"But you're not happy with 'em, are you?"

"They aren't exactly a pack of heroes," Jeff said, nodding to the four slumbering outlaws. At least two snored so that it seemed the stars might fall.

"You got to give 'em a chance, Jeff. Who's to say we won't look the same by summer's end."

"That's what worries me, Pike. All this runnin'! For what?"

"So we have a chance to even up things for Ma and Pa," Pike said, ripping a wildflower from the ground and twisting it apart in his hands. "I can't forget how they died. Can you? I want that DeMoss to bleed like

117

you bled, to see everything he cares about blown to bits."

"Even if we all die in the end?"

"If that's what it takes, yes."

Jeff frowned and fought a tear from the corner of his eye.

"Pike, I'll do my share. You can count on that. But can you trust these others?"

"Like anyone who's desperate not to get hung. You said they weren't heroes. They're not. For what I've got in mind, I don't want heroes. I want men who've got nothin' to lose, who'll do anything . . . shoot anybody . . . without questionin' or hesitatin'. These four are what I need."

"I hope so."

"I know how you feel, little brother. You spent all those years on the mountaintop, or with Iron Hand or Uncle Peter. You read your books, and you found out about the best side of people, how good they can be when they have it in their minds. But me . . . well, I've seen th'other side o' men. I've walked through the camps down by the fort, seen the gamblin' and the painted women, even sampled a bit of both. You know the best a man can hold in his heart, Jeff, but I know the worst. And it's the worst kind of men that we need to keep us alive."

"Won't that make us all the same, Pike? Will we be better than DeMoss?"

"Does it matter, little brother? Because if it does, I can still get you to Uncle Peter's mission before we hit the rail camps."

"It does matter," Jeff said, gripping his brother's

hand. "It matters because Ma would've wanted it that way. But I don't suppose we've got much choice, any of us. After you run awhile, nothin' seems to make much difference."

"I know," Pike said, glaring at the campfires in the distance. "That's what I hate most of all. But it's bound to get worse 'fore it turns better."

"Yes," Jeff said, sighing.

III

The main railroad camp was a beehive of activity. A city of canvas tents spread out along both sides of the shiny new rails. Locomotives puffed their way to the temporary depots, depositing flatcars laden with rails and crates of spikes. Elsewhere workers busily loaded stacks of wooden ties into wagons or assigned relief crews to the various construction camps out west.

"I never dreamed there'd be so many people," Jeff whispered to Pike as the two of them peered down at the busy camp from a nearby hillside. "Must be hundreds. I count thirty soldiers alone. The whole Cheyenne nation couldn't attack that camp!"

"You're right, little brother," Pike whispered as he motioned for the others to stay back. "This isn't the place. We'll have to try the work camps."

Leaving Depford and the Masseys back in the mountains, Pike and Jeff headed westward to scout the work camps. It had been possible to view the main encampment from the hills, but the construction camps were out in the open, winding along the rivers and creeks or stretched across the prairie. One crew might be clearing the route while another leveled the grade. The third crew laid the track itself.

Pike led the way as always, proudly and without fear. Jeff followed, the brim of his hat pulled down to hide his youthful forehead. Even so, his stiff left leg swung awkwardly in its stirrup, and Jeff worried someone might question why.

"Don't fret," Pike told his brother. "Bein' shot up in this country's nothin' to notice. An ocean o' trouble's rolled through here."

Even so, Jeff continued to worry. And yet the cavalry patrols that rode past had their eyes fixed on the far horizons.

"Nobody expects his enemy to ride right down on top of him," Pike explained.

No, Jeff thought, remembering how DeMoss had come to the cabin speaking of laws and agreements when, all along, the railroad people had been determined to do whatever was necessary to scratch their names across Thompson's Mountain.

Pike and Jeff visited each of the camps in turn, but it was camp number three that drew the most attention. Pike walked among the laborers, but Jeff remained atop his horse, studying the activity. A bare-backed army unloaded wagons of supplies. Three cauldrons of soup bubbled on fires built from imperfect ties and buffalo chips. The important work was performed by a half-dozen tall, broad-backed Irishmen who hammered away at spikes, securing the rails to their ties.

Jeff found his attention grabbed by the gaunt-faced boys who held the spikes in place or set the ties onto the bed. Some flinched as the giant sledges sang out as they hit the head of the spikes. Others stared off toward the mountains, their eyes half dead from a lifetime of

121

pain and hardship. The oldest were even shorter than Jeff, and more than one exhibited the stumps of fingers cleft by an errant sledge.

"What be your business, son?" a burly man suddenly demanded of Jeff. "You don't appear fit for our kind of work."

"We, my brother and I, came to see if you might need fresh meat," Jeff said, pointing to Pike. "There's game in the mountains nearby."

"There's crew already hired to shoot buffalo enough for five winters," the large man explained. "I'd like to find you work, lad. That leg of yours bears the look of bein' reb musketball shot to me. But I couldn't hire meat shot if you was Billy Sherman himself, and you don't appear up to line work."

"I understand," Jeff said, managing a smile for the stranger.

"My name's Arthur Cochrane, of Limerick, more recently o' the Armies of these United States. Why not hop along down, lad? I can find you some soup at least."

"Thank you, but I see my brother's ready to ride. I best be off, too."

Pike had observed the questioning and was now mounting his horse. As he turned the animal southward, he motioned for Jeff to follow.

"Didn't catch your name," Cochrane called out.

"Pick one," Jeff told the kind-faced stranger. "One's as good as another."

The railroader nodded sadly, and Jeff turned his horse away and headed after Pike.

"We're not so different, us and those men buildin' the railroad," Jeff told Pike once they were safely beyond

122

earshot of the camp. "Did you see those boys with their fingers gone? And that fellow . . ."

"Don't go takin' any of that to heart, little brother. We're on opposite sides of this quarrel, and it'll only cloud your thinkin'."

"So, you've decided, then."

"Soon as I meet with someone. It's not too late for you to ride along to Uncle Peter."

Yes, it is, Jeff told himself.

The rest of the afternoon Jeff and Pike hid themselves in a grove of willows near the river. An hour before dawn a smallish man of near forty appeared at the spot driving a railroad supply wagon.

"This is Tim O'Brien," Pike explained as he waved the wagon on into the shelter of the trees. "He's our other recruit."

"He's a railroad man," Jeff objected.

"By day, but come darkness, he's one of us."

For a price, Jeff thought as the thick-faced Irishman climbed down from the wagon and greeted Pike.

"The paymaster's due at dawn day after tomorrow, Pike," O'Brien announced. "Bringin' a month's wages, he is. Sure you'll be happy to see so much green in one box."

"Escort?" Pike asked.

"A corporal and a couple o' troopers's all. They'll ride all the way from headquarters."

"Meanin' they'll start before first light," Pike said, smiling. "We'll take 'em when they slow to cross Potts Creek. Then we'll come along to the camp."

"To the camp?" O'Brien asked nervously. "Why the camp? You'll have the cash."

"That's not all I'm after, O'Brien. I want the powder

123

in your supply tents. And there's the track. We mean to have a little fun with that."

"You're crazy!" O'Brien declared. "The men won't have it! You'll find yourself fightin' an army, you will. Most can handle a rifle, and you'll not have the darkness to shield you."

"They won't expect us to come in broad daylight," Pike said grimly. "And once we set off the powder, they'll be too busy pickin up the shambles of their camp to chase us."

"Maybe, but there'll be soldiers after you later."

"We know how to avoid soldiers, don't we, Jeff?"

Jeff nodded, but he was far from pleased by Pike's plan.

Later that evening when Pike informed Depford and the Massey brothers, they weren't so silent.

"We'll have the money, Pike," Depford pointed out. "Why hit the camp that same mornin' when we can slip in at night, blow the place to perdition?"

"Because to do it beforehand might warn the pay-master," Pike reasoned. "Afterward the cavalry'll be there in force."

"Well, there's truth in what he says," Tom Massey said. "An' they're not likely to expect anything. God smiles on fools sometimes, so Ma used to say. Let's pray she was right."

And so after sleeping under the willows, Pike Thompson's small band of raiders rose early. Jeff distributed cold biscuits and salted bacon. The others ate greedily, but Jeff himself had little appetite. Then Pike gave the signal to mount, and the column snaked its way into the tall grasses of the prairie, bound for Potts Creek.

"Just remember," Pike repeated again and again. "There's to be no shootin'. Catch 'em off guard. Dep and I'll take the paymaster. You Masseys take the soldier boys."

"And me?" Jeff asked.

"You see nobody gets away, little brother. I've seen you use a bow. Still remember how?"

Jeff nodded, and Pike drew a Cheyenne bow and quiver of arrows from beneath the long leather scabbard that held his rifle. Jeff took the weapon, bent the bow, and tightened the bowstring.

"I've got no quarrel with the army just now," Pike went on to say. "My fight's with the railroad."

"Well, we've got the cause to bleed 'em both," Pat Massey growled.

"You'll follow my lead, though," Pike insisted. "Nobody gets hurt if we can do it that way. It'll make the next time that much easier."

Depford nodded, and the Masseys went along with it. Jeff said nothing, just notched an arrow and prepared himself for the ambush.

In the beginning, the plan worked perfectly. The Masseys charged down on the bewildered escort. The soldiers were prisoners before they knew what had happened. The paymaster did his best to scamper away from his wagon, but Alf Depford pounced like a cougar, driving a knife through the round-faced paymaster with such sudden fury that the driver immediately raised his hands.

"I've little use for railroad men," Pike said as he pushed the driver off the wagon. And like a flash, Depford had killed again.

"Pike, he'd given up," Jeff objected.

125

"There's been blood shed, and these've seen us," Tom Massey said, pointing to the bluecoats. "Best we do for all of 'em."

Pike turned and stared at the soldiers. Jeff shuddered as he read the blazing brown eyes of his brother.

"Then, do it," Pike said, and the Masseys pulled their knives. The corporal and one of the privates were cut down immediately. The third managed to evade young Pat Massey's knife and stumble off toward the creek.

"Jeff!" Pike yelled.

Jeff aimed his arrow, but the surviving soldier suddenly froze. The private dropped to his knees and pleaded for his life.

"I can't recognize you boys," the young soldier whimpered. "What do I know? I've only been in the cavalry two months, and then only 'cause I had a debt to pay back in Kansas. Please, don't do it. I'll run off. They won't find me."

"Soon as we're gone, he'll head right for his lieutenant," Depford said.

"Jeff?" Pike called.

But as Jeff gazed into the weeping eyes of the young private, his fingers wouldn't let fly the arrow.

"Jeff?" Pike spoke again.

Jeff eased the tension on bowstring and replaced the arrow in its quiver.

"He's young still," Depford said, climbing down from his horse and marching toward the soldier. "He'll do it next time."

Then, as easily as he might have wrung the neck of a chicken, Depford drew a knife and dispatched the soldier.

"Let's finish this and get along to the rail camp," Pike said, cutting the horses loose from the paymaster's wagon. The animals trotted on down the creek, and Pike used the paymaster's key to unlock the heavy iron box containing the payroll. The banknotes were rolled and stuffed in a flour sack inside Pike's saddlebags. The gold pieces were divided among the raiders. "We'll split the rest at camp tonight," Pike explained. "Now grab their rifles and ammunition."

The Masseys gathered up the weapons, as well as a gold watch which had belonged to the corporal and a few trinkets from the pockets of the paymaster. Young Pat took the driver's boots, his own being a trifle too small, and the army horses were herded along, too.

Pike led the way on toward the rail camp, followed by the Masseys, with Depford and Jeff bringing up the rear. As he rode, Jeff tried not to remember the wide, pleading eyes of the cavalryman or the ease with which the others had been killed. Dying came so suddenly, like a bolt of lightning crashing out of a summer thunderstorm.

"I wouldn't let it worry you, Jeff," Alf Depford said from three feet away. "It's never easy the first time."

"What?" Jeff asked, staring with reddened eyes at the killer who'd become his companion.

"It's never easy killin' your first man."

"He wouldn't've been the first," Jeff said, sadly recalling that crisp spring morning when the world had gone insane.

"Then, you know it's like other things. It gets easier with the doin' of it."

Jeff winced at the thought. Oh, Lord, he prayed. Don't ever let it get that easy for me.

Pike halted his band a quarter mile from the work camp and made a final scout. Then he deployed his companions. The Masseys dismounted and formed on the left. They would provide covering fire should the need arise. Pike and Depford would ride to the supply tents, load a few barrels of powder on two of the cavalry mounts, then set a fuse to blow the remainder of the stores. Jeff would cover the right on horseback.

It's all he trusts me to do, Jeff told himself as Pike rode toward the white canvas tents. The sun was only now chasing away a heavy ground fog, and the laborers were busy eating breakfast. For a moment all appeared perfect. Then Jeff heard a voice from the distance.

"Well, so you've come again, have you?" Arthur Cochrane bellowed. "In time for breakfast. Care to share a bit o' bacon, lad?"

"I can't," Jeff said, trying to hide the Winchester cradled in his hands.

"What's that?" the friendly Irishman asked. "A boy with no stomach for meals? Don't seem right, it don't."

Only then did Cochrane recognize the object in Jeff's hands. The railroader gazed up in disbelief, then turned in time to see Pike and Depford tie the powder kegs on the cavalry horses.

"You're no better'n a thief!" Cochrane cried out. "A thief! I'll see you all hanged."

"No, you won't," Jeff said, turning his rifle on the bewildered Irishman. "And you don't know nothin' about stealin'. Whose land is this you're on? Who died so Henry DeMoss could bring his rails across the Medicine Bow? It wasn't a rebel ball that shattered my leg!"

Cochrane started to call out, but the sound of the

Winchester's lever advancing a shell into the firing chamber chased away the words.

"That's it!" Pike shouted, riding hard toward the south with Depford and the cavalry horses close behind. The Masseys opened up with a volley, and Jeff turned to go.

"Thieves!" Cochrane yelled at last. Jeff took aim, then swung the rifle to the left and shattered a water flask a foot from Cochrane's ear. The supply tents then exploded with a roar akin to thunder, and a dark black powder cloud swallowed the work camp. Canvas tents erupted in flame, and men screamed as they ran for safety.

Jeff squeezed his knees together in an effort to quiet his horse. The animal kicked its hind legs into the air and whined in terror. A second blast did little to improve the animal's temper, and Jeff stuffed his rifle into its scabbard and held onto the horse's neck with both hands.

"Jeff, let's get!" Pike cried out.

A rifle or two barked from the flame and smoke that had once been a work camp, and Jeff urged his horse into a gallop. The heavy acrid smell of burning gunpowder mixed with charred canvas in the misty morning. Shouts mingled with screams and curses in the camp, and Jeff took a final glance backward. It seemed a vision of sulfurous hell, of confusion cast upon the world.

"I'll see you hanged, you son of Satan!" Cochrane's voice rolled through the air.

Jeff spotted the big Irishman standing with clenched fist in the midst of the smoking tents.

What did you expect? Jeff silently asked as he turned

to leave. We're at war with DeMoss, and you men take his money, do his bidding.

As he galloped after Pike and the others toward the distant mountains, toward the refuge they would provide, Jeff hoped sincere, hard-working men like Cochrane would abandon the railroad, would leave the uncompleted rails to rust in the summer rains. But deep inside himself, Jeff knew it was a forlorn dream, that he had witnessed but the first of many raids, the first of many deaths.

IV

Jeff led Depford and the Masseys into the high country while Pike kept a rendezvous with Tim O'Brien. Knowing his brother was in such bad company made Jeff more than a little nervous. A man who will betray his employer once will do so again, and DeMoss might offer a generous reward to put Pike Thompson out of business.

As it happened, though, Pike paid the Irishman a share of the loot and caught up with the others by the second night.

"The army's after us," Pike said as he slid down from his horse and joined the circle around the campfire. "I passed three columns. They think it was Cheyennes hit the paymaster, but they know we're the ones burned the camp. Saw us clear enough, I suppose."

"One of them recognized me from the visit we paid to their camp," Jeff explained.

"You should've shot him," Depford grumbled.

"One or two saw us, too, Alf. You're known hereabouts, and someone's bound to've noticed our horses."

"But we're safe up here," Tom Massey said. "Young Jeff here took us up trails a goat couldn't travel."

"We're not entirely safe anywhere," Pike confessed. "We have to stay alert for anything. They'll be money on our heads."

"Already is on most of us," young Pat said, laughing.

"One thing's for certain, though," Depford said. "If your brother's goin' to ride with us, he'd best get that leg mended. His horse goes, he's got no chance at all."

"Didn't know it mattered to you," Jeff said, forcing his knee to bend slightly.

"No, he's right," Pike said. "Long as we're up here layin' low, you'd best work that leg."

Jeff nodded, though he was far from convinced the tendons and ligaments that held his knee together would ever allow him to be very nimble.

Summer, some say, is a healing time, though, and as the raiders drifted through the Medicine Bow peaks, skirting the rail camps and army patrols, Jeff began to notice improvement. The leg remained stiff and sore, but gradually he was able to bend it a little more. Sometimes he'd be swimming in the chill ponds with Pike, and the leg would seem to explode with pain. Then, lying on the rocks in the noonday sun, the flesh would brown, and Jeff would bend the leg as if it'd never known hardship.

Twice during August, Pike made the perilous ride to the work camps. There he'd skulk about until he could safely contact O'Brien. On such occasions he'd visit the shantytowns that seemed to be following the railroad camps, buying supplies and gathering information.

Each time Pike returned, the Masseys and Depford would engage in riotous drinking. Even Pike would whoop and holler, boasting of the next raid and setting it all down as a plan. But as long as the cavalry patrols crisscrossed the valley, there was little hope of venturing from their mountain refuge.

Jeff often noticed the restlessness of the others. Pike

in particular seemed like a caged grizzly, eager to get out and tear at his enemies. For his own part, Jeff was content to pass the close of summer in the hills and valleys he loved. Often as he fished the streams or hunted deer he could recall a gentler, better time. And as he did, his hatred for Henry DeMoss grew.

If not for him, we'd be smoking venison for the winter, Jeff thought. We'd be sitting at the table as Ma read the Bible. Maybe Little Heart would visit with news of Iron Hand. Perhaps I'd pass a month with Uncle Peter, reading the newest English history and learning what wondrous stories the Philadelphia Bible Society sent this year.

But just as Jeff began to dream that peace might reign over them a little longer, Pike announced it was time to return to the valley.

"Can't stay up here forever," Pike told them. "The railroad moves along each day. From now on we'll hit the supply depots. The construction camps, well, they're beyond us. Besides, the cavalry watches 'em closely."

"So where do we hit?" Depford asked.

"Any place it'll hurt," Pike said, smiling. "That means we tear up a little track, rob a payroll, burn supplies, anything and everything we can."

"I like that payroll part," Tom Massey declared. "Where and when?"

And so Pike led the way north, back to the prairies, back to where the iron road stretched across land once black with buffalo. After meeting with O'Brien, Pike planned a half-dozen strikes. Paymasters were robbed. Company offices and supply depots were torched. From time to time Pike would blow a section of rail, delaying supplies to the construction crews and forcing men that should have been breaking ground toward the Rockies to rebuild some barren stretch of track along the Laramie River.

Such raids were only a minor nuisance to the Union Pacific, though, and Pike realized that. He was always on the lookout for a bigger target, hoping to strike DeMoss directly or at least prompt inquiry. Pike finally settled on the bridge that carried the rails over the Medicine Bow River.

The bridge was DeMoss's masterpiece, an engineering marvel. Built of hundreds of tall pines, crossed and bolted into an intricate framework, the bridge stood thirty feet above the lowest point of the riverbed and stretched across some fifty-five feet of broken terrain. Moreover, it stood near the cabin's site, a painful reminder that Thompson's Mountain was no longer home.

"I don't know that we can do somethin' like that a lot of damage," Pat Massey said, scratching his head as Pike studied the bridge.

"Oh, what do you know about it?" Depford asked. "I done my share o' railroad work with Sherman down in Georgia. Nothin' was ever built o' wood and sweat that can't be burned."

"O'Brien says it took two months to build that bridge," Pike said. "It'll be even worse for 'em come winter. How's it to be done, Alf?"

"Powder charges," Depford said, "set to blow the beams on the right or left side. More charges up top to ruin the tracks. Fire ought to do the rest."

"Sounds too easy," Jeff said.

"Won't be," Depford told them. "Guards up top can

spot your charges, see you plantin' 'em. Powder's touchy, and you've a long way to run to get clear. It's an invitation to get caught. Might be possible on a moonless night, but even then, it's risky."

"Would make a nice bonfire, though," Tom said, smiling at the thought.

"We'll need lots o' powder," Jeff whispered.

"Well, the Union Pacific's always provided us with all we needed," Pike said, laughing. "We'd have to hit the supply camps first anyway. Got to throw 'em off our scent."

"They won't expect two strikes so close together," Jeff pointed out. "And they can't exactly ignore it's happenin' this time."

No, Jeff thought. DeMoss will have to send someone after us. That's clear enough. Pike was raising the stakes. It was growing serious.

O'Brien was opposed to the idea. No money was involved, and there were bound to be a lot of railroad detectives nosing around afterward. Nevertheless Pike launched the first of three raids on the supply camps, each better than thirty miles from the other, each defended by railroad guards and soldiers. And each depot handed over ammunition and powder, then vanished in a storm of powderflash and splintered crates.

When the third depot was cleaned out, Pike drew his raiders to a maze of rock and sagebrush known as Demon's Roost. It wasn't but three miles from the bridge, and no one camped there normally. The Cheyennes believed bad spirits lived nearby, and the wind howled through oddly-shaped rocks in a way that would set a man's nerve on edge. It proved a perfect hideout.

The supply depot raids had succeeded in decoying the cavalry patrols into the mountains. In spite of occasional gunfire and a hundred reports, the army found no trace of the raiders. But while the soldiers were stumbling about the mountains, Pike Thompson was preparing his greatest attack.

August nights seemed to last forever, and finding a night that lacked a moon yet wasn't plagued by rain or hail was far from easy. Wet powder rarely burned, though, and the best results would come when the bridge itself was brittle and dry. The chance came the final week of August, and Pike brought his company into readiness.

"The plan's simple," Pike explained as Depford filled several small casks with powder. "We place the casks, attach the fuses, then light them on a signal. Afterward you'd best run like high heaven or you'll go the way of the bridge!"

"This is crazy," Tom growled. "Don't you see? There are three guards atop the bridge every night. We'll have to lure 'em away. Then you have to plant the bombs, not just next to the rails, but below, near the river. Some of those beams are in the river itself!"

"I'll decoy the guards," Pike promised. "Alf, you tend the casks down in the riverbed. They're the touchy ones."

"They're all touchy so far's I'm concerned," Tom said. "We'll cover you, Pike, but I won't have Pat or Charlie lightin' fuses that're bound to blow 'em sky high."

"I'll set the ones on top," Jeff volunteered.

"You?" Tom asked, laughing. "You hobble around like a one-legged crow. You know how long those fuses burn? Two minutes!"

"I can get clear," Jeff assured them. "Pike, you know I'm steady. Besides, there's no one else."

"He's right about that," Depford grumbled, staring hard at the Masseys.

"I don't know," Pike said, scratching his head. "It's dangerous."

"Always was," Jeff admitted. "But all I have to do is get clear of the bridge, then hide in the boulders. Once the charges start blowin', no one's about to go lookin' for me. They'll be too busy with other matters."

"Could work, Pike," Depford said. "It's a throw o' the dice either way, but if it works, they'll long remember it 'round these parts."

"Yes," Pike agreed, and it was settled.

The very next night Pike led the way on horseback along the winding, treacherous route to the bridge. The three guards were there as before, but with them was a squadron of cavalry.

"You ready?" Pike asked as Jeff and Depford steadied their horses. Behind each saddle were a half-dozen powdercasks primed and fused. Depford nodded, and Jeff did likewise.

"Do what you can," Tom Massey told Pike. "If they don't all give chase, we'll hit 'em hard."

"Just see to it you don't hit us," Depford warned. "I don't plan to go up like a candle."

Pike nodded, then started toward the bridge. The Masseys readied their rifles, and Jeff headed for the far side of the river. Depford rode through the shallows of the stream itself. Then Pike screamed a command and opened fire with his pistol at the seven soldiers assisting the guards.

"It's them!" one of the guards screamed. "They're here!"

It's who? Jeff found himself asking as he slowly rode in and out of the shadows. Are they expecting us?

It certainly seemed so, for the soldiers coolly and calmly fired a volley at Pike, felling his horse and forcing him to stumble to a pile of rocks for cover.

"Let's get him!" a soldier yelled, racing forward. His companions followed. The guards hesitated, then raced to catch up. Suddenly the Masseys swooped down on the whole crew, firing and shouting, completely terrifying those not shot dead.

Now, Jeff thought as he slid down from the saddle, draped the charges over one shoulder, and limped along the track. He placed the charges along the left-hand rail as Depford had suggested, then took a deep breath. Below, Depford had placed his casks, too. Jeff lit a kerchief and dropped it from the bridge. The moment its flame vanished in the river, both raiders lit their fuses.

The most dangerous part for Jeff was lighting the four lengths of fuses and then getting away. The second fuse was stubborn and twice went out. Fortunately the others burned immediately, and Jeff stumbled back toward his horse. The loyal animal waited ten feet away, and Jeff threw himself onto the saddle. Then he slapped the horse into motion, riding like thunder to the pile of boulders that might offer safety. Jeff reached it none too soon, for the first of Depford's charges sent a tremor through the bridge as Jeff turned his pony toward the rocks. The second and third explosions came from the track itself. The third blew one end of the rail skyward, and the blast that followed sent a shower of water over the whole structure.

Dear Lord, Jeff thought as he rolled off his horse, urged the animal to flight, then covered his head. A tremendous roar split the air, and amber tongues of flame leaped skyward, consuming the great pine beams of the bridge.

"The bridge!" an anguished voice cried out.

"The bridge!" another and another screamed.

Another cask exploded, and the center of the delicate framework splintered in a hundred directions. The air filled with a terrible moaning, groaning, and the bridge gave way a bit to the right. Then, as if consumed by some ancient dragon creature, the bridge broke apart and fell in a smoldering heap into the river.

Debris continued to crash downward for several minutes, and Jeff huddled in the rocks, afraid to stir. When the air finally began to clear, he looked below at the masterpiece of construction that had suddenly become a summer campfire. Depford was already mounted. He rode away down the river. The Masseys continued to pour rifle fire into what was left of the cavalry squadron. Pike was nowhere to be seen, nor was Jeff's horse.

I guess there are healthier places to be, Jeff told himself as a pair of railroaders appeared along the broken, twisted rails. As more and more laborers appeared in their nightshirts, wildly firing rifles and cursing their unseen foe, Jeff retreated through the rocks toward the north, hoping to catch up with his horse or perhaps spot some member of the band. He half expected Pike to appear, his dark, somber eyes afire with success. But at the moment, Jeff considered his personal safety most important, so he concentrated on making good his escape.

As it happened, the faithful horse was chewing on willow branches two hundred yards upstream. Jeff climbed atop the animal and prepared to take flight in earnest. Before he could nudge the horse into a gallop, though, Jeff saw something move across the river.

Another man might have instinctively reached for his pistol and fired at the approaching shadow. But Jeff noticed something familiar in the silhouette, a long-remembered squareness about the shoulders.

"Pike?" Jeff called out, foolishly alerting the railroaders to both their presences.

"Keep quiet, you fool!" Pike hollered even louder.

The men alongside the shambles of a bridge fired toward the noise, and one bullet actually tore a button from Jeff's sleeve. Jeff paid it little heed as he drove his horse into the shallow water of the river. Soon Pike was pulling himself up onto the saddle behind Jeff, and the two of them rode cautiously back toward their camp to the north.

"Well, look's like you saved my bacon this time," Pike said, squeezing Jeff's shoulder in a manner half forgotten in that time of death and despair.

"Seems I'm not altogether useless, then."

"Not altogether," Pike said, laughing. "We hurt 'em this time, little brother."

"Yes," Jeff agreed.

But as they continued, it wasn't triumph over their success that flooded Jeff's mind. It was the notion that their arrival had been anticipated . . . no, expected. It wasn't a pleasant idea, not at all.

V

As dawn broke across the mountains to the east, Jeff and Pike waited anxiously for the arrival of their companions. From time to time bands of horsemen splashed their way across the Medicine Bow River just beyond the shielding boulders. Jeff or Pike would peer out at the riders, then duck to avoid detection. Sometimes patrolling soldiers would gallop by. At least once Jeff spotted the long black coats of railroad detectives among the horsemen. Occasionally a pair of supply wagons would roll past, always protected by a dozen armed men.

"It's goin' to be hard from now on," Pike grumbled. "They'll have an eye out for us."

"We can always head back to the high country," Jeff suggested. "Winter's not long in comin', and they'll never track us once the snow fills the passes."

"Can't give 'em that much peace," Pike said hatefully. "Got to keep after 'em."

"Even if Depford and the Masseys are caught?"

"They'll turn up in time, little brother. Likely they've taken to cover for the day. I expect 'em to wander in tonight."

And indeed they did. Jeff gazed at his fellow out-laws, then shook his head. A fine company they made! The four new arrivals fell off their horses without speaking. Each face was black from powder and smoke. Their tired eyes and wrinkled foreheads told of the difficult flight from the river bridge.

"Glad you boys made it back," Pike said, unsaddling Depford's horse. "Was beginnin' to worry."

"Well, we had a spot o' trouble," Depford explained. "Half the country's full of soldiers. Never saw so many bluecoats, not even ridin' with Sherman. Lord, but we did get their attention."

"We'll take a day or two to rest, then make our plans," Pike said, pulling the saddle off the horse and tossing Depford the blanket.

Depford nodded, and the Masseys mumbled their agreement. But there proved to be little time to rest or plan. The soldiers began searching every inch of the river, and half a company camped a hundred yards from the hideout.

So, it's ride again, Jeff thought when Pike gathered them together. As midnight cast its summer spells, Pike Thompson's raiders exchanged their weary ponies for fresh mounts drawn from the cavalry's picket line. After liberating what ammunition and food was un-guarded, Jeff and Depford scattered the rest of the mounts. Pike and the Massey brothers then rode among the calvarymen, shooting and whooping so that most of the soldiers abandoned their blankets and ran helter-skelter into the river.

"Can't call 'em bluecoats now," Pike joked as he led his companions away from the scene. "Bare-bottoms'd be more fittin'."

Jeff couldn't help laughing at the floundering soldiers. Most stumbled about in nightshirts while others sat naked in the river, totally dumbfounded. Their captain shouted curses at the sky and demanded reinforcements.

It won't always be this way, though, Jeff thought as Pike led the way into the foothills. Luck and daring only take a man so far. Dancing Lance was half shadow, could ride the wind and wrestle a grizzly. And yet a bluecoat bullet had found his heart.

The final sun of August set on Jefferson Thompson, and the coming of autumn saw him fighting off the evening chills in a hundred camps scattered through the Medicine Bow Mountains. For whole days at a time Jeff and his companions survived on stale biscuits and leathery beef stolen from the railroad depots. The rails themselves snaked off toward the setting sun, and Pike contented himself with burning bridges, torching supplies, or blowing rails.

Each raid brought more determined pursuit, though. Jeff felt as if the devil himself was after them. Railroad detectives and even bands of farmers hounded the Thompsons each and every step. The snap of a twig, the cry of an owl, or the rustling of the wind brought six fugitives to their feet. No fires were lit, and Pike stationed a guard every night.

"It's goin' to be even worse now," Pike declared as he rode into camp after the weekly meeting with O'Brien. "The army's made peace with Red Cloud, and the whole cavalry's like as not to turn on us."

"Maybe it's time we headed south," Depford suggested. "There's gold in Colorado, and plenty of opportunity for men in our line of work."

"I'm not after just anybody's gold," Pike raged. "I'm after railroad money."

"Well, we've seen little enough o' that lately," Tom Massey complained. "My boots are near rotted out from the rain, and we've got no provisions for winter. All you want to do, Pike Thompson, is burn shanty-towns and shoot up depots. I'm tired and cold. I want more."

"You can ride off any day you choose," Pike thundered.

Tom and Pat started for their horses. Jeff then stared in disbelief as Charlie Massey rose and motioned for his brothers to sit down. Charlie hadn't spoken five words all those months, but he now lashed at all of them.

"You know nothin' 'bout fightin' a war!" Charlie shouted. "You're a bit hungry, or maybe cold, so you think you'll ride on, winter down south. You forgettin' we're posted, Tom? Reward's the same in Denver City or Scott's Bluff. Hell, I never figured to be alive this winter. You don't know the country, Pat. You'd ride plumb into a cavalry patrol first day out. Look at ole Jeff here. He's still got a leg twisted 'round so it half bends. Don't hear him complainin'."

"Let him stay," Pat grumbled.

"We'll all stay," Charlie said, fingering the handle of his pistol. " 'Cause if they catch you, Pat, it won't take 'em long to track the rest of us. The thing is, we'd best get some better news from O'Brien. He sends us to burn coal oil and buffalo hides. He used to know where the gold was. Pike, you remind him he's always had his share, with little o' the risk."

"We could still winter in Kansas," Pat said, hands on his hips.

"Is it winter you're afraid of?" Charlie asked, shaking his head. "Winter's the best time to raid. Those blue-coats won't be ridin' out here once there's snow on the ground. The railroad hands'll be too busy keepin' the tracks clear."

"He's right," Depford declared. "Why, we can proba-bly build ourselves a cabin up here somewhere. There's a thousand spots to hide a place."

"Then, it's settled?" Pike asked. "Everyone's stayin'?"

Pike had gazed at each face, but it was Charlie Massey who answered for everyone.

"Thought I said that," Charlie said, gazing at his brothers with menacing eyes. "Only way to leave this gang is with a bullet through the head."

"From them," Pat asked, pointing to the distant rail depots, "or you?"

"Whatever you choose, Pat," Charlie replied with a wicked smile. "Just as you want it."

No one else spoke of leaving. As the leaves of the aspens browned and yellowed, blazed scarlet with the chills of late September, Pike grew more venturesome. Twice the payboxes were robbed, and once a cavalry supply wagon from Fort Laramie was ambushed. The most successful raid hit the Medicine Bow depot the evening after a supply train had arrived.

"This is what I call profit," Depford said as Pike tossed sacks of gold coins about as if they were boiled potatoes.

"There's somethin' else," Pike said, spreading out a stack of freshly-printed sheets.

The others grabbed at the papers. When Jeff finally gazed at one, he shuddered. They were posters, and near the bottom were six sketches.

"Would you look at that!" Depford gasped. "Cheyenne Pike. Don't even know your last name, Pike."

"I'm no half-breed," Pike growled, tearing a poster in two. "I'm three fourths white."

Jeff read aloud the descriptions below the drawings.

"This renegade band is responsible for loss of life and property in the Wyoming Territory. The Union Pacific Railroad will pay a reward of $500 for the death or capture of Cheyenne Pike. The Union Pacific and the State of Kansas will pay a reward of $500 for the death or capture of Tom, Charles, or Pat Massey. The Union Pacific and Jonas Kincaid will pay the sum of $1,000 upon proof of the death or capture of Alfred Depford."

"They left you out, Jeff," Pike said, failing in an attempt to laugh.

"No, I'm down at the very bottom," Jeff told his brother. "The Union Pacific will pay a reward of $200 for the death or capture of a renegade boy known to ride with the Cheyenne Pike gang. Said boy is known to be lame of the left leg. All these criminals ride heavily armed, and no undue risk is encouraged. Wire H. DeMoss, Laramie Junction, Wyoming Territory."

"Only two hundred, eh?" Depford said, nudging Jeff's shoulder.

"Must be payin' by the pound," Pike said, lightening the mood.

"What's undue risk?" Pat asked.

"Seems the Union Pacific wouldn't shed a lot of tears if we got shot instead o' captured," Pike explained.

"You know what this means, don't you?" Charlie asked. "There'll be bounty hunters about. Especially for you, Alf. A thousand dollars buys a lot of whiskey."

"Buys a lot o' trouble, too," Depford added.

146

"It makes no real difference," Pike told them. "We'll take no more chances than before. But neither will we hide in a hole."

The others whooped their agreement, but Jeff felt no such enthusiasm. To be hunted as a pack of wolves! And if the sketches failed to resemble anybody, it wouldn't be hard spotting Jeff's bent leg.

A rare fire was lit that next morning, and the posters were solemnly burned. Then, filled with bitterness, Pike led his band back to the Medicine Bow depot for a second strike. With a storm of rifle fire Depford and the Masseys silenced the two line detectives. Pike then battered down the door, and Jeff poured coal oil across the floor of the simple wooden depot. Minutes later the station was reduced to a scar of ashes on the autumn prairie.

Pike didn't pause at the scene. A handful of stunned supply handlers and an old, wrinkled Pawnee watched from the safety of a nearby aspen grove.

"Let's ride!" Pike yelled, and the six raiders galloped off into the mountains.

They didn't stop until the first ridge had been crossed. Then, as if guided more by memory than by intent, Pike made his way to the old Cheyenne camp on the banks of Wolf Creek.

"Remember this place?" Pike asked as the others unsaddled their horses.

"Yes," Jeff said, sighing. "We were here with Iron Hand not so long ago."

"Little Heart brought us out."

"You and me, Ma and Pa."

"Was about the last good time we had."

Jeff sank to the ground. Beside him in the sandy

riverbed was an arrowhead. Jeff turned it over in his fingers, recalling what Iron Hand had said about remembering.

"I lost track o' the days halfway through springtime," Pike said. "Seems like it could be mid-October, though. I thought you might like to pass your birthday here, in a good place, with somethin' o' Ma an' Pa around."

"Doesn't seem birthdays have much place in the world these days."

"You feelin' old, little brother?"

"White hair and no teeth wouldn't make me older."

"Then, maybe we ought to change that," Pike said, shoveling Jeff into the creek. As he shivered from the chilly water, Pike jumped in after him. Soon Depford and the Masseys joined in, splashing handfuls of water at each other in a mock duel.

For once the gloom seemed to lift. Jeff broke off a willow branch and tied a length of string to one end. Then he fastened an almost-forgotten fishook to the line.

"Been a long time since we've been fishin'," Pike whispered, handing Jeff a wriggling worm.

"We've had other things to do," Jeff said, trying to cast the memory of that long, last year from his mind.

"Ever do much thinkin' 'bout old times? Other night I thought I heard Iron Hand callin' me to the buffalo hunt."

"You just want to get little Prairie Flower to keep your lodge."

"Think she was more taken with you, little brother. She sure did fuss and fret over that leg o' yours."

"It was a better time," Jeff said sadly as he dipped his line into the creek. "Think things'll ever get any

148

better?"

"I'm not Two Humps. I don't see the future. Don't really see how they can, though."

"If there's peace up north, maybe we could head up there, hunt the buffalo, shoot elk with Little Heart. I know it won't be the same as at the cabin, but . . ."

"I never should've let you stay," Pike said, interrupting. "Now it's too late. We'll all die up here, shot down sippin' coffee some mornin' when we think no one's around to spot our fire. They don't even know who we are, don't understand why we're doin' this. We're just somethin' to be rid of, like a prowlin' grizzly or some lone wolf."

"It'll be better come winter, Pike."

"No, it'll only be colder."

Jeff tried to smile as the afternoon sun warmed his face. He warmed a bit as the smell of fresh-cooked trout drifted through the camp. He didn't really brighten until he read the shine in Pike's eyes as he handed Jeff a heavy bearskin coat in celebration of sixteen years of life.

It's really fifteen still, Jeff thought as he wrapped himself in the warm coat. The last year I haven't been alive. But Jeff kept his thoughts to himself and tried to enjoy the rare interlude of laughter. Depford played a jaunty melody on a mouth organ, and the Masseys sang sad ballads their Tennessee grandmother had brought West.

Once the noise quieted, and the weary men spread their blankets out along the creek, Jeff realized nothing had changed. Alf Depford kept watch with a loaded Winchester in his arms. The Masseys kept their guns handy as well.

"Let's go off a way tonight," Pike whispered as Jeff prepared to pull off his boots. "Up there, past the aspens, where we can see Pa's mountain."

Jeff nodded, collected his things, then followed Pike to a clearing up the hillside.

"I miss him," Jeff whispered as they placed their blankets side by side. "I know we had our differences. Sometimes I wondered if I was maybe a prairie orphan Pa took in."

"I was there the night you were born, little brother," Pike reminded Jeff. "Pa was proud o' you. I guess we both saw what was happenin' to the high country when we looked at you. Even if DeMoss hadn't come, you would've left. I envied the easy way you had with words and figures. But now I see you've got a hardness to you as well. Pa worried about that. But that mornin' when they hit the cabin, you showed us all."

"I still have nightmares."

"Me, too," Pike said, shedding his trousers. "Now we'd best get some rest. Alf won't keep watch all night. He'll expect relief."

Jeff nodded, then rolled the bearskin coat into a ball beneath his head. Within seconds he was asleep.

Jeff's eyes cracked open around midnight. He stared up in surprise at Depford's ashen face.

"Someone's down at the creek," Depford whispered as Pike hurriedly dressed himself.

"See if you can work your way through the trees to the Masseys," Pike told Jeff. "We'll cover you from here. You hear any shootin', get yourself clear."

"And the Masseys?"

"They'll know somethin's up, don't you think?"

Jeff nodded, then pulled his trousers on over his shirt and stepped into his boots. He cradled his rifle in both hands, then began creeping down the hillside toward the creek.

There was a moist, strangely muggy feel to the air. Looking overhead, Jeff watched the moon dip in and out of a heavy haze. His father had a name for it. Hunter's moon. Bright enough for stalking, and when you were ready to close with the quarry, it'd dip into the clouds and altogether disappear.

Jeff grew uneasy. His palms began to sweat, and he took care to keep in the shadows. By now his eyes picked out the dim outlines of a dozen riders. It'd been folly to build a fire, cook trout. Making camp on the banks of Wolf Creek had been insanity!

"That could be them there," a voice announced as horses splashed into the creek. "Now, boys!"

Jeff froze as the opposite bank of the creek exploded with rifle fire. Young Pat Massey, sleeping peacefully beside the cold ashes of the fire, caught the first three bullets. The young man nevertheless sat up, only to be hit in the face by a fourth shot.

Tom and Charlie were luckier. They crawled away from their blankets as another volley tore apart the camp.

"Come on in an' finish it!" Charlie shouted. "Come on!"

Tom started to speak, too, but the third round of gunfire silenced him. Three, maybe more bullets slammed into Tom's chest, and he collapsed like a rag doll.

"Jeff, get on back here!" Pike shouted as Jeff made

his way toward Charlie Massey.

Jeff halted and gazed back at his brother. Pike and Depford held their rifles ready, and yet they didn't fire. Jeff glanced at Charlie, desperately firing back at what now appeared to be twenty rifles. Pike saw it clearly. Nothing would save Charlie.

"Come on, you devils!" Charlie yelled at the shadowy figures across the creek. "Come get your due!"

As the moon emerged from the clouds, Jeff noticed Charlie's left arm hung limp. A large patch of red was already spreading across one shoulder.

It's not how I pictured it, Jeff thought as he crept back up the hill toward his brother. I thought we'd die in a heroic charge. I saw us dying together, not ambushed in the night like rabid dogs.

"Aren't we goin' to do anything for Charlie?" Jeff asked when he reached Pike.

"He wouldn't leave his brothers," Depford said, leading the way toward the horses. "It's how he'd have it, holdin' off the whole bunch while we make our escape."

Jeff doubted that. In the final moment, Charlie'd probably turn over all the gold he'd ever dreamed of for a little covering fire and a chance at one of the horses.

As Jeff followed Pike along the ridge, they both saw someone else had thought of the horses, too. A shadow or two moved among the hobbled ponies.

"What now?" Depford asked.

"Appears they're well led," Pike admitted. "Well, so are we. Jeff, you watch the creek."

"Watch?" Jeff asked. "I can't see ten feet in front of my face unless the moon's out."

"Listen for riders. You hear anything, open up on it. You so much as smell company, open fire. I'm weary o'

152

surprises."

Jeff nodded, then set down his bundle of belongings and concentrated on the creek. Moments later a terrible cry slit the air, and he knew Depford was back at work. A muffled scream followed shortly, and Pike led the horses over.

"No time to mess with saddles," Pike declared, tossing Jeff a bridle. "Tie your things to his neck. Then ride like the devil was after you. We'll meet you at Eagle Rock."

"Pike?"

"I mean to have a run at 'em," Pike explained as he slapped Jeff's horse into motion. "Wait for me!"

"Pike?" Jeff cried as he fought to control his flying pony. "Pike?"

But there was no hope of turning the terrified animal, and Jeff instead sought to control its charging hooves. Eagle Rock was only three miles distant. With any kind of luck, Pike would reach it before first light.

VI

Jeff hid himself and his horse behind the fierce granite cliff he'd always known as Eagle Rock. There was a cave halfway up that made a perfect boyhood hideout. It was too well known a place to conceal outlaws for long, and there was only one approach. It offered a good vantage point, though, and anyone attacking would pay a heavy price.

The sun was still poking its head over the eastern ranges when Pike and Alf Depford started up the trail to the cave. Both were drenched with sweat and blackened by powder smoke. Jeff asked no questions, just helped the weary men down from their horses and left them to sleep.

Jeff kept watch from the mouth of the cave, scanning the valley below for any sign of riders. He wasn't disappointed. A hair after midday, three men wrapped in buffalo cloaks and carrying deadly Sharps carbines rode by. Jeff felt their eyes examining the cliff, searching for hiding places.

"Not from 'round here, that's for sure," Pike whispered.

Jeff jumped three inches, and if Pike hadn't grabbed

his shoulders, Jeff might have flown outside. After terrifying midnight raid, he wasn't prepared for Pike's voice.

"Kind o' jumpy, aren't you?" Pike asked.

"Good reason to be," Jeff answered. "You figure they're DeMoss's men?"

"Those three? No, they'd be after the bounty. The Masseys made for a good night's work. Depford and us, well, we'd be icin' on the cake."

"We were awful careless, Pike."

"One thing's for certain, little brother. We're finished in these mountains."

"So where do we go?"

"After the railroad. We can hit 'em a time or two yet. Then maybe I can get you back to Uncle Peter. Or else we can pass the winter in Iron Hand's camps."

"The posters said DeMoss is at Laramie Junction. Ever heard of that place?"

"Bound to be a railroad depot, or maybe some new town. But a snake like DeMoss ain't apt to stay anywhere. He's up buildin' his railroad."

"We could burn the bridge over the Medicine Bow again."

"Not with just the three of us," Pike said sadly. "I'll go see O'Brien. Maybe he knows somethin'."

"I'm not altogether sure I trust him anymore, Pike. Somebody always seems to know where we'll be next."

"I didn't tell O'Brien about Wolf Creek."

"What about the bridge?"

"Likely somebody crossed our trail."

"Maybe," Jeff said, unconvinced.

An hour or so later Depford awoke. The rest of the afternoon the three of them took turns watching and

155

sleeping. Then, as the sun set in the western hills, Pike led his horse down the winding trail from the cave. Jeff and Depford followed.

The trio made their way slowly back toward Wolf Creek, back across the same rocky ground that had concealed their trail from the camp to Eagle Rock. All three held rifles across one knee as they rode warily onward. Pike uttered no warning. It wasn't necessary, not with half their band lying dead and the mountains swarming with bounty hunters.

Daylight was fast departing when Pike started down the old Cheyenne trail to Wolf Creek. It was largely overgrown by brush, but Pike had no trouble keeping his bearings. It proved a wise precaution. Down below the pine-shrouded trail five or six campfires burned along the banks of Wolf Creek.

Jeff spotted something more. A heavy smell hung over the hillside, and the wind seemed to moan mournfully as it stirred the branches of the tall pines. Finally he saw the cause.

"Pike," Jeff mumbled as he felt his stomach turn over.

Jeff's trembling finger pointed to three bundles hanging by ropes from the trees. As they swayed in the evening breeze, the bundles turned so that it became possible to identify them.

"Lord, help 'em," Depford whispered.

The Masseys, Jeff thought as he stared in horror at the three lifeless figures, hung upside down by their heels. The bloodstained corpses had been left to the birds.

"Well, their sufferin' is over," Pike said softly. "We'd best pass 'em by. Wish we could lay 'em to rest, but it'd only get the rest of us killed."

Jeff nodded sadly, reading the bitterness spreading across his brother's face. Jeff's own chest was as hollow as ever. Already forgotten was the quiet afternoon spent fishing and swimming in Wolf Creek. He tried not to imagine what tomorrow would bring. Who would die next? Pike? Jeff himself?

It seemed all too likely, for after threading their way through the mountains, Pike led the way down the slope directly into the huddle of shanties and tents that flanked the Union Pacific's Wyoming headquarters.

"Look," Jeff whispered as they passed a small wooden sign. *Laramie Junction*, it read.

"Well, that's one question answered," Pike mumbled. They rode wearily down the muddy main street, then stopped beside a large, ivory-colored tent.

"Bathhouse?" Jeff asked, reading the placard nailed beside the opening.

"We'll get ourselves scrubbed clean, shaved, outfitted with some fresh clothes. Nobody's apt to suspect who we are."

"I hope you're right," Jeff said nervously. "We won't exactly be heavily armed inside a bathtub."

Depford laughed, but Pike read the seriousness in Jeff's eyes. The brothers pulled their horses around behind the bathhouse tent, then walked back toward the door.

"Tell you what," Depford said solemnly. "I'll keep watch outside."

"Fine," Pike said. "Later, we'll return the favor. Might be best for a time if we don't keep company. Jeff and I'll make camp at Bear Springs in three nights' time. That's the same place I met you and the Masseys back in the beginnin'."

"I remember it," Depford said. "Three nights' time."

"Three nights' time," Pike echoed.

Jeff then slipped inside the tent, and Pike followed. For a silver dollar, the two of them enjoyed a bath and a shave. Actually, Pike had plucked most of his whiskers Cheyenne style, but Jeff borrowed the barber's clippers and trimmed Pike's flowing black hair. Jeff himself put the razor to better use, slicing away the beginnings of a moustache and the scraggly whiskers that sprouted from his chin and cheeks. Then it was Pike's turn to clip Jeff's hair.

"We'll never disguise you as Cheyenne now," Pike laughed as he showered Jeff with wild strands of sandy hair. "Goin' to have a bit of a beard, I'd say."

After grabbing a plate of eggs and ham at a small clapboard cafe, Pike kept watch at the bathhouse while Depford took a turn at the bathtub. Jeff meanwhile purchased supplies at the railroad store. When Pike joined him, they outfitted themselves with new boots, trousers, and shirts.

"You boys been in the high country quite a time, have you?" the shopkeeper asked.

"Down in Colorado," Jeff explained. "Got lucky at our diggings."

"So you thought you'd try the Medicine Bow country, did you? Well, best keep an eye out for renegades. Got a gang o' thieves up there. They've killed a score of good men at the Union Pacific camps."

"We'll keep that in mind," Pike said.

"Well, word around here is there's three less of them now," the clerk said, laughing. "Mr. DeMoss, one of the railroad hobnobbers, brought in some trackers, printed posters, got after those bushwhackers."

"Good for him," Pike said, banging his hand on the counter. "Ought to string the whole bunch up. That's the only way to handle stealin'."

As the clerk tallied the bill, Jeff suspected there were more thieves in town than Pike and Jefferson Thompson. Flour went for close to six times what the post trader at Fort Laramie charged, and a pair of trousers cost a full five dollars.

"I'm almost afraid to wear any of these clothes," Jeff remarked as he followed Pike outside.

"We picked the wrong line o' business, little brother."

"Well," Jeff whispered, "at least we paid 'em with their own greenbacks."

Pike laughed at the thought.

Jeff saw to the feeding and watering of the horses while Pike set off in search of Tim O'Brien. Now, more than ever, it was important to have accurate information. Pike reappeared around ten.

"Did you see him?" Jeff asked.

"He's runnin' the telegraph office now. We'll meet him outside o' town after supper. Meanwhile, I managed to rent us a couple o' beds over at the hotel. Don't know 'bout you, but I could sleep till spring."

"Yes," Jeff agreed.

And so the brothers sprawled out on straw beds at the half-finished Station House Hotel just up the street from the bathhouse. There, exhausted from the seemingly endless ride from Eagle Rock, they collapsed into a deep and restful sleep. A little before dusk the desk clerk awakened them, and Pike led his brother to where the horses were tethered on the fringe of the junction.

After tying their bundles of supplies in back of saddles bought off a pair of Kansans, they mounted

159

their horses and rode out of town. Jeff felt no regret at leaving the place. Each time he walked down the street, he bent the brim of his hat down to conceal his face from railroaders who often seemed much too familiar, and on occasion were entirely too curious.

They met Tim O'Brien beneath a pair of aspens a quarter of a mile from the junction. Jeff noticed the informant seemed a trifle surprised and none too pleased about Pike's arrival.

"I hope you know the kind of risk I'm running," O'Brien grumbled. "The countryside's alive with bounty men, all with an eye to collect on your heads."

"That's not goin' to be money easily earned," Pike said, tapping the handle of his pistol. "Now, you said something about a payroll due shortly."

"I won't have all the facts for a time, boys, but I do know the figures. There'll be ten thousand in bank notes left overnight in the Union Pacific freight offices. It's no trouble to break in there. They've got naught but a padlock on the door and no safe at all."

"Ten thousand," Pike said, whistling as he mentally counted the stacks of greenbacks. "They'd remember that, little brother. Now, when and where?"

"That's the difficulty, lads. I don't know the particulars yet. Soon, though. If I knew where to find you, I could send a friend."

"What friend?" Jeff asked. "You've never had to know our camp before."

"Hush," Pike declared. "There was never this much money at stake."

"The friend's Thomas Tolbert," O'Brien told Jeff. "We fought side by side in the Irish Brigade. He's a fine hand with a gun, and he knows how to keep his tongue in check."

"Seems all right," Pike said. "In three days' time we'll be at Bear Springs. Afterward, we'll send somebody to the springs every evening, just after sunset."

"That's reasonable," O'Brien said.

"Meanwhile, what do you know of Henry DeMoss?" Pike asked. "His office is in Laramie Junction. Where is he?"

"Off toward California," O'Brien said, clearly less than happy about it. "He wires instructions, but he leaves the management to a pack o' fools."

"We don't like him much either," Jeff said. "If he gets to town, we'd like to know about it."

"Same's as we do the payroll," O'Brien replied.

With everything settled, Jeff and Pike climbed atop their horses and headed eastward toward Bear Springs.

"Are you sure we can trust that man?" Jeff asked as they were safely out of earshot.

"No, but it's in his interest to do business with us," Pike explained.

"I believe he'd sell his own mother for a silver dollar, Pike. He knows enough to get us hanged."

"That works both ways, little brother. And just now he's sittin' in his office without a worry. We take the real risks."

"I guess," Jeff admitted as Pike turned his horse north toward the little mission Peter Ryland ran on the Laramie River. "It sure makes me wonder, though, when a man won't look you in the eye."

"He's shifty, for sure, little brother, but you'd hardly expect a turncoat and an informant to be different."

So Jeff swept away his suspicions and prepared for the visit to his uncle's mission. There'd be new books to gaze upon, and perhaps Uncle Peter would help mend Jeff's lame leg. At any rate, it would be wonderful to see their mother's youngest brother.

VII

It was a hard day's ride from Laramie Junction to the small huddle of wooden buildings that composed Peter Ryland's mission. There was a church, a schoolhouse, a small trading post, and a three-room cabin that housed the residents.

A half-dozen Sioux and Cheyenne lodges formed a cluster beside the river. The residents of those lodges attended school and worshipped at the mission. The trading post sold them the necessities not dug from the ground or cut from the deer and buffalo. An iron kettle or a box of cartridges could always be bartered for a bit of beadwork, a beaver pelt, or a buffalo hide.

Jeff found the place as always. It was comforting that something at least had not changed. All day long he and Pike had crossed once-quiet creeks now muddy with cattle, whole hillsides stripped of timber for cabins or fences. Worse, he found himself examined by the dark, curious eyes of a dozen bounty men, each of whom seemed interested in his bent left leg.

"Lord be praised!" Peter Ryland shouted from the door of the schoolhouse. "Jeff, Pike . . ."

"It's good to see you, too, Uncle Peter," Jeff said as he

slid down from his horse. "We've been awhile ridin', it seems."

"The mission seems to be prosperin'," Pike added as he climbed down from the saddle and joined his brother.

"Matthew, see to their horses," Peter Ryland told a young dark-headed boy on the back bench of the classroom. "See they have a good drink at the trough."

"Yes, sir," Matthew said, scampering past Jeff and taking the reins of both horses.

"You've grown, Jeff," the reverend said, smiling. "You'll be as tall as I am by Christmas. And, Pike, you look more like Ruth each hour."

"She's dead now," Pike whispered.

"I know," Jeff's uncle said sadly as he turned back to the dozen assorted students working away at their ciphers. "Class, that will be all for today. See you put away your books carefully and mind your manners on the way out."

"Yes, sir," they spoke in unison. After walking slowly through the door, they raced with abandon toward the river, laughing and shouting as if they were convicts suddenly set free.

They are in a way, Jeff thought as he watched.

"Who told you?" Pike asked when the last of the students left.

"Iron Hand. He came to Fort Laramie for the treaty signing."

"Another treaty," Pike grumbled. "How much land did the Cheyennes surrender this time?"

"I don't know they lost anything," Peter Ryland answered angrily. "Red Cloud won his point. The Bighorns are to be left alone, and the army's abandoned its forts."

"And what about the railroad built through the heart of the Medicine Bow?"

"I understood that land already belonged to the government."

"Too bad we didn't save the treaty cloth," Jeff said, sighing as he sat on a vacated bench. "But I suppose someone like DeMoss could always write some fancy paper, sign it, then say the place belonged to him in the first place."

"DeMoss?" the young reverend asked. "You've met Henry DeMoss? He's growing to be an important man."

"Looks like he did some o' the growin' over Ma an' Pa's bodies," Jeff growled. "He's had less luck with us."

"But he's had some," Jeff's uncle said, examining the crooked leg. "I wish you'd come here. We might have gotten the post surgeon to have a look."

"Since when was there a real doctor at Fort Laramie?" Jeff asked. "One time, I heard, they had the blacksmith cut off a man's arm. Two Humps treated it."

"You've got lodges out there with Cheyenne markings, Uncle Peter," Pike pointed out. "Iron Hand anywhere nearby?"

"Off hunting, so I've been told. Sometimes I fear that old buzzard's hunting the same quarry you're after. A survey party or a supply wagon disappears each time Iron Hand takes to the buffalo valleys."

"They crossed his land, too," Jeff explained. "And how's Little Heart? Is he well?"

"Usually comes to my classes, though I can tell he's not much inclined toward learning from books. Spends most of his time catching horseflies."

"Sure seems like you get a lot of white children here now," Jeff remarked. "Not at all like before. Then it was mostly Sioux and Cheyenne."

"Some live at the fort. Others stopped here on their way to California or Oregon. The railroad's brought work and opportunity."

"And death," Jeff added.

"Change rarely comes easy," Peter Ryland said, motioning for his nephews to follow as he left the schoolhouse. The minister then quoted scripture to prove his point. Once they reached the house, though, Peter Ryland lit the stove and began slicing a ham.

"I can do that," Jeff offered. "I'm a fair cook, remember?"

"Tell you what," the minister said. "What if we let Pike slice the meat. That way I can have a look at your leg."

"Pike?" Jeff asked.

"Can't go too far wrong slicin' meat," Pike said, taking the knife and starting at the work.

"Now, as for this leg," Peter Ryland said, working his fingers along both sides of Jeff's knee, then continuing on toward the hip. "The bone's straight enough. It's the tendons that are wrong."

"Could've told you that," Jeff grumbled.

"Do you try to bend it?"

"It's hard when you're in the saddle all night and half the next day."

"Maybe, but you'd best find a way. I think I can make a brace for you out of elkhide. It will hurt in the beginning, but it should gradually straighten the knee."

"That might just save my life," Jeff joked.

"I know. I've seen the posters. And I understand you

used to have four men riding with you. Are they all dead?"

"Only three," Pike said, placing the slices of ham in a skillet. "It was a close thing. The mountains down south are swarming with bounty men. I'd hate to be an honest trapper out there this winter."

"The railroad might be willing to grant you amnesty if you agree to leave them alone," Peter Ryland explained. "They dropped all charges against Bart Taylor, a killer out of Kansas."

"You're startin' to believe in all that forgiveness you preach on Sundays, Uncle Peter," Pike said, laughing. "Railroad won't forget or forgive. Even if they did, I wouldn't. Can you forget those two graves up on Thompson's Mountain? I can't. Those people killed my ma and pa. They have to pay for it."

"Do they, Pike?" the reverend asked. "You're not punishing DeMoss. You kill simple, hard-working folk who never did you any harm at all. They're just trying to feed their families, earn an honest wage. Only some can't, because you shoot them dead."

"Not if they stay out of the way," Jeff objected. "We never go out of our way to kill anybody."

"Even those soldiers riding escort for the railroad payroll. They were killed with knives."

"That was Depford," Jeff said, trembling as he recalled it.

"And who rode with him? That was you, Jeff. You, Pike. Killing's a cumbersome sin to carry around with you."

"Yes," Jeff agreed. "But we didn't start it."

"No, we didn't," Pike said, setting the skillet over the fire. "It's a hard life we've chosen, Uncle Peter. I know

Ma'd be grieved by it, too, but we don't have a lot of choices."

"You could stay here, help at the mission. If it's too quiet for you, go to old Iron Hand, live with the Indians."

"It's not that easy," Jeff said as he removed his trousers so Peter Ryland could examine the knee more closely. "You forget about the bounty men. We've been posted."

"Those posters don't have your names, Jeff, and the description is no help at all. Soon we'll have the lame leg solved, too."

"That's just fine," Pike said enthusiastically. "With two mended Thompsons, old DeMoss is bound to take to tremblin'. We'll raid 'em till they bleed."

"Oh?" their uncle asked, raising his eyebrows. "Tell me, Pike, how long can you last? Another month? A year? How long till one of those bounty hunters shoots you down? How long till the pictures improve, till the reward gets high enough that your own men turn you in?"

Jeff thought about O'Brien's friend, this mysterious Tolbert. O'Brien himself wasn't above betraying someone if there was a way to survive such treachery.

For several minutes a heavy silence draped the room. Then Pike responded.

"Pa used to say nobody chooses his own life. I didn't pick this out for myself. It's what I'm destined to do. Don't you think I'd rather take to the buffalo valleys with my cousins, the Cheyennes? Killin' isn't easy for me. Pa made a promise not to give his mountain up to the railroad, and now that's my promise."

"But the railroad's a hundred miles west of here."

"I can't keep every train from breakin' through," Pike admitted, "but I can make the line pay a price. I can make passengers think hard about ridin'. That's my lot."

"And what about Jeff? Pike, you can't go on dragging him across the countryside like this! His leg's sour already. Don't turn the rest of him to vinegar."

"He's not chained to me," Pike pointed out. "He's a blooded man. He's sixteen, old enough to make his own choices."

"Oh, you know he'll follow his brother no matter what."

"There's more to it than that," Jeff said, gazing intently into his uncle's eyes. "It's not just Pike's obligation. It's mine, too."

"You'll only get yourselves killed!" Peter Ryland shouted. "And in the end, nothing will change."

"You used to talk about all those saints that got burned at the stake," Jeff reminded the minister. "Just because they wouldn't say this or that. They kept faith with their beliefs, stayed true to themselves, even when it meant death. This is no different."

"Yes, it is," Jeff's uncle declared. "None of those saints ever burned and killed and robbed. You do the devil's work, and it can only end one way."

"I know that," Jeff said, wincing as his uncle turned the bent knee until the leg straightened. "I've known it from the first."

After eating a simple dinner of ham, raw carrots, and cold biscuits, Jeff and Pike spread out their blankets beside the stove and went to bed. It was a clear, calm night, and Jeff found himself unusually at rest. His mind filled with a dozen dreams, visions of chasing wild stallions through the hills, of fishing streams with round-faced girls and sad-eyed boys whose faces were miniatures of his own.

Best of all Jeff saw two bright brown eyes smiling out from a face as soft and gentle as a newborn fawn. The small, delicate figure they belonged to danced through a meadow, her yellow skirts keeping time to a half-forgotten tune.

Jeff awoke a little after dawn to find his uncle already busy preparing for the morning's lessons. Pike snored away in the far corner, lost to the world.

"Good morning," Peter Ryland said, spooning scrambled eggs beside a rich slice of bacon on a wooden plate, then passing it to Jeff. "Sleep well?"

"Wonderfully well," Jeff said, recalling the dream. It was just a dream, of course. It could never happen.

"If you haven't got other plans and feel up to it, I could use some help at the schoolhouse. Young Matthew Polk and Hadley Griffin are struggling with their numbers. Care to take a try at them?"

"We'll be leavin' before nightfall," Jeff explained. "We're to meet someone."

"Nightfall's a long way off, and you used to have a fair head for figures, Jefferson Thompson. So, can I depend on your help?"

"Until Pike decides we should leave," Jeff agreed. "Did you have any success with my brace?"

"Let's find out," the minister said, taking a piece of elkhide and fitting it to Jeff's bare leg. Then, using three buckskin straps, Peter Ryland forced the knee into a painfully awkward position. The leg, however, straightened.

"Doesn't feel any too good," Jeff complained. "If I

170

didn't know better, I'd believe it was cuttin' my leg in half."

"I know it hurts, Jeff, but you have to tolerate it. Wear it a month, maybe two, and I think the ligaments will readjust. There's not much wrong with the leg itself. Your old friend, Two Humps, must've known what he was doing."

"Yes," Jeff agreed.

Jeff's leg plagued him all morning, but he refused to let the pain interfere with the task of tutoring Hadley and Matthew in the use of figures. In truth, both boys caught on amazingly fast, and Jeff suspected his uncle had set a trap.

"You're a natural teacher," Peter Ryland remarked. "You have the touch with boys, encouraging them while having patience."

"I enjoyed it."

"Then, why don't you stay, become a permanent part of the school. You'd be quite welcome. I never find enough time for everyone, and there'll be more and more children coming in, not to mention the Indian children this winter."

"There was a time when that was all I ever wanted," Jeff said, taking a history book and thumbing through the pages. "I thought all the truth and wonder of the world was in these pages. But that's all passed. I can never be a teacher, a lawyer, a quiet man in a quiet place. My world rocks with thunder, with shootin' and dyin'. I've no more hope of escape than Pike or Iron Hand's Cheyennes. We're all of us doomed by those infernal rails. There's no room for us in Henry De-Moss's future."

"That's not true, Jeff. There's always time to change."

"Some of us can't," Jeff said, his eyes growing moist as he remembered the girl in the yellow skirts, the innocent eyes of the children. "It's not in me anymore."

"You're bound to get killed."

"Maybe. Maybe not. What's to be will be."

Shortly after midday Pike arose. Jeff saddled the horses, then joined his brother for supper. Their uncle made a final effort to persuade them to stay, then returned to his classroom. Jeff frowned, then rolled the assorted bank notes he'd accumulated into a ball and stuffed them inside his uncle's favorite coffee mug.

"Bein' awful generous, aren't you?" Pike asked.

"He'll put it to good use, Pike. We're not likely to have many occasions to spend money for a time."

"And we'll be acquirin' a good bit more of it," Pike said, laughing.

"Just remember what I said about the Tolbert fellow," Jeff told his brother. "We don't know anything about him."

"I'll keep a sharp eye on him, little brother," Pike promised as they mounted their horses and headed south for Bear Springs.

VIII

They reached Bear Springs as the evening shadows swallowed the mountainside. Alf Depford had beat them to the rendezvous, but O'Brien's old friend, the mysterious Tolbert, was nowhere to be found.

"He'll be around," Depford said, opening a provision bag stuffed with fried chicken and cornbread squares. "Sit down and help me eat this food. It's cold now, but at least it was cooked today. I've an idea that from now on it's cold beans and salt pork."

"See many on the trail?" Pike asked as he turned his horse over to Jeff.

"More'n twenty of 'em," Depford grumbled. "Bounty men. Could tell by the way their eyes wouldn't look straight at you. Good thing those posters're a poor likeness. Even so, I spun 'em a tough trail to follow."

Jeff was too busy to catch much of the conversation that followed. There wasn't much laughter, though, and he could tell Pike was clearly worried. When Jeff finished unsaddling the animals, he left them to graze on the soft grass that grew beside the overflow from the spring.

"Best get over here an' get yourself some chicken,

Jeff," Depford called out. "You're skinny enough without missin' meals."

Jeff hopped on over, and Depford gazed with wide eyes. Pike noticed, too.

"You lost your limp," Depford cried. "Boy, that leg's not half bent. Been to the medicine mountain?"

"I'm glad it looks better," Jeff said, staring at his leg, "because it hurts to high heaven. I feel like a grizzly's got hold of one end and a steam locomotive the other."

"That'll pass," Pike said, handing Jeff a wing.

It was pitch dark by the time the three renegades finished eating. Only a single square of cornbread remained, and Pike thought it only right to save that for their new recruit.

Tolbert didn't appear for another hour, though. Jeff was about ready to spread out his blankets, but the sound of a horse climbing the rocky trail drew his attention. Jeff drew out his rifle when a second animal whined.

"Hello there," a foreign voice called out. "Anybody there?"

Pike motioned Jeff into the rocks to the right, then raced to the left. Depford remained in the center.

"Hello there," the voice asked a second time.

"We hear you," Depford replied finally. "Who would that be?"

"Could be anybody," a more familiar voice spoke, "but as it happens, it's me, Tim O'Brien. Brought Tolbert with me."

"Thought he'd be comin' on his own," Pike said nervously.

"He'd never found this spot without a guide," O'Brien explained. "Didn't want me drawin' no maps o' the place, did you?"

"I guess not," Pike admitted. "Just the same, you climb down off those horses and walk in easy."

"Easy as partin' your hair," Tolbert said.

The new arrivals dismounted and continued their slow approach. Pike risked building a small fire. O'Brien's appearance was a surprise, and Pike Thompson had never known a surprise to bring good fortune.

"Got the information on the payroll?" Pike asked as Tolbert and O'Brien sat beside the fire.

"To the last detail," O'Brien said, drawing out a weathered army-dispatch case and emptying the contents.

Pike and Depford gathered in the documents and began asking about the escort. Jeff, though, saw something familiar in Tolbert's eyes.

"I've seen you before," Jeff suddenly said, staring at the newcomer's heavy eyebrows and cold brown eyes. "Not lately, but somewhere."

"I've trapped this country," Tolbert replied with an easy smile. "Hunted up north some."

"Hunted?" Jeff asked, trying to recall. Those eyes seemed menacing. And as the moments ticked by, they grew more malevolent. There was a sinister quality about Tolbert. He seemed to be lost in some private nightmare, and those eyes brooded about it.

"Jeff?" Pike asked as Jeff finally realized.

"I do remember," Jeff said, turning his rifle in Tolbert's direction. "You were with DeMoss. You came twice—once to talk, and once to kill my ma and pa!"

"Jeff!" Pike asked as Tolbert leaped across the fire.

"What's—" Depford tried to ask.

But before another word could be spoken, Tolbert

drew a pistol and fired in Jeff's direction. The bullet struck Jeff's boot and sliced off the toe. Jeff responded, and Tolbert retreated to the cover of the pines, shouting out commands.

"It's them, all right. Have at 'em, boys!"

Pike managed to clear the fire before a volley of lead tore into the camp. Depford had departed the instant Jeff stirred. Tim O'Brien was still sitting by the fire, though, and the storm of shot struck him squarely.

"Tay—" O'Brien stammered. But the name was never completed. O'Brien fell face first into the fire, scattering the ashes and smothering the flame.

"We're in real trouble this time, Pike," Depford called out as a pair of Tolbert's henchman grabbed the horses. "No way out."

"They haven't got us yet," Pike said, angrily filling his Winchester's fifteen-shot magazine. "They'll have to pay."

"We can't hope to stand 'em off, Pike," Jeff told his brother. "They'll have help come first light. Till then all they have to do is keep us here."

"Then, we'll run," Pike said.

"But not far on foot. I'll bet we can turn back on their rear, though."

"What?" Depford asked.

"Let 'em come to us, then punch a hole in their lines and shoot 'em from behind. They can't shoot back without runnin' the risk of hittin' their own men or supplies."

"It could work, Pike," Depford said hopefully. Pike nodded his agreement, and Jeff began.

"I'll hold 'em here while you try to break through," Jeff said.

"Not you," Pike objected.

"Look, I'm not much man to man, but I can shoot anything with legs. I'll keep 'em busy. By the time you get to the horses, they won't know where we are, and they'll think we've got a hundred rifles, each one aimed at one of them!"

Pike wasn't happy about it, but he continued on into the pines just the same. Then Jeff opened fire, sending his bullets slicing off boulders and ringing through the camp. Only the muzzle flashes betrayed Jeff's position, and he moved so frequently Tolbert, or Taylor as Jeff reasoned the man's name to be, would have trouble locating him, much less killing him.

"You didn't expect me to forget, did you?" Jeff called out. "I watched you burn my house. That was my ma you got killed."

"Never liked that part of it," Taylor answered, his voice seemingly amused. "I never took a hand in killin' a woman before that. You was the kid, eh? Must've weighed on my mind. I usually check my kill."

"Big mistake."

"Maybe," Taylor said, sliding through the pines like a cat on the prowl. Jeff shrank back instinctively. He hoped Pike and Depford might open up, distract the bounty men, but that was reaching a bit. The horses came first, and by the time the animals were gathered, it would be impossible to know Jeff's location.

I have to lose this Taylor, Jeff thought as footsteps seemed to splash leaves in a dozen directions. I know this country. I know where the horses'll be. It's up to me to save myself.

Saying it was one thing. Doing it was quite another. The air began to fill with smoke as trackers lit torches.

In the dim light Jeff saw shadows. He'd occasionally fire, and once he heard a cry from a target. But seeing something, knowing more than a sliver of what was happening, just wasn't possible.

Then Jeff heard a twig snap, and he turned in time to stare into the cold, wicked eyes of Taylor himself.

"I thought for sure I'd killed you the last time," the bounty hunter growled.

"You did," Jeff answered bitterly. "But sometimes the dead don't find their peace."

Taylor raised his rifle, but Jeff fired first. The Winchester sent its shell tearing through Taylor's chest, and the surprised killer found himself the victim instead.

"Jeff?" Pike called out from the spring.

"Here," Jeff answered. He turned away from Taylor's fallen corpse and raced toward his brother. A shower of bullets and buckshot splintered the surrounding pines, but Jeff emerged unscathed. Pike was waiting in the clearing just past the springs.

Never had Jeff seen a more welcome sight. He hopped along to his horse, climbed into the saddle, and rode like thunder behind his brother and Alf Depford away from the erupting hillside.

Jeff lost track of the miles they covered. The horses were near exhausted from the long journey earlier to Bear Springs, though, so it couldn't have been more than five miles or so. A small pinprick of light off in the distance drew their attention, and they coaxed a final quarter mile from the lathered horses.

They found themselves halted outside a small farmhouse. A lantern burned in the front window, but Pike motioned toward the barn.

"No tellin' who might be in that house," Pike explained. "Could be old DeMoss himself. More likely some farmer with a loaded shotgun. Never knew friends to call in the middle of the night. Let's greet 'em come mornin' instead."

Jeff nodded, and Depford mumbled his approval as well. They fell off their horses and led the weary animals in through the side door of the barn. Pike nearly struck his head on a lantern that rested on a nail over the door. He lit the wick and allowed a dim amber glow to flood the barn.

"Who's there?" a young voice called out.

"Nobody to alarm you," Pike replied to the unseen sentry. "Just wanted to rest our horses. Your pa said it was all right by him."

"You never spoke to my pa in your whole entire life," the voice answered. "He's been out huntin' horse thieves a week now."

"And who'd you be?" Pike asked.

"Annie Farley, that's who," a girl of perhaps thirteen answered, stepping into the light. A pair of barefoot boys stood beside her, still dressed in their nightshirts. Neither appeared to be half as old as Jeff. But that wasn't what drew Jeff's attention. Despite her tender years, young Annie held a shotgun as if she knew how to use it.

"Didn't mean to alarm you," Jeff said, trying to steady himself. "As you can see, our horses are spent. All we ask is to pass the night in your barn. We can pay for the privilege."

"You think we're stupid 'cause we're young, don't you?" Annie asked. "I can tell when men are on the run. Get their guns, Hallie."

179

The taller of the two boys gazed at his sister in terror. It was only then that Jeff looked at his companions. All three were scratched and torn by tree limbs and half black from powder smoke. Their clothes were tattered, and Jeff's right boot was missing its toe.

"Go ahead, Hallie," the girl repeated. "They move, and I'll blast 'em."

The boy warily stepped forward. Depford, quick as a cat, snatched little Hallie and held the boy like a shield.

"Mister, this shotgun'll spatter you all over this barn!" Annie shouted. "Let go my brother."

"You don't lower that gun, you won't have no brother," Depford replied. "You shoot, he's worse off'n me."

The girl gazed at Depford. Her eyes filled with confusion. The smaller boy hid behind her nightgown and began to cry.

"Hush that, George!" she shouted angrily. "I can't think with you bawlin'."

"There's nothin' to think about," Jeff said, sitting down in the hay. "We only want a place to sleep. Your pa's gone, and your ma, too, I'd judge. We'll be off by first light, and we'll trouble you no further. Why don't you take your brothers on into the house now?"

Annie gazed at Depford, who nodded. She lowered her shotgun, and Depford released his prisoner. The boys raced out the open door. Their sister followed, glancing back cautiously every few steps.

"A narrow escape," Depford proclaimed, loosening his horse's cinch. "You know these horses won't be in any shape to ride tomorrow, Pike. We'll need fresh mounts or another day here."

"I don't see any livestock," Pike said, pointing to the

empty stalls behind them. "As for layin' over, we didn't take much care with our trail last night."

"Well, it's no point arguin' till mornin'," Depford said, collapsing in the hay. "I couldn't take another step tonight. Maybe tomorrow somebody'll do the decidin' for us."

"Could be," Pike admitted, stripping the saddle from his horse.

Jeff tended his own and Depford's horse. There was a bag of oats in one corner, and Jeff filled a feed trough. A water barrel stood beside the front door, and Pike filled buckets for each of the animals.

"You're right, you know," Jeff whispered to Pike as they spread out their blankets. "Tomorrow they'll find us."

"Maybe they'll find that girl first," Pike said, laughing.

"I'm serious, Pike."

"Then, you're a fool, little brother. No point to bein' serious when things come to this point. What's to happen will. Now get some rest. You're apt to need it."

Jeff closed his eyes, and Pike blew out the lantern. The darkness seemed to cast a spell on the barn, and before either of them knew it, they were both asleep.

Left alone, Jeff might have slept till noon, but a cock began crowing at daybreak. He sat up and tried to shake the weariness from his bones.

"Where there's a rooster, there's bound to be a hen," Depford declared as he pulled on his trousers. "I'll see if I can find an egg or two."

Depford hummed some old tune picked up in his

army days and skipped out the door. Seconds later the door itself exploded, and Depford fell to one knee, his left side torn apart by a shotgun.

"No!" Jeff screamed, fumbling with his rifle. "Damn you, girl!"

"Wasn't no girl," a deep voice bellowed. "I'm Perkins, line detective for the Union Pacific. You Cheyenne Pike?"

"No!" Pike answered, tossing Jeff a box of shells. "It's just like you railroad killers to get your facts wrong. I'm Pike Thompson."

"Thompson, huh," Perkins said. "Yeah, that'd fit. You got a boy in there, too?"

"I'm here!" Jeff shouted, "but I can shoot. Ask Tolbert."

"His name was Taylor," Perkins explained. "We hired him to find you. Paid off O'Brien, too. Cost a few dollars, but it was worth it. You boys have been quite a bother to us."

"Glad to know we're appreciated," Jeff replied. "I imagine we'll bother you some more before we're through."

"Oh, you're through, all right," Perkins called. "The whole back of that barn's soaked with coal oil. We light it, you'll go up like Atlanta."

"Then, do it!" Pike yelled.

"Wanted to give you a chance to give it up first. Mr. DeMoss wants to watch you hang personally."

"Pike?" Jeff whispered. "We might get a trial. Maybe a judge would understand . . ."

"What judge'd side with us over the railroad?" Pike asked. "I'll not end like the Masseys, Jeff. It's hard to hang ashes."

"Then, we'd best get to it," Jeff said, sadly cocking his rifle and swinging it out the doorway. "Ready?"

Pike nodded, and the brothers opened up on the house. Glass shattered, and rifles answered. Moments later the back wall of the barn ignited, and the horses stomped restlessly as smoke drifted through the structure.

"They're cautious," Pike observed. "Can't be many of them, either. Care to have a go at 'em?"

"Sure," Jeff said, coughing as the smoke choked his lungs and stung his eyes.

"Grab the tail of your horse," Pike instructed. "Then stay as close to him as you can. I remember a ravine just past the house. Try to make it there."

Jeff nodded, then did as ordered. He knew the plan had a slim chance of success, but there wasn't much choice.

"Yah!" Pike screamed, slapping Depford's pony into motion. The horse bolted through the door, and a half-dozen rifles greeted the poor animal. It flew twenty yards down the road before stumbling to a stop, its head and chest shot to pieces.

In the interlude, Pike and Jeff chased their horses through the door. Jeff felt himself flying along as the air around him exploded. They abandoned the animals once outside and charged desperately for the ravine. A pair of gunmen blocked their path, but both flew in the face of danger.

"Keep goin'!" Pike screamed as Jeff stumbled to a halt. "They're all over."

The warning came too late. As Jeff got to his feet, a volley of bullets ripped through the ravine. One struck Jeff just above the left ankle, and again the leg seemed to go lame. Pike tried to drag Jeff along, but the shooting only grew worse. Shots whined through the air, and bullets bounced off rocks and trees. Twice Jeff heard the sickening thud of a bullet striking flesh.

"Just a little further," Pike said, somehow continuing. Jeff could see blood from his brother's wounds dripping on the ground. But ahead stood a pair of roan mares, saddled, seemingly awaiting their riders.

"I see 'em," Jeff said, fighting off the pain in his leg. "We're close to there."

"They're gettin' away, Cap'n!" a distant voice cried.

Then, just as Jeff reached for the saddlehorn, a final flurry of bullets whistled through the air. The single shot that found Jeff tore through the tender flesh just above his left elbow. The arm went limp, but somehow Pike pushed his younger brother atop the animal.

"Get to Iron Hand if you can. Don't cry for me, little brother. I've had a fair run!" Pike yelled as he slapped the horse's rear.

Jeff looked back as the terrified animal took flight. Pike stood taller than ever, the rifle in his bleeding hands. One knee was shattered; a half-dozen wounds were already depriving him of his life's blood. And yet Pike Thompson managed to scream at his attackers.

Jeff's eyes blurred with pain, and he saw nothing more. He gripped the galloping horse with both arms and prayed it would carrying him away, take him to a better place where there was no killing and dying, no shadows in the night that offered betrayal and death.

Soon he was too weak from pain and loss of blood to hold on. His fingers lost their grip, and he fell from the horse and rolled off down a hill until his body came to rest in a small gully.

"Lord, let it be over," Jefferson Thompson prayed.

The skies seemed to open up, and a bright ocean of light engulfed him. His eyes opened wide to drink in the brilliance. But already his mind had drifted off into the numb, overpowering darkness.

III. The Glory Hole

I

The darkness swallowed him totally. He became not Jefferson Thompson, but instead a sightless creature exiled to a world without taste or touch, sound or odor. He drifted as on a cloud, formless, lost.

When his eyes finally cracked open, he found himself in a dark, dank chamber no more than ten feet across in either direction. There was a smell of moldy bread, of onions and turnips blending with rosemary and sage. He could move his fingers and toes, but his back appeared numb. A woolen blanket lay over him from chin to ankles, but beneath that he was bare.

Oh, Lord, what is this place? he asked himself. His head swelled with a general dizziness, but as his vision cleared, he located an old, round-faced woman pounding herbs into powder a foot or so away.

"Hell-ow-ah," Jeff managed to say. "Hell-oh."

The woman continued with her work. He could see now she was dark of complexion, not quite Cheyenne, perhaps, but she might know the language. He tried speaking again, this time using the Cheyenne and

Sioux words he'd learned in Iron Hand's camps. But neither language drew any response from the old woman.

"Is this heaven?" he finally asked.

"You'll more likely find yourself in the other place," a voice replied from the shadows.

"Uncle Peter?" Jeff asked, turning his head. His eyes cleared a little more, and he recognized the weary face of the minister. "How? When? . . ."

"Rest easy, Jeff," his uncle pleaded, setting a hand on Jeff's chest to restrain movement. "You've lost a lot of blood."

"I should be dead," Jeff blurted. "I was shot, lying in a gully."

"Young Matthew Polk stumbled across you. He recognized you as my nephew, but he couldn't bring you here himself. He did get the bleeding stopped, and he got word to me. I sent a pair of your Cheyenne friends out with a wagon, and they brought you to the mission."

"The mission?" Jeff asked, staring at the foreign walls around him.

"We put you in the root cellar. There are men watching. I dared not go to get you myself. Railroad detectives have been asking all sorts of questions."

"Why ask you?"

"Because of Pike," Peter Ryland said, swallowing a sudden flood of sadness.

"He's dead, then."

"Matthew brought that news, too. They strung the body up like a wild animal. Poor boy was shot a dozen times, then cut up some afterward. I buried him down by the river where it's shady. We'll see that flowers are planted there come spring."

"I'll see they pay for it," Jeff vowed angrily.

"That's all over now. Pike's past his pain, and you're in no condition to fight a stray pup just now. Three men rode in this morning to tack up posters. The sketch doesn't do you justice. 'Renegade boy of sixteen,' the poster reads. Nothing more. But the reward's $500. There are people here who haven't dreamed that much money exists, Jeff. I like to think people have good in them, but money's an awful temptation."

"I can't stay, not and get better. Can somebody get me to Iron Hand?"

"They're watching the Indian camps most of all," Jeff's uncle explained. "Iron Hand sent this Shoshoni woman to look after your wounds. She traveled with Two Humps. I cleaned and bound the wounds myself, but she brewed the medicines that brought you back to us."

"Did he say where he's winterin'?"

"North. And, Jeff, he said the best thing for you to do was head south, away from the railroad, away from all this trouble."

"South," Jeff mumbled. He pictured the distant peaks of Colorado, the South Platte and the world of gold camps and frontier towns described by Zeke Thompson in another lifetime.

"I don't dare keep you here much longer," Peter Ryland said. "The railroad detectives are getting bolder about searching the mission. Besides, the air down here's not fit to heal a man. I've asked the Polks to take you into Colorado. They're bound for Denver, and Mrs. Polk is a good cook. She'll put some flesh back on you."

"Do they know I'm an outlaw?"

"They know. They're forgiving folk, though, and they'll honor their pledge."

"So, when do I leave?" Jeff asked.

"Tonight, just after sundown. And here, you'll need this."

Jeff smiled as his uncle produced a small leather pouch. Inside was the roll of banknotes Jeff had left earlier.

"I won't need it all, Uncle Peter," Jeff objected.

"You might," his uncle insisted. "I've little need of money for my work, Jeff. You'll have a hundred worries down south, especially with winter on the wind."

Jeff grasped the pouch in the fingers of his right hand, then frowned as he realized soon he'd be bidding farewell to the mission, to his uncle, to the final strand of family that tied him to the past.

"I can never come back, can I?" Jeff asked sadly.

"Never's a long time, especially for one who's still young. But it'd be wiser if you changed your name, grew a beard, kept out of sight for a year or so."

"It'll take that long to grow much of a beard," Jeff said, touching the small, whitish hairs on his chin.

"You can always write, but it's best if you don't mention where you're at. Use a code name like slaves did when they rode the underground railroad to Canada."

"How about Moses?" Jeff suggested. "He did his share of wanderin'."

"God will look after you, Jeff," the minister said, dropping to his knees and bowing his head. "You'll do all right."

"Yes," Jeff agreed. After all, he was Zeke Thompson's son!

Jeff passed those next hours in the cellar quietly. His uncle appeared twice, once to bring food and the other time to change the linen bandages that covered Jeff's wounds. The left arm seemed a bit swollen, and it hurt some, but the bullet that hit Jeff's ankle had chipped the bone. That was the more serious of the two.

"See that Matthew makes you a crutch," Peter Ryland advised. "He's got a talent for carving things. And keep inside that wagon till you're well clear of this place. Those bounty men will ride down anything and anybody to get $500."

Yes, Jeff thought, recalling the Farleys' burning barn.

Jeff's mood was no less somber when a pair of broad-shouldered men arrived with a litter and carried him from the cellar to a small canvas-topped wagon. Twelve-year-old Matthew Polk climbed into the back of the wagon, then guided Jeff's litter in. Two small girls hopped in afterward, and a tall heavily bearded man placed three planks in place to enclose the back of the wagon.

"Does it still hurt, Mr. Moses?" Matthew asked as the wagon rumbled into motion. Jeff winced, then tried to conceal the extent of the pain from the alarmed faces of the children.

"I'll get through it," Jeff said.

"He has been hurt worse," Matthew said, lifting the blanket so that the girls could see the dark red scar across Jeff's middle. "Indians do that? I heard they cut men up."

"White man's bullet," Jeff explained.

193

"Guess it's like Reverend Ryland says," the boy said somberly. "There's good and bad in us all."

"That's a truth," Jeff agreed. "Now, who would these two fine ladies be?"

The girls giggled, and Matthew shook his head in disappointment.

"Sisters," the boy grudgingly admitted. "Mary's the bigger one. She's six. Paula's four."

Jeff touched each lightly on the shoulder, then closed his eyes a moment.

"Mr. Moses?" Mary whispered.

"Who?" Jeff asked, blinking his eyes open. "What'd you call me?"

"Mr. Moses," Matthew answered. "It's what Reverend Ryland said to call you. So nobody else'll know who you are."

"But you know, don't you?"

"Sure, but the little ones'll say anything to anyone. It's best this way."

Jeff nodded, but inside he wasn't half as certain. He couldn't help feeling that he was walking away from his life, running away from the obligation he'd once sworn to fulfill.

I'll never forget who I really am, Jeff promised himself. No matter what other people start calling me, I'll always recall what it was like on Thompson's Mountain, the way we hunted and fished and cared for the land.

But as the wagon plodded along southward, the land had already taken on a foreign tint. The familiar outline of the peaks and ridges seemed distorted by the darkness. Even when the moon broke the horizon, the mountains remained ominous, menacing. The ravines and creeks that cut the broad grasslands between the two forks of the Platte River jarred the weathered wagon until Jeff thought his rattling teeth might fall out. The little girls wrapped themselves around Matthew and gazed fearfully out the back.

"You're bleeding," Matthew told Jeff after the wagon's front wheels slammed against a narrow ditch.

Jeff raised his tender left arm and noted the smear of red that now stained the bindings.

"The leg?" Jeff asked, fighting without success to lift his injured leg.

Matthew hesitated before examining the swollen leg. The girls shrank back.

"It's all right, Mr. Moses," Matthew said, taking a blanket and placing it below Jeff's leg to protect the wound from further injury. "Maybe we can tighten the bandages on your arm."

Jeff nodded, then left the boy to do just that. Young Matthew, despite his small hands and pale complexion, seemed quite at home with bandages.

"My grandpa was a doctor during the war," Matthew explained. "While we lived at the mission, I helped the reverend whenever somebody got hurt. When I'm older, I plan to go back and help at the mission."

"Once I thought to work there, too," Jeff said, wincing again as the pain mixed with a flood of memories.

"You know figures, that's for sure. The reverend says you speak Cheyenne, too."

I *am* Cheyenne, Jeff thought to say. Instead he swallowed the words and let Matthew ramble on about the dream of being a doctor on the frontier.

Once Matthew stopped the arm from bleeding, Jeff

195

faded into a light sleep. The wagon ride continued as before, but after a time a man can adjust to anything, even pain. His eyes didn't fully reopen until late the following afternoon. The wagon finally drew to a halt, and the cessation of motion brought Jeff to consciousness.

"We're makin' camp," Matthew informed him. "I've got some bread and jerked beef if you're hungry. We didn't wake you for supper."

"I'm not hungry," Jeff said as Matthew removed the planks enclosing the rear of the wagon. "I'll wait for dinner."

Matthew paused until his sisters scampered outside to speak a reply.

"Just as well," the boy whispered. "That beef's none too good. Pa bought it off a Cheyenne, and I think it must be skunk or such."

"You'll eat skunk if you get hungry," Jeff said, remembering such a winter.

"Well, I hope I never get that hungry," Matthew remarked.

Jeff met the rest of the Polk clan that evening. In addition to Matthew and the girls, the bearded man proved to be Amos Polk, Matthew's father. Mrs. Polk was a broad-hipped woman of thirty-plus years whose fierce eyes and determined brow attested to her years on the frontier. There were also two younger boys, Mark and John, born one year on either side of nine-year-old Lucia.

Jeff enjoyed the two weeks he spent heading southward with the Polks. In spite of the stabbing pain that sent shudders through his body each time the wagon struck a rock or slid into a rut, Jeff felt warm, calm,

196

secure almost. Whenever strangers happened along, the Polks would hide Jeff beneath a blanket and crowd the wagon with the little ones.

More than once Jeff had the boys carry his litter out beneath a tree. Mr. Moses would then relate stories of Cheyenne warriors, tales of fighting grizzlies or shooting cougars. Adventures Jeff had lived were like wonderful fantasies to the boys and girls, even if occasionally the littlest ones would clutch Matt's skinny arms or hug Jeff's legs. When it was all over, John or maybe Mary would race off to tell one of their parents.

"I like the way you spin your tales," Matthew remarked more than once. "It's like all that really happened."

"Most of it did," Jeff replied. "To me, or to my brother or father or uncle."

"Reverend Ryland?"

"No, my other uncle, Iron Hand, who leads the Cheyennes."

"Well, that's a story, isn't it? I thought your brother looked to be part Indian. But you . . ."

"My hair's light, and I've got a moustache. But here, deep down," Jeff added, pounding his chest, "I'm Cheyenne."

"I want to be a doctor, Mr. Moses, to help people by healing their wounds or curing their sickness. But I have to tell you. I wouldn't mind a little adventure in the bargain."

"Yes, you would," Jeff grumbled. "There's nothin' to like 'bout bein' on the run, wonderin' where you'll find your next meal or even if there'll be one! No, it's an ice-cold, lonely kind of life. I wouldn't wish it on anyone."

And yet Matthew's eyes continued to swell whenever

Jeff spoke of past exploits. The smaller boys marveled when the bandages came off Jeff's arm and leg. The resulting scars testified to the hardships of the trail, and yet they also served as trophies of war. Even the elkhide brace came to denote courage and honor.

Mrs. Polk was far from pleased by the way Matt and the others worshipped Jeff.

"Mr. Moses, I agreed to carry you along to Denver as a kindness to Reverend Ryland," she told Jeff one morning while the children were off with their father. "I'm most grateful to the reverend, but I won't have you fillin' my boys full of such tripe and nonsense!"

"I understand, ma'am," Jeff whispered. "It's mostly my way of rememberin' somethin' special that's gone from my life. I was raised on the Bible, too, you know. The trouble I've seen wasn't altogether of my own makin', you know."

"And the choosin'?"

"Nor that, either."

"I'd have you hold your tongue around my children!"

"I will, ma'am," Jeff promised. "I never forget I owe you my life and my safety. I'd sew my lips shut before I'd harm those kids."

"Well, you're not much more'n a child yourself," she said, brightening.

As they continued southward, though, Jeff ceased being the invalid boy riding along in the back of the wagon. Matthew made a fine crutch from an aspen branch, and the torn and tender flesh began to knit. Often Jeff took a turn driving the wagon. Sometimes he'd borrow Amos Polk's horse and rifle, then vanish. There'd be a shot in the distance, and Mr. Moses would return with fresh meat for the dinner table.

Jeff's biggest contribution came later, though, after the main channel of the Platte turned due south. A trio of smaller rivers had to be crossed, and though Jeff had never ridden that country, experience warned him of the dangers.

"Get on out of that wagon," Jeff told the children. "It's the best way to drown I ever saw!"

"Now hold on, Moses," Amos Polk complained. "We've always let the little ones ride across. None of 'em can swim."

"That's pure folly," Jeff grumbled. "There must be a hundred creeks and rivers out here to drown in. First chance we get, I'll teach 'em."

"And now?" Mrs. Polk asked.

"Now I'll borrow your horse, take 'em each across in turn."

"It'll take forever," Polk objected.

"The wagon can go ahead on. We'll catch up," Jeff assured them.

Matthew helped his sisters climb out of the wagonbed, but before Jeff had a chance to say another word, Polk jerked the reins, yelled, and got the wagon moving on ahead toward the sandy bank.

"No!" Jeff shouted, limping into the shallows and waving his crutch at the horses. "Not here!"

"What in heaven's name?. . . ." Polk began. But as the wheels began to sink into the soft mud, he hushed and concentrated instead on turning the horses back toward the bank.

"Matt, slap your hat at 'em!" Jeff yelled.

Little Matthew splashed into the water and waved his hat at the animals. The horses, distracted from the river, slowly turned to their left and returned to the bank. The wheels were covered with thick, oozing black mud, and the horses themselves were little better.

"This is no place to try a crossin'," Jeff explained as he leaned on his crutch and fought the pain that was cascading through his leg. "You've got to find the shallows, not try the main channel."

"I guess I'm still a tenderfoot," Polk admitted.

"Well, it's how we learn," Jeff said, biting his lip to keep from fainting.

"You oughtn't to put weight on that leg just yet," Matthew complained.

"Had to," Jeff explained as Matt helped the would-be guide sit on the riverbank. "Couldn't have you drown your family."

"Or the horses," Matt said, laughing.

Jeff located a ford the following morning, and the first crossing was made safely. The other rivers were got across as well, and time was even taken for swimming lessons in the icy water.

"Before I came down here with you folks, I'd close to forgotten what it was like to be alive," Jeff told the Polks as he watched the girls chase each other around a large pine tree. "Bein' alone, with nothin' but fear and killin' around you, can eat out a man's heart."

The following morning Jeff had his chance to do a little doctoring. The girls had picked some cedar berries, and everyone else had eaten a handful before Mary brought Jeff a portion.

"Spit 'em out!" Jeff shouted.

But it was too late. By nightfall the whole of the Polk family was down with a terrible bellyache.

"Eatin' the fruit of the land's a fine notion," Jeff said as he pounded a root into powder. "Only trick is

200

knowin' what to eat and what to leave alone. And when."

"Guess they don't teach that in a book," Matthew groaned.

"No, it's mostly learned the hard way," Jeff agreed, blending the root powder with the herbs Dancing Lance had once used to cure Jefferson Thompson of just such an ache. Two doses brought the last of the berries up, and a day of rest completed the cure.

"I feel like your debt's squared," Matt said as he helped Jeff roll up the blankets. "You saved my life for sure."

"Was just a belly grip," Jeff told the boy.

"No, I was prepared to stop that ache if I had to jump off a cliff."

"No cliffs close-by. It would have passed in a bit, anyway."

"Just the same, consider us even."

Jeff smiled as the boy offered a hand that had somehow grown larger, firmer, stronger. Jeff gripped it tightly, sadly recalling how warm it had felt to shake hands with Pike not so very long before.

I wonder how long this can last? Jeff wondered as he drove the Polk wagon along the west bank of the South Platte. That very afternoon he had his answer.

An encampment of tents spread for a hundred yards along the river. The odor of whiskey and scented soap mixed with the groans of men straining to unload freight wagons.

"Must be minin' camps about," Jeff said as Mrs. Polk frowned at the trio of bare-shouldered women bathing in the river nearby.

"Satan's playground!" Mrs. Polk declared.

Jeff tried not to grin as Matthew led his brothers toward the river. Their young faces drank in the sights until their father angrily drove them back toward the wagon.

"Can't we camp here tonight?" Matt asked as Jeff turned the wagon past the first tents.

"Upstream a bit," Mrs. Polk answered. "And you boys stay clear of that place. Hellfire waits the men and women who foul their souls with such carrying-ons."

It was Amos Polk's turn to smile, but his wife only lashed into a recitation of verse. Later, as the sounds of laughter from the tent city drifted past the Polk campfire, she drew Jeff aside.

"Yes, ma'am?" a bewildered Jeff asked.

"Mr. Moses, we only promised to carry you this far. There are people there who'll sell you a horse and provisions. I know you mean us no harm, but you see how Matthew takes to such devilment. It's not altogether your doing. The devil has a sweet voice to a boy's of Matt's age. You've paid any debt you ever owed to us, and I see your heart reaches out to the little ones. But our place is down south, in a town, with people who pray at night and go to meeting on Sunday. You were born of this high country, and it will always be in your soul. It's right you should go your own way."

"I've done that," Jeff said sadly. His eyes silently pleaded to go a little farther, enjoy the refuge a few more days. But her face was as unyielding as the Rockies themselves. He nodded, and gazed sadly at the flickering lights surrounding the tents downstream.

"I'll say my good-byes to the little ones tonight," Jeff said, swallowing the bitter taste in his mouth. "It's best I get along now. I couldn't do it in the daylight."

"It's for the best."

"I thank you for your kindnesses, ma'am."

"You're more than welcome, Mr. Moses."

Jeff nodded, then leaned on his crutch as she returned to her camp. Jeff felt the salty taste of tears reaching the corner of his mouth, and he shook them away. He wanted no more farewells, no heartrending partings to plague his recollections. Instead he steadied his step and made his way back to the wagon. After gathering his belongings, he announced to the children his decision to leave.

"You can't!" Matthew objected. "We're not safely to Denver. There might be another river. We could—"

"Nonsense," Jeff said, smiling as he felt little Mary's hands wrap themselves around his fingers. "Your pa knows what's to be done, and you all can swim."

"Wish I hadn't learned," John grumbled.

"That's no way to talk," Jeff said, painfully kneeling down so that the children could collect around him. "You gave me back my life, and for a time, I was your guide. A good guide's the one who does his job so well a party can get along on their own after a time. We've shared a good trail, you Polks and I. Let's have no tears now."

"What good are tears if you can't cry for a friend?" Matthew asked.

"You don't remember the partings," Jeff said, breaking away from the little hands that hugged his legs and pulled at his arms. "You recollect the smiles and the stories. Do that, and I won't be far off at all."

It's a lie, of course, Jeff thought as he turned away and struggled on toward the distant campfires. They'll learn that in time. But for now, maybe it will help. And soon they'll be busy with storybooks and lessons.

But what about Mr. Moses? Jeff wondered. He was headed for Egypt, for the terrible loneliness of exile in a foreign land.

II

Jeff made his camp on the hillside overlooking the tent city. Already the first hint of winter cut through the night air, but he foresook the shelter of the canvas hovels. Even now his left arm bore the thin scars of a recent gunshot, and his limp wasn't difficult to trace to the ankle.

He didn't watch that next morning when the Polks pulled out on their way to Denver. When Jeff finally pulled on his clothes, it was close to midday. The tent dwellers were stirring, and he had errands to attend to. He crutched his way into the camp, cautiously avoiding the curious eyes of anyone who might prove to be a bounty hunter. He walked as near normal as he could in spite of the crutch, and he did his best to conceal his youth behind a hard stare and cold eyes.

Jeff's first stop was a small corral. Inside were two dozen horses, most lost on wagers, and more than one eager for a buyer. He picked out a tall, broad-backed chestnut mare and a stout little pack mule. Their owner threw in a saddle in the bargain. Then Jeff purchased a long-barreled Winchester rifle from a lucky card player who had picked up three and needed only the miniature Colt stuffed in his vest pocket. Two boxes of shells were bought at the store on wheels Carl Hagen operated next to his riverside fancy house.

Actually it, too, was a tent, with blankets thrown atop ropes dividing the interior. Once or twice Jeff felt the urge to follow the inviting eyes of the girls inside that tent, but the notion of baring his wounded forearm, not to mention the long, unforgettable scar on his belly, kept him at bay. He did watch the girls cavorting in the river from time to time, though, in truth, he found their lifeless eyes and stringy hair no match for the memory of Prairie Flower's glowing smile and gentle touch.

For half a week more Jeff drifted amid the sea of drinking and gambling, all the time searching for a direction, some purpose to his wanderings. He most often found himself camped on the hillside alone, gazing around at the ragged families that seemed to collect at the rim of the temporary settlement. Each night some gambler would die in a flurry of gunfire, more often than not an accidental discharge by an intoxicated companion.

The gaunt, half-starved faces of the women and children came to haunt Jefferson Thompson. He found himself calculating the days some had left, which winter blizzard would put an end to which pain. And often Jeff stared at his own reflection, at the eyes that never looked back, at the thin moustache and scraggly beard, at the chest that seemed to sink into his back. He, too, had become a walking ghost.

I have to get out of this place, Jeff told himself. So he bought supplies, packed them on the mule, and headed out into the Rockies themselves, rode for the high peaks that had always been the last refuge for Thompsons.

He rode alone into the first snow flurries of winter, his eyes clouded with tears that wouldn't fall. He had no winter coat, only a blanket to pull tight around his shoulders. Each night as he made a lean-to to shield himself from the worst of the cold, his legs would ache, and he'd shiver until morning no matter how many logs he placed on the fire.

So, I'm alone, he told himself. There were no pursuing bounty men now, no ambushing line detectives or companies of soldiers. And yet he was running still, chased by shadows of a past, by memories of better times and grand dreams now blasted into oblivion by a year of cold, unfeeling killing.

Sometimes he'd sit beside his fire and brush the snowflakes from his hair. The white reminded him of a picture in one of his uncle's Bible storybooks.

"So, I'm Moses," he said, laughing at the likeness flashing back from his coffee cup. "Yes, I'm Moses, and this is my burning bush," he added, tossing a branch on the fire. But no voice, no answers, came from the fire. And he was as lost as ever.

The next morning he set off across another ridge, destined for another after that. The wind whined through the pines as never before, and the skies overhead threatened any minute to smother the land with the first great blizzard of the season. Suddenly his ears picked up the sound of banging on the hillside up ahead. His first impulse was to turn away from the sound. Instead he drew in his reins and frowned.

What are you doing, Jeff Thompson? he asked himself. Do you want them to find you come spring, frozen like some statue in a picture book? Pa'd never give up. Pike, shot to pieces, with a half-dozen of them closing in like hounds on a wounded stag, still fought them to the end.

"Let's go, boy," Jeff said, patting the chestnut mare on its shoulder. "Let's go see who's hammerin' to high heaven when the sky's about to fall."

Jeff wove his way across the ridge cautiously. He finally spied a lone figure atop what would soon be a small cabin. At present only the four stark walls stood completed. The beams for a roof were in place, but as for the roof itself, it was mostly air. Planks were cut and ready, but only the first two were actually in place. Jeff searched the slope for some sign of a partner, of family. But there was nothing more than a curious weasel.

"Hello there," Jeff called.

The stranger set down his hammer, grabbed a rifle, and pointed it in Jeff's direction. The old man appeared utterly fearless. His grizzled face was outlined by a beard as white as snow, and his gnarled fingers seemed more than capable of firing a rifle whenever he took the notion to do just that.

"I'm no bushwhacker come to steal your property or your life," Jeff said, dropping the reins and holding out his empty hands.

"You're stealin' my solitude!" the stranger shouted. "Stay clear!"

"Why, you old fool," Jeff said, laughing so that the valley echoed "Can't you read the sky? The whole world's about to come crashin' down on you. I've been a loner, but never in winter. First snow's about to find you roofless. Two men might just get the job done."

"And who'd be the other man?"

"I would," Jeff said, pounding his chest.

"You?" the hermit asked, lowering the rifle at last. "Why, you're no more than a sliver of a boy."

Jeff lowered his hands and dismounted. For a second his leg gave way, but he managed to steady himself. Then, using Matthew's crutch, he started toward the cabin, half smiling, half frowning.

"A sliver of a boy, and crippled to boot!" the stranger exclaimed. "Well, I've seen it all. And you're goin' to help me finish my roof?"

"Unless you talk the rest of the day away," Jeff said, dropping the crutch, grabbing a plank, and hoisting it toward the roof. The old man took it, and Jeff pulled himself up to the roof, too.

"By thunder! You're no stranger to work. That's for sure."

"If I'm not intrudin' too much on your solitude now, how 'bout helpin' me get this plank nailed down. The storm's about here, and I have to see to my horse. She's not been long with me, and I'd hate to be horseless in the high country."

"We'll put her and the mule down in the dugout."

Dugout? Jeff asked, gazing around. There, concealed by the trees, was a dugout cabin that doubled as a stable.

"You had shelter all along?" Jeff asked. "Why, you might've shot me off my saddle quick as lightnin'!"

"Thought to do just that," the old man said. "But you kind of put me in mind of myself when I was younger. And stupider."

Jeff laughed at that remark, and as so often happened in the high country, a friendship was instantly sealed.

"They call me Shep, short for Shepherd, Skelly," the old man said as he and Jeff worked feverishly to finish the roof. "I look for gold, mostly where there ain't any."

"Jeff Thompson," Jeff said, extending his hand so Shep could grasp it.

"I heard of a Thompson or two lately," the old man said, his eyes darkening. "Was troublin' a railroad."

"Was," Jeff said, taking the hammer and striking hard at the nail. "That's finished."

"Maybe not so far's the railroad's concerned. They got posters up, I'm thinking."

"Even down here," Jeff grumbled as he hammered away. "I wouldn't want to bring my trouble down on anybody else."

"You wouldn't be," Shep said. "Way I look at things, a man's past is his own business. Why, you can't be full-grown yet, and I've had some doin's with railroads myself. Thing is, you got to find a safer name, boy. Name like yours, well, it can get you killed."

Jeff recalled his uncle's advice.

"I guess there are lots of names a man can find for himself."

"That's a truth, boy," Shep said, grinning. "You'll come up with one. Now let's get this roof on."

Jeff took to his new partner right away. After living with a litter of pups like the Polks, the nights had grown incredibly lonely. Shep was a little less certain about the arrangement, but when the snows came, the roof was a comfort. And sleeping away from the animals didn't hurt either disposition.

"Have to say this to you," Shep admitted after they'd shared the cabin a week. "You cook better'n that Arapaho woman I kept year afore last, and the supplies you brought along won't be unwelcome."

"That mean you're pleased I'm stayin'?" Jeff asked.

"Well, don't know as pleased is the word for it."

"What is?"

"Don't know there's a word for everything, boy. But if it came down to it, I don't suppose I'd shoot you."

"That's a real comfort, Shep."

Gradually, though, Jeff made himself as much a part of Shep's mountain as the cabin and the stream. They shared the chores, alternately fetching water and splitting firewood. When the weather brightened, they fished the stream for trout and hunted the hillsides for rabbits.

Finding a new name came less easily. Jeff thought of Bible figures, Presidents, a hundred notions.

"What you want's something simple," Shep declared. "Short and simple. Try a name with a J. That wouldn't be so hard to keep in your mind."

"Joshua, Jerome, there are dozens of J names."

"John's easy."

"All right."

"And the rest?"

"How 'bout Wilson? John Wilson."

"How've you been, Johnny?"

"Just grand, Mr. Skelly," the new John Wilson said, making a mock bow. "Anything else I ought to change?"

"Cut the hair a bit. Looks like a female I once met in a Denver cathouse."

"I'll cut it."

"Might toss that crutch in the fireplace, too. Leg might as well mend now as later."

"It's gettin' better."

"Then, let it get well, boy! You keep walkin' on that crutch, you'll bend yourself like a saplin'. Start walkin' straight again."

A memory appeared. Little Matthew held the crutch up like a prize at a state fair. The boy flashed such pride, but Jeff Thompson was gone now, and the crutch best be discarded as well. John set it on the fire.

Shep was right about the ankle. The more John put his weight on the foot, the straighter the leg grew to be. Before long the limp disappeared. Even better, the old elkhide brace was removed, too.

Now that John Wilson was sound of limb, he began exploring the snowclad slope that was becoming home. He'd already grown weary of rabbit stew, especially when wild onions and moldy potatoes were the only vegetables. So he took his Winchester and set out to track a deer.

"A Pawnee scout couldn't find a deer up here this time o' year," Shep complained.

"That mean if I shoot him, you won't eat any of the meat?"

"Didn't say that, Johnny boy," Shep said, licking his lips. "Wouldn't want to discourage you, not for the world."

"Have the fire ready. Venison steaks'll be mighty tasty."

And true to his word, John returned two hours later dragging a deer carcass toward the cabin.

"You'll need to skin it, dress the meat," Shep said. "Best keep the carcass off a bit. We get wolves up here sometimes."

John nodded his understanding, then took out his knife and started working. Once the skin was cut away, he stretched it out on a framework of pine branches. Then the butchering began.

For three days they ate venison steaks with the few surviving potatoes. Twice John fixed biscuits to top off the meal. But it was working the deer's hide that most drew Shep's attention.

"Never saw a white man chew it soft like that," Shep remarked. "Arapaho gal did it that way. Needlework's more like Cheyenne, though."

"It is Cheyenne," John said, smiling as his mind filled with memories of Iron Hand and Dancing Lance, of Prairie Flower's wide brown eyes and Little Heart's wild abandon on horseback.

"You passed some time with 'em, did you?"

"More than that, Shep. I *am* Cheyenne, a quarter of me, anyway."

"Don't favor it much," Shep said, examining John's face closely. "Some in the eyes, but the hair's light."

"It was easier to see in my brother."

"That's the better for you, Johnny. It's not the best time, and this ain't the best place, for a man to have Indian blood."

No, John thought, or to be in the way of a railroad.

III

It might have been the scent of fresh meat that brought the bear. Or perhaps the great, hulking beast tired of the solitude of winter's hibernation. Whichever the cause, a tremendous roar split the midnight air outside the cabin, and the horses sheltered in Shep Skelly's dugout whined in terror.

"Grizzly!" John cried out as he grabbed his clothes.

"Can't be. It's too late for bears," Shep argued. "They're sleepin' off their summer fat. Must be wolves."

The beast growled furiously, and the horses reared and bucked.

"I've heard lots of wolves," John said, pulling on his trousers and grabbing the Winchester. "Never heard one sound like that!"

Shep continued to dispute the notion, but once the partners stepped out into the frigid darkness, neither spoke a word. Twenty feet away a dark gray shadow lumbered across the hillside.

"You ever know a wolf to have that kind of size?" John asked, cranking the lever of his Winchester, then firing at the monster. A horrible groan shook snow from the pine branches all around them, and the grizzly turned toward its tormentors.

"We'd best clear out for now," Shep urged, pulling at

his young friend's arm. "That thing looks none too friendly."

But to John Wilson, there could be nor more fleeing, no hiding in the shadows, fearing every sound might signal the end of life as well as the conclusion of the chase.

"Johnny boy," Shep pleaded.

John merely advanced another cartridge into the firing chamber and squeezed the trigger. Again the grizzly staggered backward, bellowing so that the sky itself seemed to fall. The bear stood for a moment on its hind legs, towering above the swirls of white powder. Then it turned and romped off to the safety of the forest.

"Lord, help us. That thing's near torn off the dugout door," Shep said, trotting to the horses. John followed, and together they moved the splintered pine door aside so that the terrified horses could escape into the open.

"We'd best keep a watch till daylight," John said, stroking the frothing nose of the chestnut mare. "He could be back."

"Sooner or later he will," Shep said, touching a splotch of sticky red liquid which stained the snow beside his foot. "You hit him square, Johnny, but he's more'n a match for a pair of bullets."

"I've got more."

"You'll need 'em."

A little after dawn the next morning John followed his partner outside the cabin. Shep headed directly for the dugout. The animals lurked nearby, and John examined his mare and the mule to assure himself neither had been harmed during the night. Neither was hurt, so John joined Shep just the other side of the dugout.

"Grizzly's got no business up here in midwinter," Shep complained. "Ought to be holed up in some cave."

John nodded, then knelt beside a massive paw print. The bear's huge foot had torn through an inch of snow and left its mark in the hard ground underneath. Gazing up at the nearby pines and aspens, John had no trouble tracing the grizzly's progress. Whole branches were torn from the trees, and a carpet of pine needles sprinkled the trail.

"He went through here in a hurry," John said, pointing to the elongated tracks left by the fleeing bear. "Was bleedin' some, too."

"That's bound to make him even meaner."

"Yes," John agreed as he started up the trail, keeping his rifle ready should the monster suddenly appear. He thought it more likely the bear had found some refuge, would let the pain subside, then strike out again.

"This looks to me like askin' for trouble," Shep grumbled as John led the way through the tangled underbrush and dense pines. "Sooner or later he'll come to us."

John stopped in his tracks, rested the rifle on his shoulder, and stared into the distance. Shep was right. What's more, John had little enthusiasm for the hunt. He understood that grizzly, lying off in the distance, his body shivering with pain. Even though he was John Wilson now, he hadn't forgotten the recent past, that life of running from ridge to ridge, turning from one ambush to another. He still recalled the pangs of hunger, the overpowering daggers of loneliness tearing at his heart.

What was it Zeke Thompson had said to his son that

first autumn when they'd set off after deer? It's our lot to be the hunters, and their lot to be the prey. It's the way the world is, boy, and it's not for us to change it.

Truths don't change just because a man alters his name. John Wilson knew that as well as Jefferson Thompson had.

"You ready to turn back, son?" Shep asked.

"I've got a bear to kill," John answered grimly.

So they continued tracking the creature. For a time the tracks slashed at the snow in desperation. But gradually the bear slowed, and the splotches of blood ended. John spotted the fresh carcass of a rabbit, probably caught unawares early that morning. Only a bit of bones and fur remained. Afterward all signs of panic left the bear's movements.

"We'll come upon him soon," Shep said, drawing John's attention to a series of small caves on the opposite side of a gully. "He's in one of those."

"Does seem likely," John agreed.

But actually the bear was fishing a small stream farther east, and when the two men started across the gully, the beast caught their scent.

"Good Lord!" Shep shouted when the grizzly tore through the pines above them.

John pulled his partner up the opposite slope, then coolly and calmly opened fire on the bear thundering down the gully.

The grizzly reared up on his hind legs and shook its huge paws at the air. Its growl rolled down the gully and echoed out across the mountainside.

"I hear you, bear!" John hollered back at the devil. "I'm here, waiting for you."

But as the mammoth beast clawed its way painfully

up the side of the gully, John retreated to the trees. Then he leaped in and out of shadows, shooting again and again. Each time the lead projectiles tore their way into the grizzly's vitals, the creature would scream out in pain.

Shep stared in disbelief as John slowly and methodically saw to the creature's killing. By now John Wilson had become half phantom, appearing and disappearing as the weary grizzly groped its way first to one side, then the other. Its eyes were already clouding with the onset of death, and yet still it struck out blindly at the enemy.

It's like with Pike, John thought as he closed in on the tormented beast. He can't give up. He knows he's dead, but he strikes out even so, hoping to take somebody else down, too. Finally, though, with the Winchester's magazine nigh empty, the grizzly fell. Its blood stained the snow, and its dying gasps echoed down the gully toward the cabin.

"He's gone now," Shep said, pulling John away.

"Almost," John said, motioning at the left paw. Even now the claws tore at the earth. Shep raised his rifle and fired point-blank into the grizzly's head. The shot sent a shiver down John's spine. A deathly silence followed.

"It's time we headed back," Shep whispered.

"And the bear?" Shep appeared confused, and John pulled a knife. "He'll make a good coat, and we'll have steaks and grease to last us half the winter."

"Boy?"

"Nothin' ever happens up here by chance, Shep. My cousin once taught me the spirits know a man's every need. They provide for all if a man has the eyes to see

218

and the will to act. I was cold, and the bear came to give up his fur. I never in my whole life left meat to rot on a mountaintop," John added, staring bitterly out across the peaks to the north.

"Who are you, boy?" Shep asked, stepping back a few feet.

"I'm not altogether sure I know anymore," John admitted. "But I haven't forgotten everything."

Later that week as John worked the heavy fur of the grizzly into a coat to hold at bay the worst chills of winter, Shep poked at the fire with a stick.

"You really believe that bear was sent by spirits, boy?" the old man asked.

"It came, didn't it?" John asked in turn. "I don't know what to think anymore, Shep. There was a time when I said my prayers every night. Ma was religious, her father bein' a preacher and all. I knew the Bible almost as well as I knew the mountains. Then the railroad people came and killed everybody."

"Everybody?"

"Well, I might've been breathin', but that was none of their doin'. And I'm not altogether certain what I've been doin' since could be called livin'."

"Never saw a grizzly out this late in the year."

"Me neither," John said, scratching his head. He gazed at the bearskin. A tear appeared in his eye when he remembered that other bearskin coat, the one Pike had handed him not so very long ago.

"I never had much use for religion myself," Shep said, poking the fire so that a plume of sparks erupted toward the chimney. "I used to pray some, mainly that I'd make a real strike, hit a glory hole maybe."

"A glory hole?"

"Well, that's what the miners call it. You dig all along a river. Then one day some fellow stumbles on a sea of nuggets so thick they appear to be one big fist of gold."

"Did you ever find yours?"

"Think I'd be up here if I did?" Shep asked, laughing loudly. "No, I pan a bit of dust, a few nuggets, enough to get me through the next winter."

"Then, why stay out here, work yourself half to death?"

"Well, Johnny, the company's not so bad. There's the eagles and the elk in summer. Winter, well, it's mostly quiet 'cept when I take in a renegade Cheyenne or tangle with a grizzly."

"Are you ever sad you didn't take a wife, raise a family?" John asked, studying the lines in Shep's forehead as the old man pondered the question.

"Well, I do wish there was somebody to miss me, but I never had much luck with the gals. I was always wantin' to go deeper into the mountains, and they always wanted to settle in some town, sell flour and oats. I've made my own trail, I suppose, and nobody's the worse for me havin' come their way."

"That's more than I can say," John said, sighing. "Men have died because I crossed their path."

"You're a strange man, Johnny Wilson," Shep said as he gazed deeply at John's face. "One minute I see a boy born to climb every mountain in the Rockies, chase the wind to the Pacific Ocean and back, laugh so the frownin' moon himself starts to smile. Then I look over and see a lifetime of sadness in those eyes."

"I know," John whispered. "I don't know myself who I am half the time. I keep hopin' I'll figure it out one of these days."

"You've time yet."

I hope so, John thought as he worked on the coat.

In the weeks that followed, John was glad to have that coat. The heavens emptied, and deep snowdrifts blanketed the Rockies. A dozen times John tunneled his way to the dugout to tend to the animals. The grass Shep had set by for his horse fell far short of what the two horses required, not to mention the poor pack mule. So John would take to the meadows each afternoon and dig down to where the frozen grasses lay. Once thawed, the horses would eat that grass greedily.

"I never knew a time when the horses couldn't find their own grass after a week's sunshine," Shep complained.

"Hasn't been three days of sun up here since October," John grumbled. "We're not long on supplies ourselves."

And then the great blizzard hit. Snow fell continuously for three days. The whole world seemed drowned by whirlwinds of the white powder. Rockslides carried away whole hillsides. Even the bearskin coat failed to fend off the nighttime chills, and John often huddled beside what little fire remained, feeling the daggerlike cold drive its blade between his ribs.

There was no hope of venturing outside, and the whining of the horses was worse than the howling of the wind. Food was rationed, and a single log was placed on the fire each morning and evening. Finally even the furniture and the bowls were burned.

"Was there ever a time as hard as this?" John asked. "Was there ever since the world began a cold that ate a man's fingers and toes, choked his breath, and starved

221

him at the same time?"

"It's like this sometimes," Shep explained. "And it's worse when you're alone. You said the spirits provide what a man needs, John Wilson. They gave you that coat. Well, they sent me you, to listen to an old man's stories and remind him of what it was like when his heart was young. Next time you feel sorrow for the death you've brought, consider I owe you for a roof, for the food I've eaten and the company you've shared."

"The roof's kept me warm, too," John reminded the old man. "It's been a fair bargain, our partnership."

But as the white fog swallowed the earth, the sky, the universe, John began to wonder if either of them would survive to see the first robin.

"Lord, I haven't done a lot of prayin' lately," John whispered as he stared at the dying embers of the fire. "You sent me the bear to give me warmth. Seems like it'd be kind of a waste if I was to starve now, or freeze, either."

He fell asleep to the mournful tune of the north wind whistling through the treetops. He dreamed of swimming with Pike in the river, of chasing buffalo with Little Heart and Dancing Lance. He saw Prairie Flower's shining eyes as she brought him his morning coffee.

No chills penetrated the bearskin coat that night. No hunger rumbled through John's belly. There was nothing but the dream, the bright vision of a better life, a better world. That was enough.

IV

John didn't recall ever seeing a brighter morning. The inside of the cabin dripped with melting ice, and the deep drifts of snow that blocked the door seemed to shrink each moment. By early afternoon John was chopping firewood, and Shep found grass for the starving animals.

"Spring!" Shep hollered to the mountainside.

"Spring! Spring! Spring!" it echoed and echoed.

Soon the icy surface of the river began cracking. It wasn't long before melting snow transformed it into a roaring torrent. The aspens began budding, and the birds sang out their annual greetings.

Best of all, the trout in the stream seemed eager to bite at anything dropped their way, and the skillet filled each night with tasty rainbows. Deer and rabbit appeared as well, and more than one contributed its meat to the near-starved partners.

"Good thing spring came when it did," Shep told John. "Look at those ribs. I can count 'em. You're lucky as it is that you can keep your britches up."

"Yes," John agreed, tracing the bones of his forearms from wrist to elbow. "But a bit of venison and fried trout will tend to that quick enough."

And as the snow gave way to green hillsides blanketed with splashes of wildflowers, John felt his shoulders broaden, his chest swell, the power return to his arms and legs. The thin, almost delicate moustache of winter began finally to darken and thicken.

"You're comin' to be a man," Shep declared. "So it's fittin' I should put it to you. Soon as the ground hardens, I'm headin' upstream. Will you stick with this old man?"

"Dig for gold?"

"Pan, dig, pick it out of the streams with your toes if that's what's called for. I know it's a life of chasin' rainbows, Johnny, but sometimes you happen upon that pot of gold. Once is all it takes."

"Can't say I've got anything better to do," John said, smiling broadly.

In a week the worst of the mud brought by melting snow hardened, and the stream returned to its banks. John loaded what meager provisions had outlasted winter on the back of the mule, then saddled the chestnut mare. Soon he was trailing Shep Skelly as the old man headed upstream.

For two springs and two summers, John Wilson followed that golden trail up one played-out stream after another, over one ridge and down another. He endured two autumns and two winters of cabin life, withstanding blizzard and hardship, half starving and near freezing. And in that time he grew tall and confident the way his father once had. But in spite of the years and the peace, he never entirely forgot what had come before or the pledge he had made to an aging Cheyenne in what seemed sometimes to have been another lifetime.

The spring of 1871 found John and Shep camped along a winding stream someone had named Putnam Creek. Putnam himself, along with most sensible miners, had long since departed the diggings. Only a couple of dozen stubborn goldseekers remained, and most of those looked longingly north or west to other mountains, richer streams.

John sifted through the sandy creek bottom from dawn to dusk. Each time he swirled the pebbles and sand around in his pan, he grew more discouraged. A month earlier at least one or two golden flakes could be plucked from every panful. Now a single grain of gold seemed a real find, and a nugget would send half the hillside scrambling back to the creek.

"It's like all the other places," Shep finally growled as he slung his pan across the camp. "Played out! The only one to make any money's the man who gets there first. And then half the time he digs in the wrong place."

"Gets himself shot or loses his claim in a card game," John added. "There's no end to the foolishness takin' place in these camps, Shep."

"And what'd you do if you struck it rich, Johnny?"

"Oh, first I'd buy myself some new clothes," John said, sticking his fingers through the holes in his woolen trousers. "Then I think I'd buy some land, good land where I could run a few horses, raise some kids."

"Kids?" Shep grumbled, kicking a rock at the discarded pan. "Why, you could pick up three dozen of 'em 'round this camp a week back, glad to join you for a square meal and a decent winter coat."

"I'm not talkin' about these camp orphans," John said, gazing at a pair of ragged boys rummaging through the remains of old Frank Ritchie's sluice box. "I mean kids of my own."

"You need a wife to get that kind," Shep said, smiling. "Got any likely prospects?"

"I did once, in my uncle's camp up north. Her name was Prairie Flower, and she was as beautiful as her name."

"Cheyenne?"

"Yes, but she'd be married by now. Girl turns fourteen or fifteen, her father puts out the word. And a girl like Flower, one that's pretty and can cook, isn't likely to be passed up."

"Sometimes I've a mind to turn my horse north and take to the Cheyenne trail myself, Johnny Wilson," Shep said, smiling. "I listen to you tell how it was, and I don't know that I wouldn't pick it over diggin' up one stream after another for nothin' more'n a few pieces of quartz and a nugget or three."

"Think it's time to move on?"

"Should've left a week ago, with the others," Shep confessed. "I sure did think this was the place, though. The hills are just like Kettle Creek, and they dug whole hillsides of color out of that place."

"Well, I guess we've got enough put by for supplies," John said, taking the money pouch from his pocket and feeling the weight.

"Prices might be down a bit for lack of customers. You might even pick up some new trousers."

"I wouldn't turn 'em down," John said, locating still another hole. "May have to turn back to buckskins again."

Shep laughed, then began gathering up their gear. John checked the provision bag, made a mental note of what was needed, then headed downstream toward the clapboard supply store.

"Headin' out, Johnny?" one miner after another asked.

"Seems time," John answered each.

There'd be a solemn moment of shared disappointment, a funeral of sorts for a buried dream. Then John would continue toward the store.

"Any bargains to be had, Mr. Cleghorn?" Johnny asked as he passed the storekeeper fishing in the creek.

"See for yourself," Cleghorn said, pointing toward the store. "Clerk'll take your dust."

"Any chance of gettin' the prices down, what with most people movin' along and all?"

"No chance," Cleghorn said, pointing downstream. "There are other camps to move along to. I'll get my price there if not from you."

John thought to ask a third question, but there was no point to appeal to Cleghorn's sympathies. The shopkeeper had been too long in the gold camps. Avarice eats a man's heart, and it rarely grows back. Instead John continued toward the store, swung open the door, and stepped inside.

"Any bargains?" he asked.

"None I can see," the clerk replied from behind the counter.

John hadn't been there in a while, and he didn't recognize the clerk by voice. He tried to catch a glimpse of the speaker, but all he saw was a worn felt hat that was clearly three sizes too big and a pair of overalls draped over shoulders skinnier than John's had gotten in the worst days of midwinter.

Probably some camp orphan old Cleghorn's hired, John thought. Most of those boys would work for next to nothing, just to get fed regular and have something to cover themselves with. It was like Cleghorn to take them in, work them half to death, and set them afoot without a penny for their trouble.

John shook his head sadly as he caught another glimpse at the gaunt clerk. Then he filled a box with a sack of flour, a tin of coffee, and a small sack of sugar, some shells for the rifles, and a slab of bacon.

"Can you weigh my pouch?" John asked, setting the box on the counter and handing over his gold. "I need to know how much more I can spend."

The clerk nodded, then took out Cleghorn's scale and poured the contents of the pouch on one tray.

"Not much here," the clerk said, placing weights on the opposite tray to determine the value. "Cleghorn's cut the price per ounce, too."

"Not much I can do about that," John said, frowning. "A man's entitled to gouge his neighbors."

The clerk nodded, then tallied the gold.

"That's all?" John asked, looking at the numbers on the pad. "I've already spent all but seven dollars of it. Look at these trousers, would you? They're all but fallin' apart. Next thing you know I'll be naked as a jaybird!"

The clerk laughed loudly as John ran his fingers through the holes in the fabric. John might have laughed along had not the hat fallen from the clerk's head. Instantly he covered up the bare spots and retreated toward the door.

"What's wrong?" the clerk asked, brushing back long strands of thick blond hair. "You'd think you'd never seen a girl before!"

"I . . . uh . . . I . . ."

"Don't talk so good now as before."

"Well, how'd you feel if you'd just shown parts of yourself to somebody you thought was—"

"I've been in mining camps the last three years," she said, laughing. "I've seen a lot more than a few holes in a pair of trousers."

"Maybe so," John said, catching his breath. "How come you to hide your hair? Truth is, I haven't seen too many girls lately. Only ones since winter've been a scarecrow of a granny back at Shermanville and a pair of little ones runnin' bare-bottom through the creek here a week or so back."

"That's why," she said, avoiding his eyes.

"Well, anyway, I'm sorry if I act like a fool, I guess it's all that time spent with my legs in the creek, sloppin' sand around in a pan. People call me John Wilson. Some make it Johnny. I'm partnerin' with Shep Skelly."

"My name's Marie, Marie Beaumont," the girl said, brushing back her hair again.

"Well, I'm glad to meet you, Marie," John said, gazing at her with a shy, hesitant smile. "You don't know if seven dollars might buy some wool, do you? I can maybe patch these trousers."

"If you don't mind wearing something that's been used, you could look through that box in the corner, Johnny. Sometimes Mr. Cleghorn takes things in trade. One of the miners left that box. His family drowned crossing the South Platte."

229

John nodded, then headed for the box. As he went through the contents, he fought off a terrible sadness. Most of the clothes were small, wonderfully delicate dresses of lace and soft cotton, made lovingly for little girls not half grown. He hadn't thought about the Polks for a long time, but the small faces of those children suddenly overwhelmed him.

"I cried when I went through it the first time," Marie said from across the room. "But Mr. Cleghorn said to get what I could for them, and I remember the man had a son about your size. I recall at least three shirts and a couple of pairs of decent britches. You can have 'em all for two dollars."

"Thanks," John said, smiling in gratitude as he picked out the aforementioned garments. He also found a pair of cotton drawers which he wrapped inside the trousers. No point to increasing his embarrassment! With the remaining five dollars John bought three scoops of beans, a jar of honey, and a used hunting knife.

"Guess you're heading out," Marie said as she stuffed the clothes into John's box.

"We haven't dug a pound of flour's worth the whole last week," John told her. "No point to lingerin'. The only ones around here gettin' rich are the shopkeepers."

"Cleghorn's leaving himself before long. He heard there's a big strike out west of here. Maybe you and your partner will head that way, too."

"Not likely. Shep likes to move north. It's fresh country there, mostly rivers the rest haven't gotten to yet. He says the real strikes get made by the ones who get there first."

"The secret's to find the gold first," Marie told him.

"Well, we've been at it three years now. Luck's bound to change."

"Bound to," she said, balling her hair up and pulling the hat down over it. "It's not likely we'll run into each other again."

"No, not likely," John said, lingering a moment. For just an instant he thought to ask her along. But what life could a girl have heading north into the high country? What would Shep say? Likely laugh his teeth out."

"*Via con Dios*," Marie told him sadly.

"What?"

"It's Spanish. Go with God."

"*Via con Dios*," Marie."

She smiled her answer, then turned away as John opened the door and carried his heavy box of supplies outside. Always before he'd headed into the high country with a light heart, with an eagerness to return to what he knew best, living off the land away from people. But suddenly he wasn't so sure.

"Looks like you did all right at Cleghorn's," Shep said when John began packing the supplies. "No more holes in the trousers for a time. How much he rob you for them?"

"Two dollars for the clothes."

"What?" Shep asked, coughing in pretended amazement. "That old miser's losin' his touch."

"He didn't sell 'em to me. A girl did."

"A girl?" Shep asked, raising his eyebrows. "Pretty?"

"I guess you'd say so," John admitted as his face turned slightly pink.

"Surprised you didn't ask her to come along."

"I almost did. But then when I told her you snore,

she lost interest."

"Oh, I should've known you were makin' it up," Shep said, shaking his head. "A girl at Cleghorn's! What'll the boy dream up next?"

V

As they headed north into the heart of the Rockies, John stared at the abandoned remains of a half-dozen mining camps. Splintered sluice boxes lay here and there. John frowned as he gazed at the holes torn in the earth, at the scars eaten away by picks and shovels.

The wounded land won't ever yield up its treasure, John thought as he wept inside for the spoiled mountainsides. It was so different from riding through the Cheyenne camps with Iron Hand. It was often hard to notice anyone had been there a week after the Indians had departed.

"The spirits provide all things," Iron Hand had said a hundred times. "But they punish those who take without giving, who kill without giving life."

The ruined framework of a supply store stood to one side, and for a moment John was tempted to ride over for a closer look. Then he caught sight of a flash of black and white . . . and another.

"Skunks," John muttered, turning his horse away.

"Don't tell me you're shy when it comes to polecats, Johnny," Shep joked. "You go a month between baths, so it's probably them that'd complain about *your* scent, not t'other way around."

"Smelled your feet lately, old man?" John asked as he nudged the chestnut mare into a trot. "I'm not the one who could do with a bath!"

The partners continued to exchange insults as they rode ever higher. Not until they were well clear of the played-out streams and abandoned diggings did Shep start to study the rocks and streams. Finally the old miner located a streambed flowing out of an elbow-shaped ridge.

"Another Kettle Creek?" John asked as Shep dismounted.

"A likely enough spot for us to try, anyway."

"Looks like we're the first miners to get up here," John said, climbing down from his horse. "From the looks of the place we might be the first white men to pass this way."

"You think we could have Indian trouble, Johnny?" Shep asked, sliding his rifle out of its saddle scabbard.

"I'd say the Arapaho were up here once, but they've mostly been chased off. Could be a band or two left. Some Utes, too, but they wouldn't be likely to bother us."

"Then, I guess we'd best start to work."

Work it was, too, for springtime in the Rockies brings rain and hail, cold, wicked winds that cut through a man's ribs followed by bright sunny afternoons that bake flesh and drive a man half to distraction. John's dark complexion absorbed the sun, but Shep's face and shoulders reddened till the old man howled in pain. But not once did the two men pause from their labors.

By summer the isolated spot had been transformed

into a home of sorts. Shep and John constructed a simple log cabin, together with a small supply shed nearby. A shelter for the horses nestled among the pines closer to the stream. And down at the water's edge a sluice box helped the miners work the streambed.

"This stream's a bit miserly, Johnny," Shep remarked each day as they collected a few flakes from the sluice box. Now and then a nugget would emerge from a shovelful of mud, but most days a bit of dust was all they found.

But whenever the sweat and fatigue began taking their toll, John would sprawl out in the river and let the swift, cold current wash away the weariness.

Of greater concern were the nocturnal visitors who plagued the camp. Sometimes skunks and raccoons upset the sluice box or dug up the garbage. Occasionally a bobcat or a wolf appeared, chasing the horses halfway down the stream and sending their unearthly cries resounding through the mountains. Each threat was dealt with in turn. Traps were set out on the trails, and twice John stalked wolves through the timber. By mid-June night had become as peaceful as day.

Even so, John wondered if there was any gold left in Colorado to be dug from the ground. As he and Shep worked their way upstream, it seemed more doubtful every dawn.

"You sure we're doin' this the right way, Shep?" John finally asked.

"It's the only way I know, and I've been at it since the world began, Johnny boy. A man's got to have patience."

"Three months we've been diggin' in this stream,

and what have we found? A couple of pouches of dust and five or six nuggets!"

The following day John took off into the pines in search of fresh meat. The supplies were dwindling, and he'd lost his taste for trout. He brought down a deer at the edge of a wondrous green meadow, but the thought of venison steaks did little to cheer him.

"What sort of life is this?" he asked the clouds swimming along in the azure sky overhead. "Scratchin' away at the land, hopin' to find a fortune when all I ever really wanted was a little peace, a chance to live without somebody shootin' bullets at me or chasin' me off my land."

Clouds rarely give answers, though. Life remained as great a puzzle as ever.

"We haven't had biscuits in a week," Shep complained a day or so later. "You forgot how to make 'em?"

"Hard to make biscuits without flour," John explained.

"How much do we have left?"

"Just a few spoonfuls. We'll be out of coffee in a week, too."

"Why don't you ride down to Cleghorn's, buy what we need?"

"With what?" John asked, holding his empty hands out.

"We've got three pouches full now. Some nuggets, too. More than we dug back at Putnam's."

"He may well have raised the price, too, Shep. If we spend everything now, it could prove a long winter."

"Winter's always long, boy. Saddle your horse and take the mule, too. Clean out that skinflint."

John laughed, knowing it would probably be the other way around.

Early the following morning he set off alone across the ridges and streams that separated him from Putnam's Creek and Cleghorn's trading post. His path swung westward some, and he found himself riding through a beehive of miners at a place called Henry's Folly.

"Only folly old Henry had was leavin' this place," one old-timer told John. "I dug out five hundred dollars' worth yesterday alone."

"Congratulations," John said, fighting hard to hold back the bitterness. If only Shep had gone along with the others instead of blindly heading north, groping around like a fool when the treasure rested just beyond his fingers.

Cleghorn's store had found Henry's Folly easily enough, and John almost wished it hadn't. With gold flowing like rainwater in August, the prices were steeper than ever. John managed little more than two bags of flour and a small tin of coffee.

"What happened to your clerk?" John asked Cleghorn as the storekeeper tallied the bill. "The girl you had working for you back at Putnam's Creek."

"Oh, she didn't have a head for business," Cleghorn grumbled. "She was forever buying something we had no use for, then selling it off again for nary a penny's profit. She was quarrelsome, too. When I left, I gave her some honey, a bit of flour, and sent her on her way."

John frowned. He liked the girl better than ever. And when he left the gold camp that same afternoon, he found himself heading east, toward Putnam's Creek.

He camped overnight on a ridge five miles or so

down the trail. As he spread his blankets, he gazed at the flickering campfires of Henry's Folly. To the east there was only the darkness that came with unraveled dreams, with dead hopes and abandoned diggings.

The following morning he was up early. By midday he rode through the shallows of the creek itself. Only a single wall remained of the store, and except for two sheets of canvas inhabited by forlorn families bound for the big strike out west, John detected no sign of life.

You can't blame anyone for leaving, John told himself. There was no future in a played-out stream. And yet something bid him pause a moment, climb off his horse, take a closer look. The same something led him to the store. As he bent over to examine a discarded dinner fork, he heard something move behind the wall.

"Who's there?" John asked, stepping back toward his horse. He started to withdraw his rifle from its scabbard, but a small, mud-splotched face popped out from behind a rock. Two other slightly older children appeared near the wall. Their clothes were mere tatters, and none possessed a pair of shoes. The younger ones were near starved, and with their long, scraggly hair John couldn't tell whether they were boys or girls.

"We mean you no harm, mister," the oldest said, pulling the rags that once were a shirt together so that his bony chest was less apparent. He wasn't more than fourteen, though his eyes seemed ancient.

"Nor I you," John replied, leaving the rifle in its place. "Your folks leave you here?"

The little ones nodded. The older one gazed sadly toward the west.

"We're awful hungry, mister," one of the little ones

said, holding out his diminutive hand.

"I'll see if I can catch us some supper," John answered. "You can build a fire."

"You've got a generous heart," a new voice spoke from the far side of the wall. "Knew it from the first."

"Who's that?" John asked, feeling uneasy.

"See those trousers fit you."

"It's you," John said, staring in disbelief as the clerk from Cleghorn's store stepped out into the open. "Well, I sure figure you smarter than to stay here."

"Got nowhere to go," she explained, straightening her hair a bit. She was thinner than ever, and her arms were scraped and sunburned. Her eyes glowed with life, though.

"And these three?" John asked.

"Just camp orphans. They dig around the store. Sometimes they find a coin, a little cloth, or some food."

"And you?"

"Well, you didn't dig all the gold out of this creek after all," she said, holding up two pouches.

"Marie, you know him?" the older boy asked.

She nodded, then motioned for the youngsters to collect wood for the fire. John meanwhile took some fishing line from his knapsack and found a worm for the hook.

"So, you've got a motherin' instinct," he told her as he tossed the line into the creek.

"They don't need a mother," she declared. "They've been getting along just fine without anybody."

"And you?"

"I'm no different."

John frowned. He searched for something else to say,

but her blazing eyes sent shivers through him. He couldn't seem to put his thoughts into words. Instead he concentrated on the fishing.

"Don't suppose you've struck it rich yet," she finally said.

"No. I'm still tryin', though. My partner, Shep, is up north. They're diggin' plenty out west at a place called Henry's Folly."

She smiled sympathetically, but John's attention shifted to a trout fighting to free itself from his hook.

"Not this time, fish," John said, pulling a beautiful rainbow out of the creek. Marie instantly grabbed the fish, pulled the hook from its mouth, and set it beside her.

"We'll need five or six," she told him. "You'll find there are worms under most of these rocks."

"You sound like you've done this before."

"Fished? You get hungry. You learn how to find food."

"I've got a spare line."

"No, I'll watch this time."

She did just that until John had snagged a third trout. Then she pulled out a knife and began cleaning the fish. From somewhere she produced a skillet and some flour, and minutes later she was frying the trout and making dough balls.

"Drop biscuits?" John asked.

She nodded as he pulled another trout from the creek.

"Do much cooking yourself?"

"Most of it," John admitted. "Shep, well, he's not much of a cook."

"I cooked for my papa after Mama died. But I don't

think he ever took to me much. One day I woke up, found he'd pulled out with my brothers during the night."

"I lost my family, too," John told her. "Almost three years ago now."

The little ones gathered around, expecting John to spin a tale, but he remained mute. It wasn't wise to speak too freely among strangers.

After sharing a supper of fish and biscuits, John prepared to continue his journey. The little ones dashed off to the woods as if they were afraid there'd be a bill to pay. Marie stayed behind.

"You cook wondrous well, Marie," John told her.

"Not much to it."

"I know better. You lookin' after those three?"

"I told you. They look after themselves."

"Well, I've been thinkin'. If you've got nowhere else to go, you might care to come with me."

"Where?"

"Up north. Now, I know it's no gold mine. We'll be lucky to dig enough to get us through the winter. But it's honest work, and Shep's not a bad companion."

"What exactly would I be asked to do?" she asked suspiciously.

"Just cook," John said, trembling slightly as she gazed into his fearful eyes. "I promise. I'd have to talk it out with Shep, but you could even share in the gold."

"I don't know," she said, scratching her head.

"You can't have anything all that important to do. And if we're not good company, you can always leave."

"That's true enough."

"So?"

"I suppose I'm bound to go with you."

John smiled so that his teeth seemed to outshine the sun. He then rearranged he supplies so that Marie could ride atop the mule. When he finished, he helped her up and started northward. From the woods came three sad figures, each silently waving farewell.

"They'll get on," Marie said again. "You'll see."

"Yes," John agreed, knowing that was the way with orphans. They learned to look after their needs because no one else would. And if they failed, they died.

VI

For three days John Wilson and his new companion rode north into the Rockies. Not since his childhood on Thompson's Mountain had John shared his camp with anyone his age. Whether swimming or fishing or watching the evening stars, he felt younger, more alive.

Marie was a wonder. She never seemed to tire. Most might have complained about riding a mule, especially with only a rough woolen blanket in place of a saddle, but Marie merely laughed and told stories of the mining camps.

"Why should I complain?" she asked. "I walked from the South Platte to Putnam's Creek. Most of it barefooted, in late winter, with only a wool shawl of my mother's to keep me from freezing."

Iron Hand had said it once. A boy who faces hardships grows into a better man. The same held true for women. If they survived, that is.

When they arrived at Shep's cabin, John slid down from the chestnut mare and greeted his partner.

"I brought somebody with me," John told the old man. "You recall I mentioned the girl at Cleghorn's."

"You brought a female?" Shep asked with raised

eyebrows. "Boy, sometimes I think you must've spent too much time in the sun without a hat. Why'd you bring another mouth to feed!"

"She's a good cook," John pointed out. "Besides, she can do her share of the work. She's panned for gold."

"Well, she's your worry, Johnny. You see she pulls her load, and I'll have no quarrel with either of you."

"That's only fair. Once you get to know her, you'll come to see it's our good fortune she's here."

"I hope you're right, boy. Many's the time a woman's broke up a good partnership. But then you're not a starved pup of a boy anymore. It's time you chose for yourself."

"I always have," John said, smiling.

As it turned out, those warm summer days were lighter and happier with Marie there. She worked as hard as a Cheyenne, shoveling sand into the sluice box, hunting and fishing, cooking and mending.

"I don't know what you did before I got up here," she complained more than once. "Your clothes have more holes than pockets! Bigger ones, too."

And in the evenings, when the valley grew still and quiet, she'd sit beside the fireplace and sing soft ballads that brought John right out of his skin. Old Shep would smile, hum along, then yawn. Next thing you knew the old man would be sprawled out on his blankets, snoring away.

"I used to sing my brothers to sleep," Marie said, frowning as a memory flooded her mind. "They usually joined in."

"I'm not much on singin'," John told her. "Ma used to teach me hymns, but most of 'em ended up soundin' like Cheyenne war cries."

244

Eventually he did sing along, though his voice provided little harmony. The melodies drew them closer, though, and the sharing of each new day forged a bond stronger than either of them thought possible.

It wasn't all sunshine and song, though. It didn't take too long for Marie to tire of the musty cabin and her muddy, sweat-streaked companions.

"Last I heard, nobody died from taking a bath," she announced one morning. "So if you're not too attached to all that dirt, and you're tired of smelling like a pair of hogs, I'd consider it a favor if you'd go down to the creek and scrub yourselves."

"You sayin' we need a bath?" John asked.

"Well, it's either that or you get your own supper from now on," she said, putting her hands on her hips and scowling. "Wouldn't hurt to find a razor, too."

"Shave?" Shep asked, feeling his brittle white whiskers. "No man shaves in the high country. That's craziness, girl!"

Marie proved to be utterly unyielding, though. John finally surrendered, taking a square of lye soap and heading for the stream. Shep proved more stubborn. But faced with the prospect of eating his own cooking, the old man took a turn at the stream around dusk.

"Tomorrow," Marie told them as she meted out their dinner, "I want you shaven."

"With what?" John asked. "It's been a long time since I've seen a razor."

"I found one," she said, producing a steel blade. "Tomorrow, agreed?"

Shep grumbled, but John took the razor and sighed. Next morning he shaved the unruly hairs from his chin and cut away the darker growth of his moustache. Shep

Skelly refused, though, and no argument would sway the old man.

"I've had this beard longer'n you two've been alive," he declared. "An old man's entitled to a few comforts."

"I suppose he is," Marie said, grinning. "Keep your beard, Shep. Truth is, we wouldn't know you without it."

From that time on, John would occasionally find the cake of soap on the table or the razor lying atop his boots. The hint was sufficient to send him to the stream toward midafternoon. And though he let the moustache grow again, he did keep his chin as smooth as when he'd been ten.

By autumn, John had a hard time imagining life without Marie's good-humored prodding and gentle laughter. It seemed her smile took the edge off life, tamed the wind and quieted the storms.

"She's good luck, too," Shep declared as the stream finally yielded up larger nuggets. "Since she's been here, we've dug five pouches' worth of dust. I've got a coffee tin full of nuggets too."

John wasn't sure luck had much to do with it. Now that three people were working the stream, you'd expect better results. And Marie badgered them into working longer and harder, though often as not she'd be at the diggings before and after either of them. Sometimes she'd make a contest of it, challenging John to shovel more sand into the sluice box, or else offering an extra biscuit to the person who found the most nuggets that day.

"She's got a way of turnin' work into a game," John told Shep as the two partners headed up the hillside in search of fresh meat. The leaves on the aspens were turning, and the first chill winds of the season were blowing down from the north.

"She's a bit fussy for my likin'," Shep grumbled. "Always after a body to wash. Makin' a lot of noise 'cause you scratch your arm on a branch or slice a finger choppin' kindlin'."

"I kind of like the way she rubs salve into my shoulders when they ache," John said, smiling as he recalled the soft fingers working the tightness out of his back. "And her cookin'! I never knew a trout could taste so good."

"There's truth to that, Johnny. But winter's comin'. Have you done any thinkin' 'bout what she'll do then?"

"I figured she'd stay here."

"Boy, there's a difference between sharin' your camp with a girl who's got nowhere to go and keepin' a woman in your cabin all winter."

"I don't see that."

"Up here winterin' with a man's the same thing as marryin' him, Johnny."

"You're here, Shep. It'd be different if it was just the two of us."

"Would it? Take that little gal you told me you knew in the Cheyenne camps. If you asked her up here to cook for you, had her in your cabin all winter, wouldn't her pa expect you to provide for her like a wife? Wouldn't she consider you her man?"

"Marie doesn't."

"Have you asked her, Johnny Wilson? I see how she looks at you sometimes when you're asleep, all hunched up like a little ball of fur. She'll sit down beside you, brush your hair off your eyes, whisper to you . . . that's more'n a partner'd do, boy."

"How come you never said anything before?"

"Wasn't winter. But now it's time you did some decidin'. If you want to send her down to the settlements, it's time you got started. Snows'll be here 'fore too long. If you want her to stay, she deserves to be asked."

"I sure didn't expect this," John said, scratching his head. "I'm confused. Pa never said much about such things. I'd miss her if she was to go, Shep, but what business do I have takin' a wife? I've got no money, no land. Even my name belongs to somebody else."

"I can't help you much, either."

"Did you ever winter with a woman, Shep?"

"Once," the old man said, sighing.

"How was it?"

"Fair, in the beginnin' at least. I ate good. She looked to my comforts. I'll give her that. But in the end, she wouldn't leave the cabin come first thaw, so I left her to it."

"Ever go back and see if she was still there?"

"I never go back, Johnny. Once you turn down the trail, it's best to keep goin' and not look back."

"I don't know that I could put her on a horse and let her go, Shep. I care what happens to her. We're a lot alike. I wouldn't mind havin' her for a wife, settlin' down, raisin' a family."

"She's the kind of a girl who'll do that, boy. She's strong-minded. She won't give out on you when the tough times come. Well, you've got your dreams, you two. You're young. You can afford 'em. Me, I'm past dreamin', past wonderin' what's ahead. I just try to see myself through till mornin', from one summer to the next."

"You're not so old as you let on, Shep Skelly. And I'm not so young as you'd have me think."

"Think on this, Johnny Wilson. If she stays to winter and won't leave the cabin come spring, will you stay here?"

"Don't know," John admitted. "It'd be hard if we haven't struck a vein by then. If we did, would you?"

"You know me by now, Johnny. I'm not one to stay once the stream's played out. I'd head on north, climb higher and higher."

John nodded as he read sadness in the old white-haired man's tired eyes. But in the end he asked Marie to stay.

"I hoped you'd ask me," she whispered. "I feel like I belong up here now."

"Winters are hard."

"So am I," she reminded John.

VII

John and Shep spent the final weeks of autumn preparing for another harsh Rocky Mountain winter. Every morning one or the other of them was up chopping wood. Log was stacked atop log until a pile the length and height of the cabin was made. Then a second row was started.

Venison was dried and salted away for the months ahead. Marie contributed her daily string of trout. Onions, turnips, and the wild fruits and berries that appeared in late summer and early fall were put aside, and John gathered those herbs he'd learned were useful in curing a cough or easing a fever. Grass was cut and dried for the stock, and shutters for the cabin's three windows were crafted.

When the first snow flurries of the season arrived, John felt like celebrating. His only regret was of not having a bearskin coat for Marie, but he did manage to trap enough rabbits for her to sew the pelts into a passable garment.

"May not be as warm," she admitted, "but it's soft as anything I've ever owned."

John comforted himself with the knowledge that

there'd be plenty of wood to keep a fire all night, and their bellies, for once, would remain full even in the blizzards.

At it happened, that winter of '71 was a nightmare of wind and snow, sleet and hail. The mountains fended off the worst of it, though, and Marie worked her magic to dispel the rest. Her games, her songs, her stories . . . they made the difference. Each time John's eyes darkened with gloom, she'd sit beside him, resting her soft head on his cheek.

"It'll pass, Johnny, and soon we'll be digging more gold than ever from the stream. We'll have a big house in Denver, a dozen kids for you to chase up the stairs, and none of us will know another sad time."

"Is that what you dream of?" he'd ask.

"Dreams are free. You might as well make them wonderful."

Sometimes Johnny would add to her dream world, weave a rich carpet of golden moments and tender days. More often he'd content himself with listening to her voice, studying her bright blue eyes, and feeling a warmth he didn't think possible in the depths of winter.

Once Marie took out an ancient red carpetbag and pulled out a half-dozen masks.

"Here, Shep, pick out one," she said, dancing over to where the old man sat beside the fireplace.

"What's this nonsense?" he asked.

"Masks. We're going to act out a story."

"A what?" Shep asked, shaking his head.

"After my family left, I traveled with a theatrical company, Marie explained. "We used to do this all the time. You hold the mask in front of your face and make up a character. It's fun."

251

Shep grumbled more than ever, but in the end the old man had a better time than anyone. His mask showed the face of a king, and John was stuck switching back and forth from a dim-witted count to a court jester. Marie played the lovely princess. By the time they finished their tale, all three were laughing till tears ran down their cheeks.

After Shep took to his blankets, John sat in the far corner with Marie and gazed at the winter sky.

"Sometimes I look up there, and I think we're the only people in the whole world," she whispered.

"We're not, you know," he told her. "We're just hiding out up here, hoping the good times last a little longer."

"Is that really what we're doing?"

"It's what I'm doing, Marie. I had a family once, too. They didn't exactly leave me. They were killed."

"Is that how you got that awful scar?" she asked, gently touching his belly. "I've wondered about that."

"I've been shot. Twice bad enough I thought I'd die."

"By outlaws?"

"No," he said, sighing. "Once by some killers hired by the railroad to run us off our land. The second time by the same kind of men. Only that time they were the law."

"Tell me about it."

"I can't," he said, lowering his chin. "It's not something I want to remember."

"Can you forget?"

"No," he said, pulling her closer. "I made a promise once, and the time may come when I'll be able to keep it. You ought to know that much at least."

"Know what?"

"I can't explain any of it without telling you everything, Marie. You ought to know my name's not really John Wilson, though. I've done things I'm not proud of. I've killed men, and there are those who'd pay money to see me dead."

"You're making this up," she said, laughing.

"No, I'm not," he told her, his eyes darkening with the seriousness of it.

"It doesn't matter," she whispered. "It's been over a long time now. Besides, nobody will care when we have our big house with the golden staircase."

He laughed as she recounted her dream world again, and the gloom that had surfaced was eaten by her smiling eyes and tender touch.

The rest of the winter passed in much the same way. The cabin remained warm with shared laughter, and John almost hated to see the stream begin to thaw.

"It's time we were working the sluice box again," Shep announced at last. "And I wouldn't mind some fresh meat."

Those words, as much as the melting ice or the noonday sun, brought an end to winter and a return to long days of seemingly endless toil.

That evening while Marie started dinner, John motioned Shep outside.

"What is it, Johnny boy?" Shep asked. "I'm hungry."

"I was wonderin' about somethin', Shep."

"Oh?"

"I guess you know I've got strong feelings for Marie."

"Was suspectin' it anyway," the old man said, trying not to laugh.

"Well, the thing is, Pa never talked about such things, and I don't . . ."

"Don't what?"

"Don't know what to do next. If we were back in some town, I guess maybe I'd talk to a preacher."

"A preacher!"

"Get him to marry us maybe."

"Oh," Shep said, grinning. "You want us to build you a church maybe. Do it up proper."

"It's not a joke, Shep. I haven't seen a preacher or even a Bible in three years!"

"Tell you what, Johnny. We'll have a look for one when we move along. Maybe one of the minin' camps'll have a preacher."

"You give up on this place?"

"Got to admit we'd been better off headin' west. We could dig some more nuggets here, get a little dust, but I've not seen a sign of a real strike hereabouts."

And so the snows melted away, Shep took to staring longingly toward the north. As days came and went with few fresh traces of the precious yellow powder, John grew less anxious to depart. They'd shared some fine moments there, and who was to say the same awaited them at the next camp?

"Trout tastes different tonight." Shep said one evening at the dinner table.

"We're out of salt," Marie explained. "Before long we'll need flour, too."

"Soon we'll head west. There's bound to be a trading post out that way, maybe even a town by now."

"What?" Marie asked. "Leave this cabin?"

"We always head on come first thaw," John explained. "Cabin's for winter shelter. This stream's close to played out."

"We haven't covered half the bed. There's still the northern stretch. If the gold's coming down from the

254

mountain, the richest part would be there."

"Unless it's washed downstream already," Shep pointed out. "If we wait too late, all the likely spots'll be taken 'fore we get there."

"Then stay!" Marie said, slamming her hand against the table. "Miners are all fools. That man Henry had a fortune if he'd stayed. Instead years later somebody happens along and gets rich on the very spot Henry abandoned."

"She's got a point," John agreed.

"You're old enough to make up your own mind about such things," Shep said, his eyes growing moist. "Johnny, you've been like a son to me, but the time comes when even a son's got to make his own way."

"You dissolvin' the partnership, Shep?" John asked, his fingers trembling.

"Could be the time for it, boy."

"I don't know that I'm a year-round cabin man yet, Marie," John said, turning toward her. "We could get awful hungry up here if the stream's got no more gold to give up."

"Try it another week," she pleaded. "Just a week. What do you say, Shep? Is that fair?"

He nodded his agreement, then stood up.

"But remember," Shep warned. "Seven days, and I'm on the trail. You two'll have to make your own minds up as to whether you go with me or stay."

John clutched Marie's hand, then nodded.

Three days later the two of them shifted through the sluice box till an hour past sunset without finding a single nugget. In half a week, they had taken a pinch of dust and three tiny nuggets.

"Well?" John asked. "What do we do if it isn't better

255

tomorrow? Leave? Stay?"

"I've been in gold camps before, Johnny," she said sadly. "I've seen what happens there. This is a good place, a wonderful country even if there's no pile of nuggets, no instant wealth. If we leave, we'll end up like those others. I've seen men desert their wives, leave their children to wander the creeks, crying, wondering if they'll starve. That's no kind of life! It's walking death. I want something more. I want to share my life with a man, have children . . ."

"There aren't a lot of men around here, Marie."

"Just the one I want," she said, grabbing his hands.

"I'm still not full grown, you know."

"You're getting there."

"What about your house in Denver?"

"It's not the house I want, Johnny Wilson. It's you. Besides, we might still find that pot of gold here. I saw a rainbow across here the other day, and I could swear it dropped right into this stream."

He laughed, and she wrapped her arm around his waist.

"Don't give up yet," she whispered.

"I won't," he agreed.

As three more days passed, though, Shep spent more time packing supplies and exercising his horse. John would have abandoned the sluice box himself if it hadn't been for Marie's stubbornness.

"Ever been married, Shep?" John asked as he watched the old man divide the gold into three equal pouches.

"No. Never been with but one woman, that gal I wintered with back in what, '62?"

"I'm close to twenty now. I'd have my own lodge in

the camps of the Cheyenne."

"Isn't years makes a man, Johnny," Shep said, resting a gnarled hand on the young man's shoulder. "It's what he's got inside of him. You've had it there all along. Only regret I've got is that I can't leave you with somethin' more'n a pouch of dust. I feel sort of like the father of the bride, so to speak. Ought to leave you a dowry."

"You've left us with more than you think, you old coot."

"I'm old, Johnny, and a man as old as I am gets to where he thinks back on things. I haven't got a lot of regrets. I've had it my way. I've seen the tops of the mountains, and I've watched the eagles soar. I've held the whole world in my own two hands. Still, I'd like to think you and that wisp of a girl could have somethin' more, somethin' better from life."

"Is there anything better?"

"Maybe," the old man said, sighing. "But I suppose that's for you to discover on your own. Some secrets are best found in their own time."

John didn't really understand, but the distant, somber look in old Shep's eyes foretold there was something grand out there, something not to be missed.

VIII

"Johnny! Shep! Gold! This is it! Lord, help us, Gold!"

John was busy filling Shep's provision bag with what supplies could be spared when Marie screamed the news across the whole valley.

"I think she's turned crazy on us, boy," Shep said, staring out the doorway toward the stream. "She's jumpin' around like a loon, throwin' rocks in the air . . ."

"I'd best go see," John said, abandoning his work and heading toward the diggings. By the time he was halfway there, Marie was digging into the sandy fringe of the stream, hopping around, tossing her hat into the air.

"Have you lost your senses?" John asked when he reached her at last. "They can hear you in Denver."

"I hope not," she said, leaning against him and fighting to catch her breath. Then she reached into the sand and deposited a handful of bright, shining golden nuggets in his hand.

"Where?" he asked. "How'd you—"

"They've been here all along," she said. "Not in the

water, but here, in the sand. Look at this! We're rich!"

"It's a little early to say that. Could be just a few nuggets."

"Look," she said, dragging him along as she pointed to trenches dug in the sand. Gold nuggets collected in the roots of plants, mixed with sand and rock, speckled the ground for a hundred yards. Best of all, a long splash of gold stained an outcropping of quartz that Marie had exposed on the nearby hillside.

"It's a vein," John said, dropping the nuggets in his hand as he tried to absorb the news. "I've never seen this much color. Lord, Marie, we *are* rich!"

They joined hands and danced around in a circle, laughing and shouting like two fools escaped from an asylum.

Shep finally came down to investigate, and John was beyond words. He jabbered away so fast his words became unintelligible. But the nuggets shining in the holes told the story. The old man dropped to his knees and began kissing the earth.

"After all these years, I've finally struck a vein!" Shep shouted. "And to think we almost left. Little gal, you've saved us."

Shep twirled Marie around, and the three of them danced the better part of the afternoon away. When they finally collapsed into the sand, John gazed into the clear blue sky overhead and spoke a brief prayer.

"You've brought so much to us, Lord," he whispered reverently. "We're grateful. Thank you for bringin' us this good fortune, and for lettin' us share it."

John turned his eyes to Marie. Her smile seemed brighter than all the nuggets heaped together, and she crawled to his side.

"So, what do we do now?" John asked.

"First thing is to cover the holes. Don't want somebody movin' in on us. Next thing is to collect enough for supplies. We'll head down to a trading post, buy what we need in the way of provisions and powder."

"Powder?" John asked nervously.

"To blast the rock," Shep said, pointing to the hillside. "That's where the real treasure lies. Then we've got to get title to this place. You'll never dig this vein, children. It'll take equipment, men."

"How do you know all this?" John asked.

"I know lots of things," Shep told them. "Didn't turn my hair white dancin' in the river, Johnny boy. No, sir. Looks like you'll have that big house of yours, gal, and a half-dozen to spare. We're rich!"

If John and Marie had been the first to turn crazy, Shep Skelly was the one to stay that way. He walked across the camp cradling a rifle, and he'd raise an alarm at the drop of a hat. A dozen pouches of nuggets were collected, but only five were left in the cabin. The rest of the gold was hidden beneath the floorboards of the supply shed.

"I wish we had somebody to leave up here as a guard," Shep said when they prepared to head west toward the supply camp. "But I suspect we'll need all three of us once we open up our pouches. Got to guard against bein' followed, too."

Shep's precautions sent shudders through John. He knew only too well what men would do to snatch land they wanted.

"Maybe we ought to dig out all we can, then head somewhere safe," John suggested.

"You couldn't scratch the surface of this strike in a

year's time," Shep explained. "No, we've got to blast her open. Then you can ride to Denver, hire help, and get clear title. That's the only way, boy."

John wasn't half as sure, but Shep's face filled with confidence, and there was no arguing with experience.

They headed west a week later, John leading the way on the chestnut mare, Marie following on the mule, and Shep bringing up the rear on his tired old pony. For three days they wove an elusive path through the mountains, carefully concealing their trail by riding through streambeds and over rocky hillsides. By the time they finally came upon a settlement, all three were near exhaustion.

"Look there," John said, waving to a simple wooden structure with neatly stenciled letters on a sign over the door. ALONZO'S. "Must be the store."

"You tend the horses, Johnny," Shep said, dismounting. "I'll tend to the supplies."

"Take Marie along," John suggested. "She knows what we need better'n you or me, and havin' a woman along might quiet some suspicions."

Shep nodded, and Marie hopped down.

"And don't forget," John added. "We need a pair of mules at least, and a horse and saddle for Marie."

"I know what we need," Marie said, shaking her head. "You tend your own business, Johnny Wilson."

John smiled. Give a girl a little gold, and she turned bossy. But as he thought about it, he decided she'd always been that way.

"Well, it's little enough of a fault for somebody so pretty," he told the horses. They seemed to nod their tired heads in agreement, and John laughed till he nearly fell to the ground.

Once the horses were unsaddled, John left them to graze on the grassy hillside. He then exlored the settlement.

Beyond Alonzo's, there were two neat rows of tents leading to the river. Diggings spread out on both banks as far as the eye could see. On a small hillside between the tents and the river stood a lone aspen, spreading its branches out like a welcoming mother. A crowd had gathered there, and people were laughing and shouting.

John thought it was probably like other camps he'd visited. The edge of the diggings was frequented by gambling tables and fancy women. But the more he studied the scene, the less convinced he became. When Shep and Marie finally returned with the animals and supplies, John left them to watch the camp, and headed down for a closer look.

He took care to stay clear of the diggings. More than one shotgun blast had greeted a careless visitor to a gold camp. John finally stood at the edge of the river and stared at the scene on the opposite bank.

"Rejoice, neighbor, for drowned away are the sins of the world!" a deep-voiced giant of a man bellowed from the shallows. Then, with a great, bearlike hand, the giant pushed the head of a boy of eight or so under the water. The child reemerged shortly gasping for breath, and the crowd shouted, "Glory be! He's saved!" Others across the river would laugh and jeer, but the line leading toward the river topped the crest of the hill.

"Blamed dunkers got nothin' better to do than muddy the river," a miner complained to John. "They could go upstream a bit where the gold's already been dug."

John nodded, but he couldn't help watching the wilderness preacher continue his baptisms. Sometimes the drawn face and bloodshot eyes of a miner would stare at the giant.

"He's my husband, brother," a woman would say. "Lately he's taken to strong drink and harsh words. He beats the children, and he plays cards."

"Lord, save this sinner!" the preacher would yell, and the gathering would echo the words. The poor wretch's wife and children would gather as the preacher dragged his unwilling charge to the river. Then, the huge hand would plunge the miner's face into the stream, calling out for forgiveness and salvation.

"Don't see how he keeps from drownin' 'em myself," Shep spoke up suddenly from behind John. "Don't seem proper, nigh drownin' kids amid laughter and amens."

"Everybody's got his own style," John explained. "Truth is, they remember it this way. When times get hard, it's a comfort to feel there's a better world waitin' for you."

"Could be," Shep admitted. "Couldn't catch me standin' in line to swallow a chestful of river, though."

"Wouldn't hurt either of you," Marie said, joining them. "Especially you, Johnny Wilson."

"I've been dunked," John told her. "I've got an uncle who's a preacher up north."

"Do you?" she asked. "Well, I guess you know preachers are good for other things, too."

"Like for weddings, you mean?" John asked. "Think you're ready for one?"

"I am!" Shep declared, pushing them together. "How 'bout havin' a talk with that preacher later on, boy."

"Feelin' like the father of the bride again, Shep?" John asked.

"Sure am," the old man confessed with a smile. "And I've got a shot gun should the need arrive to use it."

John touched Marie's hand, then pointed toward the preacher. She nodded, and Shep clapped his hands together with a resounding whack that echoed across the river.

It was nearly dusk when the preacher finished his baptizing, and John had no trouble persuading the man to join them for dinner. The burly man gobbled up a plate of biscuits, two venison steaks, and a berry pie.

"Guess preachin' doesn't feed you too well," Shep remarked.

"I'm not hurtin'," the preacher said, laughing as he tapped his rounded belly. "Can't always tell when the next meal's goin' to happen your way, though."

"Ever do weddings, Brother Thomas?" John asked. "Marie and I want to get ourselves married."

"All the time," the preacher answered. "I've got papers in my saddlebags. Just need a pair of witnesses, and we'll send a copy to my church in Denver. That's just in case the one of you with your copy chances to lose it, and the other might happen to need the proof."

Brother Thomas smiled, and Shep laughed loudly. Marie was less amused.

"Tell you what, children," the preacher said. "You say you want to be man and wife. Talk it over tomorrow, and if you're still of that mind, I'll read the words over supper. Agreed?"

"Agreed," Marie answered, poking John in the back.

"Sure," he added.

After Brother Thomas headed back toward his camp beneath the aspen on the hillside, Shep began scrubbing the dinner plates.

"Preachers sure like to eat," the old man complained. "He's willin' to wed you if he gets another meal in the bargain."

"Seems a fair price to pay," John said.

"Likely you'll pay more'n that, boy," Shep added.

The next morning John found out just how much. The papers would cost ten dollars, and the wedding, in spite of supper, was another ten. Ma and Pa Harper, the witnesses, also expected ten dollars for their services, which included the singing of a hymn when the vows were exchanged.

All in all, it's a fair bargain, John decided. Marie was worth more than a sack of flour and a tin of beans, which was exactly what thirty dollars bought at Alonzo's.

"Must be hard for poor people to get married, though," Marie pointed out.

Following the simple ceremony and the supper that followed, John and Shep packed the supplies on the mules, and Marie scrubbed the supper bowls. Soon they were mounted up and riding northeastward.

"Bless your happy union!" Brother Thomas bellowed as they left. "May you find every happiness."

John waved in reply, feeling in his heart that with Marie as his bride, they'd find just that.

For the present, that happiness was postponed. Shep had them on the trail from dawn to dusk, and there was hardly time to eat. Each of them watched the slopes behind them for signs of stalking horsemen.

"I guess Alonzo wasn't much impressed by our

takings," John said finally. "A few pouches of dust and nuggets when he sees a sea of the stuff every day probably didn't cause much of a stir."

All the same, Shep backtracked carefully through creeks and across steep hillsides, concealing the trail at every opportunity.

"Best to be safe," the old man said over and over.

Once they returned to the cabin, John expected his old partner to relax. But Shep worked furiously to set powder charges on the hillsides and restock the supply shed. Rifles stood loaded and ready to face any intrusion.

"I wonder if we're ever goin' to feel married?" Marie asked as she fried trout over a campfire. "Maybe we can go off by ourselves, put up a tent on the mountain."

"I guess I should think about addin' a room to the cabin, too."

"That would be nice, Johnny."

When John brought the matter to Shep's attention, the old man slapped his thigh and frowned.

"Guess you two haven't exactly had a weddin' night, have you? Old man like me gets to forget 'bout bein' young. We'll have us a holiday, a sort of celebration. You two can have the cabin all to yourselves tonight. And me, well, I'll see you're not bothered."

John wasn't quite sure what to say, but as Shep abandoned his powder kegs and took to dancing around, shouting up a storm, it was hard to tell who enjoyed the holiday more.

"He does seem happy," Marie said as Shep produced a few surprises after dinner. He'd bought Marie a gingham dress, and he'd found a shirt for John complete with collar and bow tie. To top it all off, the old

266

man produced a bottle of bourbon and three glasses.

"We'll drink to success and happiness," the old man declared. "In all things and for all times."

"In all things and for all times," John and Marie agreed.

As night fell, John led his bride of a week inside the cabin. Shep had stuffed grass under a large blanket, making it into the closest thing to a bed any of them had seen in years. The fire blazed lightly, adding a subtle warmth to the cabin.

"I feel like a boy about to ride his first horse," John admitted as he knelt beside the blanket.

"A horse?" Marie gasped.

"Swimmin' his first stream?" John asked, his face filling with panic. "That better?"

"I think you'd better quit talking and try to relax," she advised.

As they sat together, the quiet of the evening was suddenly broken by a loud, terribly off-key melody.

"Won't you sit by the fireplace, darlin',
Be mine when the summer sun sets?
Won't you love me till snow's on the prairie,
And time's crossed the mountains an' gone?"

"Is that Shep?" John asked, laughing.

"And the bourbon," Marie pointed out.

The old man continued his singing, and his drinking. Shep was like an aging grandfather, but John warmed knowing there was someone out there wishing them well.

"It's been a long time since I felt like I was home," John said, slipping out of his shirt and letting the dim

267

light from the fireplace illuminate his smile. "I didn't think I'd ever know a night when I felt this good."

"It's been a long time for me, too," Marie said, turning so that John could open the back of the gingham dress. "We've been awful lucky, Johnny. I'm almost afraid I'm going to wake up and find it's all been a dream, and I'm back at Putnam's, all alone, with winter bearing down."

"You're here," he said, touching her bare shoulders. "So am I."

As they lay together quietly, John listened to the peaceful sounds of the mountainside. The songs of the birds whispered through the treetops, and the rush of the stream carried across the hillside. Most of all he heard Marie's gentle breathing, and as he pulled her closer, he felt her warmth spread through him so that an ancient hollowness inside his chest was filled with a new, wonderfully precious belonging.

"Don't ever leave me alone again," he whispered.

"I won't," she promised.

It was close to daybreak when the world exploded. At first there was a low rumble. Then the air was split by fragmented rock, by splinters of wood and fists of sand and smoke.

"Oh, Lord!" John said, jumping to his feet. "Oh, Lord!"

"What's happening?" Marie asked, wrapping herself in the blanket.

"Shep!" John shouted. "Shep!"

John stepped into a pair of britches and raced out the door in his bare feet. Upstream the universe was choked with rolling powder smoke and debris. Pieces of pine branches and bits of sluice box peppered the valley. A single tongue of flame licked the remains of the sluice box. Shep Skelly had disappeared entirely.

"What have you done, old man!" John shouted. "You drunken old fool! Where are you?"

"Johnny!" Marie called from the door of the cabin. But his ears paid no attention. His feet carried him across splinters of wood and sharp rock spurs to the hillside. The earth itself had been split apart, opened up like a hog at butchering time. Amid the smoke and dust John spotted a patch of white hair.

"Shep?" he called, racing across the tortured hillside to his old friend.

"Guess I did it this time, eh, boy?" Shep asked as he struggled to rise from beneath a sea of debris. "Been drinkin', you know. But would you look at it? A glory hole. An honest-to-God glory hole."

John gazed at the glittering hillside. A golden waterfall seemed to cascade down the mountain.

"A glory hole, boy," the old man repeated, coughing. Blood trickled from his lips.

"You're hurt," John said in alarm. "Let me—"

"Not much point," Shep whispered, his eyes watering. "Set the charges just fine, you see, but I wanted to see 'em go off. Got to get clear . . . when you . . . when you use . . . powder."

"Don't try to talk," John said, scraping the dust from the old man's forehead, then pulling the first rock fragment from atop Shep's chest.

"Got so little time now," Shep mumbled. "Got to tell you what to do."

"We'll worry about that later," John said, working

269

furiously to free Shep from the rocks.

"No, now," Shep said, gripping John's hands tightly. "There's a man I know. Name's . . . Jennings. Arthur . . . Jennings. He knows the . . . knows the . . ."

"Shep, you've got to—"

"Knows the mining business, boy," Shep said, coughing blood. "Get to him. He'll help you file the claims, treat you square."

"You'll talk to him yourself, you old fool," John said, tears appearing in his eyes for the first time in years. "Let me just get these rocks off."

"No point," Shep mumbled, his grip loosening. "She's a fine gal, boy. Look after her."

"Shep?"

"Look after her, Johnny Wilson."

"I will," John said as he watched the old man's eyes grow heavy with approaching death. There was a rush of wind across the mountain, and it seemed as if it carried Shep Skelly off with it. John closed his partner's eyelids, then stood up and screamed at the heavens.

"Johnny?" Marie called out as she started toward him.

"He's gone," John said as tears began to weave their way down his smoke and dust-covered cheeks.

Marie joined him, then gazed with terror-filled eyes at Shep's shattered body.

"The whole mountain's opened up," she whispered, pointing to the scarred hillside that glittered like a sea of diamonds.

"Yes," John said, swallowing the pain that tore at his heart. "There's a price to be paid to the spirits when the earth gives up her treasures. Shep knew that, and he paid it."

"I don't understand," she said, gripping him tightly.

"Doesn't matter," John whispered. "We'll heal her wounds."

"Johnny?"

"I'll explain it all sometime. Now let's tend to Shep."

She nodded, and they began to dig the old man out from the rubble.

IV. Denver

I

Eight winters came and went, and with their passage the world itself seemed to be reshaped, molded by unseen hands into a softer land. The harsh, jagged peaks seems to grow round, less threatening, and the virgin wilderness was tamed with the coming of roads and towns.

John Wilson himself changed. Maturity brought with it a softer speech, refined manners, and tailored clothes. Just as a weekly appointment with a barber cast the wildness from his dark brown hair, soft feather beds and warm fireplaces had erased the gaunt cheeks and blazing eyes.

Though the transformation of John Wilson from haggard miner to wealthy businessman was great, it was nothing to the alteration of the land. The gentle, rolling stream now known as Shepherd Creek had been dammed to form deep pools in places. The town of Mariesville nestled along the banks of the largest pond. A neat line of wooden row houses quartered a legion of miners and their families. Across a dusty street stood two churches, a town hall, even a school, all built by the booming Wilson Mining Company's generous president, John Wilson.

At the edge of Mariesville stood two tall wooden houses, brightly painted in yellow with blue trim. Bright gardens of wildflowers and lush green fields warded off the encroaching fingers of the town and lent a quiet solitude to the structures. The smaller of the two had been built early on by John Wilson to house his growing family. The second, built more recently, housed the Shepherd Skelly Home for Abandoned Children, a project born and nurtured in the mind of Marie Wilson, herself a camp orphan, or so the legend said.

For legend was the word for the Wilson story. The couple not yet out of their teens had made the biggest gold strike in a decade, and even now the rich vein showed no hint of fading. Three parallel shafts now reached into the heart of the mountain, quietly clawing away at the golden treasure. The twin chimneys of a smelter blackened the horizon, filling the weekly wagon train with refined gold ready for the buyers in Denver.

Three years back John and Marie Wilson had become strangers to the little town they'd given birth. Instead Marie had bought a lot on Millionaires' Hill in Denver, and shortly thereafter the house she'd envisioned while starving winter after winter rose to dominate the swaying aspens and majestic spruces that spread their branches over its courtyard and walkways.

For Marie it was a dream come true, a fairy tale brought to life, a wonderland of crystal and tapestry, music and parties. To John it became a nightmare of idle conversation, double-talking strangers out to pick his pocket or misdirect his ideals. If not for the monthly journeys to the mine, John Wilson thought he might go mad!

As he stood on the hillside a hundred yards from the company office, he couldn't help feeling the smoke-clouded valley was his legacy. True, he'd insisted the mounds of slag generated by the smelter be buried out of view, and the rock torn from the tunnels was being used to build the walls of the new courthouse and library. Even so he couldn't help feeling he'd violated that mountain, wounded it in a way that might not be forgiven.

"You understand, don't you, Shep?" he whispered toward the lone grave high above him on the mountainside. "This was never my plan. I only wanted—"

John couldn't finish, for he'd long ago lost sight of a goal, a direction for the future, a notion of tomorrow or next week, much less next year.

"It's good to see you, Mr. Wilson," spoke Arthur Jennings, the graying engineer who'd built the mine from a tear in the mountainside into a fifty-million-dollar business. "Come along inside the office. It's a little chill out here this morning. We'll find you some coffee."

"Thank you," John said, following the mine's manager inside. In his heart John wished they'd remained out on the mountain. A little April wind was nothing to a man who'd wintered in the high country, who'd felt the bite of hunger or the desperation of loneliness. But long ago he'd learned to follow Art Jennings's lead. Shep's dying words had brought the two together, and their teamwork had made a fortune.

"Well, as I wrote in my letter, the third shaft's paying off," Jennings said as he poured them both a cup of steaming liquid. "It should double our output. We'll be able to process $50,000 a month now, and we won't have to cut the payroll."

"I'm glad of that," John said, sipping the coffee.

"We're cutting back the hours some, too. I know you were worried about the men, Johnny, and ten hours is long enough to keep a man at his task."

"I noticed the orphans have their crops in."

"Knew you'd ask about that," Jennings said, laughing. "I turned the home over to my boy Winfield. He knows more about farming than an old tunnel man like me, and the children seem to like him better than that old miser Shotfield."

"He was a mistake," John agreed. "Managed a church home in Kansas City. Brother Thomas recommended him, but he only knew how to keep boys on a leash."

"That doesn't work on those outlaws your wife keeps rounding up."

"No," John said, smiling for the first time all morning as he loosened his necktie and opened the tight collar on his Philadelphia shirt. Then he kicked off his shiny new St. Louis boots and sighed.

"Tired?" Jennings asked, refilling John's cup. "It's still a long ride up from Denver."

"It's not the ride, Art. It's Denver, the fancy house, the cold-hearted company we keep. I wish I could enjoy it more for Marie's sake. Truth is, I was happier with mud sucking at my feet down at the creek. I felt better doing an honest day's work, slaving away in the noonday sun, feeling a bond with the earth and sky."

"Now you're a man of property. You have responsibilities."

"I know," John whispered as he sipped his coffee. "I'm not cut out for it, though. I thought buying the hotel in Denver would help. But shoot, I didn't know anything about making people comfortable, picking out curtains, that sort of thing. Then there was the flour mill. And the newspaper. I got them started, but . . . well, I guess I don't really know much of anything!"

"You know how to hire the right people, Johnny, and that's more important to a business than anything else. Even the orphanage raises its own food."

"Sure, I know how to make money. And how to spend it. I just wish I knew how to keep busy."

"I'm hiring again," Jennings said, laughing.

"If I could talk Marie into it, I'd grow a beard and move into one of those row houses tomorrow. But she'd throw a fit. She doesn't like me coming up here for a few days."

"The men like to know you take an interest. The orphans, too. This is your valley, Johnny, your town."

"I know."

"Tell you what. You still own all that acreage upstream. I had the men build a little lodge up there, sort of a hunter's cabin. Why don't you come out here in June with the family, live off the land a bit. It'd get you clear of Denver, and the little ones would get a taste of the high country."

"Maybe," John said, closing his eyes momentarily so that he could picture it.

"Talk it over with Marie. She ought to get out here and see the orphanage anyway. I'll wager she'll jump at the chance."

"I'll ask her," John promised.

That evening John sat alone at the dinner table in

the big, silent house. Mrs. Fitch, the round-faced housekeeper, soon appeared with a sizzling plate of roast beef and potatoes, topped off by her famous apple pie. As John ate, he gazed out the window at the boys and girls from the orphanage chasing each other across the hillside.

That's how it was for us, Marie, he thought. Those first weeks all alone we had the world for a playground. Then I rode to Denver, and Art Jennings came with his men to dig the first shaft. Soon there was a town, and we had responsibilities.

John thought back to an even earlier time, a day when a straw-haired boy chased his older brother through a river now lost to memory.

Pike knew, John told himself. There could be no tomorrow.

"Is there something wrong with the dinner, Mr. John?" Mrs. Fitch asked from the kitchen doorway. "You've hardly touched your beef."

"No, the food's wonderful, as always," John said, motioning her to come closer. "It's just that it's so quiet."

"I know," she said, patting his hand and sitting down. "When there's no one here, I like to take my meals with the wee ones. They're always a-jabbering and laughing. You shouldn't come here without Miz Marie and the little ones."

"I do miss them," John said, his fingers growing cold for lack of a small shoulder to squeeze, a tiny cheek to touch.

"Bring them next time, sir. Young Tim's likely to lose his baby cheeks soon, and me not seeing him in months!"

"We'll have to come for a visit. That's certain."

"Bless you, sir," Mrs. Fitch said, beaming. "Now eat your dinner. Isn't like you to waste a woman's efforts."

John laughed, then devoted himself to his dinner. But once Mrs. Fitch departed, his mind again flooded with memories. Once more he fled with Pike through the trees. He lay in Iron Hand's lodge, tended by Prairie Flower.

"That's long finished," he mumbled as he stuffed a bite of potato in his mouth. The Cheyennes had helped the Sioux ride Custer into the dust of the Little Bighorn back in '76, and now the cavalry had erased both tribes from the plains. The rails of a dozen lines were choking what remained of the wilderness, and farmers were breaking up the buffalo range. As for the great woolies, their bones spread across the prairies from Texas to the Dakotas, and the tribes who once followed their wanderings were now starving on reservations down in the Indian Territory.

It's all over, John told himself. It's but a half-forgotten shadow of a long-buried past.

He broke off a fragment of pie with his fork and lifted the wonderfully-spiced mixture of crust and fruit and cinnamon into his mouth. It was such a stark contrast to the dinners of fried trout or salted venison he'd survived on for so long.

Oh, how we've changed, Marie, he thought, closing his eyes and envisioning her soft smile as she descended the marble staircase into the parlor of the house in Denver. Little Michael, his sandy brown hair the image of his father, stood at one elbow while Peter, fair-haired, with the bluest eyes in Colorado, sat as usual on the bottom step. They'd celebrate their birthdays in

July, Michael his seventh, and Peter his sixth. Joanna, barely three, would giggle as she played with two-year-old Timothy, their soft, yellow hair matching their mother's delicate tresses.

What did you want, Johnny? Marie's voice flowed through his thoughts. We're your pride, your future, all you and I dreamed of during those cold, half-starved months of winter. Shep died so that we could have something better. We've got it!

Yes, John thought as he finished the pie and stepped away from the table. We have wealth and power, fortune and friends. But do we have happiness? Are we really content?

John knew his own reply, but he wasn't sure Marie would agree. She'd found her dream, hadn't she? She had the big house in Denver, the crystal chandelier and the covered carriage.

And me? John asked himself as he walked to the front door and stepped outside. What did I want? Peace? Love? Don't I have them?

As he gazed at the orphans, laughing and singing and waving once they spotted their benefactor's slender figure on the porch, he wondered. And somewhere, deep within himself, he envied those poor, stick-thin youngsters the dreams they still held in their hearts, the struggles that had yet to be waged, the secrets that waited to be discovered.

"I feel old," John whispered, "so terribly old."

II

Although a good road wound its way from Mariesville to the state capital at Denver, few cared to travel
the distance on horseback. Some journeyed by wagon,
and others endured the jarring, jolting route of the
Denver & Western Stagecoach Line. As with many of
the trails and roads threading their way through the
Colorado goldfields, the Mariesville road was subject
to road agents, and the gold shipments from the
Wilson mine always carried an escort of armed guards.
Lone riders offered a tempting target to any outlaw.

John Wilson had grown up on horseback, though,
and he carried a pair of new six-shot Colt revolvers
under his coat in addition to the veteran Winchester in
its saddle scabbard.

Whenever Arthur Jennings offered to send an escort
along on the long journey homeward, John only
laughed.

"Truth is, I look more like a highwayman myself
than a target ripe for the plucking," he'd tell Art.

Actually, as John set out on the road, he almost
wished someone would pop out of the shadows, break
the tedium of the long ride. But except for a pair of

bankers who shared the same inn overnight, he met no one at all until he reached the outskirts of Denver itself.

The city was crawling with people, even on its fringes. Carts brought food from the outlying farms and fields while wagons headed out with mining supplies toward the gold camps. The afternoon resounded with the hammering of planks on new buildings, and there was a scent of fresh paint and sawdust in the air. A great city was springing to life at the base of the Rockies, and John Wilson was doing his part to aid its growth.

He could never resist the temptation to visit *his* Denver, those buildings that bore the John Wilson stamp. He always began with the Columbia Hotel, the ornate five-story hostelry that towered over its neighbors on Mountain Street. Nearby was the Colorado *Herald-Courier*, the survivor of two frontier weeklies merged into the state's leading daily newspaper.

There were a half-dozen other businesses, among them a boot factory, a flour mill, and his personal favorite, a printing house. John never tired of stopping by, leafing through the pages of the latest volume and listening to Kell MacFarlane describe upcoming projects.

After nodding to the Statehouse and its accompanying government buildings, he turned his horse and headed for the imposing mansions of Millionaire's Hill. As he rode, he waved to neighbors and acquaintances, smiling at the hard stares of the ladies in their hooped skirts and fine gowns. The fashionable people enjoyed an afternoon promenade along the street. Some rode high in their fur-lined carriages, the men dressed in top hats and long coats while their ladies wrapped themselves in fox furs. None was eager to recognize as a neighbor the unshaven horseman with the pair of pistols bulging from under his coat.

"I do wish you wouldn't ride up the street like an outlaw escaped from the county jail," Marie had complained more than once. "They all think we're a pair of saloon rowdies from the gold camps."

"Maybe we are," he'd answer, but that hadn't kept him from going along with her plans to improve their social standing. It started with diction lessons, with private tutors and elegant clothes. Next came fine paintings, a library of books, and finally the house.

You can't buy respectability, though, John thought as he passed other strolling neighbors. Except for a few aristocrats who'd brought their dollars west, most held no more claim to social standing than a gray wolf howling in the mountains. He supposed it was their own insecurity that produced the frowns. None of them enjoyed being reminded how short a time it'd been since they wintered in the musty interiors of log cabins.

So, why am I so proud of that past? John asked himself. I cling to it like a drowning man grasps a rescue branch. But he was too close to home to start searching for evasive answers.

The house, like most on that hill, spoke of affluence and power. But it was unique in its combination of towers and gabled rooftops. The walls were of yellow brick, highlighted by a delicate sky-blue trim. The grounds were surrounded by a tall iron fence.

John slowed his horse, then nudged it into a slow trot. The animal required no further direction. It recognized the open door of the stable and whined a greeting to the other horses.

"Well, Mr. John," Ezra Gregg, the stablemaster, called out. "Been sort of expectin' you in today. Good trip?"

"Good weather," John replied, climbing down from the horse and handing the reins to Ezra. "These days one trip's about the same as another."

"Well, we're glad to have you home again, sir."

"Thank you, Ezra."

John left Ezra to his duties and continued up the stone walkway toward the big oaken front door of the house. He reached for the doorknob, but it eluded his grasp. Instead the twin doors retreated, and he found himself staring into the wide, eager eyes of his young sons.

"You boys look after your mama like I said?" John asked, bending down to confront the children eye-to-eye.

"We did our best, Papa," Michael said.

"Me, too," Peter chimed in.

"Well, I don't suppose a pair of fine strong boys like yourselves would be interested in a ride upstairs?"

"Please, Papa," the children begged, and John hoisted each up to one shoulder, then started toward the staircase.

"Did you shoot a grizzly bear this time, Papa?" little Peter whispered.

"He doesn't shoot bears anymore," Michael declared. "He just makes sure the gold mine's all right."

"That so, Papa?" Peter asked.

"Grizzlies aren't much fun, Peter. But if you have to shoot one," John said, gazing seriously up at the boy, "you never do it in the warm months. His hide's no good for a coat till fall."

John reached the top of the stairs and lowered the boys to the floor. He squeezed their necks lightly, and they ran their small hands along his weary back.

"I'm glad you're back, Papa," Michael said, holding onto John's hand.

John hugged them against him, then shuffled them along down the hall. He then turned and gazed below as Marie approached the first step of the staircase.

"I wondered what had become of you," she called out. "We heard you ride up."

"You left me in good hands."

"They're always anxious to see you again."

He nodded, then smiled at the picture Marie painted climbing the stairs. She'd pinned her hair up so that only a pair of curls on each side fell across her forehead. She wore a lovely yellow gown with swirling red roses embroidered on the skirt.

"I missed you," she said, embracing him warmly.

"I missed you, too," he whispered.

"You usually say it's good to be home."

"Is that what this is, Marie? Home? It doesn't feel like it. Lately more than ever I feel like I don't belong."

"Don't belong? Your children are here, Johnny. I watch you with the boys, holding them on your shoulders, telling them nighttime stories, and I can't imagine you being anywhere else."

"I love them, Marie. I love you. But I just don't feel that I know who I am anymore. I was more at home on the trail back from Mariesville than I've been in this house. We don't belong here."

"Of course we do," she argued. "We built this house. Why, I remember how you insisted we put in the ballroom so we could entertain our friends."

"Friends? These neighbors of ours?"

"Well, they might be a little friendlier if you'd leave your horse at the Columbia and take a carriage to the house. Wearing pistols may be wise on the trail, but it doesn't attract many friends in Denver."

"Are you ashamed of me?'

"I'm not, and I could never be, Johnny Wilson. You've made me proud more times than I can recall. I know it's difficult fitting in, becoming a part of society, but we're rich now. If we are accepted, the children will be, too. That's what I want for them. They should never have to scratch for their survival like we did."

"That's funny," John said, sighing as his mind filled with a dozen memories. "When I was at the house in Mariesville, I kept gazing over at the orphans. There I was, eating apple pie, sitting in a dining room bigger than any cabin I ever wintered in, and I couldn't help envying those orphans."

"What?"

"Their world's just beginning, Marie, and I feel like mine's over. What do I do? Buy other people's businesses, play with them for a while, then find somebody who really knows what he's doing and turn the work over to him."

"You just haven't found what interests you," she told him. "In the beginning, I was nervous about coming here. I wouldn't be cooking and cleaning, not with maids and a cook. We even hired a nurse to tend the children. But I became interested in the house. Now I work buying furniture, redecorating rooms, making everything perfect. There's the orphanage, too. Soon we'll open one here in Denver, I hope. There's such a need."

Yes, John told himself. She occupies herself redecorating rooms, swapping one piece of furniture for another. And me? I'm equally useless here in Denver or riding back and forth to Mariesville. Why go at all when I know Art Jennings has everything in hand?

"Nancy will have dinner ready soon," Marie finally whispered. "Come on. Let's see if we can find you a bath. You're filthy from the trail, and you haven't seen Joanna and Timothy. They're in the nursery."

She took his hand, and John followed her meekly toward the nursery. He sat on a soft couch cradling little Tim in his arms while Joanna played with his boot.

"Glad Papa's back?" he asked.

"Yes, Papa," Joanna said, hugging her father tightly.

John scratched Tim's chin, and the boy smiled an answer. Their mother soon collected the children, though, and John left to get his bath.

Neither the bath in lilac-scented water nor the wonderful dinner of pork chops and mashed potatoes made John feel more at home. He bid Marie and the children an early good-night, then crawled onto the big feather bed in his bedroom and tried to catch some sleep.

It proved to be anything but a restful night. The lilac fragrance annoyed him first, and the bed was so soft he felt as if the world were turning him over every few minutes like a fried egg. He was staring at the plain white ceiling when Marie slid under the blanket and rested her head on his shoulder.

"Still awake?" she asked. "I thought you'd be fast asleep. You appeared so tired at dinner tonight."

"I am tired, but . . . I don't know. After sleeping on

a slat bed last night and on straw the two nights before, this is all too soft, too easy."

"Well, I'm sorry, Johnny. I'll see a slat bed's brought here tomorrow for you."

"I don't mean to complain," he said, sighing. "It's not your fault. I'm just feeling old, seeing so many things change, so many of our old friends gone with no one their equal happening along."

"You have to give the neighbors a chance, Johnny. They're not all snobs."

He sighed, then closed his eyes. But when sleep finally came, it wasn't peaceful. Soon John found himself in a dream. He was walking beside the stream eight years before. There were no row houses, no town, no mine, no big house or nest of kids.

He waded into the water, then shoveled sand into the sluice box. There was no gold, not even a hint of a nugget. He worked away until sweat ran down his bare arms and chest. He slaved away as if there were no tomorrow. But the gold remained as elusive as ever.

Yes, that's how it was, John told himself. He expected any moment to strike the vein, for Shep to appear with his powder charges, to blast away the face of the mountain and revel in the glory hole beneath.

In the end, though, there was nothing. No gold, no fortune, no future. Instead a dark-eyed figure appeared on horseback, swinging a scythe at John as though John were a stalk of wheat at harvest time.

"Death," John mumbled as the nightmare unfolded. Death chased only John at first, but soon it appeared willing to stalk Marie and the children as well. The dark figure struck out with its harsh blows, sending drought and famine, pestilence and hardship, a November snow or a breath of sunlight on a rocky ridge.

"Johnny?" Marie whispered as he shook violently. Death chased the little ones, shrieked terribly so that Michael and Peter shrank back in horror. "Johnny, what is it?"

"Nothing," he said, shaking the nightmare away. Its horror persisted, though.

"Then, go back to sleep," she told him.

"Just how do I do that?" he asked. "It's funny, but I never had trouble sleeping on the hard floor, with nothing beneath me but a blanket and the cold, cruel earth."

"You really do miss it, don't you?" Marie asked. "Are you forgetting what it was like, how we could never be sure a passing stranger might not kill us for our flour? We never ate properly. I spent those years praying we'd escape the hardships, that my children would have something better."

"I've been thinking about that, Marie. What will they have? Nancy cooks them almost anything they desire, including pies and cakes on a regular basis. They have more books to read than I would have imagined. Timothy has more leather in his tiny boots than I had in a pair till I was twenty-five. I wonder if we're not making it too easy for them. What will they do when they run up against a problem? Nancy and you and I won't always be around. How will they develop self-reliance."

"They'll have money to rely on."

"Money can be spent, can be lost, can disappear faster than you'd believe possible. I was talking to Art, Marie. He's built a lodge of sorts on that piece of land upstream from Mariesville. I want us to go up there for the summer. It'll be cooler than Denver, and the children will have a chance to learn the ways of the high country."

"Timothy and Joanna are too young for that kind of experience. Maybe you should take Michael and Peter."

"And you?"

"I couldn't leave the little ones, Johnny."

"It would be nothing if you didn't come," he said sadly. "Marie, we can leave Joanna and the baby with Mrs. Fitch. She was pestering me for a chance to look after Timothy, and she loves Joanna like her own. If you get too lovesick for them, you can ride down to the house."

"You're sure you want to do this?"

"Yes, Marie darling," he said, pulling her over against him. "See, I was raised on a mountain, and there are things I want to pass on. I want that part of me that my father and uncle put there to grow within the children, to give them a sense of belonging to something greater than they've known before."

"Are you sure they're ready?" she asked. "Fishing and swimming may sound like a great adventure, but living among rattlesnakes and wolves and bears is a lot more than a challenge for a seven-year-old."

"We'll be along to see they come to no harm, Marie. You'll love it. Mornings we'll fry ham and eggs. For dinner we'll have venison and trout."

"Provided you catch some," she said, laughing.

"We will. You'll see, Marie. It will be wonderful."

III

Those remaining weeks of spring flew by. Where before John had drifted between meaningless tasks, he suddenly found himself concentrating on the family trip to the mountains, dreaming of introducing Michael and Peter to the power and majesty of the mountains and the magic of living a simpler, if often harder, life.

John had hoped to leave Denver in early June, but spring had arrived late, and heavy rains toward the end of May turned roads into quagmires. Marie had to provide for the upkeep of the house, and John had to meet the hotel managers and newspaper editors, factory managers and attorneys. It was July by the time all the details had been dealt with. Eager to escape the capital before some other calamity delayed their departure, John kept the servants up half the night loading luggage and supplies into the two wagons that would carry the family westward.

"Quite a contrast to heading north with everything we owned packed on the back of a mule, huh?" John asked Marie as she sat beside him on the driver's seat of the first wagon.

"Don't forget," she whispered as he started the wagon in motion. "I rode that mule."

They left an hour before dawn, largely to appease Marie. She dreaded rumbling down the avenue with the neighbors staring in wild-eyed wonder. The children sat on a bench behind their parents, slumbering away without a care in the world. The second wagon was driven by Philip Gregg, Ezra's oldest boy, and Aaron Stamp, an ex-territorial marshal hired by Art Jennings as a sort of unofficial bodyguard.

"You needn't give your safety another thought," Stamp had said as they'd left. "I've taken payrolls to the mine a half-dozen times along this road, and no one's touched so much as a nickel of that money. Ran across a few venturesome types once, and we attended to them easily enough. Since then the outlaws leave my wagons be."

John had smiled. Stamp was as out of place in Denver as John himself. Behind the ex-marshal's winning smile and thick blond hair were eyes as cold and deadly as a rattlesnake's. It was a comfort having a man like that around.

Actually, the only incident on the three days to Mariesville that marred the journey was Philip Gregg's twisting of an ankle. Marie bound the foot quickly, then drove the second wagon several hours while Philip sat with the supplies, his foot suspended atop a flour barrel.

"I never knew Mama could drive a wagon," Michael told his father. "When'd she learn?"

"Before you were born," John told the boy. "You'll find she can do quite a number of things. Pretty soon you'll be doing a few your own self."

Once they arrived at Mariesville, Stamp took his leave, and Art Jennings sent a handful of men from the mine to take the supplies to the cabin. Beforehand Marie had them unload two crates of new pewter plates at the orphanage, along with some new schoolbooks and several bolts of cloth which the girls at the home would convert into clothing. Marie then busied herself introducing Joanna and little Timothy to Mrs. Fitch. John took the older boys with him on a tour of the mine.

Michael was impressed by the miners.

"I thought you just picked it up off the ground," Michael told one of the brawny workers.

"Only if somebody puts it there, littl'un," the miner said, smiling a toothless grin. "Mostly we digs it out."

Peter clung to his father's side as they followed a more venturesome Michael down the dark corridor.

"Nothing to be afraid of, Peter," John assured the six-year-old. "We'll be back in the light before long."

"And I'll be glad," Peter replied.

That night Mrs. Fitch treated them to fried chicken and roasted ears of corn.

"What? No apple pie?" John asked as he emptied his plate.

"With cream on top," Mrs. Fitch said, producing the pie as if by magic.

"You're a wonder, Mrs. Fitch," Marie declared. "You keep the house sparkling, and the dinner's simply marvelous. We have a staff of five back home who don't do as well. Ever considered leaving Mariesville?"

"Well, ma'am, I take that for a compliment, but to tell you the truth, I'd miss the orphans. I'm a little like a granny to them all, and I admit to enjoying that part of the job. I've little to spend what money I make on, what my own dear Daniel in his grave these ten years and the children all grown and married off."

"Mariesville couldn't do without Mrs. Fitch," John said, shaking his head. "If she wasn't here, no telling what trouble I'd get myself into when I visited here."

"Don't you believe a word of it," Mrs. Fitch said, laughing so that her rotund belly shook. "He's a saint, that one. It does a woman good to hear all this chatter in her dining room, though. A house misses the ring of children's voices."

"You may be glad of the quiet after Joanna and Timothy," John said, laughing. "The good Lord never intended little ones should walk or talk. I'm convinced of that!"

Joanna looked up at the mention of her name, but little Tim only went on playing with his slice of pie. Peter and Michael laughed and whispered to each other. Marie lightly tapped her fork on the table and nodded in their direction. The whispering stopped.

After a sound sleep and a generous breakfast of ham and eggs, biscuits, and string potatoes, John gathered up the children and prepared for the journey on to the cabin.

"You behave Mrs. Fitch now, little ones," John said, giving a farewell kiss to Joanna, then cradling Timothy in his arms as he walked onto the veranda. "We'll be just over that hill there, so don't you fear. No grizzlies will bother your dreams."

The child giggled, and John hugged him.

"I'd best leave you to your mother now," John told Timothy, setting the boy on the decking and waving Peter and Michael toward the awaiting wagon.

Marie spoke her good-byes, and Mrs. Fitch handed John a lunch basket.

"Aren't many chickens on that mountain, Mr. John," she whispered. "Now, don't you work Miz Marie too hard. And use a gentle hand with the lads."

"I promise, Mrs. Fitch," John said, raising his right hand as if in a courtroom. "You watch the little ones. They haven't often been away from their mama."

"They aren't far now, Mr. John. It's not so far you won't want to visit."

John nodded, though in his heart he hoped to wall himself off from Mariesville, from the world of row houses and smoking chimneys, roads and cities.

"It's time we were off," he finally called out, stepped down from the veranda and walking to where two boys from the orphanage had brought the wagon.

"Thanks, Henry," John told the older of the two, taking the reins from the boy and leaving a half-dollar in their place.

"Have a good journey, Mr. John," Henry said, making a series of exaggerated bows as he showed the coin to his companion. Then the boys raced off toward town.

"They really don't have a mama or papa?" Peter asked as Marie lifted the boys into the wagon.

"None at all?" Michael asked.

"Oh, most of them had parents once," Marie explained as John shook the horses into motion. "Some of their mothers and fathers abandoned them, just rode off and left them on their own. Other parents died, or took ill."

"You wouldn't ever leave us, would you?" Peter asked, huddling against his brother.

"Who'd we leave you with," John joked. "Nobody'd take you. Besides, how would I get along without my sidekicks?"

"We're never leaving you, boys," Marie said more seriously.

"You've leaving Joanna and Tim," Michael reminded them.

"Oh, not exactly," Marie objected. "We just thought you two don't always get enough attention, and Mrs. Fitch gets lonely. So for a while Joanna and Timothy are staying with her. And we're going back there. That I'll guarantee."

"I thought so," Michael said, nodding his head firmly. "It wouldn't make much sense for you to leave us when you build a big house for all those other kids."

"You're right, Michael," John said as he turned the wagon past the orphanage and down toward the creek. "The orphanage was your mother's idea. When we lived in the gold camps, we used to see a lot of those abandoned children."

"Yes," Marie said, sighing. "Dozens of them."

John had prepared a funny story about the first pair of urchins Marie had taken in at Mariesville, but something in her eye quieted him. Instead he waited for her to speak.

"I remember the first time I came up here, boys," she said, rubbing a tear from the corner of her eyes. "I'd been down at a place called Putnam's Creek. I was a camp orphan of sorts myself at the time, and your father asked if I'd care to head north with him to his cabin."

"And you said yes," Michael spoke up.

"I was hard to turn down," John explained. "I was

such a handsome devil."

The boys laughed, but Marie scowled.

"The truth is, I was worried he might starve if he wintered on his own cooking," she told them. "Now, let me finish. We rode up here, the two of us, supplies hanging off our animals, your papa on a big yellow-brown mare and me on a worn-out pack mule. I thought then, and I still do, that this was the most beautiful place on the face of the earth. The mountains to the north towered one over the next, and the creek was bluer than the sky. Deer used to run in and out of the pines, and an eagle flew in a great circle overhead."

She paused long enough for the boys to imagine the scene. Except for the deer and the eagle, nothing much had changed.

"We had a little flour, some sugar and coffee, salt, and powder. But mostly we lived off the land," she said, suddenly breaking into a wide smile. "I'm prouder of that time than any other period of my whole life."

"Me, too," John added. "That's why we brought you boys here, to share a little bit of that life with you."

"It's special here," Marie said, resting her head on John's shoulder. "For us, at least. I hope it will be the same for you."

John glanced back at the boys. Both were smiling, and he reached back to touch their shoulders.

Once they reached the cabin, though, John began to realize he'd brought his children to a foreign world.

"Who's going to unload the wagon?" Michael asked. "Where's Philip?"

"Staying at the orphanage to help Mr. Jennings with some repairs," John explained. "We're going to unload the wagon and tend to the horses. All the heavy things are already in the cabin. All we have to bother with are our clothes, a few boxes and—"

"We didn't have servants when your father and I first arrived here," Marie said, drawing the boys to her. "Think of this like a game. Pretend we've opened up a magic door and gone back in time."

"I don't want to," Peter complained.

"It won't hurt you a bit," John said, waving Michael over. "To start with, we're going to unharness the horses. I'll show you how it's done. Then you'll be able to help next time."

But as John explained his actions, the boys shrank back in terror. The horses had seemingly become dragons, belching fire, tearing the earth with their claws.

"Come here, Peter," John said, pulling the smaller boy over so that he could touch the steamy nose of the animals. "See. She wouldn't hurt you."

Peter remained unconvinced, and Michael wouldn't even lead the second horse over to the rope corral the miners had thrown up in the nearby meadow.

It got no better. Michael and Peter both grumbled about carrying boxes of food inside the cabin, and they refused to tug the heavier flour sacks. John sent them off with their mother for a talk while he unloaded the wagon by himself.

"It's all foreign to them, Johnny," she explained as she filled a cupboard with supplies. The boys sat on the steps, tossing rocks at a nearby pine.

"I don't know what to do," John admitted. "I fell like they're strangers, like I don't even know my own sons."

"It must seem that way to them, too," she said, softly squeezing his hands. "We've never told them anything about our life out here. All they've known is that we have money, that we wear fine clothes, eat off china plates, sleep on feather beds. They don't understand this life. That's our doing, Johnny. It's what we wanted for them."

"It is not!" John shouted so that the boys looked up.

"We wanted for them to have it easier, to be loved and nurtured."

"I never wanted them to be lazy," John said sadly. "I never dreamed they'd feel above doing simple work. Do you suppose they look down on Philip, on us? Are we raising another pair of snobs who'll look down their noses when their father rides his horse up the hill?"

The notion tortured John, tied his insides into knots. He couldn't bear it. These were the grandsons of Zeke Thompson. Their roots were in the mountains, in the land of the Medicine Bow and its Cheyenne magic. Their blood was the same shed by Crook and Mackenzie a half decade before in the Bighorn Mountains.

Have I waited too long to tell them? John asked himself. Have I buried my past so deeply that I've robbed my children of their heritage?

That night John spread out blankets beside the fireplace, then helped the boys arrange their clothes in neat piles against the wall.

"Can't we put something soft underneath us?" Michael asked, hesitating to crawl between the blankets. "Some straw maybe?"

"Tell you what, Michael," John told the seven-year-old. Tomorrow you go outside, round up all the pine needles you can find. They'll make you a soft bed under your blankets."

"And tonight?"

"You sleep like the rest of us. Trust me. It will be warm enough with the fire going."

An owl hooted in the distance then, and Peter grabbed John's arm.

"Are there wolves out here, Papa?"

"Of course not," John said, laughing. "That's an owl. In a week you'll learn that for yourself."

"If a grizzly doesn't eat us," Michael grumbled.

"It won't," John told them as he slipped Peter back into bed. "I know this place seems frightening to you, boys, but it shouldn't. Your people have always lived in the mountains. Your grandfather was a giant of a man, tall, strong, proud. Once he wrestled a grizzly bear with his bare hands. There wasn't anyone around to do it for him. It was fight or die.

"When I was little, my father thought I spent too much time with books. I loved to read about the wider world, and he always knew I'd one day leave his mountain. Even so, he took care to show me how to hunt and fish. He sent me to my uncle to learn the Cheyenne ways. My cousin taught me how to stalk game, how to ride like the wind and vanish like a shadow into the forest."

"Where was all that?" Michael asked, taking interest for the first time.

"In a place to the north, far away from here," John said, a great sadness gripping his heart. "I left there when I was sixteen. All I knew as family were dead, and the place I'd called home was taken away."

"Did you ever go back?" Michael asked.

"No," John admitted. "It proved too far a journey, and nothing remains of the world I once knew. Even here, in these mountains, I can smell the town over the hill. There won't be many more chances to know the earth, to become one with the land as your mother I were once one with this place. It's why we brought you, to teach you."

John gazed at the faces of the boys reflected in the dancing light of the fire. Michael, his Cheyenne grandmother's deep brown eyes flashing beneath a forehead overrun by strands of delicate walnut-colored hair, looked lost and bewildered. Peter, his face full of fear, his bright sky-blue eyes lacking his mother's boldness, trembled like a leaf in the autumn breeze.

Yes, John thought as he lay on his blankets, feeling cold in spite of Marie's tender touch. Thompson's Mountain lies a lifetime away, and that's very far indeed.

IV

The following morning John awoke to find the boys nestled against his side. He sat up slowly, carefully, to avoid disturbing their rest. Maybe Marie was right. They seemed so small, so vulnerable. Even Michael, who could put up a brave front at times, seemed terribly defenseless just now, clutching the blankets in his small hands, the nightshirt swallowing his slender shoulders.

"It's time we woke them," Marie whispered. "I'll start breakfast."

She crawled out of her blankets and slipped into her clothes as John drew the blanket back from Michael's chin.

"Son, morning's here," John whispered, cradling the boy's head in his hand. As John drew Michael forward, the dark-haired child crawled up his father's arm and rested against John's chest.

"Hey, what's this?" John asked, resting Michael on one shoulder like a flour sack. "Is this a bag of potatoes?"

As his father tickled his ribs, Michael squirmed with delight.

"It's me," Michael managed to say between giggles. "Stop, Papa, please."

John saw a different plea in little Michael's eyes, though. It'd been weeks, maybe months, since they'd joined in such foolishness, and there was a comfort in feeling the power in John Wilson's large, rough hands.

The frolicking woke Peter, and the smaller boy quickly crawled over and joined in the fun. John found himself beset by a pair of little demons, and he finally surrendered.

"We'd best clean ourselves up," John declared. "Your mama'll have breakfast cooking soon enough."

The mention of food brought instant obedience. The three shed their nightclothes and dressed themselves. The boys followed their father's example and rolled their blankets against the wall. Michael even rolled up his mother's bed.

John nodded his approval, then filled a wash basin with water and rinsed his face and hands. The boys eagerly followed suit. Washing up before breakfast was a long-established ritual. But when Marie spooned portions of bubbling oatmeal in bowls, the youngsters' eyes filled with disappointment.

"No eggs?" Peter asked. "I thought . . ."

"There are no chickens here," Marie explained. "I want you to eat as your father and I did."

"I could've sworn I packed a basket of eggs," John said, scratching his head.

"You're not the king of the pantry, sir," she told him. "You know how easily eggs turn in the July heat. I returned them to Mrs. Fitch's larder. You haven't lost your taste for oatmeal?"

"No," he said, sprinkling sugar over the sticky glop

and spooning a bite into his mouth. Lose my taste? he thought. Never had it in the first place.

"I wish we were back home," Peter grumbled when all the bowls had finally been emptied. "Nancy always cooked us bacon and flapjacks or ham and eggs."

"Wait till dinner," John said, laughing at the frowning boys. "We'll go down to the creek and pick us up a string of rainbows."

"You can't eat a rainbow," Peter said, laughing as he sketched an arc in the air and tried to gobble it.

"Trout," John explained. "Come on. You can help."

John headed away from the table and waved for the children to follow. Michael bounded along at his father's side, but Peter hesitated.

"Maybe I can help Mama," the little boy mumbled.

"Get along with you," Marie said, sweeping him out the door with a broom.

John drew a length of string and some hooks from his chest in the back of the wagon. He then led the way down the creek toward a stand of willows.

"They're perfect for poles," John explained. But as they arrived, they discovered the willows shielded a favorite swimming spot. Two dozen boys from the orphanage were putting it to good use before morning chore time arrived.

"Somebody's comin'," one of the older boys cried out in alarm.

"It's only Mr. John," another announced, and the boys continued their splashing and shouting.

"Good morning," John told them as he searched for a trio of branches suitable for fishing poles. "Seen any trout?"

"Caught one with my feet!" a boy of ten shouted,

306

waving the fish in the air.

"Don't catch them all," John said. "I plan to do that myself."

"Yes, sir," the scrawny fisherman answered with a broad smile.

"You don't really catch them with your feet, do you, Papa?" Michael asked as John broke off the branches and stripped off various leaves and twigs.

"Only if they happen by while you're swimming," John said, laughing.

He then nudged Michael and Peter upstream to a rocky bend of the creek. Two aspens offered shade, and John motioned for the boys to sit down.

"Papa, is that their bathtub?" Peter asked, pointing back toward the orphans.

"They're swimming," John said, laughing. "Of course I know some boys that never get much closer than that to a bath."

"I've never seen anybody swim like that," Michael declared, shaking his head. "They're all naked."

"That's how it's done, Michael. We might even try it ourselves a little later, when the sun heats things up."

The boys exchanged glances, then shook their heads. John only smiled and began tying a line to each pole. He then added a hook and dug around the base of the trees for worms. A handful of long, squirmy creatures was quickly located, and John baited the hooks.

"Now hold onto your pole, boys," John said, handing Michael a rod and helping the boy sling the line into the creek. "Wait for a tug. Then turn the pole so that the string winds around it. That way you draw the fish to you bit by bit."

"That looks easy," Peter said, eagerly reaching for his

own pole.

"It's easy if the trout are cooperative," John said, smiling as the youngsters stared in anticipation at their lines.

"Does it take a long time?" Peter asked.

"Sometimes," John said, kicking off his boots. "Might be best if you shed your shoes and stockings. It's cooler, and if you have to wade in after a fish, you won't ruin your shoes."

John set the example by peeling off his stockings and rolling up his trouser legs. He then held the poles while the boys did likewise.

Peter was the first to get a nibble. At first the boy wasn't sure what to do. John set down his own pole and helped the boy shorten the line. Then as the trout moved into the shallows, John waded out, cradled the fish to shore and removed the hook. He then tied the fish off on a string anchored securely to the closest aspen.

"How big is he?" Michael asked.

"See for yourself," John said, pulling the string out of the water long enough for the boys to stare at the long, shimmering body of the trout. "Another three or four, and we'll have our dinner."

"We're going to eat him?" Peter asked, his eyes filling with alarm. "He's too pretty."

"It's that or go hungry," John explained. "Now grab a worm and bait your hook."

"I can't," Peter said, backing away from the bloody hook.

"This isn't just for fun, boys. It's how we get our dinner. It's how we survived out here. The mountain provides all a man needs to grow tall and strong. There are roots and berries, fish and birds, deer and elk."

"Nancy never hunts," Michael pointed out.

"No. In Denver we buy our food from someone who raises the animals or hunts the game. But here we rely on ourselves."

John shook his head and again showed Peter how to bait the hook. But even after a half-dozen trout had been pulled from the stream, neither of the boys showed any inclination toward baiting a hook. John knew better than to suggest they clean the trout. He and Marie would do it later.

"Now, how about a swim?" John asked, shedding his sweaty shirt. "I'm hot."

"Me, too," Michael said, unbuttoning his shirt. But when John shed his trousers and drawers, Michael grew less ambitious.

"Come on, boys," John said, plunging into the cool creek.

Michael carefully searched in all directions, then slipped out of his clothes and tiptoed into the water. Peter, staring at his brother in disappointment, finally shrugged his shoulders and followed.

"Feels good, doesn't it?" John asked, sitting in the shallows and resting one boy on each knee. "Now, do you know how to swim?"

Michael shook his head, and Peter did likewise.

"Want to learn?" John asked.

The heads continued to shake.

"It's not so hard," John said. "Let me teach you."

He then started toward the deeper stretch of the creek, balancing each boy carefully so that they remained atop the surface.

"Papa, no!" Peter cried when John released his hand.

Peter grabbed John's shoulder and whimpered.

"Michael?" John asked.

"You sure it's safe?"

"I'm right here," John assured the boy as he swung Peter around so that the smaller boy rested on his father's shoulders.

Michael thrashed about a little, but there was too much panic in his strokes. John relaxed the boy, then held out his arm. Michael took the arm and practiced his kicking.

"That's the way, Michael," John declared. "Now take a deep breath, then release it." Michael did so, and soon John felt the tension in the seven-year-old's arms ease. Finally John told Michael to draw the water toward him, and Michael was swimming.

"I'm doing it!" Michael said, splashing awkwardly. "Hey, Peter, it's not so hard!"

But Peter wasn't convinced. The frail little boy clung to his father's shoulder, and John finally abandoned the effort.

"Did your papa teach you to swim?" Michael asked as they returned to the shallows.

"My brother," John answered sadly.

"I didn't know we had an uncle," Michael said, leaning his head against his father's chest. "Does he live on that faraway mountain?"

"He died there," John explained, swallowing the sadness that was threatening to engulf him. "He was shot and killed when I was only sixteen."

"Is that when this happened?" Michael asked, running his small hand across the great, purple scar on John's stomach.

"I was hurt, too," John said, nodding. He pointed to

the smaller, rounded scars on his arm, the misshapen leg.

"It must've been terrible," Michael said after John told of the long, lonely journey south.

"It wasn't so bad," John objected. "Each time I thought I couldn't continue, wouldn't survive another mile, another minute, I held on. That way I knew I was stronger, that even when things turned against me, I could carry on. Afterward, I met your mother, and we made a good life for ourselves."

John babbled on about cold winters and scorching summers, about days spent digging till the dust choked half the life from him. But the boys understood none of it, and John finally stopped.

"I guess we'd better get back to the cabin," he announced.

"Yes," Michael agreed. "Those girls from the orphans' home might come here."

John tickled the skinny ribs of his sons, then pulled them close. He wanted so much to share himself, to give them the best part of their father born of mountain hardship and a lifetime of pain. But those things had to be learned in moments of trial and suffering. They couldn't be passed down like a war bonnet or a medicine arrow.

Back at the cabin, John turned the boys over to Marie. She fed them dried beef and slices of bread Mrs. Fitch had sent along. John, meanwhile, cleaned the fish. When he finished, he walked off alone across the hillside, gazing below as a hundred memories raced through his head. But as he turned back toward the cabin, he realized that the past he treasured above the present must remain buried, set aside, lest it sweep him away from Marie and the children, shatter the world so carefully crafted those last few years.

Over a dinner of trout and biscuits, Marie recounted episodes of their life on the mountain. The boys listened, but clearly their thoughts were elsewhere.

John tried again that next day to impart some sense of the past, some particle of the rich heritage to the boys he loved more than life. But in the end, it was a failed project.

"We'll go back tomorrow," he told Marie as they spread out their blankets. "I can tell you miss the little ones, and we're only making Michael and Peter miserable."

"I wouldn't be so sure."

"I am," he said, sighing. "It's not the same, Marie. We've tried so hard, but it was a fool's errand to try and go back to something best left behind."

"But Nancy and Ezra won't expect us for another week."

"We can stay at the house in Mariesville. I wouldn't mind visiting the orphanage, and Art's been after me to ride after elk in the high meadows."

"It wasn't a fool's errand, Johnny," Marie whispered as she pulled him against her. "I found out I miss it, too. Maybe when they're older, they'll open up more, see what's in our hearts."

"Maybe."

But inside he wondered.

V

With a heavy heart John repacked the wagon that next morning and set out for Mariesville. Once the tall house with the blue trim had been home, but that, like so much, had been swept away by the winds of change. He listened to the laughter of the boys that cut like daggers through his heart. They weren't born of the mountain. They'd never been touched by the spirits of the clouds and the sky, of the sun and the moon and the stars.

Now I know what Pa felt, John told himself. He thought I was cut off from the earth. He was wrong, though, and maybe I am, too.

That was the sole flicker of hope. Maybe, somewhere deep within them, the chill of a mountain stream or the voice of a midnight owl might kindle an ancient, half-buried instinct, a respect for the earth and those who walked it.

It didn't take long for word of John's return to reach the mine. Mrs. Fitch was serving supper when Art Jennings arrived at the door.

"Come along in and join us, Mr. Jennings," Mrs. Fitch said, a warm smile spreading across her face. "It's a treat indeed for me to serve a full table."

"Thought I might be in time to eat," Art said, removing his hat and following the old woman into the dining room. "Can't imagine anyone passing up the chance to taste one of Hanna's pies."

"Today it's peach," Peter said, turning his fork over in his small, thin fingers. "I looked."

"Young people ought not to venture into strange kitchens," Mrs. Fitch said, shaking her finger at the boy. "Could be you'll poke your nose right into a mousetrap one of these days."

"It's not good manners to spy on people," Marie scolded. "I don't want to hear of a repeat performance, understand, young man?"

"But Nancy—"

"We're not in Denver," Marie said in the unmistakable tone that always ended discussion. "Now let's attend to our supper."

Peter nodded, and Michael cracked a smile. Little Tim and Joanna seemed delighted to find their older brother in trouble.

"Hope you're not planning to head back straightaway," Art said once the conversation had settled down to less serious matters. "The Gregg boy's far from finished with his labors, and I sent Stamp off on an errand."

"No, we still won't leave before Thursday," John said. "Mrs. Fitch wouldn't let the little ones escape before that, would you?"

Hanna Fitch blushed, and Marie joined in the laughter.

"There are some things I had in mind to talk over with you," Art explained. "But more important, young

Donald O'Keefe says the far ridge is swarming with turkeys. I haven't had a proper turkey roasted for dinner in better than a year now. I thought if we bagged a pair, Hannah might—"

"Simmer it in my oven," the cook broke in. "Boil some of those little potatoes and slice some carrots, top it off with greens. It'd be a feast fit for a king."

"Does sound tempting," John admitted.

"Then, why don't you join me at the bridge around dawn. You do still have that Winchester?"

"Sure do," John said, smiling as he envisioned the hunt.

"Bring the boys if you like."

John glanced at Michael, then at Peter. Neither seemed eager to go. John shook his head.

"Well, there'll be time another year," Art said, devoting himself to his supper.

"Yes, there's always time," Marie agreed.

John didn't share their optimism, though. He finished his food, then walked Art to the door.

"Don't expect too much of them," Art warned. "I've got three boys myself, and none of them took to my work. One, as you know, is a teacher. The others read the law. Fine professions all, but I've little in common with any of them."

"That's what I worry about, Art."

"It's the nature of boys, John. Don't let it occupy your thoughts. All a father can really hope for is health and happiness for his children."

"I suppose," John grumbled.

He spent the rest of the day cleaning and oiling the Winchester. The rifle felt cold in his hands, and again he recalled other times when he'd readied himself for deadlier confrontations. Shooting turkeys was nothing compared to raiding railroad supply wagons or facing bands of bounty hunters.

An hour before daylight John saddled one of the spry young stallions kept at the orphanage. He felt strangely young. For the first time in weeks he'd managed to escape the shadows of despair that had been choking him. Hunting required concentration, caution. It chased other thoughts from the mind. John was actually smiling when he slipped the old Winchester into a saddle scabbard and mounted the tall ebony horse. He tapped the horse's rear and broke into a gallop.

"You look fit to ride in a parade down State Street," Art announced when John reached the bridge. "Beautiful horse."

"The boys at the home take good care of him," John explained. "It's a good craft, handling horses."

"A dying one, though," Art commented. "Like candlemaking or spinning cloth. Factories are doing it all. As for horses, well, the range is half fenced already, and it won't be long before there's a railroad stretching between every two towns with a name."

"Could be," John admitted. "It'll be sad, though. A man with a horse has independence. I hate the notion of being chained to railroad schedules and innkeeper's hours."

Art laughed, then led the way past the simple wooden buildings that lay on the west end of town.

"Shep and I hunted elk up here," John said, recognizing familiar rocks and trees, warming as he passed meadows that had once crawled with deer, caves where bears had once lurked.

"Haven't seen an elk up here in years," Art said, frowning. "We shot a grizzly two summers past. Likely she was the last. Soon the turkeys'll leave, and there'll be only—"

"Us," John said, sighing. "Just the old-timers, the last ones who haven't moved on or been laid to rest."

"Maybe, but I think there'll always be a place where a man can stand tall, can make his own decisions, fight his own battles."

"I hope so, Art. But I look around me, and all I see is change. You walk down the streets back in Denver with a pistol on your hip, and people look at you like you're Jesse James, out to rob a bank. I've never fought change, but it's happening too fast. It's taking away some of the good things, part of what it's always meant to be alive."

"You mean the freedom," Art said as they started up the slope toward the far side of the ridge. "It's taking a lot of the danger, too. Now people don't risk their lives traveling a few hundred miles. Thousands died making the Oregon crossing."

"That same trail made a lot of others strong, though. You knew they could be counted on."

"For what? We've got laws now to send outlaws to prison. Shopkeepers don't have to join posses now."

John nodded his head and sighed as Art went on to list a hundred comforts people now enjoyed. But for each innovation, John thought of an ill effect. Only a blind man or an idiot could fail to recognize the plight of the poor and the homeless.

It was midmorning by the time they reached the meadow where the turkeys were suspected to roost. John and Art stepped down from their horses and wove a semicircle through the dense underbrush. Just as they'd begun to be discouraged, John heard the faint gurgle of a turkey call.

"There," John said, pointing to the right.

Jennings nodded, then stepped back so that John could lead the way.

Hunting turkeys in July wasn't easy, especially on a mountain littered with rock fragments and boulders, dotted by tall pines and graceful aspens, snarled by tangles of vines and brambles and haunted by shadowy figures. The birds fluttered through the forest, blending in with their surroundings. Only a trace of red amid a splash of green pine needles betrayed the presence of a turkey.

John spotted the first one not by sight but by sound. A slight movement through the underbrush, the awkward chortle, and John raised his rifle, advanced a shell into the firing chamber, then squeezed the trigger. The rifle barked, and the turkey cried out. Then, after flapping its wings, it fell lifeless.

The shot aroused the other birds, and several raced through the trees. The Winchester blasted again, and a second turkey dropped. Art Jennings fired, too, hitting still another bird.

"Not a bad day's work, eh?" Art asked as the remaining turkeys fled.

"Not much to it."

"Don't know that I'd say that," Art objected. "It's not every man who could slip through these woods, move like a whisper on the wind."

"I haven't forgotten everything."

"Come on. Let's gather the birds and head back."

John nodded and started toward the first turkey.

Before he'd taken three steps, he froze.

"Johnny?" Art asked.

"Shhh," John whispered, pointing toward the rocks to their left. A moment later a mountain cat appeared, growling so that the ground beneath their feet seemed to tremble.

"Lord, where'd he come from?" Art gasped.

"You gather the birds," John said, staring into the cougar's cold green eyes. "I'll watch him."

"Johnny?"

"Do it," John said impatiently.

Art Jennings collected each turkey in turn and dragged them along to the horses. John watched as the cat nudged ever closer.

I hold your death in my hands, John silently told the cougar. But I don't have the heart . . .

The cougar leaped, and John instinctively raised the rifle, fixed the cat's flying body in the sights, and fired. It all took but a second, the leap, the shot, the cougar's final step before a splinter of lead tore into its heart and ended life.

"Johnny!" Art screamed, racing over.

"He came right at me," John mumbled. "He gave me no choice."

"Cougars have a way of doing that. Nice shot."

"Sure."

John walked over and gazed down at the lifeless cat. Why hadn't it backed away, vanished back into the rocks. The way that cat had come on, there was no escape. For either of them.

"Aren't many of these old cats left up here," Art whispered.

"No," John said sadly. "Nor old creek panners like

you and me, either."

"Everyone has to grow with the times. Nothing stands still, not even the tall pines."

Yes, John thought as he dragged the cougar's carcass toward the horses. Maybe that cat just got tired of watching the elk, the deer, everything he knew, disappear. Sometimes the pain got so that you had to strike out at something, anything. Or maybe it was just time to have it over.

"You all right, Johnny?" Art called.

"A little tired," John confessed. "Nothing a good brisk ride won't cure."

Art had the three turkeys stuffed in a game bag and tied onto the back of his horse. John tied the cougar's still body across the back of his saddle. The horse shied, but John calmed it.

"I can find someone at the mine to skin him for you," Art offered.

"I'd like to see if I can't make a couple of vests from the pelt. For Michael and Peter. Kind of make up for them not having such a wonderful time up here."

"They're awful young, Johnny."

"I know. And lately I've been thinking I'm awfully old."

That thought still weighed heavily on John's mind the next day when he met again with Art Jennings, this time at the mine offices.

"Yesterday we talked about the past," Art began. "Now I'd like to bring up something else."

"The future?"

"We've got too big an operation up here to be carting gold bars to Denver in the backs of wagons. Supply takes forever, too."

"So what's the solution?"

"A rail spur."

"Spur?"

"I talked to some surveyors. They're planning a new line into the Rockies. The Denver and Rocky Mountain Railroad. The main line isn't far from Mariesville, and I'd guess they would agree to the spur."

"Wouldn't it be easier to swing the route through Mariesville?"

"You're talking about big money now, John. You'd have to buy into the line to convince them to make a change like that."

"Isn't that what you had in mind, Art?" John asked, smiling.

"Might be an investment you'd come to regret. A railroad will bring more people, development, change this valley more than the mine ever could."

"Progress," John muttered. "Bound to come sooner or later."

"A rail line would speed our supplies. The gold shipments would be safer, and you could come out here anytime you want and be there in half a day's time."

"I never mind the ride."

"I know," Art said, laughing. "But you'll still go along with the rail spur?"

"Or the line."

"The man you'll need to see is Franklin Hardy. He's the new line's president."

"And his office?"

"Is in Denver. But you'll be more successful seeing him at his home. You'll hear from him soon. I'm fairly certain you'll get a dinner invitation."

"You know how I hate doing business that way, Art.

All that small talk. It's just idle chatter and a waste of time."

"But that's how it's done, Johnny. Wait and see. I'll wager he's as eager to have your money as you are to have his railroad."

VI

Art Jennings had a gift for prophecy. John and his family hadn't been back in Denver three days before the invitation arrived. It was hand-delivered, briefly written in gold letters stamped on fine watermarked paper.

"I know you detest dinner parties, Johnny, but we are going to this one, aren't we?" Marie asked. "I've heard stories about the Hardy house. The interior's like a museum."

"Does that mean we'll be redecorating again?" he asked.

"Oh, you know how I am when I get a new idea. Now, are we going or not?"

"We have to," John told her. "Art won't have his rail spur otherwise."

Marie immediately sat down and wrote a note of acceptance. Then she dragged John to the tailor to have him fitted for a new suit.

"These are important people," she reminded him daily. "We have to look our best."

By the time the day of the dinner arrived, John was ready to forget he'd ever heard of Franklin Hardy. The new suit confined his knees, hurt his back, and its tight collar was enough to choke a normal man. Marie, on the other hand, seemed to bloom like a flower in her flowing pink gown.

"We won't be getting any business done around you," John told her. "Too much of a distraction."

"You don't think it's too showy?"

"Couldn't blame it if it was. You've got a right to show yourself to best advantage."

When they arrived at the Hardys', John was startled to discover he and Marie were the only guests expected. A tall, white-haired butler took Marie's shawl, then led them into a parlor.

John stood uncomfortably beside Marie. She pointed out the rich furnishings, the ornate masonry of the walls and the lovely paintings. John marveled at the beauty of the room, but he couldn't help feeling terribly out of place. He wasn't good at polite conversation, at flattering addle-minded idiots just because they happened to have a pile of money or a big house.

"Mr. and Mrs. John Wilson, sir," the butler then announced.

"Good evening," a distinguished man in a gray suit said as he approached John and shook his hand. "I'm Franklin Hardy. My wife Virginia's just a little late. Forgive her."

"I'm John Wilson," John replied, "and this is my wife, Marie."

"Charmed," Hardy said, taking Marie's hand and kissing it lightly. "If Mrs. Wilson doesn't object, I'll steal you for a time, John. My wife will be in shortly, and she wants to show you her house. I feel tours can become tiresome, but Virginia never lets a female guest escape without a grand tour."

"I'd enjoy that," Marie said. "You have such beautiful furniture."

"Well, then I assume we're pardoned, and we'll take our leave," Hardy said, leading John out a side door.

After passing through a narrow corridor, Hardy led the way inside a magnificent library. Books lined all four walls, stack upon stack of them from floor to ceiling. Other shelves three feet high occupied the center of the room. At the far end was a desk, table, and several chairs.

"I don't believe I've ever seen so many books," John told his host. "Histories of France and England, the plays of Aeschylus and Sophocles. I've only heard those names. I never thought I'd actually see their work."

"Yes, it's quite a collection," Hardy said, nodding to the books. "I'm partial to Mark Twain myself, though I rarely have time anymore for literature."

"A railroad can keep you busy," John said. "I suppose it's sometimes a challenge to acquire the right-of-way."

"Not so much as in the old days. Out here we place our route through public land much of the time. And many owners are so delighted to have the tracks pass through their town that they'll buy up the land and give it to us. Back in the old days it was tough. I've heard stories about how the old Union Pacific had the cavalry chase farmers off their land."

"Yes," John said, fighting back the bitterness that was boiling up inside him.

"This is my first route to manage, though, and we've acquired most of the right-of-way already. But I gather it's the route itself you wanted to discuss."

"You invited me," John reminded Hardy.

"Ah, well, I don't know that it really matters," Hardy said, opening a small box and drawing out a cigar. "Smoke?"

"No, thank you," John said, slowly shaking his head. "I've never taken to tobacco."

"Virginia deplores it, and I ought to give it up for her sake, I suppose. But the doctors have sworn me off alcohol, and a man is entitled to at least one vice."

"At least one," John said, laughing along with the railroader.

"So, let's take a look at the line," Hardy said, spreading out a map of the fledgling state of Colorado on his desk. He held the chart by placing a gold-plated miniature locomotive atop each corner.

"Mementos?" John asked.

"Vanity. I'm afraid I've become a collector. The railroads and I've grown up together, and I like to have little reminders of the past around me. Keep me from losing sight of my goals."

"Which are?"

"Likely the same as your own, John. To be rich, and to do what others say couldn't be done. I've crossed the Rockies once, working the line north out of California toward Salt Lake. Now I plan to open up Colorado."

"I'm not so concerned about the money, Mr. Hardy."

"Please, call me Frank."

"All right, Frank," John said, leaning over the map and pointing to Shepherd's Creek and the uncharted point where Mariesville should have appeared. "Mariesville needs a supply and shipping medium. Your line can provide it. You'll need fuel and water. There are plenty of both at Mariesville. You'll also need freight and passengers. Mariesville can provide those, too. What's more, I understand you might be thin on capital. I'm prepared to buy into the line to see my town prosper."

Hardy laughed loudly, and John frowned.

"Excuse my amusement, John," Hardy said, trying to steady himself. "My vice presidents told me you were an uneducated man, a buckskin-clad oaf from the gold camps who still wore pistols on the streets of Denver."

"Sometimes I am," John said, his eyes chilling Hardy so that the graying railroad president became silent. "But I never walk around an issue. It's plain we can serve each other's interests, and I see no reason for spending a year getting acquainted."

"Please continue."

"It seems to me the obvious choice is to swing your route up and cross Shepherd's Creek at Mariesville. I know that creek. It never floods so high a bridge would be in danger, and the route west follows the creek, then climbs gradually through a pass. It's gentle grade the whole way."

"Now you really are surprising me, John. You know something about routes and grades, do you?"

"I've had a previous experience with a railroad. It wasn't successful."

"I certainly hope that won't prejudice you against our venture. It's going to take some time to build, and we won't make a quick profit, but it'll be a steady money-maker fast enough."

"How long will it take you, and how much of an investment are you looking for?"

"We'll start in a week or two."

"You'll face rough weather after September."

"Yes, but we'll be at least to Mariesville by then."

"And the amount?"

"I hold forty percent myself. Ten percent is already public, and another twenty-five has been offered to a group of Denver businessmen."

"So it's the other quarter we're discussing."

"That's right, John. Of course, you need not take on the whole portion yourself."

"What do you figure the company's worth at present?"

"Once the stock's sold, two million."

"So you're wanting a half million for a quarter-interest."

"That's what we're asking, yes."

"And you'll take what, four hundred thousand if it's in cash?"

"You have that amount in cash?"

"My company digs gold from the ground, Frank," John said, smiling. "Even so, that's quite a sum."

"But you're prepared to offer it if we revise the route?"

"That's the deal."

"Then, I believe we're in agreement," Hardy said, taking a long, rich draw on his cigar. "I'll have the papers drawn up and the certificates issued. It's been a pleasure dealing with so straightforward a business-man."

"You were closer to the truth before," John said as

they shook hands. "My wife keeps at me to work on my manners, but I'm more at home on a mountainside than I am in a house like this. I do envy you the books, though."

"Then, I suppose I ought to make a confession myself," Hardy said, laughing even louder than before. "They were here when I bought the place. Borrow any you like."

"You mean . . ."

"I got my start swinging a sledge on the old Rock Island line. Truth is, I've always found it best to deal with men who've known hard work. They appreciate the value of a dollar, and they understand the limits you can impose on men and get the job done. Truth is, I sought you out not only because I had something of value to offer, but because you're lucky. Every time you do business in this town, you hit paydirt."

"I have been lucky," John admitted, "but I've also relied on the people who run my companies. I'm relying on you, Frank. I can usually trust a man who puts his own fortune on the line."

"That does encourage me to make this line a success," Hardy agreed, laughing and clasping John's hands with his own. "Now, what would you say to some dinner? My cook does a wonderful job with a goose."

John followed his host back down the corridor. There they met Marie and Virginia Hardy. The four of them entered the dining room, and two young women wearing matching white skirts and speaking in thick Irish brogues began serving the dinner.

The goose was as good as Hardy predicted, and the meal was topped off by a marvelous dessert of frozen cream and fruit.

"Guard your cook, Virginia," Marie warned. "Someone's bound to steal her away."

"Nonsense," Mrs. Hardy replied. "They'd have to hire half the Irish population of Denver. We employ most of Katy's family to keep her content."

"It's worth it to have a good cook, though," Hardy added.

They then adjourned to the sitting room, another marvelously ornate chamber, where they shared opinions on the latest national news as reported in the newspapers.

"I envy you, dear," Mrs. Hardy told Marie. "Having your own newspaper. It must be wonderful to have all the news at your fingertips any day of the year."

"Actually, we don't bother the people at the Herald-Courier," John explained. "I have a good editor down there, and I let him run the show. We get our information in the morning like everyone else."

"A pity," Mrs. Hardy said, sighing. "I'd love to have a few tidbits of gossip ahead of Agnes Swinbourne."

"Can't very likely do that," John said, laughing. "She makes most of it up, doesn't she?"

Mrs. Hardy seemed a little displeased with the remark, but her husband laughed loudly.

"I tell her that myself," Hardy said, regaining his composure. "But she never listens."

Marie flashed a warning with her eyes, though, so John kept his comments to himself the rest of the evening. On the way home he told Marie the news concerning the railroad, and her frown faded immediately.

"I'm so proud of you, Johnny," she said, hugging him tightly. "A railroad in Mariesville is splendid. We'll be able to visit there more often, and your trips won't take a full week now."

"I'm glad I was useful. You know this will change the valley even more, though."

"It would have happened anyway," she said, sighing. "It's all changing, Johnny. Everything but us."

"I know, Marie."

"Maybe we should go away for a time, travel. The Parkes went to Europe. I understand France is lovely in the autumn."

"What about the children?"

"Nancy can look after them. Or we could send them out to Mrs. Fitch. She was so good with Timothy."

"Maybe," he said, frowning as he looked down the brightly lit street at the lights still flickering from the tower bedroom occupied by Michael and Peter.

"You're still thinking about the mountain, aren't you?" Marie asked. "You can't worry about that, Johnny."

"I can't help thinking I've robbed them of something, kept them from knowing and feeling the power, the freedom, of the high country."

"You kept them from knowing the hunger, too," she reminded him. "In a few years they'll be older. They'll beg you to take them hunting and fishing, to let them spend a summer in a cabin."

"Maybe," John said, not really believing it. And even worse, he wasn't sure there'd be any mountains, any free-flowing streams full of rainbow trout, any wild turkeys gobbling on a hillside, any . . . any of the old days left.

And I'm helping to reshape it, aren't I? John asked himself. The answer echoed again and again through his mind as he recalled the cold, deadly eyes of the cougar.

I am, he thought, and I have no choice! No choice at all.

VII

It wasn't long before the papers were signed, plans were finalized, and the first rails of the new Denver and Rocky Mountain Railroad were laid. John rode only once along the route. The canvas tents and sweaty, bare-chested workmen heaving their sledges brought back too many memories.

It wasn't possible for John Wilson to totally ignore his involvement with the railroad, though. He and Marie were frequent guests of the Hardys, and when Virginia decided to host a banquet in honor of Colorado's fourth anniversary, the Wilsons were high on the invitation list.

"Oh, Johnny, we are going, aren't we?" Marie asked as she read an accompanying note from Virginia Hardy. "The governor will be there. I can wear the new blue gown Mrs. Gundarson just finished."

"Well, I certainly wouldn't want that poor old woman to have worked her fingers to the bone for nothing."

"Then, I can accept?"

"Yes," John mumbled.

In truth he hated parties and banquets, especially ones likely to be fraught with political speeches and tiresome prattle. But a little after six on the first of August, he found himself climbing the steps to Franklin Hardy's gilded mansion with Marie on his arm.

"What a lovely dress!" Virginia announced when Marie stepped through the door. "Come along and meet everyone, Marie. You're the real gem in this crowd."

John reluctantly released his wife's hand, and Virginia whisked her off into a huddle of middle-aged socialites. John wandered off toward the library, escaping the throng of jabbering businessmen and officeholders that choked the house's main hall. He was three pages into a story collection when the door swung open.

"Hiding again?" Franklin Hardy asked as John glanced up from the book.

"Caught me."

"Well, you'd better follow me to the dining room. You wouldn't want to miss the governor's speech."

"I wouldn't?"

"I think you'll enjoy this particular speech," Hardy said, motioning John toward the door. John reluctantly replaced the book on its shelf and joined his host in the corridor. Soon they were sitting with their wives at the center table in the Hardys' huge ballroom, enjoying a dinner of roast beef and boiled potatoes more than the governor's remarks.

"Now, as we look forward to a boundless future, let us raise our glasses to those who have brought peace and prosperity to the Rockies," the governor chuckled. "To four years of statehood!"

John raised his glass as the others did, then sipped

the heavy California wine. Others clapped, loudly murmured their agreement. John shared none of their enthusiasm. The governor's words echoed through his mind.

"Gone are the days of wild Indians preying on our innocent children. Gone are the long winters alone in the mountains, the desperate months spent searching one stream after another for wealth."

John was none too happy with all those changes, and the governor's praise for Franklin Hardy's new railroad brought further misery. Marie noticed immediately, and as the guests began circulating around the room, she leaned on John's shoulder and smiled.

"You can't spend the rest of your life worrying about what's past," she whispered.

John nodded his agreement, but he wasn't at all sure either of them was convinced.

"Well, well," the governor suddenly spoke as he extended his hand in John's direction. "Mr. Wilson. I was hoping we might meet at last."

"How are you, Governor?" John asked, shaking the wily politician's cold hand.

"Fine. Just fine. More to the point, how are you?"

"Equally fine," John said, gazing around the room in hope of deliverance.

"I was greatly pleased to learn that you'd invested in Franklin's new railroad. A man like you, Mr. Wilson, should take a more active interest in politics. You own one of our leading newspapers, and your companies employ hundreds. Should you desire to run for Congress, you'd find many willing supporters in the city."

"I'm afraid I wouldn't make much of a politician,"

John confessed. "I have a hard time talking in circles."

"Ah, but you've got wit," the governor said, laughing.

Franklin Hardy rescued John, then led the way to a nearby huddle of businessmen. Hardy introduced the men, and John shook hands and exchanged polite remarks.

"Here's a fellow railroader, John," Hardy said as a tall, graying man stepped forward. "He helped survey the route for the Union Pacific across the great plains to California. Meet Colonel Henry DeMoss."

John gripped DeMoss's hand and gazed at the hated face, the dastardly eyes half hidden by an easy charm.

"Have we met before?" DeMoss asked, noticing the sudden change in John's eyes.

"I don't believe you've been to . . . Mariesville, have you?" John asked.

"No."

"I've spent most of my adult years there. Or here in Denver."

"Then, we couldn't have met," DeMoss said, shaking off an uneasiness.

"I'd certainly remember," John said solemnly. "I never forget a face. I remember . . . almost everything."

"That's a gift," DeMoss said.

"Frank called you 'Colonel.' You've been in the military, then?"

"Oh, the title's strictly honorary," DeMoss said, chuckling. "When I started building the line north into Wyoming, the men on the line took it up. Grenville Dodge was a general, so I suppose they thought I should be a colonel. My military experience is limited to a few brushes with Indians and renegades."

"Oh?"

"Yes," DeMoss said, relaxing. "Haven't you heard of Cheyenne Pike? An outlaw from the old days, clever as a cat. He got careless, though, and we managed to trap him."

"He was an Indian?"

"Had a white mother, so they say. Father was an old trapper. Felt he had a score to settle. Men like us make enemies."

"I suppose," John echoed.

"I've heard a lot of talk about you, Wilson. They say everything you touch turns to gold. Sometime you'll have to extend to me the opportunity to participate in one of your projects."

"I don't generally take in partners."

"Well, there are always exceptions, aren't there? Sometimes you have a need for someone who gets things done. I'm quite good at handling delicate problems. Especially when you, let's say, need to skirt the edges of the law."

"I see," John said, fighting to control his emotions.

John backed away from DeMoss, then wove his way through the crowded room to where Marie stood with Virginia Hardy.

"Who is that man?" Marie asked, pointing to where DeMoss remained, smiling brightly and nodding toward the Wilsons.

"Oh, that's Henry DeMoss," Virginia said, laughing. "He's harmless enough. He fashions himself another Dodge, but in truth he's just a surveyor with an eye for greater things. He organized the financing for the

337

Northern Colorado Railroad, the one that runs up into the Wyoming Territory. DeMoss is ambitious, but his latest ventures have been none too successful."

"So he's now at loose ends?" John asked.

"He's still president of the Northern, but there've been rumors that the line's finances aren't in good order."

"You mean they're losing money?" John asked.

"Well, I ought to leave the financial world to Frank," Virginia said nervously. "But the talk is, the books aren't kept carefully."

"Meaning?"

"Someone might be borrowing from company funds."

John smiled for the first time since leaving the governor. Marie clasped his hand as she always did when he worried her.

"Have you had dealings with DeMoss before?" Virginia asked.

"I've heard of him."

"Be careful, John. He's got few scruples, and he deals with men that . . . well, don't always operate within the law."

"I'm always careful," John said, leading Marie away.

"Johnny?" she whispered.

"A face from the past," he told her. "Nothing to worry yourself about."

But that night as they lay together in the big feather bed back in the turreted house on Millionaire Hill, John was far from certain. He shook from head to toe, and a feverish sweat broke out on his forehead. Over and over it had come. The dream.

It was as if half his life had been erased, and he was back in the Medicine Bow Mountains, riding along behind Pike as they desperately picked their way through the pines. A dozen times he shook with terror as powder blasted apart the timbers of the railroad bridge. He saw again the hated faces of O'Brien and Taylor, the pale, death-stricken corpses of the Masseys swaying in the morning breeze. He saw Alf Depford fall, felt the hot bullets tear through him. Most of all he saw his brother, that last scrap of family, the single thread that bound him to a gentler world on Thompson's Mountain.

I'm not Jefferson Thompson anymore, John told himself as he fended off the weariness that beckoned him back into the darkness, back into the nightmare cloud that sleep would bring.

His eyes closed, and he huddled beside the barn door as Depford fell again, dropped to the dusty barnyard while the railroad detectives prepared to do DeMoss's bidding.

"No!" John shouted as the bullets peppered the air, as the choking fumes began to consume the barn. But if that scene vanished, the other appeared, and he saw the shattered bodies of his mother and father lying outside the blazing cabin.

"No!" John shouted again as he felt the bullets tear through his insides.

"Johnny, wake up," Marie pleaded as she shook him out of the nightmare.

"No!" John screamed so that the roof shook, so that every inch of his being filled with a deathly chill.

"It's all right, Johnny," Marie whispered as she

stroked his head, massaged his shoulders.

"No, it's not," he told her through eyes filled with tears. "It'll never be right."

"What won't?" she asked.

"Anything," he cried. "Not as long as he's still alive to haunt my dreams."

"Who?"

"Who? DeMoss!"

"The man at the banquet?" she asked, drawing him closer. "Johnny, what is he to you? What's he done?"

"Oh, Marie," he whimpered, hugging her tightly. "I wish I could tell you."

"You can."

"No, it's too late," he said, moaning as he stared out the window. His body shook with fury. He was wracked by hatred, and he couldn't stop his hands and shoulders from trembling.

"Let me help you," Marie pleaded. "We've been through tough times before."

"I know," he said, calming slightly. "But this is something I have to do alone."

Alone! Alone! The word seemed to echo through the room until he thought it would deafen him. It was a terribly hollow, icy word, one that chilled him to the bone, cut him off from everything warm and wonderful about his life.

Alone? Oh, Lord, not alone again, he thought, staring into the black emptiness beyond the window.

"Don't fence me out, Johnny," Marie begged. "I'm part of you, Johnny. You can't separate your past, whatever it is, from my present."

"I have to," he mumbled. "Don't you see? Otherwise

it'll taint you and the children as well. But maybe, just maybe, I'll be able to put it all to rest myself."

"Johnny?"

"I know," he said. "I remember what it's like, too, walking alone, shaking with fear every time I heard footsteps in the darkness. But it's the only way I know."

VIII

John never did get much rest that night, and he rose early the following morning. August in the Rockies is a rainy month, but it often features clear, bright mornings. John slid out of bed without disturbing Marie, then rapidly threw on his clothes and descended the steps. In another moment he'd raised the bolt from the back door and escaped out into the heavy dew of the rear court.

What would you do, Pa? John asked the faint glow on the eastern horizon. Ma would try to forgive, even though her Cheyenne blood would burn for revenge. And Pike? Didn't he fight them to the death?

The bigger question was, How could he get to a man like DeMoss? Pike might have shot the devil on State Street, in broad daylight, but Pike had always been an outlaw of sorts. And that sudden, clean kind of death wasn't much retribution for the slow, lingering pain that had haunted John Wilson for a decade and a half.

No, to do a proper job of it required finesse. John knew only one man who might be able to help. He walked to the stable, saddled a horse, and rode down the back streets to the small two-story rooming house where Aaron Stamp dwelt.

The ex-deputy marshal was both surprised and pleased to discover his sunrise visitor to be John Wilson.

"Yes, sir?" Stamp asked as he cracked the door and stared up at John. "Mr. Wilson? What can I do for you?"

"Sorry to disturb you so early, Aaron, but I thought it better not to ride here at midday."

"Oh? Well, then, you'd best come along in," Stamp said, swinging open the door and motioning John inside. Stamp then threw a robe around his nightshirt and led the way to a small table.

"Is it safe to talk here?" John asked as he sat down.

"I live alone, Mr. Wilson. There's no one to hear."

"Have you ever had dealings with a man named DeMoss?"

"Railroad man?" Stamp asked, his foggy eyes clearing instantly. "Yes, sir. I never could prove it, but I had evidence back in Kansas he had some folks killed 'cause they stood in the way of the railroad."

"Up in Wyoming, too."

"And who'd that be, sir?" Stamp asked, leaning slightly forward.

"People I cared about."

"And might I suggest this happened before you came to your good fortune, sir?"

"Yes," John admitted.

"Then, I have to say this, sir. Keep that knowledge to yourself. When I was a younger man, I saw a wanted poster that described a certain limping boy. A friend of mine, now gone to his reward, said that boy had a scar across his belly that would raise your hair. I've heard—"

"Then, we understand each other."

"Yes, sir."

"I'm trusting you more than I've trusted anyone in a long time," John told the former lawman. "That's because Art Jennings said you were a man that could be trusted with anything."

"Just you try me, sir."

"For reasons you suspect, I'd never be able to formally accuse DeMoss in a courtroom. He's too slippery to let himself be convicted anyway. What I need is—"

"Another crime," Stamp said, smiling. "My Kansas farmers would do, but Kansas is a railroad state. You'd never get a conviction to stand up at appeal. If you'll pardon the expression, what we need is a good steel trap. My papa used to say that snaring a clever fox wasn't all that hard. You just had to use the right kind of bait."

"So, what would you suggest?"

"DeMoss, he's like an old catfish cruising the river bottoms. He'll nibble on most anything, but unless he's sure there's something worthwhile, he won't strike."

"So we use money."

"Sure, we do, but not greenbacks. Gold."

"I don't understand."

"He knows you're a miner, Mr. Wilson."

"So?"

"He'd kill to get in on a gold strike. You find yourself one, let word leak out you're investing in a mine. He'll beg on all fours for the chance to buy in. Once he does, you've got him hooked, and most of the bait's his very own money. Only don't let him buy from you direct.

You need a partner."

"Know anyone who'd like to lend a hand."

"I do, indeed," Stamp said, smiling. "Name's Aaron Stamp."

"I'd still put up the front money."

"It might be thirty thousand, Mr. Wilson. Quite a price to settle an old score."

"Not much at all."

"One thing more. You've got to be careful not to get yourself too tangled up in this thing. Don't buy the land yourself. Purchase the mineral rights."

"This isn't a game, is it? We'd best be cautious."

"You write me a bank draft for ten thousand dollars. I'll get things rolling. Before the week's out, Denver'll be full of rumors. You'll see DeMoss. Remember. Play him like a shy schoolgirl. Make him want it so bad he tastes it before you agree to let him in."

"That ought to prove enjoyable."

"One last thing. What spot do you have in mind?"

"The Medicine Bow Mountains," John said, bitterly gazing northward.

"There's danger in that."

"It has to be. The Cheyennes and the railroad have kept people out of that country. Colorado's been over-run by miners. No really big strike's been made recently."

"I was thinking more about your danger. Someone could recognize you."

"I don't see how. Most of the old ones are dead, and I'm not the same person who left there. I'm ten years older and then some."

"You watch yourself just the same. I'll keep an eye on you, too."

"I'd appreciate that."

John rose and shook Stamp's hand. Aaron Stamp's eyes blazed with energy as John took out his wallet and wrote the requested draft. There weren't many like Stamp left, men you could trust, men with a sense of justice.

The rest of that week John's thoughts were rarely far from DeMoss. John dreamed a dozen different fates for his old enemy. Marie, meanwhile, thought John had put it all behind him. So she was surprised when Henry DeMoss appeared at the house toward the end of that next week.

John met DeMoss in the library.

"Forgive me the liberty of calling on you at your home, Mr. Wilson, but I have to be leaving Denver soon, and I couldn't do so without speaking to you."

"I don't discuss business at my home," John explained. "Certainly not without an appointment."

"I know you're busy, sir, but it's a matter of grave importance. I understand you are looking into the development of certain mining operations, and—"

"Stop right there," John said angrily. "Who told you I was interested in mining property? I have a gold mine that's only operating at a third of its potential. I need no second fortune."

"Come now, Mr. Wilson," DeMoss said, sitting on the arm of a nearby chair. "We both know about needs, but more to the point, there's the game."

"The game?" John asked.

"The game of making money. It's what keeps us making and losing fortunes."

"If I was to find another mine to develop, I wouldn't need a partner."

"Can you be so sure?" DeMoss asked. "I'll be frank. I find myself somewhat embarrassed financially. But I could still raise some $200,000 pledging my rail stock as security. That would make a fair-sized capital investment."

"I told you before. I don't do business this way!" John declared.

"I do!" DeMoss said, sliding between John and the library door. "I need this opportunity."

"You impose on my hospitality is what you do," John said, glaring at his old enemy. "I don't know who you think you are, but to intrude on a man's privacy, test his patience, and then pretend to tell him his own affairs is not what we call in Denver good manners."

"Look," DeMoss said, stepping away. "I didn't build a railroad across the Rockies by using good manners. I moved whole mountainsides, not to mention Indians and outlaw bands. I'm not a man to be put off."

"Then I'll explain it to you one final time," John said, taking a deep breath and hiding his fury. "I never involve partners in a gamble, especially ones who clearly can't afford to lose. I take on the risks."

"And garner the profits."

"Naturally."

"But you involved yourself in the Denver and Rocky Mountain Railroad."

"That was the price of bringing the route through Mariesville."

"I pay my debts, Mr. Wilson."

Oh, yes, you will pay, DeMoss! John thought as he studied DeMoss's anxious, hungry eyes. John remembered the plan, though. It was too early to give in.

"I'll certainly keep you in mind, Colonel," John

347

finally said. "And now I must insist. I'll discuss this no further. If you force me, I'll summon someone to escort you out."

DeMoss's face betrayed surprise.

"You're serious about not accepting my offer?" the old surveyor asked.

"I couldn't be any more serious."

DeMoss scowled, then stalked out the library and down the hall toward the front door.

"You were right, Stamp," John mumbled as he gazed through the window as DeMoss muttered and cursed all the way to his carriage. "We're playing him like a fish. Give him line. We'll draw him back in later."

And yet that night the nightmares were worse than ever. John screamed out twice, waking the little ones. As John sat up in bed, shaking like a leaf, Marie hurried down the hall to quiet little Timothy. Joanna peeped in through the open door. Then Michael and finally Peter arrived.

"You're not sick, are you, Papa?" Michael asked.

"Just had a bad dream," John said, motioning for them to return to their beds. Instead, led by Michael, the three walked slowly to the bed and gathered around their father.

"I have bad dreams sometimes, too," Peter whispered.

"He thinks giant ducks are chasing him," Michael said, laughing.

"Ducks can be pretty frightening," John said, pulling Joanna over next to him with his left hand, then sliding the right around the boys. "But they never get as big as you, Peter. You just have to stand up to them, show them you won't be run off."

"What was you dream about, Papa?" Joanna asked.

John gazed into the girl's small, fiercely bright eyes and smiled. His fingers still quivered, but he fought off the spectre of swaying bodies and exploding bridges long enough to pull the children tightly to his sides.

"Maybe, when you're all older, I'll tell you about it," John promised. "It was something very terrible I saw a long time ago."

"When you got the scars?" Michael asked, touching John's nightshirt near the belly, then pointing to the thin red scars on John's ankle and leg.

"Yes," John told them.

There were no more requests for explanations. Instead Michael escaped his father's arm and crept around the bed to massage John's tense shoulders. Little Joanna crawled onto John's lap, and Peter reached a small arm around his father and hugged tightly.

"So, there are my escaped convicts," Marie said, standing in the doorway with hands on her hips. "To bed, prisoners!"

Joanna and Peter bowed their heads and obediently started for the door.

"We were worried about Papa," Michael explained. Then the older boy gave John a rare kiss on the forehead and slid off the bed.

"Thank you, Michael," John said, hugging the child. The others immediately rushed back to get a similar hug, and Marie smiled. "Now off with your mama," John told them.

After tucking the children back in bed, Marie returned.

"Don't you think it's time you told me?" she asked.

349

"That Colonel DeMoss appears, and you try to tear the bed apart."

Only now did John notice the rips in the sheets and the goose feathers torn from his pillow.

"I'm not sure you'll want to know it all, Marie."

"I'm your wife, Johnny, the mother of your children."

"And as much a part of me as anyone ever has been," he told her. "Or ever will be."

And so he told her of Jefferson Pike, of the Cheyennes and Thompson's Mountain. Last of all he narrated the sad saga of Zeke and Ruth Thompson's final morning, and the fate that had awaited their sons.

"Why didn't you go to the law?" she asked.

"What law?" John said sadly. "The same law that rules a gold camp? The strong survive, and the weak die. That's the only law we knew out there. That and the Cheyenne law. Blood must be avenged."

"From what you've told me of your mother, that wouldn't have been her way."

"It was her uncle's way. Pike's, too. I rode with him, Marie. When DeMoss talks of hunting down Cheyenne Pike, he's speaking about my brother. I was with him. There's still a reward out on me, on Jefferson Thompson. That's me, Marie, not John Wilson. That knife-in-the-back son of the devil DeMoss stole my family, my home, even my name! I'm Jefferson Thompson!"

"No," she said, tenderly stroking his head, "that man's been dead a long time now."

"I'm not so sure," John whispered. "Maybe he's been here all along, lurking in the shadows."

"But you sent DeMoss away."

"He'll be back, Marie. The trap's been baited. He'll

stumble into it as sure as a mouse nibbles cheese."

"Don't do this, Johnny," she pleaded.

"I have to. I've put it off too long. Don't you see? It's why I can't sleep. I owe Pike, Ma, and Pa. Their spirits don't rest. It's time the ghosts had their rest."

Two days later John Wilson boarded the northbound train, headed for Laramie Junction and a long-delayed appointment. Marie and the children stood at the station platform, sadly waving farewell to a husband and father that none of them could be certain would return.

5. Revenge

I

A shrill blast from a train whistle roused John Wilson from his sleep. He stared around him at the foreign walls of the hotel and tried to blink away the haze of a decade's remembering. It was hard to believe it had been less than a day since he'd arrived in the little town straddling the railroad tracks at the base of Thompson's Mountain.

And I thought I'd put it all behind me, he mused as he threw off the sheets and shivered away the morning chill. Thirteen years he'd been running, almost half his life. But in the end the ghosts had slipped through the cracks in his wall of secrecy, and he was Jeff Thompson now as much as ever.

John dressed slowly, carefully. He rubbed the ancient scars as if they could somehow be seen beneath a shirt and coat. He pulled on his riding boots and straightened the leg that had lately begun to bend awkwardly, betraying a deadly past. Lastly he buckled on a leather gunbelt and cautiously checked the cylinders of his shiny new Colt revolver. The piece was clean.

"No, it's not for you, DeMoss," John whispered as he peered out the window. "Nothing quick and painless for you. No, I plan a long, lingering fate, much like the one you spun for me."

While John sat at the dinner table downstairs and ate a slice of ham and two fresh eggs prepared by Mrs. O'Hara, he caught a glimpse of something near the stairway. A moment later John saw it again, a thin elbow hanging from a cotton shirt three sizes too big. When the matching face appeared, John waved it over.

"Didn't mean to disturb your meal, Mr. Wilson," the boy from the day before whispered meekly.

"Your name's Jeff, isn't it?" John asked.

"Yes, sir. Jeff Kelly, sir. I only came to say that I found you a horse."

"That's fine news, Jeff. Come, sit down, have a biscuit."

"Oh, no, sir," the boy said, bowing so that his long, shaggy blond hair fell across his forehead into his eyes. "Mr. O'Hara would skin me. I'm not supposed to enter the dining room at all."

"I told you yesterday I'd have need of someone's help," John reminded the boy. "How old did you say you were?"

"Sixteen," the boy said, forcing his voice as low as possible.

"That'd seem a little generous, wouldn't you say?" John asked, examining the boy's thin frame.

"Fourteen?"

"More like ten?"

"Twelve," Jeff said, sighing. "Too young?"

"Not if you've an eye for horses," John said, laughing.

356

"Now let's go have a look."

John placed coins on the table to pay for the meal, then smiled as young Jeff stuffed the uneaten biscuits in an overalls pocket. The two then headed out the front door of the hotel and made their way to the stable.

"Just how much might this new job of mine be paying?" Jeff asked as he swung open the door of the table."

"A dollar a day, and Sundays off."

"I'd not be doing anything illegal?"

"No. You'd be my eyes and ears in town."

"A spy, is it?" the boy asked, his eyes lighting up.

"Let's call it a detective. I might need some information from time to time. I'd have a horse to exercise, and there might be other errands from time to time."

"And when I wasn't attending to those errands?"

"You're your own man. Just leave word where I can find you."

"You've a bargain, Mr. Wilson," Jeff said, extending his hand. John shook the frail hand, then followed Jeff into the livery.

"You must be Wilson, come to see a horse," a tall, grimy-faced young man of perhaps twenty-five said, setting aside a half-mended bridle. "I'm Ryan Fitzpatrick, and this is my stable."

"Are you the smith as well?" John asked.

"Ay, and sometimes doctor," Fitzpatrick said. "I've only a pair of horses just now, the bay mare and the charcoal stallion."

John started toward the indicated animals. Jeff whispered, "The stallion's wild and fast, but the mare's

357

steady."

Fitzpatrick enumerated the merits of both animals, but John ignored both voices and examined the horses personally. The mare was sound enough, but her teeth hinted she might have seen her best days already. The stallion was perhaps three, and his feet were as sound as a dollar. He stirred restlessly, whining for the feel of the wind in his mane.

"I'll take the stallion," John told the liveryman. "Now, I'll also need a rig and a team."

"That could pose a problem, sir," Fitzpatrick said, leading the stallion out from its stall. "I've none to sell."

"Mrs. Murphy's got a carriage and a matched pair of grays," Jeff declared.

"She the widow with the house down the street?" John asked.

"That's right, sir," Fitzpatrick declared. "She's away just now."

"Her brother's the banker, sir. Mr. Andrews," Jeff whispered. "He'll sell it fast enough, though he's apt to ask a high price. But he'll haggle."

John grinned, then dickered with Fitzpatrick over the price of the stallion.

"Horses come high out here," Fitzpatrick complained when John's offers continued to fall short of the mark. "You won't find anyone else here offering stock."

"And you won't find many buyers," John said sternly. "For what you ask, I can have ten horses freighted all the way from Mexico and still have the best dinner in town."

Jeff nodded his approval when the two men finally settled on a sum half Fitzpatrick's original asking price.

"I'll be at the bank," John told Jeff after paying the smith for horse, a saddle, bridle, and blanket. "Saddle him up for me. I won't be long."

"Yes, sir," Jeff said, eagerly stroking the stallion's nose.

John crossed the street and made his way along the plank walkway to the bank.

"Yes, sir?" the teller asked, slightly alarmed to spot a stranger, especially one carrying a pistol on one hip.

"I've come to inquire about the Murphy house," John announced. "I understand the bank's handling the sale."

"Sale?" asked a thin-faced man from inside a small office to John's right. "Are you interested in buying?"

"I might be," John told the banker. "Are you Mr. Andrews?"

"Joshua Andrews," the banker said, motioning John inside the small office. "And you are . . ."

"John Wilson."

"Oh, Mr. Wilson," Andrews said, clearing papers out of a chair and urging John to sit down. "I've heard much about you. My old friend Welles Barrett from Denver wired a bank draft in your name only yesterday. It's not often a sum like that crosses my desk. Except for the railroad . . ."

"Can we have a look at the house, Mr. Andrews? I'm in a bit of a hurry."

"Of course," the banker said, grabbing his coat. "It's my sister's place. A nicer house isn't to be found in town. Seven rooms, including a fine front parlor for entertaining, with kitchen, privy, and stable in back. There's a pump inside that draws on its own well, and another in the kitchen. Mary Elizabeth left a carriage and team, together with three saddle horses. Those may be included in the purchase price, if you wish."

"Let's have a look, then decide."

"Of course," Andrews agreed, leading the way.

The house proved to be all Andrews boasted and more. In truth the two main floors gave it more space than the house in Mariesville, and the attic rooms, now given way to cobwebs, could easily be restored to usefulness.

The saddle horses were no match for the charcoal stallion, but the rig and team were just what John had had in mind.

"I realize you'll possibly need the house but a short time, Mr. Wilson," Andrews said as they headed back to the bank. "But my sister is in need of cash, and I'm prepared to offer you generous terms for purchase."

"Such as?" John asked.

Andrews computed figures in his head, then scribbled on a blank page. When he recorded the final price, John nodded.

"If you'll accept my personal draft, you can consider the sale closed," John said. "Or if you'd rather—"

"Your draft will be more than adequate, Mr. Wilson. Perhaps you'd choose to open an account here in town to ease your dealings with the other merchants. Not everyone knows Welles as I do."

"I'd be happy to sign the draft over to you and deposit the funds accordingly."

"Wonderful," Andrews responded. "I'll get started on the paperwork immediately."

"One more thing," John said, eyeing the banker

sternly. "I'd prefer our dealings be kept strictly confidential. No one's to know my business or the extent of my finances, understand?"

"Oh, yes, sir, Mr. Wilson. Of course not."

John smiled as he left the bank. By midday he was confident everyone in Thompson's Mountain would know John Wilson had bought the Murphy house. Most would even know of the quarter-million-dollar bank draft. Bait like that was bound to attract Henry DeMoss.

Young Jeff Kelly met John in the street. The boy rode the tall black stallion as if born to the saddle, and it pained John to see the twelve-year-old's sad face slide down from the animal.

"You ride well, Jeff," John said, squeezing the boy's shoulder. "I bought the Murphy place. But it needs some cleaning, and I'll have to hire a cook and housekeeper. You mentioned you have a sister. Do you suppose she'd be interested in the position?"

"Oh, yes, sir!" the boy shouted.

"She's to have ten dollars a week plus the room back of the kitchen. First week in advance, with twenty dollars to stock the larder. And here's another twenty. See if you can round up some help to clean that house from cellar to attic."

"Yes, sir!" Jeff said, jumping with excitement as John handed over the money.

"Mr. Andrews at the bank will give you the key. Tell him I sent you. I'll be back before nightfall."

"I'll tell Katy to expect you for dinner."

"No, don't hurry her. We'll start her off with breakfast. If you have a chance, could you take my things from the hotel over?"

"I'll do it straightaway, Mr. Wilson!"

Jeff flew up the steps to the bank, and John frowned. If only Michael or Peter possessed a hair of that enthusiasm! But there was no point to pondering such matters. A far more important task lay at hand.

John Wilson mounted the stallion and nudged the horse into a slow trot. As he traversed the dusty main street, he examined the neat, freshly-painted shops and stores of the town, nodded to dour-faced ladies and children chasing each other around watering troughs or hitching posts. Only on the outskirts of town, where the shanties and hovels still remained from the railroad construction camp, could John glimpse the bands of shoeless, shirtless, dispossessed children, staring at their gaunt-eyed mothers, or hoping some crust of bread or bit of oatmeal might break the aching curse of hunger. The mothers stared up at John, pleading for some salvation from the scourge of poverty. And at the same time the cold, lifeless eyes acknowledged no such salvation would come.

John made a mental note to wire Welles Barrett. The bootery in Denver was expanding. Surely it could employ another four dozen such women, and perhaps some of the older children as well. Zeke Thompson would have bellowed out in anger to see his valley come to such ill use!

It was Zeke and Ruth Thompson who John thought of as he urged the stallion into a gallop. The two small wooden crosses didn't lie far from town, just across the river and halfway up the slope. John wished Pike had been buried there as well.

362

"I'll make my peace with him another day," John whispered to the wind.

The mounds of earth John recalled had long since blended into the gentle contour of the land. The crosses seemed bent, twisted by wind and rain, snow and ice. Later a common stone might take their place. For a little longer, though, John Wilson must conceal his relation to the slain frontiersman and the gentle half-Cheyenne mother.

John drew the big black to a halt, then dismounted. He tied the reins securely to a nearby aspen, then slowly, sadly, walked to the graves.

"Ma, Pa, I've come home at last," John whispered as he sat beside the crosses and gazed at the mountain that suddenly seemed foreign, hostile. "I've come back to punish the man who did this, who shattered our world like a stone fragments the glass of a window. I didn't forget. I couldn't."

The wind seemed to sigh in answer, and John sniffed away a tear.

"Iron Hand, if you can hear me, know that I kept my promise. I'll always remember."

John then walked to where the cabin had stood. Pine saplings had recovered the clearing, and a sea of grass had swallowed the scars left by fire. Only a few splinters of rotting timber remained, and those were only spotted by the sharpest of eyes.

Time endeavors to heal old wounds, John told himself as he opened his shirt and let the wind sting the long red scar across his belly.

"But I loved them," John said, tasting the bitter tears that slithered down his cheeks into the corners of his mouth. "I won't forget . . . I can't forget!"

There's a price to be paid, Pike had said, and the debt remained. As John stared at the soft, cloudlike plume of smoke floating across the valley behind a locomotive, he found himself staring bitterly at the railroad bridge across the Medicine Bow. A vision of that bridge exploding into dust and splinters filled his mind. The cries of the dead and the dying haunted him even now. And deep inside him, where there once was softness, love, pity, there grew a rock-hard fist as cold as a January blizzard.

"I've come back, DeMoss," John said, grinding his teeth so that the wind itself seemed to step away. "You don't know it, but you're already dying. Soon the hounds will be at your heels, and you'll know what Pike felt, what I've lived for thirteen long years. I only hope you feel half the pain, suffer a tenth the loss!"

John untied the reins from the aspen and mounted his horse. The better part of the afternoon he rode along the crest of the mountain, his father's mountain, searching for the lost fragments of a world now lost, even as the gentle boy he'd been was gone now forever. Finally, as the sun started to settle in the west, John turned the horse back toward town and quickened its pace into a gallop.

For a moment the wind swept the tears away, and he felt young again, felt as Jeff Thompson had once felt riding that valley. But the sensation was a temporary one, and John soon slowed the stallion into an easy trot. He splashed across the river and sadly continued down the dust-choked road into town.

"Welcome back, Mr. Wilson," Jeff shouted when

John rode the weary black around to the entrance of the Murphy house stable. "I'll take him."

John passed down the reins, then rolled off the side of the horse.

"You can still grab some dinner at Mrs. O'Hara's," the boy said. "I'll brush him up real fine, sir. I moved you into the front bedroom, but Mr. Shea at the hotel says you need to sign out."

John nodded his understanding, then plodded back out the door and stumbled toward the hotel. He settled his account with the clerk, then sat down in the dining room and picked at a plate of stew.

"Can I get you something else, Mr. Wilson?" Mrs. O'Hara asked. "I hope you're not displeased with the dinner."

"No, just not very hungry," John confessed.

"Well, I understand you've had quite a ride this afternoon. Maybe you'll feel like something later."

"Perhaps," John said, motioning for her to remove the plate.

He then placed a silver dollar on the table and headed toward the door. As he reached the stairway, an old gnarled hand pulled him aside.

"They watch you," an ancient voice whispered.

In the faint light John recognized the old Cheyenne scrubwoman.

"Do I know you?" John asked.

"Once," she answered, leading him down a corridor and through a back door into the valley. "I was called Lost Antelope."

"The Pawnees carried you away. You escaped and returned to Morning Star's camp."

"It was long ago."

"What can you tell me of my mother's uncle, Iron Hand?" John asked, sitting with the old woman in the darkness."

"Iron Hand is a long time dead," she said sadly.

"And Little Heart, his son?"

"He rode into the dying land in the south. They call it Indian Territory, but it is a hot place where sickness walks the wind. Little Heart is dead. The children are dead. It is a bad place."

John gripped her hand as he felt a knife turn inside him. First Dancing Lance! Now Iron Hand himself. Even Little Heart was gone.

"I remember how it was," Lost Antelope mumbled, the sadness in her eyes as deep as that in John's. "Everything has changed. The white men swallow all the world. They will swallow you, too. I listen. They talk. Already they wonder why you come here. Be careful."

"I'm always careful," John assured her. "Let me get you away from this hotel. I'll find a job for you at —"

"I make my own way," she said, stepping away from him. "Have you forgotten so much? Would you offer me white man's money?"

"Forgive me," John said, lowering his head. "I've been away a long time."

She nodded, then vanished back inside the hotel. John slipped down the alley and made his way to the Murphy house. He stepped through the open door and smiled at the clean floor, the shining tops of the furniture in the front parlor. Once in his room, he kicked off his boots and unlocked a small case.

"Ah," he sighed, spreading out a map of the Medicine Bow country. Thompson's Mountain was no more than a speck beside the railroad tracks. A small *x* appeared on the mountainside not far from the river.

Yes, DeMoss, it won't be long now, John thought as he envisioned the plan. Stamp's wire would arrive, and then the final plans could be made. Soon. Yes, it would be soon.

II

John never slept well in strange surroundings, and the heavily starched linen sheets and coarse woolen blanket on the lumpy bed didn't help. It was on toward midnight before he finally set aside the map and closed his eyes. He drifted between nightmare and recollection. Sometimes he found it hard to tell which was which. Finally, though, a knock at the door woke him.

"Yes?" John called out.

"Mr. Wilson," young Jeff Kelly said, cracking open the door. "Olie Finn brought a telegram over. He said it was important."

"Bring it in," John told the boy.

"Yes, sir," Jeff said, stepping cautiously inside. The boy's hair was disheveled, and he still wore a nightshirt stuffed inside a pair of trousers. Jeff blinked twice at the bright sunlight seeping in through the open front window, then stumbled over a pair of boots.

"You all right?" John asked as the boy picked himself up.

"Yes, sir," Jeff said, carefully rearranging the boots. "My, those are fine boots, Mr. Wilson. I never saw a pair to match 'em."

"It's the leather," John said. "My factory in Denver makes them. I'll see if I can't have a pair your size sent up."

"Oh, no, sir," Jeff pleaded, his face turning ashen. "I wasn't fishing for favors, really I wasn't."

"I know that," John said as he took the telegram."

"I don't know you'll make any sense of it, Mr. Wilson," Jeff said, pointing to the telegram. "If you ask me, the telegrapher must have been up all night, or else he takes to the bottle."

John smiled and read the brief message.

GOD IS STILL IN HEAVEN AND A STAR IS IN THE SKY STOP ORION 2 STOP GRAY

"See what I mean?" Jeff asked, leaning over John's shoulder and gazing at the message. "Never saw such nonsense."

"Don't you worry over it," John said, setting the telegram on the nightstand. "It tells me what I need to know."

"How?"

"I'll teach you one of these days. For now, it's just as well you don't know."

"There's talk in town you're here to open a factory. Or else start a gold mine."

"People like to talk, Jeff."

"It's something like that, though, isn't it?"

"Fishing for something else now, are you?"

"You're right," the boy said, laughing. "I ought to mind my own business."

"Which right now ought to be getting dressed. Would you do me the favor of joining me for breakfast,

369

you and your sister both? I hate to eat alone."

"I'll tell Katy," Jeff said, pausing long enough to nod his head before racing out the door.

It proved to be a quiet breakfast. Aside from meeting Katy Kelly, the freckle-faced girl of nineteen who somehow seemed completely capable of managing the house as well as she had herself and her twelve-year-old brother, John accomplished little that entire morning. After eating a simple supper a little after noon, he walked to the bank and signed the transfer deeds.

"I suppose you'll be sending for your family soon, Mr. Wilson," Andrews said after the sale was completed. "My wife would be more than delighted to show Mrs. Wilson about town, introduce her to the other ladies."

"Thank her for me."

"Then, are we to assume Mrs. Wilson will arrive shortly?"

"You're welcome to assume what you will," John said, smiling. "I learned a long time ago that a prudent man keeps his own council."

"You can trust me to keep my tongue," Andrews assured him. "I'm your banker. What proves lucrative to you will certainly benefit me as well."

"Maybe I should explain," John said, frowning. "I'm leaving some operating funds in your bank. They won't be there forever, and all I ask is that you insure their security. If I needed your advice, I would've asked for it. Do we now understand each other?"

"Yes, sir," Andrews said, sighing. "It's just that I . . ."

"Yes?"

"Nothing, Mr. Wilson."

"Good day, then. I do appreciate you handling the

house for me, but that hardly constitutes a business partnership."

"No, sir."

As John left the bank, he heard the teller whisper something to a customer. John couldn't escape the feeling those whispers followed him halfway down the street. But he paid little attention. Instead he devoted the remainder of the afternoon to his maps and a stack of papers he also removed from the locked case.

He might have spent a week studying the various reports had not Jeff Kelly knocked on the door shortly before six o'clock.

"Mr. Wilson, sir," the boy said. "Katy's got dinner on the table. If you're hungry . . ."

"Since when did that have anything to do with it?" John asked. "A man's supposed to come when dinner's on the table, isn't he?"

"Well, that's the way it always was when Mama was alive, but you're . . ."

"The master of the house? When I'm back in Denver, I don't eat if I'm not at the table when called."

"I always figured, when you were rich, you could eat whenever you wanted."

John smiled, then carefully replaced the maps and papers in the case and attached the padlock.

"Care to join me for dinner tonight, Master Jeff, or do you have other plans?"

"Actually, I already ate," Jeff said, slightly embarrassed. "I'd sit with you, though."

"No, you go along. You might take a moment, though, and saddle the big black for me. I'll be taking a ride tonight."

"Alone?"

John nodded, and the boy seemed concerned.

"I don't know that I'd do that, Mr. Wilson. Men've been robbed hereabouts."

"I'll be all right," John said, pointing to his pistol.

"But you don't know your way."

"I know this country better than you might think, Jeff. Don't concern yourself."

Jeff nodded, and John shoveled the boy on down the hall. Jeff departed through the back door while John sat himself at the table. Katy arrived within a minute with a bowl of steaming soup and an apology for eating earlier.

"I only hired you to keep house, Katy," John told the young woman. "I never intended to run your life. What's more, you ought to decide upon a day off."

"I have to cook for Jeff and myself, don't you think?" she asked. "Surely it can't bother you if I prepare something for you at the same time."

"Surely it can't," John said, smiling as her face reddened. "But if you need some time off . . . maybe to see a young man, feel free to ask."

"And if you feel the need for company at dinner, feel equally free," she said, brightening. "You've a soft place for children, or so I hear. Certainly you've proven it with Jefferson. It's only proper you shouldn't dine alone."

"Thank you," John told her with a smile. "I've four little ones of my own, and I miss them most at mealtime."

"Four? Well, no wonder! The quiet must near deafen you. I'm from a family of eight myself, though Jeff and I are all that's left here. Boys or girls?"

"Three boys and a girl."

"You're a young man. Sure you'll have to give the poor girl a sister. Three brothers!"

John laughed so that he nearly choked. But when Katy left to bring the second course, the awful silence of the big empty house nearly swallowed him. Already he missed Marie's tender touch, the stories and pranks of the boys, Joanna's good-night kisses, and little Timothy's attempts at words.

"You miss them, don't you?" Katy asked as she replaced the empty soup bowl with a platter of roast beef and vegetables.

"Very much."

"I'm surprised you didn't bring them along."

"I never bring them with me on business," John said, fighting off the loneliness. *Especially not when there's a business of the kind I have with Henry DeMoss,* he thought.

Katy sat with him through the rest of the meal, leaving only to bring in a tray of biscuits and refill his coffee cup. When he'd finally eaten his fill, John excused himself and left through the back door. Moments later he was atop the charcoal stallion riding south.

John took great care not to be followed. He carefully recited from memory the words of the telegram.

God is still in heaven.

It was a simple enough code. Aaron Stamp had gone over it before John left. God was indeed still in heaven. More importantly, Peter Ryland was well and riding with Stamp toward a rendezvous. John knew the latter from the second cryptic line.

A star is in the sky.

The star was Stamp, who not so long ago had worn

373

one on his chest.

Orion 2 denoted the place. North was one, south was two, and so on. *Gray* told the time. *G* being the seventh letter of the alphabet, and gray being a dark color, Stamp would be south of town at seven in the evening. So would John.

The big black seemed to sense the eagerness in John's knees, and it sped through the deer thickets and the aspen-covered hills. Soon John spotted the small campfire, and he slowed his pace.

"You're two minutes late," Stamp announced when John finally rode into the camp.

"I'm sorry if I kept you waiting," John said to the ex-lawman before turning to his uncle. Peter Ryland's face was lined now, and he appeared to have aged past his forty years. But nothing had slowed the minister's step.

"Jeff, I don't believe it, son," the reverend said, hugging his nephew as though thirteen long years had been erased in the blink of an eye. "Oh, Lord, I've prayed you were safe."

"I thought to write, but I wasn't certain you'd know who John Wilson was, and I dared not say too much in a letter."

"It'd be best if you took care to call him Mr. Wilson now," Stamp urged. "From this moment on, we're in danger, all of us. I've dealt with DeMoss before. He's no fool, and he rarely plays by the rules or does the obvious."

John and his uncle nodded, and Stamp motioned for them to join him beside the fire.

"I'll leave you time to have your reunion later," Stamp explained. "For now, I want you both to be clear as to the plan. I've arranged to purchase from Peter Ryland the mineral rights to Thompson's Mountain. Understood?"

"Not really," Ryland said. "No one's found a trace of gold or silver, either one, in these mountains. And as to the deed . . ."

"You're the nearest surviving kin of Ruth Thompson," Stamp explained. "I took care of the deeds of ownership personally. Zeke Thompson was granted title by treaty. There were army officers present, and I got their testimony."

"You have been busy," John said, smiling.

"Now, what I worked out with Welles Barrett was this. We have formed the Thompson's Mountain Mining Company. I had 50,000 shares of stock printed. Reverend, you receive 5,000 as payment for the mineral rights. Mr. Wilson, you receive 20,000, and I keep 5,000 for, shall we say, consideration of services rendered. The balance, 20,000, will be sold to generate additional operating funds."

"Additional?" Ryland asked.

"I put up the initial funds, Uncle Peter," John explained. "We needed equipment, an office in Denver, and there were expenses such as title fees, printing, and the like. We'll sell the remaining shares at ten dollars to raise money to pay our workers, buy supplies . . ."

"Then, you expect to find gold there?" the minister asked.

"Well," John began nervously, "that's not really — "

"To be frank, Reverend Ryland, we'd be happier if we didn't," Stamp explained. "What we're after isn't gold. It's Henry DeMoss."

"The railroad engineer? I thought surely he was dead by now," Ryland said grimly.

"No. You see, Uncle Peter, the shares are bait. If DeMoss has been keeping an eye on me like I suspect, he'll waste no time in following me here. Once he learns the shares are available, he'll snap at them."

"But 20,000 shares? Does he have that kind of money?"

"That's the thing," Stamp said, grinning. "He can raise it if he sells his Northern Colorado Railroad stock. He'll have to pledge his Union Pacific bonds, too, I'd guess. The only other assets he has are a house in Nebraska and some cash in various banks. I checked carefully."

"I don't like this," Ryland said, shaking his head. "It sounds like fraud."

"No!" John objected. "It's a simple business venture. Nobody's making DeMoss buy in. We have money to lose, too."

"But from what Mr. Stamp has told me, Jeff—"

"John!"

"John, you're prepared to lose money to ruin De-Moss. Can't you forget this? It won't bring your parents back."

"Can you forget, Uncle Peter?" John asked, his eyes growing wild. "You saw Pike's body. You saw mine! Look at my eyes. I can't sleep. It's time Ma and Pa and Pike had their revenge."

"I can't believe you're the same person as the gentle boy I used to read stories to at the mission."

"I'm not the same, Uncle Peter. DeMoss changed me, stole away my family, even my name! I'm past forgiveness."

"I wouldn't grieve over Henry DeMoss," Stamp said, shaking his head. "He's got a lot of ghosts haunting his trail. Pray for his victims, Reverend, not for the devil himself."

"Uncle Peter's right about one thing, though," John admitted. "If we seed the mine, DeMoss might wriggle out of the whole mess by claiming fraud."

"I don't think we'll need to seed," Stamp said, passing John a telegram.

UNDERSTAND YOU ARE WORKING FOR WILSON STOP CONSIDER MY OFFER STOP THOUSAND DOLLARS FOR MINE LOCATION STOP MORE IF I GET IN ON DEAL STOP DEMOSS

"Did you answer him yet?" John asked.

"Tomorrow," Stamp explained. "I'll tell him no, but I'll send other dispatches as well. He'll have little trouble locating us. I'll bet he's here within the week."

"And what about the NCRR? What has Welles been able to do?" John asked.

"Oh, there's no question funds have been borrowed," Stamp said, drawing some papers from his pocket. "But as long as DeMoss is line president, he's untouchable. Once he sells his stock, though, the board can fire him. Then a federal investigation can nail DeMoss's hide to the wall."

"I understand why my nephew hates this man so much," Peter Ryland said, interrupting. "What's your grudge, Mr. Stamp?"

"It's a matter of pride, I suppose," Stamp admitted. "Years ago I was supposed to find a killer. This man shot a farmer, his wife, and their three small children back in Kansas. Everyone in the state knew the railroad was behind it, and most told me to my face it was Henry DeMoss did the shooting. But when I took the proof I gathered to a judge, I found myself shy a job and laughed out of town. Reverend, I try to be a forgiving man myself, but there's such a thing as justice in this country. A man shouldn't laugh away the lives of five people. And there've been others."

"We'll never convict him of murder, Uncle Peter. But to a man like DeMoss, facing scandal and ruin might be worse than getting hung," John explained. "We're not doing anything but letting a greedy man dig his own hole."

"Why involve me, though? I don't see how I fit in."

"We needed someone to sell the mineral rights," John explained. "More important, DeMoss will want to control the company. It's the way he operates. He'll want to buy your stock."

"And I'm to sell?"

"At fifteen dollars a share. More if you can get it," John told his uncle. "He'll not have the money he needs, so he'll have to borrow from a bank. Welles Barrett has made sure no bank in the country will advance money to Henry DeMoss."

"So he'll go to his own private bank," Stamp said, smiling cruelly. "The NCRR. Once he dips his hand in the till, he's mine! He will, too."

"How can you be so sure?" Ryland asked.

"I don't always have to see a skunk to know there's one about," Stamp said. "I know DeMoss. He'll take the bait, and he'll jump head first into our snare."

"I don't know," the minister said, scratching his head.

"Reverend, I've seen your mission," Stamp said sadly. "You yourself look half starved, and those people you look after are all in rags, eating cornbread and beans. You'll have $75,000 for your trouble if all goes according to plan. That'll feed a lot of hungry mouths."

John could tell those words bore heavily on his uncle.

"I suppose I've little choice in the matter, then," Ryland grumbled. "But I don't wish to deal with DeMoss personally. He will no doubt remember me from when I claimed Pike's remains."

"I'll arrange for someone at Laramie Junction to handle your business," Stamp said, making a note of it. "It will be simple for DeMoss to learn about it. He has lots of ears at the junction."

"So, we all know what's to be done," John said, smiling as the others nodded. "Now, tell me about the last dozen years, Uncle Peter."

John and his uncle sat beside the fire and exchanged photographs and stories. The minister had taken a wife the same winter John had formed his partnership with Shep Skelly. Now there were half a dozen children, plus four Cheyenne orphans adopted following Mackenzie's slaughter of Morning Star's band.

"You know old Iron Hand was killed then," John's uncle whispered. "I tried to convince his youngest, Little Heart, to stay and help me at the mission, but he felt his duty lay with his people."

"And now he's dead, too," John mumbled, "The hills will miss the sweet song of the Cheyenne."

"Yes," Peter Ryland agreed. "When this is over, John, you'll bring your family to the mission?"

"Or you to Denver, Uncle Peter. It's time the cousins met."

"It's time you made your peace with the past, too."

"I will," John promised. "As soon as DeMoss knows how it feels to be hounded and hunted and destroyed.

He's earned that, Uncle Peter, earned it a hundred times over."

John sat with his uncle a moment longer, but he knew there was nothing left to be said. The spider had spun its web, and it was only for the fly to appear. As John returned to town that night in the darkness, he saw the fly's face a dozen times, in every flicker of moonlight, in every dancing shadow. And each time it was Henry DeMoss!

III

Stamp underestimated DeMoss. The villain appeared in town two days later, and it took little time for him to corner John Wilson near the mercantile.

"Well, well," DeMoss said. "Quite a coincidence meeting up with you here, Wilson."

"Oh?" John asked. "I'd guess it was more than that. I can't see why the president of the Northern would come to a backwater like Thompson's Mountain."

"I try to get out here whenever I can," DeMoss explained. "I spent a good deal of time in this region. You might say I was the architect of all this," he added, waving his hands about to indicate the buildings, the rail station, the tracks. "I'm especially proud of the river bridge. It's actually the second structure we built."

"Oh?"

"The first was destroyed in a fire. But tell me, Wilson, why have you come here?"

"Oh, I visit a lot of places," John said with cold eyes. "I'm always on the lookout for business opportunities."

"As we all are. We've been looking at adding a spur to the Northern. It'd cut an hour or two off the travel time west."

"That hardly seems worth the expense."

"Time is money, Wilson. Speaking of which, why don't you join me for supper?"

"I have plans," John said, slipping away from DeMoss and escaping down the street.

Throughout that next week it seemed DeMoss lurked everywhere. Each time John ventured out from the house, DeMoss would appear from the shadows like a snake.

"I think it's time you met with him," Aaron Stamp told John finally. "I'll have the office open tomorrow, and the first work crew will be here midweek."

"Then it's time we got on with it."

"I'd say so. There's something else you ought to think about, too. We've planned carefully, but keep in mind. DeMoss is capable of anything. From now on we'd best meet using the Orion code."

"I agree. You take care, too, Aaron. At the moment, he may view you as a likelier target."

"I'll tell you something, Johnny Wilson," Stamp whispered. "I've taken to carrying a pocket pistol to church."

Another time John might have laughed at the thought. Instead he nodded grimly. And when a package arrived from "Orion," containing a small five-shot Colt Paterson revolver, John loaded the pistol and tucked it in his coat pocket.

The pistol was still in that pocket when John accompanied Henry DeMoss the following afternoon toward the railroad station.

"The best place to eat is at the hotel," John pointed out as they continued. "Mrs. O'Hara—"

"I think you'll find what I've arranged is a good deal

more satisfactory," DeMoss broke in.

John shortly discovered exactly what DeMoss meant. Sitting on a siding at the railroad station was a long, elegantly-adorned private car. A pair of porters wearing the uniforms of the NCRR were on hand to greet them. Once inside, John stood in amazement as DeMoss pointed out the Italian tapestries on the walls, the Persian carpets spread across the floors, the fine maple paneling and silk-cushioned chairs.

"This must have set you back some," John commented.

"Belongs to the Northern," DeMoss explained. "As its president, naturally it's available for my use."

"Seems like it'd be hard for a company to make money that way."

"Well, most railroads understand the importance of entertaining politicians and businessmen."

"Is that how I fit in?" John asked.

"If your new enterprise was along the Northern line, I'd be remiss in my duties not to try and obtain your freight business. But our current dealings are of a more personal nature."

"Are they?"

DeMoss started to explain, but the appearance of a slender-shouldered youth in the doorway momentarily silenced him.

"Mr. DeMoss, sir," the youth spoke. "Mrs. Tolliver has supper ready."

"Thank you, George," DeMoss said, nodding to the boy, then leading John into the next compartment. A long walnut table dominated the room. The youth and an elderly woman were busy spreading out platters of rich food at the far end. DeMoss pointed out a chair to

John, then sat across the table.

"You do travel in style," John noted.

"Men like you and I, Wilson, are entitled. There'll be time for talk once we've eaten. For now, enjoy yourself. You'll find the wine particularly interesting."

DeMoss was true to his word, this time at least. Supper consisted of a half-dozen rare treats, each perfectly spiced to complement the others. There were pheasants and elk steaks, salmon from the Northwest, even lobsters from Maine. Franklin Hardy might have been envious. And all this in a railway car!

The wine was almost sweet, a blend of Italian grapes, properly aged and well-traveled according to the label.

"If you like it, I'll have a case shipped to you," DeMoss offered as John sipped a second glass.

"Excuse me for being ungrateful, but I've learned to be wary of gifts," John replied. "Maybe it's time you spell out what you want from me."

"The same thing I wanted in Denver. I'd like to participate in your next business endeavor."

"And I told you that I don't take in partners."

"Ah, but you often include investors. I'll be honest with you, Wilson. I have my eyes and ears hereabouts. I know, for example, you've purchased 20,000 shares of this Thompson Mountain Mining Company. In addition, there are 20,000 shares outstanding. My question is, if you don't like partners, why haven't you bought those shares?"

"I don't generally explain my business dealings."

"I understand your need for secrecy. I admire it. Let me suggest a reason. Your assets are spread fairly thin, and these shares are a way of attracting cash to the business. I intend to purchase those shares within the week. That will make us partners."

"Those shares are being offered at ten dollars. That's a lot of cash. I wouldn't've guessed you had that much available to you."

"You might be surprised about a lot of things."

"I might," John said, nodding his head as he sipped a fresh glass of wine. "I do know gold mining, though. This particular operation is high risk. You could wind up with nothing to show for your investment."

"I understand that. All ventures are in their nature speculative. This Stamp fellow's worked for Art Jennings, though, and Jennings makes few mistakes. I don't think you'd be pouring your resources into too much of a gamble."

"If I'm gambling, it's with money I can afford to lose," John said, peering into DeMoss's eyes. "I have other sources of revenue. I'd say you're risking most of your savings, not to mention your reputation. If this project fails . . ."

"It won't."

"I don't see how you can be so sure of yourself."

"Of myself? No, it's you I'm betting on. You won't let this mine fail. In Denver they say you have the Midas touch. Everything you touch turns to gold. I intend to share your good fortune."

"Luck can turn."

"If I thought it was luck, I'd leave here tomorrow," DeMoss said, smiling. "You hire good people, Wilson. And you know gold country."

"And you're ready for a change? Is that it? You see, Colonel, I've got eyes and ears, too. I hear that Northern Colorado Railroad of yours is in trouble.

The stock's falling, and most of the original ownership is selling. With profits down, I'd guess investors might question the value of private railway cars and generous salaries for the president."

"Hang them all," DeMoss said angrily. "I built that line! As long as I care to, I'll run that railroad."

John merely smiled and sipped the wine.

The following day DeMoss purchased the outstanding stock, and young Jeff Kelly brought John a small envelope. Inside was a hastily sketched note.

Orion 3 Gray.

So John met the ex-marshal at seven in the hills east of town.

"He's taken the hook," Stamp declared. "Now we can really get rolling. We'll double the manpower, make a lot of progress."

"I don't want the mountain scarred. You understand that?" John asked.

"I'm familiar with what you've done at Mariesville. Most of the men are, too. We'll use the rock for buildings, and we won't cut all the timber from the same sections."

"You'll move your office out there, too, won't you?"

"And we'll put a crew to work on a warehouse for supplies. That ought to drive DeMoss crazy. He'll want half the mountain blasted away."

"Oh?"

"I told you he'd have to sell his railway stock. What he did was pledge it all as security for a loan."

"I thought Welles Barrett . . ."

"That's the thing, Johnny. DeMoss's note is payable on demand. All we do is let Welles know, and it will be called."

"So . . ."

"Welles will control the railroad. He'll move the investigation forward. Those hounds you're talking about are already snapping at his heels. Pretty soon they'll sink their teeth in."

John grinned in satisfaction.

And as each day passed, the smile broadened. DeMoss looked rattled, confused. By midweek DeMoss was making daily trips to the telegraph office. On one such occasion he cornered John at the bank.

"Does it always take this long before you have ore to process?" DeMoss asked. "When will we know something?"

"In a month or so," John replied. "The shaft is progressing. You have to understand there may not be any minerals at all. If there's gold or silver as there should be, we ought to find signs when we branch the tunnels."

"I understand you did a lot of blasting to find the vein back at Shepherd's Creek."

"That was entirely different. We'd already found placer gold in the stream. We were hunting for a vein. When you tunnel, you blast within the mountain, then dig out the rubble."

"It just seems to me we could bore into the rock the same way we blast out a railroad tunnel."

"It would collapse the shaft."

"Even so, if you found the gold . . ."

"It's not that easy," John said, shaking his head. "A man's got to have patience."

"Patience," DeMoss grumbled. "Time. Some men don't have a lot of either."

John noticed the deep lines etched in DeMoss's

forehead, the nervous way the aging engineer played with his necktie. Yes, the hounds were snapping. And there wasn't so much as an ounce of sympathy inside John Wilson for their victim.

IV

John did his best to occupy himself with correspondence in the days that followed. In Denver it had been a simple matter to keep up with the newspaper, the bootery, the mine, and the other assorted enterprises. Now it seemed everyone had problems, the exception being Franklin Hardy's railroad. The only one who didn't write was Welles Barrett, and John hungered for news from him. Direct contact was dangerous for both of them, and Aaron Stamp had been clear about it.

As John sat at the desk in the little office at the Murphy house, he answered each query. Except for the one from Marie, that is.

"When are you coming home?" her voice echoed through his ears. He could read between the lines her concern. Sometimes as she described Timothy's antics or Joanna's newest dress, he felt his heart close to splitting in two. And as he sat alone day after day at the dinner table, he became more restless than ever.

It's like the old days, John thought as he stared out the window at Henry DeMoss walking past the telegraph office. I'm as lost as ever.

After breakfast the next morning John slipped out the back door and entered the stable. The charcoal stallion stirred in its stall, and John spread a blanket across the big horse's back.

"That's my job," Jeff Kelly said, swinging the front door open. "Off for a ride?"

"Thought I might travel out to the mine, see how the work's coming along," John told the boy. "I feel like the walls are closing in on me."

"Then, it's best I come along, Mr. Wilson. You're liable to lose yourself up there."

"You'd be surprised," John said as he placed his saddle on the big black. "I can find my way."

But when Jeff trotted over and began saddling a spotted pony, John didn't object. In truth he was starving for company. And as they rode together out of town, John found himself remembering his own twelfth year, riding across the Medicine Bow, chasing Pike through the river, hunting deer and fishing for trout.

"There are legends about this place," Jeff said as they splashed their way across the river not far from the railroad bridge.

"Oh?" John asked.

"Have you seen those two crosses up on the hillside?"

"Yes," John said, trembling.

"Ever wonder how they got there, who they are? I've heard a dozen stories. One's all about two lovers, a white man and his Indian sweetheart. Her father forbade her to marry, so they jumped from the cliff. Now they lie there side by side."

"Doesn't seem too likely," John said, shaking his head.

"There are other legends."

"And what do you believe?"

"I'm not certain. There was a man who lived on that mountain. It's named for him. Zach Thompson, I believe, was his name."

"Not Zach," John said softly. "Zeke."

"That's right. You've heard the story then."

"And you think that's who's buried there, old Zeke?"

"And his wife maybe. Papa thought so."

"He did?"

"Papa worked on the railroad, Mr. Wilson. He told me once that after some of the men had been drinking, one told all about how Colonel DeMoss hired some of them to ride up there and kill Zeke Thompson."

"Is that what you think happened?" John asked, suddenly drawing his horse to a halt. "Is it, Jeff?"

"Papa said it was to get the land for the railroad," Jeff explained as he gazed at John's blazing eyes. "There's a graveyard at the edge of town full of railroad men who died. Papa's buried there, too. So's my brother Wash. Mama used to say the railroad's route was marked in blood."

"Blood," John mumbled. "No, more than that. Suffering, and remembering, too."

"Nobody ever told me that before," Jeff asked, his eyes growing red. A tear rolled down one cheek, and the boy rubbed it away. "That's how I feel, though."

"The suffering passes," John said, nudging his horse forward. *The remembering doesn't*, he thought.

They rode up the mountainside, then wove their way through the trees atop the ridge. Finally Jeff waved toward the half-built warehouses of the mine.

"I've got some business to attend to now," John said,

pausing long enough to rest a tired hand on young Jeff's shoulder. "I can find my own way back to town. If you'd like to ride on a bit, maybe spend some time with your friends, I have no objections. Autumn's coming, and there won't be many more bright afternoons suitable for swimming or running about."

"The fishing's good down by the bridge."

"Catch a trout for me."

"I wouldn't mind some company."

"I appreciate the invitation, Jeff. It'll have to be another day, though."

"Yes, sir," the boy said, reluctantly pulling away and turning his horse toward the bridge.

John continued on to the mine. He passed among the men, many of them long-time employees of the Wilson Company at Mariesville.

"How are you, Mr. Wilson?" one or two asked.

"Sure don't seem to have a winner this time, Mr. Wilson," another added. "All we dig is rock and more rock."

"Well, maybe deeper," John told them.

The miners shrugged their shoulders. John knew what they were thinking. The fool's paying us, so what do we care?

The mine had another visitor that day. Henry DeMoss rode over and greeted John warmly.

"I see you're equally concerned, Wilson. I was just speaking with Stamp. He says they've not even run across quartz clusters. Seems odd, don't you think?"

"More like disappointing," John said, trying to keep the memory of the earlier ride along the ridge from his mind.

"Why don't we take a little ride, Wilson? I know this

country. There are some interesting spots not too far from here. I'll show them to you."

"I was planning to return to town, have myself some supper."

"I'm packing some cold meats and a bottle of that Italian wine you enjoyed. Ride along. I know a wonderful place not too far from here."

"That sounds like a good idea," Aaron Stamp spoke up, suddenly emerging from amid a huddle of miners. "It's always a good idea for the majority owners to get together."

The last thing John wanted to do was share another meal with DeMoss, but the look in Stamp's eye told him it was necessary. John reluctantly nodded, then followed DeMoss out across the hillside.

"All of this once belonged to Cheyenne Indians," DeMoss began. "This little piece was sold to an old trapper, though. Zeke Thompson was his name. Pioneered this country, even helped map out the route for the railroad. Story is the Indians found out and killed him for it."

"I've heard another version."

"Well, people will spread all sorts of stories," DeMoss said, grinning. "I've even heard talk that I killed the old man myself."

"And?" John asked, spitting a bitterness out of his mouth.

"People will say anything."

DeMoss continued pointing out features of the countryside John knew better than any other person on earth. When they reached the river two miles or so from the railroad bridge, DeMoss climbed down from the saddle, tied off his horse, and took a flour bag from his saddlebags in one hand, the promised bottle of wine in the other.

"Hop down and join me," DeMoss called out.

John reluctantly did just that. The lunch proved to be good, though, meats and cheese with half a loaf of fresh bread. DeMoss jabbered away all through the meal, but John kept his thoughts and opinions to himself.

"There's just one more place I want to show you," DeMoss said when the food had been consumed and the wine bottle emptied. "It's called Arrowhead Creek. The Cheyennes favored it as a campground."

Wolf Creek, John thought as they continued. Why take me there? Does he knew? How could he suspect? Jeff Thompson is long dead. Uncle Peter would never tell.

It took close to two hours to reach Wolf Creek by DeMoss's route, and then the pace was harder than John would have chosen to force on his stallion. The horse was well lathered when they reached the creek. John dismounted and left the horse to drink.

"I meant to show you something a little farther along," DeMoss said.

"My horse needs a rest," John explained, "but I can follow on foot."

"You're a younger man."

"Also one who doesn't plan to walk back to town because his horse gives out."

DeMoss gazed at his own animal, then sighed.

"See your point," the railroader admitted, sliding off the saddle.

John knelt beside his horse and picked an arrowhead out of the sand.

"You found one!" DeMoss shouted. "They're scattered through here all over the place. Sometimes the boys from town come up here and dig around. They come up with all sorts of things. But the most interesting place is up the hill."

John followed DeMoss along until they reached the old campsite on the creek where John had enjoyed a hundred adventures. But the darker memory of that other time, the sudden bark of rifles tearing apart the poor sleeping body of Pat Massey, the cries of terror and desperation that even now rang through his memory.

"It was here we dealt our first blow to Cheyenne Pike," DeMoss boasted. "I discovered one of my supply clerks was passing along information. We persuaded him to give us the half-breed's whereabouts. Pike himself escaped, but we caught three of his gang here, shot them to pieces. Look over here."

DeMoss led the way to the three tall pines that even now sent shudders through John's body. DeMoss pointed to the rotting ropes that hung from the upper branches. Then, to John's horror, the devil found a skull.

"We hung them up there to warn the others. The birds and the wolves ended up making a meal of them, I suppose. Wonder which one's which."

John started to speak, but he bit down on his lip and kept mute.

"I tell you this for a reason, Wilson," DeMoss continued. "I generally have my way about things. You own forty percent of that mine. So do I. Up to this point, you've been making all the decisions. It's your idea to tunnel till you get to China. I'm for blasting the whole mountain if that's what it takes to expose the vein."

"You're forgetting," John said angrily. "Aaron Stamp will vote my way."

"You sound awfully certain. Stamp could get to be a rich man."

"Even so, there's still Reverend Ryland."

"I've dealt with him before," DeMoss said, tossing the skull aside. "He was Cheyenne Pike's uncle, see. Scandal can sorely plague a school like his. I've got friends in Philadelphia."

"So what will you do, buy them out? I hope you have the funds, DeMoss. And what if you're wrong? What if you blast, and the whole shaft gives way? Can you afford to lose it all?"

"I won't."

Leaving DeMoss to recount his earlier triumph to the pines, John returned to his horse and led the weary animal down Wolf Creek toward where it emptied into the Medicine Bow River. Once the animal appeared refreshed enough to bear his weight, John climbed up into the saddle and began the long ride back toward town.

It was well past sunset when John finally rode the tired stallion into the small stable back of the Murphy place. Jeff Kelly appeared almost at once, and John rolled off the horse and passed the reins to the boy.

"We were worried about you, Katy and I," Jeff said, leaning against John's sweat-soaked shirt. "I saw you ride off with DeMoss."

"You don't seem to like him very much."

"Papa died building his railroad, Mr. Wilson. We had to hire someone to bring him home. Those railroad men threw the body beside the tracks, they did, just went along with their work."

"He's a cold one, all right."

"Be careful, Mr. Wilson," the boy said, staring up into John's tired eyes. "He kills people."

"I'll keep a wary eye out, Jefferson Kelly," John said, laughing as the boy loosened the cinch and stripped the saddle from the panting stallion.

"And I'll see he gets rubbed down, sir. Katy has dinner ready."

"I'll go right on in."

After washing up, John met Katy in the dining room. She spooned portions of chicken and dumplings beside a mound of mashed potatoes.

"We were concerned about you," she whispered as she filled his cup with steaming hot coffee. "Jeff was about to go out after you."

"He's something, that boy. Reminds me of someone I used to know."

"He likes you, Mr. Wilson. Since his papa died, he's been at loose ends, I'm afraid. I've tried my best with him, but I fear the hotel was a bad influence. And this town . . . well, there is an army of Jeff Kellys in this place."

"They're everywhere these days, Katy," John said, pausing between bites. "In the mining towns and railroad towns, in Cheyenne villages and lonesome prairies. I was one of them myself."

"I thought so."

"It's a hard way to grow tall sometimes, but if you have the heart it takes to survive, you find your path."

The next morning John received another note.

Orion 1. Gray.

So it was north this time, he thought, yawning away the fatigue that even now remained. But he also knew things were coming to a conclusion. It was time. Oh, Lord, it was time!

That night Stamp kept no fire, and John had difficulty locating him at first. The two finally met on horseback, two riders pausing but a minute to discuss the weather.

"You have a good talk with DeMoss?" Stamp asked. "I was half of a mind to shadow you, but there were too many eyes about. Besides, as I recall, you used to be able to handle yourself in a scrap by all accounts."

"He wants to blast."

"He'll get his way, Johnny. I got a wire from Laramie this afternoon. DeMoss bought all five thousand from our church friend."

"And from you?"

"Three thousand, at twenty dollars a share. There's only one place he could've got that kind of money. I'd guess he dipped mighty deep into the Northern treasury."

"Wire Welles Barrett."

"I already did. They're calling a stockholders' meeting. And the bank will call his note in the morning."

"It's almost over, then," John said, sighing.

"Been worth the run?"

"It's so the running can end."

"It can end right now if you'd like," Stamp went on. "I've made my share of friends over the years. Some are in Washington. I've made some arrangements. Those old warrants on Jeff Thompson have been set aside. A pardon's been issued."

"I'm not certain I understand."

"Call it a bonus. For aiding justice."

"Justice?"

"Yes," Stamp said, grinning somberly. "Justice a long time coming."

V

Two days later Henry DeMoss suddenly disappeared from Thompson's Mountain. John no longer spotted his old enemy at the telegraph office or the bank, and the private railway car had simply disappeared during the previous night. John had never felt particularly comfortable having the villain around. And yet seeing DeMoss meant the old surveyor wasn't off weaving webs of intrigue or formulating schemes. John was almost relieved when DeMoss reappeared later in the week. DeMoss looked suddenly old as he stepped off the afternoon train in the company of an elegantly-dressed woman in her forties. Behind them walked two young men in their late teens.

"He registered them at the hotel as his wife and sons," Jeff informed John later in the day. "It's a bit of a surprise, him staying at the hotel when he had that railroad car all to himself just last week."

"Last week he was president of the Northern Colorado Railroad," John replied with a satisfied smile.

The smile faded a little later when Aaron Stamp

dropped by.

"From the look of the trunks and furniture moved into the hotel, I'd say DeMoss has lost his house as well," Stamp said. "More importantly, he's called a meeting in my office to discuss the future of the mine."

"That, or he's trying to sell his shares," John commented.

"He could have done that easier in Denver. No, he's sure there's gold there. He can't imagine you investing in a worthless mountainside.

Stamp was right. Shortly after the meeting was convened, DeMoss took over.

"I have no objections to you remaining president, Stamp, so long as you follow my instructions," DeMoss began. "They are—"

"Hold on there," John interrupted. "Just who do you think you are? Forty percent . . ."

"I'm afraid you're slow to get the news, Wilson," DeMoss said, laughing. "As of this moment, I am majority stockholder. Here are the certificates," he added, emptying the contents of his briefcase. "Fifty-six percent."

"There must be some mistake," Stamp said in pretended surprise. "I only sold you 3,000 shares."

"And Reverend Ryland sold me his 5,000," DeMoss explained. "It seemed some of my Philadelphia friends contribute generously to his mission school."

"Go on," John said, allowing the genuine bitterness inside him to reveal itself for the first time.

"So, I spoke to some engineer friends of mine in Grand Island. They said it's accepted practice to blast

401

the surface."

"Not when you've already got a shaft dug fifty feet into the heart of the mountain," John objected. "All you'll accomplish is blistering the surface. It'll cave in the shaft. You'll have nothing to show for all these weeks' labor. Worse, your capital will be spent. With no funds to pay the men, it'll all grind to a halt."

"Not if we expose the vein," DeMoss insisted. "And we will. You know it's there."

"Even so," Stamp said dourly, "you may not have the men to dig ore without more funds. Where would we get the money? I'm not about to pour another nickel into this project once the shaft's gone."

"Nor will I," John pledged. "Have you the money personally, DeMoss? I would think you're overextended now."

"Men have underestimated me before," DeMoss declared.

"If we follow your plan," John said, eyeing DeMoss with a kind of deliberate intensity, "we could end up back at the beginning with our capital spent. With nothing to show for it."

"But there's always more capital to be found," DeMoss insisted.

"Not from me," John said sternly. "A long time ago I learned it's better to fold a bad hand than play it out to the finish. You go ahead and do it your way, DeMoss, but don't forget that I warned you. When it all comes crashing down on top of you, it's nobody's fault but your own."

John stomped out of the room, leaving a smug

Henry DeMoss to examine the mine plans and go over with Stamp the procedure for blasting.

But that wasn't all John saw of DeMoss that day. DeMoss and his family showed up at the Murphy house just after dinner that night.

"I don't believe you've met my family," DeMoss said, bowing slightly to his wife. "This is Claire, my devoted wife."

"I'm John Wilson of Denver, ma'am," John said, kissing her gloved hand.

"I'm delighted to meet you, sir," Claire answered. "Allow me to present our boys, Grant and Christopher."

The older of the two shook John's hand, then retreated immediately.

"I'm called Chris," the younger said as he greeted John warmly. "I understand you keep horses. Might I have a look?"

"Surely," John said. "Jeff? You around?"

Jeff Kelly appeared instantly. His sweat-streaked face and unkempt clothes drew a frown from Claire DeMoss. Worse, the boy smelled of stable muck.

"Jeff, take Chris here out to have a look at the horses. If he'd like, feel free to take him riding with you tomorrow. The horses want exercise."

"Yes, sir," Jeff said, grabbing Chris by the hand and leading the boy through the dining room toward the back door.

"I hope I wasn't stepping out of line there," John said. "A town like this one can try a boy's patience. A ride will work wonders."

"We shouldn't even be here," Grant mumbled. "If we hadn't been pulled out of school . . ."

"That's enough of that," DeMoss barked. "Grant, be so good as to take your mother to the hotel. It's been a trying day."

The seventeen-year-old gazed at John with cold, dark eyes, then shook his head so that a stray strand or two of coal-black hair fell back from his forehead.

"Grant?" Claire asked, extending her arm to her eldest son.

The young man took it and led his mother out the door. John expected DeMoss to retire also, but such was not the case.

"I'm afraid I'm forced to disturb you twice today on account of business," DeMoss said, seating himself on one of the big leather chairs that dominated the parlor.

"Oh?"

"I'm afraid I need a slight favor."

John studied DeMoss carefully. The railroader was unable to conceal the panic from his eyes. Sweat broke out on a deeply lined forehead, and one foot tapped nervously.

"I really can't imagine why you should come to me," John said, sitting in a rocker on the far side of the room. "Surely I haven't encouraged you to consider me a business associate."

"We are working together on the Thompson Mountain Mine."

"Apparently we're working at opposite purposes there. You plan to explode six weeks' labor and a year's planning, don't you?"

"I need a quick profit."

"Ah," John said, laughing. "I'm afraid you should have invested in some other enterprise, DeMoss. The kind of mining operation we're engaged in takes years to turn a dollar. You have to build the smelter, and—"

"No, we'll ship the ore to Denver, let them process it there."

"You cut out all the profit that way," John said, throwing his hands in the air. "Why don't you return to your railroad, let mining people oversee the mine. We don't want a tunnel through that ridge! We want to locate its mineral deposits."

"Not me!"

"No, you wanted to find the goose that laid those fanciful golden eggs. There's no such bird. What you're planning is akin to cutting the goose open. You'll end up with nothing, and neither will the rest of us."

"That decision's been made!" DeMoss shouted.

John walked to the door and opened it slowly, all the time concentrating a terribly vengeful stare at Henry DeMoss. But DeMoss only grumbled and shook his head.

"I must beg your pardon, Wilson," DeMoss said, pulling out his handkerchief and running it over his forehead. "I'm under a strain. I learned recently that a loan I had taken out has been called. I have until tomorrow to raise the money or forfeit the security."

"And what security might that be?"

"Practically everything I own. My shares in the Northern, my Union Pacific bonds, even my Thompson Mountain Mining stock. I need a favor. Only my

UP bonds are at peak value. The Northern stock went up, but now it's falling."

"So you want me to buy you out of Thompson Mountain?"

"Oh, no," DeMoss said, clutching the arm of his chair. "I know the dividends alone will put me back on my feet. I've seen what your company in Mariesville yields."

"This isn't Mariesville," John reminded his old enemy. "I warned you it was speculative."

"The problem I have is that I need to come up with $200,000. That way I can pay the note."

"And you want me to loan it to you?" John asked, laughing even louder than before.

"It's far from humorous."

"Put yourself in my place, DeMoss. You come in here and tell me you have a note you can't pay. Then you ask me in effect to assume that note, knowing it's not likely to be paid. You must not think much of me as a businessman."

"I'm asking you because you're the only one certain of the profits we'll bring in with the mine."

"I'm certain of no such thing," John said, drawing back. "Even less, with you planning to blast half the countryside. I don't understand you. You want me to loan you money when you've just put a quarter-million-dollar investment of mine in jeopardy? I think you must be a lunatic."

"I ask you as a friend."

"A friend?" John asked, shaking with ill-concealed rage.

"Look, I realize we've had a disagreement concerning the mine, but that's minor. You know what it's like to be in a tight spot."

"Yes, I do," John said with blazing eyes. To himself, he thought, yes! And you put me there!

"You'd throw a drowning man a rope, wouldn't you?"

John scowled. If DeMoss were drowning, John would be more likely to pray for rain than to throw a rope.

"Tell you what I'll do, Colonel," John said, using the title with not a little bit of scorn. "What's the note valued at?"

"Two hundred thousand, with interest due of another five."

"How many shares of the Northern did you pledge?"

"All I have left."

"Which is?"

"Twenty thousand. It's the largest single block."

"And I understand the NCRR is currently selling at—"

"You know it's gone down. Six weeks ago I sold shares at twelve dollars."

"And yesterday in Denver I'd guess you might have gotten what, six or seven? No wonder the bank's called the note. They want to get something back."

"You forget the bonds."

"Their value?"

"With interest, I'd estimate thirty, thirty-five thousand."

"So what you're saying is that disregarding the

Thompson Mountain stock, which frankly doesn't interest me in the slightest until something's struck, you have at best a hundred seventy-five thousand dollars to pay a note for two hundred."

"You talk like a banker. You know the Northern could double its value tomorrow."

"Or drop to five. I've heard rumors that you haven't managed that line any too well. You've been here for weeks. But I've got faith in the future of freight service from Denver into Wyoming. I'll buy your Northern stock and the Union Pacific bonds for the value of the note."

"That's larceny?"

"Good night, DeMoss," John said, walking to the door and angrily kicking it open. "I think our business is concluded."

"No, wait," DeMoss said, jumping to his feet and blocking John's retreat. "That stock, those bonds . . . they're my only assets besides the mining stock. I've even sold my house. And once the stock's gone, the other stockholders are sure to remove me as president of the line. They've already impounded the rail car and closed my office."

"Then, I'd agree it appears likely."

"You leave me little choice."

"You forget that I have one, though," John reminded DeMoss. "I'll be honest. If it wasn't for your family being here tonight, I'd leave you for the buzzards. But I have great sympathy for destitute or deserted women and children. I'm hardly interested in creating any new ones myself."

"I suppose I should be grateful. The bank would seize the stock at any rate, and the largest block of my mining interest, too."

"Then, I'll wire my attorneys in Denver in the morning. They'll acquire the note, and you can sign over the securities in a day or so. Who currently holds the loan?"

"First Security Bank in Denver."

Too easy, John thought. Welles Barrett had even issued the note personally. John hoped his satisfaction wasn't too apparent.

"I'll attend to it all first thing in the morning," John promised. "And again I'd caution you about the blasting. If it was me, I'd sell off half that mining stock and be patient."

"Patience never got this railroad built," DeMoss said, opening the door and pointing to the tracks at the far end of town. "If patient men had been in charge, you'd still be crossing these plains on horseback!"

Yes, John thought as DeMoss left. And I would be camped up there with Pike, swapping tales of a dozen summers, chasing bare-chested sons around Prairie Flower's lodge. It's you who brought it on yourself, DeMoss!

John's thoughts were interrupted by a disturbance inside the stable. He immediately closed the door and darted through the house and out the back door. The noise proved to be Jeff Kelly trying to calm the big charcoal stallion enough to mount it. Christopher DeMoss sat atop a roan mare.

"Trouble, Jeff?" John asked, smiling with approval at the small boy's determination to pull himself atop the restless beast.

"I'm about there, Mr. Wilson," Jeff said, tugging until his neck muscles bulged with the strain. Just as John stepped forward to offer support, though, the boy succeeded.

"You ride much as a rule, Chris?" John asked the older youngster.

"Oh, just at school, sir," Chris said, grinning as he maneuvered the mare along the fence.

John marveled at the likeness of the two DeMoss boys. Chris was simply a younger version of his brother Grant. But where Grant's dark eyes had seemed calculating and sinister, Chris's were friendly, inviting. The dark hair bounced about the boy's ears as the mare trotted to and fro.

"You look like you know what you're about up there," John said. "A little like a soldier, stern and serious. Look at the way Jeff relaxes, feels a part of the horse."

"That's not how I was taught, sir," Chris complained.

"Didn't know riding was a science, to be taught," John said, laughing. "It's something you have to feel, like the wind and the sun."

"I suppose," Chris said, sighing. The boy was clearly at home on horseback, but something held back his instincts.

"Chris says he wants to have a ranch out here one of these days," Jeff explained. "I'm going to be his foreman."

"Oh?" John asked.

"Just thinking out loud," Chris admitted. "I've always loved animals, especially horses. But Father says I'm to read the law."

"There are worse labors to put your shoulder to," John said. "Still, I've always found that a man's got to find his own path. He can't always fit in the boots his pa picks out for him."

Chris nodded. Then Jeff nudged the stallion into a trot, and the boys raced off down the road.

"I thought that was tomorrow you were going riding," John grumbled as a cloud of dust rose, half choking him to death. The boys failed to respond. Instead, when the air cleared, John found himself facing Aaron Stamp.

"I was down at the telegraph office," Stamp explained. "Heard DeMoss wired Denver that you'd agreed to buy his note."

"Mainly I'm buying the NCRR stock and the bonds."

"So, he's more than swallowed the hook, Johnny, my friend. It's beginning to turn inside him, tear at his innards."

Yes, John said, remembering the feeling. It was grim satisfaction to know DeMoss was learning what it felt like to be a hunted man, to know fear and pain. Soon the scoundrel would understand what happens when a man sees his world torn apart, everything swept away in a whirlwind.

"It's funny," Stamp said, watching the sun disappear into the western range. "I thought I'd feel better about this than I do. But then, when I used to bring men in, I never went to the hangings."

Yes, John thought as they stared at the two boys

riding across the adjacent hillside. Nothing's ever what you expect.

"I know," John finally whispered. "But I can't find it in my heart to forgive a man who's brought me so much sadness, who would've ended my life a dozen times."

"I guess it's best not to forget the hatred, Johnny. A man can't let his thinking get clouded. He becomes careless. And DeMoss isn't the kind of man to put in a hole and then turn your back on."

"No, he's not," John agreed.

VI

The first real chill of autumn hung in the air that next morning. John sent his wire early, taking care not to notify Welles Barrett directly. The lawyers would attend to that. John spent the rest of the day reading a handful of dispatches and two dozen letters Jeff Kelly had stacked neatly on the desk. John normally enjoyed the sporadic mail deliveries, but this time there was no letter from Marie, no scratch of a note from Michael or drawing from Joanna. No "we all miss you" printed in Peter's uneven letters.

The mystery was solved the next day when Levi Nolan arrived with the papers transferring DeMoss's stock certificates. Marie and the children accompanied the lawyer.

"Have you forgotten the date?" she asked angrily. "It's your birthday."

"Didn't give it any thought," he said as he held her tightly.

"Birthdays are important," she declared as Peter wrapped himself under John's right arm and little Joanna snuggled against her father's leg. Michael led

Timothy by the hand.

"Your birthday, is it?" Jeff Kelly asked with a devilish sparkle in his young eyes. "Oh, Katy will have to bake a cake."

"She's liable to be too busy," John said, motioning to his brood. "There'll be a house full of children."

"Leave them to me," Marie declared. "And besides, Nancy is back there somewhere. She refused to abandon the luggage."

John laughed. Nancy was forever proclaiming railroad porters the greatest thieves west of the Mississippi. In truth he'd never had so much as a button disappear.

"If I'd known you were coming, I'd had a carriage waiting," John apologized. "I'll try and hire a wagon."

"We've got a wagon," Jeff objected. "I'll go back and bring it up. Don't worry about the baggage. I used to work here in my off hours. I'll have it all loaded before you can whistle."

John started to object, but the boy charged off down the platform.

"Well, I see you haven't given up collecting strays," Marie said, hugging him tightly. "Shall we walk to the house?"

"If you don't mind the breeze. October's making herself felt," John pointed out.

He then directed Nolan to locate Nancy and tell the woman of Jeff's expected arrival. John then returned to the family. The children seemed a little bewildered by their strange surroundings, so John drew them aside a moment.

"This town is called Thompson's Mountain," he told

them. "One of these days I'll tell you about the man who once lived here, his Indian wife, the children who used to hunt and fish and swim in the river."

"It's too cold to go swimming, isn't it, Papa?" Michael asked.

"It wasn't for them," John answered. Michael looked somehow smaller after the long weeks away. There was a melancholy tint to the boy's usually bright eyes, and John pulled him closer. "Lord, it's so good to see you all."

The children clawed and hugged their father, and John warmed so that he half expected to find the station afire. Then he picked up little Timothy, letting the boy ride like a sack of flour on one shoulder as the gaggle of Wilsons headed for the Murphy house.

Poor Katy Kelly greeted them at the door, aghast at the thought of preparing supper for five new guests.

"Don't forget Nancy, Papa," Michael whispered, and Katy nearly expired.

"Tell you what," John said, lifting the young woman's chin. "Why don't we have supper at the hotel. That way you can plan a nice dinner."

"Oh, wonderful, that'd be, Mr. Wilson," Katy said, brightening considerably. "My good friend Amanda Ehrens is on her way to help straighten the rooms, and Jeff's convinced Mrs. Hyatt to hurry the washing. I'll have time to bake a cake."

"Don't trouble yourself," John told her.

"What? Would you have a birthday and no cake? Why, it's bad luck for sure. And besides, Jeff'll be after me to give him what icing's left. Wouldn't hurt him to fatten up some."

"You convinced me," John said, laughing.

He then showed Marie the house, leaving Katy to attend to curious little ones who needed a bit of scrubbing or a shoe tied.

"I've missed you so much," he said when they were alone. "I can't remember when I've felt so glad to see someone. You're a wonder, Marie."

"I'd hoped you'd come back to me."

"It won't be much longer."

"I wish you'd abandon this revenge, Johnny. I know you were hurt, but will it really end with DeMoss?"

"I can't turn back," he muttered sadly. "It's not in me."

Supper at the hotel turned into a minor ordeal. Poor Mrs. O'Hara was as ill prepared as Katy, and it took close to an hour to complete the meal. Timothy refused to eat the potatoes, and Joanna declined the greens. Only Peter emptied his plate, and that was only because Michael wagered a nickel Peter couldn't do it.

"Never knew children to let good food go to waste," Mrs. O'Hara grumbled. "There are those in this town who'd take such leavings and be glad to have them."

Michael started to reply, but a stern glance from John silenced the boy. Mrs. O'Hara went on clearing the table, and John paid the bill. He also left a generous reward for her trouble.

As Marie ushered the children toward the hotel lobby, Henry DeMoss appeared with his family.

"Well, well," DeMoss said, descending the stairs with a quickness of step that surprised John to no small degree. "Is this your family, John?"

"My wife, Marie," John said, forcing a smile. "My

children, Michael, Peter, Joanna, and Timothy."

"Charmed, madam," DeMoss said, bowing. "Let me present my own dear wife, Claire, and our sons, Grant and Christopher."

Claire stepped past her husband and drew Marie aside. The two quickly warmed to each other, and a cheerful conversation ensued.

"Oh, dear," Claire called. "It's John's birthday."

"Well, this is cause for a celebration!" DeMoss declared. "I wish we hadn't sent the private car back. The hotel's scarcely the proper place for such a celebration."

"All the celebrating we're going to do will be back at the Murphy place," John explained. "In our family, birthdays are private."

Marie scowled, but John wasn't in the least interested in turning their reunion into an encounter with DeMoss.

"Congratulations, sir," Chris called down from the stairway. His brother Grant glanced away.

"Thank you," John responded. "All of you. But now I'd like to get this brood home before the hotel suffers structural damage. Mr. DeMoss, if you'd stop by around one, Levi Nolan brought some papers for you to sign. He's hoping to return to Denver tonight."

"Certainly," DeMoss agreed, his face paling. "Perhaps we'll have a chance to share dinner with your charming family before they have to leave as well."

"Maybe," John said, leading the way toward the door.

That afternoon John devoted almost totally to the children. It seemed they'd become partial strangers in his absence. Joanna was gabbing away now, and Tim, once he warmed up, could babble out whole groups of words before growing confused.

DeMoss arrived close to two o'clock, an hour late, but John refused to be upset. Nolan had the papers all ready, and Aaron Stamp witnessed each signature. John had already performed his part of the transaction.

"The Northern's a good line, Wilson," DeMoss said before leaving. "Find a good man to run her. I poured ten years of dreams into those rails, and I've little to show for it now. Help her prosper."

John might have felt sympathy for anyone else. But along with the papers, Welles Barrett had sent a report on the NCRR's books. Shortages appeared everywhere. The Northern had served as DeMoss's personal wallet, and the stockholders, now aware of that fact, wanted blood.

I don't see how a man could be so stupid, John thought. It's one thing to prowl the night like a panther, killing a man's family and stealing his dreams. But to take and take, leaving a record of it on paper, was pure lunacy.

John refused to let Henry DeMoss or anything else ruin that day, though. He wound up with an aching back from hauling the little ones around the house on his back, but it was a small price to pay for the joy that filled his heart. Fortunately, before he suffered any other misfortunes, Jeff swept the children off to the stable.

"Can Michael and Peter handle a horse?" Jeff had asked earlier. "I can take the tiny ones with me. We won't go far, just up the hill and back."

Jeff had agreed, and the children showed an enthusiasm for riding with their new friend that they'd never showed when their father had extended a similar offer in Denver.

It wasn't altogether a successful enterprise. Timothy managed to roll through the straw, and Joanna fell in the muck. Michael and Peter soaked themselves trying to help Jeff water the animals, and their mother had a minor fit.

"Johnny, I've never seen such a mess!" she exclaimed, pointing to the four wet, dirty, odorous youngsters. "There's only one solution. Baths!"

The boys in particular screamed to high heaven, but when Jeff volunteered to lend a hand, the rebellion settled down to a quiet rumble.

"You don't know how well off you are," Jeff told them. "I used to have to scrub myself every morning back at the hotel. Only bathtub I had was a bucket of cold well water. Most times I'd shrivel right into a ball so you'd hardly know I was there."

"Well, there's enough hot water so you can have a turn at the tub as well, Jefferson Kelly," Katy declared.

And the rebellion resumed, with Jeff its loudest advocate. In the end all were scrubbed and dressed for dinner.

"I'd be particularly pleased if you and Jeff would join us tonight, too," John told Katy as she iced the cake. "You've almost become family here of late, and I believe the children have adopted you officially. Nancy usually sits at our table in Denver, and to be truthful, you're prettier."

"Oh, sir," Katy said, blushing. But John could tell

she'd been pleased with the invitation. Jeff seemed a little hesitant, though.

"You've got your family here," the boy explained from the far side of the door. "I'm just the help, after all."

"Is that right?" John asked, scowling. "And here all along I thought maybe you were a friend."

"Oh, well, if you're inviting me as a friend, that's a different matter. I couldn't very well turn you down on that account."

"That's better," John said, smiling.

The smile grew wider as Katy brought in two roasted ducks and a honey-baked ham. Nancy, who'd quickly captured Katy's confidence, presented a tray of vegetables. The meal was topped off by sliced melons and berries. And, of course, the cake.

"How many candles are there?" Peter asked.

"Twenty-eight," Michael counted. "That's right, Papa?"

"Afraid so," John confessed. "Pretty ancient, eh?"

"That's not so old," Peter announced. "Unless you were a horse."

The room resounded with laughter, and Peter hid his face.

"It's getting to be a challenge to blow them all out," John said as Nancy touched a burning straw to each small wick. "But I believe I can manage."

John blew out the candles, and the children clapped with approval. Soon they were gobbling their slices and, led by Jeff's delicate tenor, singing away the evening. Finally fatigue set in, and John helped Marie get the little ones into nightclothes and tuck them into bed.

"I've missed this, too," he told her after Joanna kissed his forehead. "I felt so cut off from everything."

"We've felt it, too, Johnny," she said, gripping his arm. "We're not going back without you."

"But Michael has his schooling."

"I'll keep him up with his lessons. I might have a try at young Jeff, too. He seems awfully bright."

"I think that would be nice, Marie. He's a little like a clerk I once met in a trading post off in the wilds of Colorado. No folks, only a sister to look after him."

"He's fallen into good company here," she said, kissing him warmly on the cheek. "Now, let's leave the little ones to their rest and find some for ourselves."

They descended the stairs toward the front bedroom they'd share, but as John's foot touched the bottom stair, there was a hard rap at the front door.

"I'll get it," John called as Katy and Nancy stirred in the kitchen. When he opened the door, he found Henry DeMoss waiting.

"I need . . . to talk . . . to you," DeMoss stammered.

"It's late," John said, turning aside to avoid the heavy alcoholic mist surrounding DeMoss.

"I've got to know," DeMoss said, stumbling through the doorway. "Did you know?"

"Know what?" John asked, blocking DeMoss's further entry.

"The railroad investigation. I could've . . . could've stopped it if . . . if I'd had a vote."

"I don't understand."

"We've had problems. Bookkeeping . . . bookkeeping problems. They think there's a . . . a shortage.

They'll blame me. Miles says you ordered it!"

"Levi brought a proxy. I signed my vote over to Welles Barrett. I've done business with him at the bank, as apparently you have. I didn't give it a second thought. It's how I handle the newspaper, the flour mill . . ."

"Not your fault," DeMoss said, leaning against the door. "Bad timing's all. When the mine—"

DeMoss collapsed, and John sent Jeff to the hotel for help. Pat O'Hara arrived shortly and helped DeMoss to his feet.

"We'll take it from here, Mr. Wilson," O'Hara said, shaking his head. "I suppose he's entitled. Been quite a donnybrook up on the second floor with himself and the oldest boy."

"Good night, Mr. O'Hara," John said as Jeff and the hotel owner got DeMoss headed back down the street.

"Night, sir," O'Hara replied.

"What was that all about, Johnny?" Marie whispered as John closed the door.

"I'm guessing, of course, but from what I know, DeMoss bought mining stock with funds borrowed from the Northern. Without the consent of the minority owners, I'd guess."

"You mean he stole it?"

"That's not what he'd call it."

"He could go to jail, Johnny."

"Yes."

"He'll be ruined personally and financially."

"Yes."

"It's what you planned, isn't it?" she asked.

"Yes," he said, staring with cold eyes at the drunken

422

man stumbling toward the hotel. "What I planned and what I wanted. What he deserves."

"Johnny, I've never seen this side of you," she gasped.

"You never stared down as I bled half to death on this mountainside, scarcely older than young Chris and maybe not as big. You never bragged about hanging corpses in trees for the birds to pick at. He doesn't deserve sympathy, Marie, especially from me. Or you."

"I was thinking of Claire," she said sadly. "Would it be so very much to forgive?"

"Yes," he said bitterly. "Far too much!"

VII

For half a lifetime John had looked forward to the moment when he would at last avenge the cruel deaths of his parents. But as Henry DeMoss began to crumble, John found little contentment. Marie was still on hand like a spectre become flesh, a human conscience which reminded him DeMoss was not the sole sufferer. The tired solemn faces of Claire and young Christopher seemed to be everywhere. Only Grant kept out of sight.

John tried to keep busy, either corresponding with Art Jennings or the Denver businesses. Often the children would insist on a trip to the mountain, and John would bundle them up, then hitch a team to the wagon and set off for an excursion to Wolf Creek.

He never took any of them to the mine or to the simple graveyard on the mountainside. Sometimes he rode there alone, but he feared more than anything an explosion of pain, a revelation of his past that might even now pluck DeMoss from disaster's path.

And yet DeMoss flirted with ruin as a boy might dance along the rim of a high canyon wall, feeling somehow invincible. It would never happen, he must have thought, not to Henry DeMoss.

John was sitting alone on the porch of the Murphy house when Aaron Stamp greeted him an hour after dawn one morning.

"We've placed the charges," Stamp said. "I wish you'd ride out there with me."

"All right," John agreed, not really sure why.

The two rode side by side, John on the charcoal stallion, Stamp on a graceful bay mare. It was cold, and the horses' breath formed little misty clouds as they rode. It was as if the riders sat atop a pair of fire-snorting dragons.

"He's already there," Stamp declared, pointing to a carriage on the hillside ahead. With DeMoss was his whole family. John wished Claire and the boys had stayed in town.

"I brought them for luck," DeMoss explained moments later. "Well, are we all prepared to be rich men?"

"I feel duty bound to tell you one more time," John spoke up. "This will never work. You'll scar the mountain. Nature never yielded a treasure without a price being paid. You can't expect her to give up her gold when you tear at her side like a mountain cat wild with fury."

"You speak like a fool Indian," DeMoss said with contempt.

"It will all come to nothing," John warned. "Give it time."

"I have no time!" DeMoss suddenly screamed. "My back's to the wall. I need it now."

Stamp grinned, but John couldn't escape the tortured, fear-contorted faces of Chris and Claire. Grant remained haughty, but John noticed the young man's hands trembled.

"I've got no choice," DeMoss said as he motioned to Stamp. "Let's get on with it."

Stamp climbed down from his horse and left its reins in the hands of a dusty-faced water boy. John did likewise, and the boy led the animals off to the shelter of a nearby aspen grove.

"Best leave that carriage, ma'am," Stamp warned. "Horses can get mighty skittish when blasting's going on."

DeMoss helped Claire down, then motioned the boys to follow. A miner drove the carriage off, and Stamp waved the huddle of spectators behind a wall of rock debris that encircled the mine office, the warehouses, and a long barracks built to house the workers.

"Won't be long now, son," DeMoss said to Grant in particular. "We'll be swimming in gold, and then you can have your choice of schools to attend. You'll see."

Claire rubbed a tear away. No one appeared convinced.

The first explosion shook the earth seconds later. It was followed by another and another. The world itself seemed to sway like a boat upon the sea, and clouds of dark gray smoke rolled across the mountainside. Tongues of fire spit skyward, and jagged fragments of rock hurled themselves hundreds of feet in the air.

John felt as if a knife was being twisted inside him. His beloved mountain was torn and abused in a hundred places. Trees he'd once lain beneath on a warm July afternoon broke into pieces or were buried beneath rockslides. The gentle slopes were opened by great gashes.

"That's the last of the charges," Stamp finally announced.

John leaned against the rock wall, his whole being shaken so that he feared he might collapse. As the dust and debris settled, he gazed upon an apocalyptic sight. The mouth of the shaft had been swallowed, its location recognizable only by splintered timbers and a tired swirl of smoke. The barracks remained intact, but one wall of the back storehouse had collapsed, and the windows of the office had been shattered.

"Well, now we'll find the gold," DeMoss declared, racing forward to pick through the rubble for the exposed vein.

"It's the worst I've ever seen," Stamp blurted out. "I didn't believe it possible!"

The miners stared at the shaft and muttered to themselves.

"Weeks of sweat and pain wasted! And for what?" one grumbled.

"You can't claw gold out of the ground!" another growled.

"Proud of yourself, mister?" one cried out defiantly.

DeMoss paid no heed. He ran from one crater to another, searching for a cascade of golden flakes, a bright flash of yellow in the morning sunlight.

"Best have a close look, boys," Stamp finally instructed. "I want each spot examined. Bring me even a speck of color, a trace of quartz. Watch for silver, too."

The miners nodded, then reluctantly trudged off to check out the mountain's deep scars. But in the end there were no surprises. Only fragmented rock and empty gorges awaited their inspection.

"Here!" DeMoss would cry out. "What about this? Isn't it gold ore?"

"That's just a limestone rock, Mr. DeMoss," a miner would declare, tossing it away like a shred of grass. "Don't you even know what gold looks like?"

DeMoss finally sank to the ground and gazed into the sky.

"Well, Johnny?" Stamp whispered as he led John off to one side. "Hooked and landed. Now I'd say our trout's sizzling in the fat of his own frying pan."

"Yes," John agreed. His eyes crept back down the hillside. Claire stood with her arm around Chris. Tears streamed down her cheeks. Grant gazed at his father in disgust. Finally Chris escaped his mother's arm and raced to DeMoss.

"Come on, Father," the youngster pleaded. "Let's go."

DeMoss followed, a broken man if ever there was one.

"What now?" Claire asked, turning to Aaron Stamp. "Do we try again tomorrow?"

"The powder's gone," Stamp explained. "Besides, we're unlikely to find anything. If there was gold, it's buried under two hundred feet of rubble deep inside that mountain. There's no point to continuing. I'll pay off the men. All we can do now is mend the scars on the mountain and try again another day, in another place."

"We can't!" DeMoss shouted.

"What else can we do?" Stamp asked. "After we meet the payroll and settle our accounts, we might have enough left to return fifty cents a share. It wouldn't begin to get us started on a new shaft. With winter coming . . . no, we're finished."

"But . . ."

"Look, DeMoss, you hold 28,000 shares. You'd have $14,000. That's a start."

"It's not enough," DeMoss said, trembling. "Wilson? Talk to him. You've got funds. I'll sell you half my holdings."

"It's over," John said, avoiding DeMoss's grasping hands. "I have other affairs to manage. It's time I returned to Denver."

"You can't!" DeMoss cried furiously. "I need your—"

"Help?" John asked, his eyes flashing with hatred. "Look at this mountain! It's your handiwork from top to bottom. You tear at the land like a fool, and when fate failed to reward your recklessness, you ask for help?"

DeMoss drew back as the bitterness exploded through John's heart.

"It's best you head back to town," Stamp whispered, turning John toward the horses. "I'll get the men started at clearing away the debris. That ought to give them another two weeks' work."

"Tell them I'll send word to Art. They'll have work back in Mariesville."

"That'll settle a lot of minds, I'm sure."

"You will do what you can to mend her wounds, won't you?" John asked, trembling as he examined his beloved mountain, the home of his childhood, the setting for recollections good and bad.

"Leave it to me."

John paused on his return to Thompson's Mountain long enough to take another tour of the shantytown. His eyes filled with tears as he watched the half-naked skeletons of the dispossessed rumage among the scraps of food and clothing left for them by the townspeople. One little red-haired girl no larger than Joanna trod the cold, hard ground in bare, battered feet.

John stopped at the telegraph office and sent word to Art Jennings about the miners. He sent two other dispatches, one to Levi Nolan about the shoe factory they'd discussed building down by the river. The other requested that food and clothing be shipped at the first opportunity to Thompson's Mountain.

John stumbled wearily across the street then and made his way to the Murphy house. Young Jeff Kelly opened the door, his sad eyes suddenly grown old.

"You'll be leaving now, I guess," the boy said, gripping John's arm in a rare show of emotion.

"The mine's finished," John explained. "It's best I go back to Denver. I have responsibilities there."

"I could go with you. I've gotten to be a fair hand with horses."

"I have a man in Denver to handle the stable," John said, enclosing Jeff's small fingers in his own larger hand.

"Oh," Jeff muttered. "I suppose I'd best see Mr. O'Hara."

"I've given that some thought, Jeff. Seems to me Katy's an awfully good cook to be sewing her life away. This house, well, it's just beginning to take shape. With a little paint and some furniture for the attic rooms, it could hold, I don't know, forty or fifty people."

"A hotel?"

"Well, I don't see there's much need for that. But down at the edge of town I've seen twenty or thirty boys and girls even younger than you. Nobody's taught most of them how to take a bath. I thought we might just turn this place into a home for them."

"An orphanage?" Jeff asked, the word seemingly

430

bitter to his tongue.

"Let's call it a refuge. Some of those kids have mothers. I imagine a few of those ladies would be willing to cook and clean, mend, and sew for the ones that don't. There'll be work here by spring for them in a shoe factory."

"And me?"

"Got to have somebody around to pick up supplies, teach the little ones how to handle stock. More importantly, we'll need someone to teach the dirty ones how to take a bath."

"Who'd run things?"

"I've got an uncle. He's a minister. He has his own mission up on the Laramie River, but I'm sure he can find someone with a fair mind and the proper temperament. How does all that sound to you, Jeff?"

"Fine," the boy said, hesitating. "I suppose you'd come up now and again yourself?"

"Have to. Wouldn't want you getting too tall between visits. Besides, I have something to teach the little ones about this mountain."

"Then, you've hired yourself an odd-jobs man, Mr. Wilson."

"There's something more, too, Jefferson Kelly. I want to hear you're going to school. A man can't spend his whole life with horses and old washed-up miners."

"Mrs. Wilson's been working with me on my figures. She says the same thing about school."

"Then that much at least is settled," John said, patting the boy's back before heading toward the kitchen to pass the news on to Katy.

By midafternoon the news was all over town. A few of the urchins from the railroad tracks had already trickled by to see if it was true, and Marie had quickly seen to it they had a hot meal, a bath, and a haircut. Where possible, a pair of shoes and a simple cotton dress were provided the girls. A few of the boys inherited a pair of trousers from Michael or Peter, with a shirt to match. Jeff rounded up other odds and ends from the townsfolk.

It didn't take long for half of the shantytown to reoutfit itself. The youngest of the orpans were housed in the dusty attic rooms.

"I suppose they'll have taken over the entire house by dinner," Marie joked. "But I'm glad we're doing this, Johnny. Even Michael and Peter are helping out."

"I think it's best if we return to Denver as soon as possible. Do you think we ought to stay until Uncle Peter sends someone to oversee the house?"

"Why don't we ask Nancy to stay a week? I think she'd like that, looking after the girls especially. Katy can handle the rest."

"Who'd cook for us?"

"I thought I might handle that chore myself for a time. I used to get us through the winter, remember?"

"Yes," he said, smiling as she held him.

They then opened up the trunks and began packing up those belongings not needed immediately. The work had barely started, though, when Jeff appeared to announce John had a visitor.

"It's Chris and his mother," Jeff whispered. "They're outside."

John turned to Marie, and she silently nodded for him to leave. He then followed Jeff to the door.

"Won't you come in, Mrs. DeMoss, Chris," John urged.

"No, I think it might be better if we spoke out here," Claire said, her speech slightly shaken.

"All right," John agreed, stepping outside and closing the door behind him. "What is it I can do for you?"

"I've just learned of your plans for the house. You're a most generous man, especially considering you lost a small fortune this morning."

"I'll make it back next time," John assured her.

"You will, too," Claire said, forcing a smile onto her face. "It's said you're lucky."

"Not always," John said, trembling as he gazed at the mountain beyond the edge of town.

"I came here to ask of your generosity, Mr. Wilson. Henry hasn't said anything, but, unlike Marie, I've always been either a wife or a daughter. Never in my life have I worked in a gold camp or labored as a seamstress. I've been forced to make first my father and later my husband's career and the welfare of my children into my world. I know Henry borrowed heavily to buy his mining stock. He sold our home, borrowed from friends, sold his Union Pacific bonds and his holdings in the Northern Colorado Railroad. Even so, he needed perhaps another $80,000."

"I suspected so," John said nervously.

"Do you know where he might have gotten that kind of money?"

"I assume he borrowed it."

"Do you really? Or do you think he took it from the Northern? I know Louise Barrett. She speaks highly of you, especially of the way you assisted Welles in buying into the Northern. Why did you go after Henry? Was he just someone to destroy, another challenge, something you had to prove to yourself?"

"Much more than that," John said bitterly.

"You did this on purpose?" Chris asked, glaring angrily at John. "You ruined my father?"

"No," John replied sourly. "That wasn't within my power. You might as well know the truth. He's been playing fast and loose with Northern funds for a long time. He protected himself by controlling the board of directors."

"That's why you had Welles Barrett seize control," Claire noted. "He bought every share on the market."

"That still wouldn't matter if the books balanced."

"So you had to trap him into borrowing."

"Trap?" John asked. "Is that what I did? I twice turned him down when he asked to invest. He begged to get in on this deal! He walked into it blindly. Mining has always been high risk. It's not some kind of game to play."

"He trusted you," Chris mumbled. "We all did."

"He should have listened more, then," John explained. "Let me tell you what he tried to do. He wanted to follow me into a venture, slip in through the side door, then maneuver himself into control. Isn't that what he did?"

John frowned as the truth sank in. The solemn look on Claire's face and Chris's trembling fingers betrayed them.

"I've seen it before," John whispered, helping Claire into a chair. "Gold blinds a man. Dreams can lead you right off the side of a cliff."

"Yes, Henry walked into this with his eyes wide open," Claire confessed. "But you knew it would destroy him, didn't you? You still share the blame."

"Blame?" John replied bitterly. "Don't talk of blame

to me!"

Chris placed a sweaty palm on John's arm and gazed intently at the older man's blazing eyes.

"If you'd done it your way, continued with the shaft, would you have found gold?" the young man asked.

"I don't know," John admitted.

"But you would have been surprised if there'd been any, wouldn't you. I listened to the miners. They never could understand why you brought them here. That's the truth, isn't it? There wasn't any gold. But why here, Mr. Wilson? Why of all places Thompson's Mountain? You have to know Father put the railroad through here, built the bridge over the river. Why smash his dreams here, where he did the finest work of his entire life?"

John turned away, but Chris pulled him back.

"Why did you ruin my father?" the boy asked with tears streaking down his cheeks. "What'd he ever do to you?"

John's face paled, and his hands fended off the boy's grasping hands.

"You might not want to know," John said, his eyes pleading with Claire to take the boy away.

"He has a right," she whispered.

"All right, then," John said, bitterly pointing toward the mountain. "You remember the two crosses on that slope?"

Chris nodded, and Claire gasped.

"Under them rest my mother and father," John told them as his whole face blazed scarlet. "Your father murdered them, Chris! Shot them down as they fled their burning cabin!"

"It's not true!" Chris shouted so that people across

the street suddenly froze and stared.

"I saw it," John said, opening his coat and loosening the buttons on his shirt. "Look," he continued, exposing the red scar across his belly. "I still bear the mark his hired killer put in me when I was but fifteen myself!"

Chris touched the scarred flesh, then shrank back in horror. Claire stumbled to her feet and leaned against her son.

"Don't ask pity of me," John told them as he refastened his shirt buttons. "It's far too late."

"Forgiveness, then?" Claire pleaded.

"I'm sorry," John said, turning away. "It's not in me."

VIII

Two mornings hence John prepared to leave Thompson's Mountain. Jeff Kelly enlisted the help of three other youngsters, and the boys loaded the luggage aboard the wagon and headed for the station. Nancy herded the children along, warning them to be on their best behavior while she was away.

John stood in the parlor with Levi Nolan, signing the last of the papers and instructing the lawyer in a few final details. They were interrupted by a knock at the door.

"I heard you were leaving," Henry DeMoss spoke when Katy opened the door. "I've come to make my peace."

Nolan glanced up in alarm. John motioned his old enemy inside, though. DeMoss had clearly gone without much sleep. Deep circles appeared beneath his eyes, and the man seemed thinner, a mere shadow of his former self.

"Levi, will you walk me on to the station?" Marie asked.

"I've got biscuits to put in the oven, sir," Katy said, excusing herself as well, When the others had left,

DeMoss leaned against one of the big leather chairs and sighed.

"Claire told me," he mumbled. "Funny. I always prided myself on being able to judge men. I never figured you for a Thompson."

"Pa always thought I came up a little short, too."

"He was wrong. A Cheyenne couldn't have peeled me rawer with a knife. Tell me. If I hadn't jumped for the mine scheme, would that have been the end of it?"

"I don't know," John said, scratching his chin. "I never considered you'd pass it up."

"That's the hardest part of all this," DeMoss admitted. "Knowing it was so easy."

"You had a fair ride while it lasted. At least nobody sold you out."

"You know, Wilson or Thompson or whoever you really are, what I did to old Zeke Thompson had to be done. One man can't be allowed to stand in the way of a country's progress. Look at this valley. As long as that old man stayed up there—"

"You murdered my family!" John shouted. "Do you think reasons will ever change that? You make it sound like you performed a service. You can't hide killing behind words. Every man on earth is valuable, not just for himself, but because he touches others. My children will never know their grandfather. You stole my name!"

"And what about my boys?"

"I'll see they don't suffer, not because I pity you somehow, but because I think everyone has a right to grow up, even sons of Cheyenne Indians or rail-camp harlots."

"Did you know there's a federal marshal at the hotel

waiting to serve me a warrant? Appears he's a friend of Stamp's. That was another mistake of mine. How'd he fit into this?"

"You'll have to ask him."

"I don't suppose it really matters," DeMoss said, sighing. "Will you go back to the hotel with me, walk the final mile, so to speak? See it's done properly?"

"All right," John agreed. "I'm heading in that direction anyway."

"Leaving?"

"Yes," John said, leading the way toward the door. "My business here is done."

They crossed the street and slowly made their way along the plank walkway to the hotel. A tall man in a dark blue suit stood beside Brian Shea at the front desk. A shiny revolver rested on each hip.

"Are you DeMoss?" the stranger asked.

"I'm ready to go along with you, marshal," DeMoss said. "Just let me have a moment with my family."

The marshal nodded, and DeMoss continued up the stairs. John stopped in the doorway. He started to leave, but DeMoss called for him to stop.

"Just another minute now, Wilson," DeMoss said as Claire and the boys joined him on the staircase. DeMoss clasped a trembling Claire, then patted young Chris on the shoulder. Grant avoided his father's touch, but DeMoss smiled nevertheless. The four of them descended the stairs together. Then, quick as a cat, DeMoss slipped into a small parlor across from the desk.

"What in heaven's name—" the marshal began.

Any other words that might have been spoken were drowned away by two rapid pistol shots. The marshal pulled his revolvers and charged into the parlor. But even before the lawman dragged DeMoss's blood-stained body into the hotel lobby, John knew his old enemy was dead.

Claire screamed as she beheld her husband's lifeless face, and Chris dashed across the room to his father's side.

"Thank God it's over," Grant declared. "He's spared us the scandal of a trial."

"Sure, Grant!" Chris shouted at his brother. "Now you don't have to be inconvenienced. Can't you see he's dead? That's our father."

"I see him," Grant said, turning away. "As to his fate, I'd say he earned it."

Chris returned to his mother and helped her to a nearby couch. The marshal and Shea wrapped De-Moss in a blanket and carried him past John and on down the street toward the undertaker's office. But before John could turn and exit the hotel, young Chris darted over.

"Well, are you happy now?" the boy asked. "Isn't this what you wanted, to see him dead?"

John frowned as he recognized the anguish in Chris's youthful eyes. Another fifteen-year-old had once stood in that valley with similar eyes.

"You said he murdered your father," Chris said bitterly. "Is what you did any different? You didn't pull the trigger, but you murdered him just the same."

"No, not the same," John objected. "You've still your mother, Chris. And your name. And a home. I'll be an outcast all my life no matter where I am. That's the difference!"

"Wilson!" the boy shouted as John turned toward

440

Claire.

"I'm sure Aaron Stamp will have a bank draft ready for you soon, Mrs. DeMoss," John said simply. "If you run into any difficulties, I've instructed Levi Nolan to be at your disposal."

Claire said nothing, just dropped her head into her hands and sobbed. John turned again, this time walking past Chris's hostile face and continuing on down the street. He never looked back.

Epilogue

It had never been easy to leave the Medicine Bow country, not when the last embers of the cabin were still smoldering and not when, his body shattered, Jeff Thompson had fled southward toward a new life in Colorado. Now, riding along the powder-blasted hillsides toward the two distant graves, he felt some unseen hand holding him back, pulling him from the wife and family huddling together at the railroad station. They were waiting for him . . . Marie and the children, eager to continue with their lives, to put an end to the mystery and pain that had so suddenly and completely disrupted an otherwise calm and ordered universe.

It's time, John told himself. Perhaps there ought to be a third grave marker, one etched with the name Jeff Thompson, a memorial to a past that could finally be laid to rest. But that wasn't why he rode onward. No, markers meant little enough when all was said and done.

As John wandered along the mountainside, nudging his horse first east, then west, next south, and finally north, he lost himself in a hundred recollections. For a time he sat in old Zeke's cabin, reading to his mother some adventurous story from faraway lands. Later he fished for trout with Pike, jabbering away at the brother that now seemed oddly close.

"Sure, Pa, I'll split more wood," he whispered as he saw the ghostly shape of Zeke Thompson scowl. "I don't mean to be forgetful."

And for the briefest of moments, a wild-eyed boy named Jefferson Thompson chased phantom buffalo beside cousins long since swept away to a world of shadows and spirits.

"It's all over, Pa," John whispered as he knelt beside the graves of his parents. "DeMoss is dead, but so are you. And so's Jeff Thompson. The railroad's there to stay, and the buffalo are all gone. The Cheyenne, too, just as you knew it would be."

For an instant, a sad-eyed old mountain man appeared on the hillside, and John reached for a weathered hand. There was a touch of leather . . . then the spectre vanished.

Ours was a better world, a finer day, John thought as he gazed out over the valley. The gray-white smoke of a train drifted over the river, and the distant echo of hammers mingled with the wild cry of a hawk overhead. Life was change, he'd learned painfully, and often what is best, most loved, is swept away as a wild rose is drowned by a summer flood.

"Good-bye, Pa. Good-bye, Ma," John said, gently touching the cold black earth. "I miss you still, and I'll always remember."

He then mounted his horse and headed back toward town, back to Marie and the bewildered little ones. One task remained, perhaps the most difficult of all. How could he explain it all, reveal a past full of death and killing?

"They won't understand at first," John mumbled. "But Marie will help. And perhaps, in time . . ."

Yes, he told himself. Time, which so often had been the enemy, the faceless rider who'd swept through a hundred nightmares, bringing change and robbing first Jeff Thompson and later John Wilson of the tenderness, the belonging he so needed. Now time offered hope, a chance to watch the children grow and understand their past, to appreciate their heritage. That would be his gift, John thought.

He suddenly gave the horse a gentle pat on the neck, then urged the animal into a gallop. As the wind swept back the hair from his forehead, he inhaled a scent of prairie grass and black earth. He felt oddly young, somehow reborn. The wrinkles departed his forehead, and his grip on the reins grew solid, unwavering.

He longed for the feel of Marie's head on his shoulder, for the tiny fingers of Joanna and little Tim. It was time to face the questioning eyes of Michael and Peter, to draw them close again. Perhaps, in time, they'd adopt his love for the streams and mountains.

Yes, there was time, he realized as he raced toward the river. For he was young again.

THE UNTAMED WEST
brought to you by Zebra Books

THE LAST MOUNTAIN MAN   (1480, $2.25)
by William W. Johnstone

He rode out West looking for the men who murdered his father and brother. When an old mountain man taught him how to kill a man a hundred different ways from Sunday, he knew he'd make sure they all remembered . . . THE LAST MOUNTAIN MAN.

SAN LOMAH SHOOTOUT   (1853, $2.50)
by Doyle Trent

Jim Kinslow didn't even own a gun, but a group of hardcases tried to turn him into buzzard meat. There was only one way to find out why anybody would want to stretch his hide out to dry, and that was to strap on a borrowed six-gun and ride to death or glory.

TOMBSTONE LODE   (1915, $2.95)
by Doyle Trent

When the Josey mine caved in on Buckshot Dobbs, he left behind a rich vein of Colorado gold—but no will. James Alexander, hired to investigate Buckshot's self-proclaimed blood relations learns too soon that he has one more chance to solve the mystery and save his skin or become another victim of TOMBSTONE LODE.

GALLOWS RIDERS   (1934, $2.50)
by Mark K. Roberts

When Stark and his killer-dogs reached Colby, all it took was a little muscle and some well-placed slugs to run roughshod over the small town—until the avenging stranger stepped out of the shadows for one last bloody showdown.

DEVIL WIRE   (1937, $2.50)
by Cameron Judd

They came by night, striking terror into the hearts of the settlers. The message was clear: Get rid of the devil wire or the land would turn red with fencestringer blood. It was the beginning of a brutal range war.

Available wherever paperbacks are sold, or order direct from the Publisher. Send cover price plus 50¢ per copy for mailing and handling to Zebra Books, Dept. 2042, 475 Park Avenue South, New York, N.Y. 10016. Residents of New York, New Jersey and Pennsylvania must include sales tax. DO NOT SEND CASH.